The Missing Italian Girl

The Missing Italian Girl

Barbara Corrado Pope

PEGASUS CRIME
NEW YORK LONDON

THE MISSING ITALIAN GIRL

Pegasus Crime is an Imprint of
Pegasus Books LLC
80 Broad Street, 5th Floor
New York, NY 10004

First Pegasus Books cloth edition 2013

Interior design by Maria Fernandez

Library of Congress Cataloging-in-Publication Data is available.

ISBN: 978-1-60598-408-7

10 9 8 7 6 5 4 3 2

Printed in the United States of America
Distributed by W. W. Norton & Company, Inc.

For my mother Edith, my sister Catherine Jean,

and my daughter Stephanie

Clarie's Paris

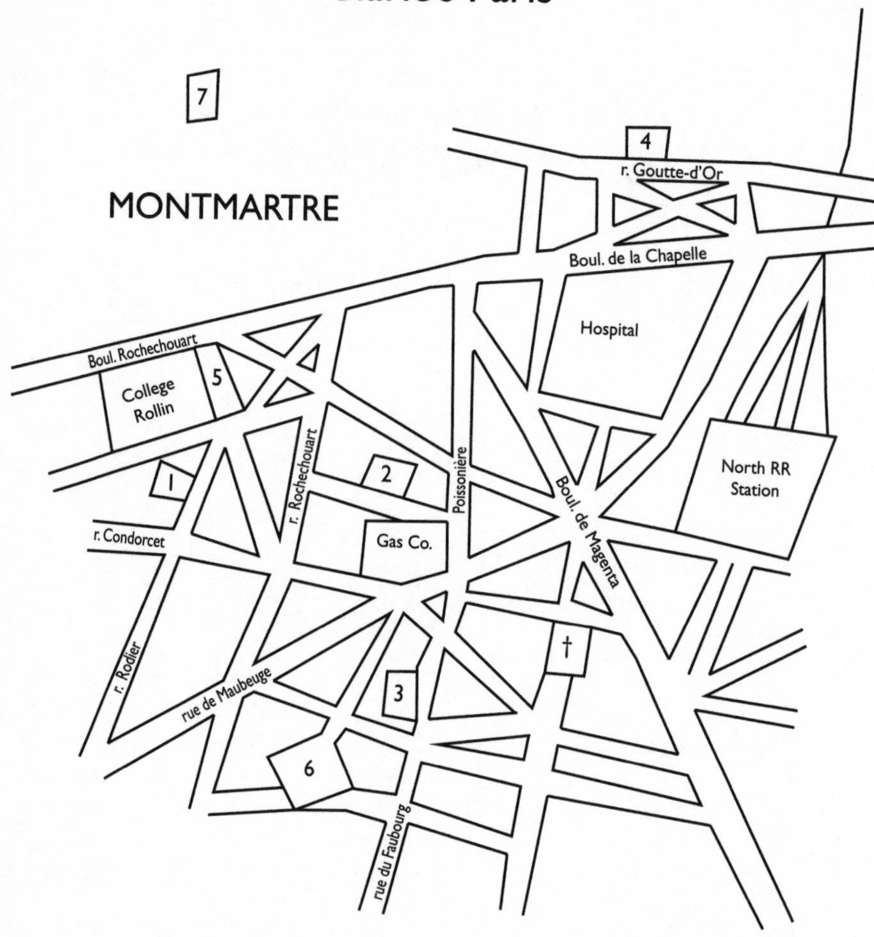

Grand Boulevards

1. Clarie's apartment
2. Emilie's apartment
3. Lycée Lamartine
4. Maura's tenement
5. Anvers Square
6. Square Montholon
7. Sacré-Coeur

I

Thursday, 24 June 1897

1

THE RAILROAD TRACKS OF THE Gare de l'Est stretched and curved beneath the bridge in gray, eerie silence. It was after midnight, the time of poor carters and night porters hauling their loads of garbage and human waste to the Basin de La Villette, hoping to make the last boat to the dumping grounds on the outskirts of Paris. Maura Laurenzano and the young Russian, Pyotr Ivanovich, were transporting a much deadlier cargo. The two of them stopped and watched as Maura's sister, Angela, ran ahead, flitting from shadow to shadow like a frightened, wounded bird. When she signaled that no one was coming, they grasped the poles of their cart and continued across the bridge.

At seventeen, Maura was a year younger than Angela, but bigger and stronger. In the steamy June night, her sweat trickled down into the sleeves of one of Pyotr's rough muslin shirts, prickling her arms. His vest veiled her femininity. She liked wearing his clothes, feeling him on her skin, smelling him. And besides, it was necessary. To complete her disguise, she had tucked her unruly black curls under one of Pyotr's caps. Any passerby might pause and gawk at a girl hauling a cart. But not at two slender youths making their way in the night.

Angela waited in the dark, far from the flickering yellow light cast by a gas lamp. When Maura and Pyotr reached the end of the bridge, he motioned with his head to turn right into a narrow cobbled street. Under the moonless sky, they barely made out the warehouses and sullen dark shacks that lined their path. Maura's arms burned with the strain of lifting and pulling the cart to keep the wheels from rumbling over the stones. Her heavy breathing filled her with the stink of Paris. Pyotr, too, panted silently as he led them zigzagging through the narrowest and most deserted streets. Finally, under the gaslights, they saw the wide, shimmering expanse of the Basin. Maura gasped when they got to the edge of a building that bordered the wharf. The first thing that caught her eye was the fiery glow of cigarettes as workers in caps and smocks stood around their wagons talking and laughing after their night's labors. Pyotr had told her that La Villette would be empty after the last sewage boat left. There were even a few bourgeois in bowlers lingering along the quays and a hatless man with a fishing pole at the edge of the water. The covered mounds in the barges bringing supplies into the city teemed with hidden threats.

"Pyotr, are you sure this is right? There are people here. Shouldn't we take him down to the canals?"

He held up his hand to calm her. He was like a prince. A young, anarchist prince, who had given up his nobility to live among the poor and learn about revolution from the French. Maura did not understand this golden-haired boy. She only knew that he was the only man she would ever trust.

"They'll think we are dumping garbage illegally," he whispered. "They are workers like us. They won't tell the police."

Sometimes Pyotr was so trusting she thought him stupid. But he wasn't concerned about what she thought. He went over to her sister and smoothed a lock of hair, fairer even than his own, under her flowered scarf. "Don't worry, my Angelina. He can't hurt you anymore. No one will hurt you," he said in the slow, careful cadence that marked him as a foreigner.

Maura did not have to see her sister's face to imagine the bruises. It made her heart surge with hate again. Hate against the boss who had seduced Angela with a promise of marriage and then kept her in his room as if she were his slave. Maura's chest began to heave. Not from effort this time, but from everything else: her hate, her shame that at this moment she felt jealousy, and, most of all, her fear. Her cheeks puffed out as she pressed her lips together to hold back the tears. What had they done? They were in so much trouble.

Suddenly she felt Pyotr's hands on her shoulders. "It will be all right," he said, looking into her eyes. "We aren't going to the canals because we don't want the body to move when they open the locks. We don't want anyone to find it." She wished her eyes were blue like his and Angela's. She wished he would stay there forever, touching her, caring for her. She nodded as he took two bundles of clothes from the cart and left them with Angela in the dark. Then he signaled to lift the cart's poles once more as they rolled it to a deserted section of the Basin.

Marcel Barbereau, who had been so hot-blooded, silver-tongued and tempestuous in life, had become stiff, heavy and mercifully silent in death. Even so, the monster moved as they took hold of him. A rigid arm jerked upward under the sheet they had torn from his filthy bed. Maura thought she would faint. Pyotr froze, then composed himself. He even smiled. For Maura, again. "A revolutionary must get used to death," he said, although his rasping voice and trembling hands belied his bravado.

"Yes." That's all she, the girl he called bold and brave, managed to utter. As if of one mind, they swathed the corpse more tightly, then, shaking a bit and cringing, Maura helped Pyotr lift Marcel Barbereau out of the cart. Counting one-two-three under their breath, they swung the body into the water. She closed her eyes until she heard the splash.

It was only right that the dense, hard muscles the bastard had used on her sister would sink him into the deep. Yet the sinking seemed to take forever. And when they finally sensed his disappearance, under a rippling disturbance of the calm waters, a chill coursed through her body. Damp with the sweat of June heat and terror's cold, Maura tasted the nausea erupting in her belly. But she had to suppress the bile. She had to be brave, act the part, be a boy. Or a man, like Pyotr.

Maura stood by the cart as Pyotr went back to get Angela. Suddenly a tall, thin man emerged, with quick, definite strides, from the very street that they had taken to the Basin. Maura crouched down behind the cart and watched, peeking between the spokes of a wheel. She saw her sister recoil as the intruder noticed her and tipped his hat. Maura held her breath as Pyotr approached them. When she saw Pyotr thrust out his hand in greeting, she allowed herself to breathe again. *A friend. Maybe he is a friend*, she whispered to herself. Still she clutched the wheel, praying that he'd go away. At last, he gave a wave and started to stroll in the direction of the canals. Shaken, but relieved, Maura slid into a hard seat on the cobblestones. She did not move until Pyotr beckoned her.

"Come," he whispered.

"Who was that? What were you talking about?" she asked as she struggled to her feet.

"Someone who comes to our café. I had to talk to him. He wanted to meet Angela, because he thought she was my girl," Pyotr said, as he laid a calming hand on her shoulder. "He even asked about the dark-haired girl who comes to listen to me make my little speeches. I told him I didn't know where you are. And I don't," he said smiling, "since you have become a strong, brave boy."

Maura thrust his arm away. She was not in the mood for one of Pyotr's gentle jokes. "How can you be sure he is not a police spy? Didn't you tell me they haunted all the workers' cafes? Maybe he saw us, maybe he—"

This time Pyotr took her hand as he peered into her eyes. "I have seen his wounds. He was injured at the gasworks. He is a worker who is learning about his oppression. Soon he may become one of us."

Maura shook her head at the pride she heard in Pyotr's voice. How could he think about anyone else's problems when they had so many of their own?

"Come," Pyotr urged again. "Day breaks quickly on a June night."

He led her and Angela under a gas lamp where he pulled two folded pieces of paper from his pocket. He had drawn a map to guide them across the river to his comrades. He had talked to them about the Russian girls many times. They were anarchists like him, believing that the rich ruled and oppressed the poor, and working for the day when everyone would be equal and live in decent, sanitary conditions. He spoke about them with admiration, for they were women studying to be doctors, so that they could go back to Russia and minister to the peasants. Tomorrow and the next day and the next, Pyotr explained, they would hide Maura and heal Angela.

The second sheet was their introduction to the Russian girls, written in a language that, under the undulating light, looked like chicken scratches. Maura stared at the sheet. This was Pyotr's language. One of the worlds he lived in. She dreamed that one day he would take them far away and become a nobleman again, although he said that he did not care about land or wealth. She did not understand him. If she had been born with a silver spoon her mouth, she would have kept it there and enjoyed all the comforts of a great estate. Perhaps, she thought, he did not love her because he knew how selfish she was.

"Maura," he was saying, "this is important. Stay in the shadows, and when the sun comes, act like two lovers as you cross the bridge and go into the Latin Quarter. Then no one will stop you."

"But what about you?" Angela asked, reaching for Pyotr's arm. "Come with us."

Once again he tucked an errant lock of hair under Angela's scarf. "Don't worry. You'll be safe."

"No, come." Even though they had made a plan, suddenly Maura also wanted him to join them. She wanted to be sure that he would be safe.

"No, no. I must take the cart back to the courtyard before my patron wakes up."

"Why?" Maura wanted to shake him. He was always speaking out against the bosses. "He's a boss."

"Yes, a patron, but a good man, and poor like us. We must not involve him. Go," he urged. "I will join you in a few days."

With trembling fingers, Maura folded the two sheets of paper and pocketed them. She rubbed her hands along the pants she was wearing, Pyotr's pants, as if by magic they would give her courage. Then she picked up the heavier bundle of clothes from Angela's side and threw it over her shoulder. "Come," she barked. "We have to go." She ignored the tears in her sister's eyes and waited impatiently as Angela picked up the other bundle and folded her arms around it.

Behind them, nearer to the water, Pyotr had already grabbed hold of the two poles and was pulling the cart back toward the railroad station, like a beast of burden. Maura did not know whether to be sad or angry or afraid. Tingling with an awareness that someone might be watching, she strode ahead of Angela, acting the part of a swaggering lover as they began their journey.

2

Clarie Martin was in a hurry that Friday afternoon. Eager to get home to her little boy, happy that the school year was coming to an end.

She flew out of the teachers' meeting, intending only to gather her papers and stuff them in her sack. But when she entered her empty classroom, she heard a low, guttural moan. Someone was on her knees at the front of the room below the blackboard.

Claire pushed past her students' desks to reach her. It was the charwoman, Francesca. "Are you all right? Are you hurt?" Clarie asked as she bent down to help the woman to her feet.

Francesca panted and gasped, then shook her head, unable to speak.

"Here," Clarie took her gently by the arm and led her to a desk in the front row. "What happened?" She sat down across from her.

Standing, Francesca was a head shorter than Clarie. Shrinking into the student chair, she seemed even smaller. She covered her face with her hands and began to cry. The knotted bun on the top of her head held together strands of hair as dark as Clarie's, but streaked with gray, oily and unwashed. Catching the pungent smell of the woman's coarse gray dress, Clarie realized that she had never been this close to Francesca before and knew nothing of her beyond her Christian name. To the Lycée Lamartine's overworked teachers, the charwomen were mere shadows, appearing at the end of the day to dust and scrub the rooms, readying them for the onslaught of well-fed young ladies who swept in each morning in starched, clean uniforms. It wasn't right that one did not notice those who toiled into the night. Still, Clarie hesitated to delve into Francesca's troubles. She had to get home to Jean-Luc.

"It's all my fault. She did it because of me."

The sobbing had stopped. The charwoman spoke as if she were in a trance. Clarie folded her hands in her lap, determined to listen for a moment. "You couldn't have done anything so terrible," she said soothingly.

Suddenly, Francesca reached for Clarie's arm. Startled, Clarie pulled away. Then she was ashamed.

"*Per favore*, please, *professoressa*. Maybe you could help me. You have such a kind face." Francesca's dark-ringed hazel eyes bore into Clarie's.

"I really don't know what I can do." This was true. Clarie meant to be kind, but. . . .

"Per favore, please."

It was Francesca's accent, reminding Clarie of her dear Italian father, that overcame her hesitations. Clarie could not imagine Giuseppe Falchetti ever refusing a cry for help. She took hold of the charwoman's hand to comfort her. It was rough and chapped, another sign, like her worn face and hunched shoulders, of a life filled with hard labors. "Tell me," Clarie urged; "tell me what's wrong."

"It's my daughter, Angela. She's gone. He took her. I'm afraid he's going to kill her."

"Someone stole your child?" Alarmed, Clarie sat back in her chair. "Go on," she whispered.

"He said he was going to marry her. He said if he married her, we would not starve. He said . . . he promised. . . . But he's cruel. He beats her. Now he's taken her away somewhere. I'm sure of it." Francesca's voice grew stronger as she spoke of the man who had hurt her daughter.

"Who is he?" Clarie asked. Her heart began to pound as she tried to understand. Murder. Kidnapping. It could not be.

"He lives in the next building. He works for one of those big new department stores. He hired my daughters, Angela and Maura, to finish shirtwaists. My girls stay in our room and work all day, every day, every single day, sewing on buttons, tying up seams, and still we did not have enough." Francesca sniffed and wiped her face with a handkerchief she retrieved from her pocket. "He promised that when he married Angela, he would rent sewing machines for us, so we could make more money. Maybe he kept some of the money he should have given to us and used it to bring us presents, so that we would believe him."

Clarie sensed an undertone of anger and resentment in the Italian woman's words. Against whom or what? Clarie wondered. The man, her life, or teachers, like Clarie, who came to work every day in the starched, white shirtwaist blouses her daughters labored over? Clarie fingered one of the tiny buttons on her cuff and tried to imagine spending all day sewing them on.

"I let her do it. Let her be with him. She begged me. She wanted to make it easier for me," Francesca murmured.

"How do you know he beats her?" Clarie asked, hoping that some part of this story was not true.

"Everyone in the building can hear him," Francesca said as she stared at the floor and began to breathe heavily. "They hear her cries in the courtyard almost every night."

Clarie gazed at Francesca, picturing what her life must be like. The teachers at the lycée were occasionally assigned to take students to crowded, sewerless tenements, to teach them how to make charity visits. Clarie shook her head. What folly, as if an hour's "visit" on a bright sunny afternoon would teach privileged young women what poverty was really like. Fortunately, she and her students had never heard shouts or blows during their forays. Yet anyone who even occasionally read a Paris daily had an inkling of what went on in rooms occupied by entire families and common-law liaisons. The thin walls and curtainless windows opening onto dank, dark common courtyards must hold few secrets.

Most of all, Clarie knew what it was to see a child suffer, and then to lose a child. She had lost her firstborn a week after his birth. This was a pain, an ache in her heart, that would never go away. She leaned toward Francesca and waited until the charwoman met her eyes.

"You must go to the police. This man should not be hurting your daughter."

The older woman pulled away. "Oh no, professoressa, no. We cannot go to the police, they don't like Italians. They think we are all bad people. No."

"Then your husband. The girl's father. He must go to the man and—" Clarie stopped. When Francesca turned away from her, she realized there was no husband.

The neighbors? Did they distrust Italians too? How different it had been in Arles when Clarie was growing up. But that was before the assassinations and bombings, before Frenchmen labeled Italians anarchists and criminals. It was all so unfair. "You are an honest, hard-working woman," she insisted. "The police will help you."

"No, no. No one can help. I am alone. Even Maura is gone. She's probably looking for her sister." Francesca's chest began to heave. Clarie could not bear to hear the anguished moans again. To stave them off and calm the charwoman, Clarie asked her to tell more about her daughters and where she thought they could have gone.

Twenty minutes later, Clarie emerged from the cool vestibule of the Lycée Lamartine onto the busy, steamy rue du Faubourg Poissonnière, the long street named for the fishmongers who centuries ago had traveled the road to the Paris markets. Although relieved to leave Francesca and her sorrows behind, Clarie was again struck by the ambivalence that hit her each time she stepped out of the school's enclosed intellectual universe. Because the neighborhood was close to both the Gare du Nord and Gare de l'Est railroad stations, it was dense and growing denser by the day. Long gone were the women taking fish to market, and the fields and estates that used to line their path. Instead, the street was occupied from end to end by shops, restaurants, and sellers hawking from carts. And everywhere—beside, above, and behind the constant commerce—apartments, new and old, crowded down upon the lycée, which was housed in the one of the few mansions that had survived the transformations.

This was not the Paris that Clarie remembered from her days at the teachers' college in Sèvres when she and her fellow students visited the city to tour its ancient cathedrals and museums. This Paris wore all that was modern and raucous on its sleeve, or rather pasted on pillars, newspaper kiosks and the exposed walls of buildings in the form of posters promoting the latest products and the most risqué entertainments. The famous Medrano Circus, Folies-Bergère and Moulin Rouge lay just outside the *quartier* where the Martins lived. In the poorer districts to the north and east, Clarie knew there were countless café-concerts and dancehalls enticing exploited girls like Francesca's daughters with the promise of fun and adventure.

Clarie sighed as she began the ten-minute ascent to her home. Her husband, Bernard, professed to love their surroundings, which he called the "true Paris," ever remaking itself and open to all: bourgeois and workers, artisans and merchants, Christians and Jews. More and more, she wondered if it was a good place to raise a child. Or to be a mother.

A year ago, when they left Nancy, Bernard had pledged to find an apartment close to the school and near to the pocket parks squeezed into the fabric of the modern city. A sharp pain shot through Clarie's chest as she remembered how one of these oases had become a bitter disappointment.

When the weather had gotten warmer, she had asked her devoted housekeeper, Rose, to bring Jean-Luc to the Square Montholon park during her lunch hour. Clarie would run down the block, around the corner, to the head of the stairs that formed part of the rue Baudin, and look for him. She always hoped to catch him unaware, longing to see that he was happy even without her. Whether she saw him or not, she would race down the three flights of stone stairs to find and embrace him. But her leaving became too heart-breaking. He cried Maman, the very first word he had learned, over and over again. So she stopped going to play with him, feeling him, smelling him. Instead, the faithful Rose came at the appointed hour and Clarie observed from the head of the stairs, hoping to catch sight of his dear head smothered in dark curls, his chubby fingers pointing to a bird or child or toy, his sturdy legs under his gown moving forward to have his turn on the swings with the bigger boys. Oh, how she loved her son.

I am full of good fortune, she insisted to herself as she distractedly waved away a hawker selling used pots and pans from his cart. *My boy is safe at home*. Unlike Francesca's daughters. Without ever having seen them, Clarie could almost imagine what they looked like from their mother's descriptions: Maura, dark and wild; Angela, blond, mild and obedient, so obviously the favorite. Perhaps, Clarie thought, when Francesca finished her work and crossed the outer boulevards to her neighborhood, she would find her girls safe and sound. Perhaps. Somehow Clarie doubted this and hated the doubting. *No*, Clarie thought, hugging her sack to her chest as she stopped to avoid the carriages and carts clattering down the rue de Maubeuge, *wherever she is, she will not be safe if she is still with that brute*.

Skirting around shoppers with baskets and men in bowlers, Clarie hurried forward, even though she dreaded the moment she would have to fulfill the promise she'd made to Francesca to seek Bernard's help. He already had so much to think about, and so many cases like Angela's. Since his decision to step down from his judgeship, he had had to jump through countless hoops to become an *avocat*, to fulfill his dream of being a lawyer for those who needed justice the most. In the strict hierarchy of the Paris Bar, with all its rigid requirements for becoming a member, he was being treated as an apprentice, getting only charity cases. These paid practically nothing and often came to naught, because the courts cared little about the fate of the troublesome poor. Bernard, Clarie knew, came home to escape his frustrations, not to add to them.

Almost without thinking, Clarie followed the inviting aroma of warm bread into the *boulangerie* at the corner of her street, the rue Rodier. She always picked up two baguettes for their dinner, and if she were really hungry would have bitten off the crusty narrow end of one of them by the time she reached the middle of the block. This time she slowed her steps and chewed while plotting her approach. She would remind Bernard of Rose, of the fact that they had agreed to bring their housekeeper to Paris from Nancy in part because one of her sons had beaten her (and, of course, because Rose had become indispensable, almost a grandmother to Jean-Luc). Yes, Rose, she thought triumphantly. They had performed this bit of justice for her, they could do it for others.

Clarie paused for a moment before entering her building. Although it dated from the 1860s, a small enameled navy blue sign beside the entrance announced in blazing, white letters that the apartments had "Gas and Water on all Floors." Clarie smiled as she recalled how Bernard had proudly insisted on finding these conveniences for her *and* Rose. She pushed her way into the entry between the *passementerie* store and the pharmacy. The Martins lived on the third floor across the small inner courtyard. One more climb. Just enough time to prepare herself before Bernard got home.

3

As soon as Clarie unlocked the door to her apartment, she sensed that something was amiss. Her twenty-month-old did not run headlong to greet her in the foyer, and Rose was nowhere to be seen. When Clarie heard low voices from somewhere inside, her heart almost stopped. She caught her breath and smiled. She realized then, how deeply Francesca's tale of violence and kidnapping had affected her.

"Bernard?" she called as she went into the parlor. It must be him. She heard laughter and hurried into the kitchen, where she discovered the three of them, Rose sipping a glass of wine, and Jean-Luc in his father's arms, pulling on Bernard's beard. Puzzled, she put her sack on a wooden chair and lay the bread on the round table that took up most of the room.

"Maman." Jean-Luc thrust his arms toward Clarie as soon as he saw her.

Her husband beamed cheerfully. "Darling," he said. Then kissing his son, murmured "There's your Maman, at last" and surrendered the child to Clarie.

Still in a state of perplexity, Clarie hugged Jean-Luc to her chest and kissed him on his forehead. "Bernard, I didn't think you would be home yet." Clarie bit her lip. What a thing to say. She should be happy that Bernard was home early and in such a good mood. If only she didn't have to burden him with Francesca's troubles.

"Let's all go into the parlor," he said expansively, although for someone as shy and serious as Bernard, expansiveness came with a kind of touching awkwardness.

There was nothing to do but follow along. Even if Bernard had won a case, which he often did, he'd hardly be so elated. Clarie sat down, bouncing Jean-Luc in her lap and blowing into his neck, making his hair rise to tickle him, as if her boy and his giggling pleasure were all she was thinking about.

"Rose, sit, please." Bernard offered their housekeeper the other armchair across from the fireplace. Rose demurred, then acceded to his wish. "Thank you, Monsieur Martin," she said as she glanced apologetically at Clarie, clearly embarrassed at having been found drinking and knowing something her mistress did not.

Bernard took center stage in front of them, his suit jacket open to reveal his vest, his arms spread out, as if her were about to deliver a soliloquy, or mount a brilliant defense, or, if he were another kind of man—bullish, full of himself and confident—about to declare his love. All he needed was his cue.

"So when is your Papa going to tell me what is going on?" Clarie said in Jean-Luc's ear, while never taking her eyes off her husband's uncharacteristic dramatics. Suddenly she felt her very insides contract with an overwhelming love for her husband. He was so good, so modest. He always described himself as an ordinary man. And in some ways, he was: of average height and build, a thirty-eight-year-old whose light brown, close-cropped hair and beard were already flecked with gray.

Yet, truly good men, Clarie knew, were quite extraordinary. And to see him so happy! She kissed Jean-Luc again, because it was not yet the moment to kiss Bernard Martin.

"As Rose knows, my dear," he announced, gesturing toward their housekeeper with one hand as he tucked the other at his waist and bowed to Clarie, "I have found a position."

Clarie's mouth fell open as she placed Jean-Luc upright on his two sturdy legs. "A position?"

"Yes, a *salaried* post."

This was so unexpected. "In someone's office? Not just the cases they give you?"

"A salary, a real salary. No more waiting around the courthouse like a serving boy to pick up what they throw at me. And it's what I've always wanted to do. Help the working man get his rights."

As her whole body suffused with joy, Clarie rose from her chair. Bernard had worked so hard, had given up so much. She reached to embrace him, and almost stumbled over her son. She and Bernard burst out laughing.

"Jean-Luc," she said, kissing the toddler on his forehead, "wouldn't you like a piece of the baguette?"

The boy nodded, even as he held on to her skirt, his big brown eyes searching her face for clues about what was going on. Clarie ran her hand over his head, fluffing his curls. "I'm sure Rose can tear one off for you."

Their short, broad, grandmotherly housekeeper, undoubtedly glad to be of use, got up immediately and led the toddler into the kitchen.

Clarie, who was almost the same height as her husband, laid her head on his shoulder and held on so tight that she could feel his heart beating. "I'm so happy for you. The Bar, the way they've been treating you. As if you were a novice."

When they broke the embrace, she urged him into his usual seat, the armchair vacated by Rose, which was divided from hers by a small, round mahogany table holding their kerosene reading lamp. She sat down and begged him to tell her everything.

"It was unbelievable," he explained. "I didn't want to say anything until it really happened, because it was too good to be true. I'm working at the *Bourse du Travail*."

"For the Labor Exchange?" Clarie shook her head. "How? I thought that was a place for carpenters and bakers and butchers—"

"They had a position for a lawyer. They were suspicious, of course, because I had been an examining magistrate. But then I convinced them that I would be their best advocate. Having been a judge, I knew all the tricks, all the rules, how the other side thinks. My greatest defense ever!" He slapped his hand on his thigh, punctuating his triumph.

Before Clarie could formulate another question, his enthusiasm carried him further. "And just think, no more getting involved in family squabbles; no more vulgar, sordid stories to piece through. I can roll up my sleeves and do some real work against those who break the laws to make a profit."

The smile faded from Clarie's face. She had heard just such a "sordid story" that very afternoon. And she had given her word to tell Bernard about it.

"And, my dear," Bernard continued without noticing her unease, "we are going to go out and celebrate tonight. We're going to one of those café-concerts!"

"Oh, no. I can't." Bernard's euphoria was really taking him too far.

"And why not?" he said as he reached for her hand.

"You know why not. Because I teach tomorrow morning and, being a teacher, I have to be respectable at all times."

"Because we've never taken any time to have fun for ourselves since we've lived in Paris?" Bernard countered with a question, which, she knew, was his very reason for insisting. "We won't stay out late, I promise. Besides," he said, getting up, "I should get to know more about the lives of the men I'll be working with."

There was that, Clarie thought, as she slumped back in her chair. How would her methodical and proper husband adjust to working at the Labor Exchange with people who were so unlike his former colleagues in the courthouses of Aix and Nancy? Yet she knew that this was what he had always wanted: to help those who were exploited by the rich and powerful.

"I'll let you think about it, and you'll see I'm right. We must celebrate." His words resounded distantly, an echo breaking through the jumble of Clarie's thoughts. "I'll go see to Jean-Luc's supper, and when he is in bed. . . ." Bernard trailed off, leaving Clarie staring at the fireplace.

So this was going to be their life in Paris. If all worked out, it was settled. She rubbed her hand along the flowers embroidered into the lilac fabric of the worn armchair, which had traveled with them from Nancy. There were times when she longed for that place, where she had lived through the worst and best moments of her life. The death of her first infant son is what had driven them to try to leave, but then the birth of Jean-Luc had drawn her to want to stay. Yet she had accepted a new post, weaned her baby as soon as his first tooth came in, and they were gone. To Paris, where the sun did not stream in every morning, and their lives were not punctuated by the shouts and clatter of Nancy's gayest street. Instead, they lived in the shadow of a peaceful, narrow courtyard, where only the voices and footsteps of the building's staid inhabitants broke the quiet. A Paris apartment, crammed to the gills, paid for mostly by her salary. Now, at least, they wouldn't have to worry about how to make ends meet every month.

Clarie lifted her head and leaned it against the top of the curved line of the chair. This was no time for regrets. They already had good memories, right here, on the rue Rodier. Like the time the Parisian Bar committee had come on inspection to make sure that Bernard's living quarters were respectable enough to allow him to be admitted to that austere and pretentious body. The thought of all their preparations made Clarie bite her lip to keep from laughing out loud. The big question had been, should they try to get a piano? But, of course, being a blacksmith's daughter, she had never, like a proper young lady, learned how to play. And where would they put it if they got one: In the middle of the room?

In front of the fireplace? Or in the far corner of the parlor beside her desk? Perhaps in Jean-Luc's tiny bedroom with his crib on top of it. Or on their marriage bed. How she and Rose had giggled afterward at the officiousness of the three "inspectors." Yes, she and Bernard were different, would always be different from their colleagues. Yet they had succeeded against all odds. A blacksmith's daughter becoming a professor in a high school. A clockmaker's son being a judge. A motherless girl and a fatherless boy falling in love, finding happiness and making a family together. Bernard, finally, finding work that matched his republican ideals.

Clarie got up and repinned her thick black hair securely into the bun on top of her head. Bernard was right. They should celebrate. She smoothed out her navy blue skirt. With her starched white high-necked shirt, who could possibly think of her as unrespectable? And besides, if they picked the right café-concert, perhaps she would spot two girls, one blond and delicate, the other dark and bold, dancing together. Perhaps by some miracle she would see Francesca's daughters and know they were safe. And, if not, she would have to work up the nerve to ask Bernard's advice on the very day he had finally rid himself of "sordid cases."

4

"LUCA, LUCA," CLARIE COOED AS Jean-Luc surrendered to sleep. This peaceful moment at the end of the day always filled her with a confusion of joy and apprehension. Because she had lost one child as he slept, she had to be sure that her little boy was full of life, even as his eyelids grew heavy, fluttered and finally shut her out of his world. Only then, as his mouth fell open, slowly, steadily breathing, did she know her son was safe. "Luca," she murmured the pet name her Italian father had given her baby, then leaned over the crib to smooth away the matted curls from his brow and brush his forehead with a kiss.

Clarie tiptoed to the parlor, where Bernard was waiting to celebrate his triumph. "I think he got caught up in our excitement," she whispered to Rose, who stood by, Clarie's paisley Indian shawl already in her hand. Bernard laid down his newspaper, leaped up and put on his bowler. "Ready?" he asked.

"Yes, for an adventure and for your new life," Clarie answered, as she tied the shawl around her shoulders. They were actually going to make a night of it.

After thanking Rose for staying with Jean-Luc, the two of them descended the stairs and hurried through the courtyard onto the rue Rodier.

"Which way?" Clarie suddenly realized she had no idea where they were going. The rue Rodier sloped gently up toward the outer boulevards and Montmartre with its famous cabarets in one direction, and down toward the center of the city in the other. Bernard linked his arm in hers and gently directed her downward. "Not the Moulin Rouge, my dear. A much more humble place. A workingman's place, remember?"

"Good," she laughed. She wasn't at all prepared for the raucousness and lifted skirts of the cancan.

They descended toward the lights of Paris and a sky streaked with whispers of rose and lilac and tangerine. All around, shouts and slams signaled a bustling street closing up shop for the night. The air was filled with the smell of burnt oil, cheeses and decaying fruit, of things sold, cooked, and consumed. Seeing the delicate colors of the sunset made Clarie suddenly long for Provence, where she had grown up, where she had met Bernard, where they had strolled on grassy hills redolent with the fresh scent of lavender and thyme. How young they were then! She hugged closer to Bernard as they reached the curb of the wide rue de Maubeuge. Even as the day wound down, one needed to pay attention to the horse-drawn cabs and omnibuses clattering by.

"It's between here and the Exchange," he announced as he guided her through the busy intersection toward the eastern part of the city. As they walked through unfamiliar narrow streets, Clarie grew apprehensive. "Do you think we'll meet someone you know?" she asked. When he answered that he hoped so, she felt a slight tremoring in her chest. What if Bernard's new employers did not like the fact that he was married to a teacher of upperclass girls? She wanted so to make a good impression, or the right impression, whatever that might be.

"It's off this street," Bernard said, as he stopped and pointed to a sign for the rue du Paradis, "and called The Little Paradise. Let's hope it is," he laughed and patted her arm.

The café proclaimed itself as soon as they turned into the alley. The doors stood open, emitting a fog of smoke and the sound of a piano lilting over a din of talk and laughter. Except for the small stage holding the player, and a space in front of it, presumably meant for dancing, it was packed with men, women, and children, most sharing long wooden tables covered with red-and-white-checkered wax cloths. A few couples occupied small round tables. Clarie hesitated, wondering where they would fit in, but Bernard plunged ahead.

They had to squeeze past a bar, where men stood with their backs to the crowd, drinking with sullen seriousness. A tall, red-headed waitress, carrying a tray of brimming beer steins, spotted Bernard and jerked her head toward a small round table. Clarie nodded a thanks. At least the waitress did not seem to find anything remarkable or out-of-place about them. Almost before they were settled, a man with rolled-up sleeves, a striped shirt, and burly arms placed his thick hands on their table and asked what he could get them. It was even hotter in the café than outside, and the effort evident in his sweating, balding head and ruddy face made his mustache droop in the heat. When Bernard ordered beer and sausages, the man assured them that Colette would be back soon with their food. And then, before taking his leave, he winked at Clarie. Taken aback, Clarie glanced at Bernard, who raised his eyebrows in amusement.

"Does it make you think of Chez l'Arlésienne?" he shouted over the noise. Indeed, it did not. Her aunt and uncle's restaurant in Aix, where she had met the young and inexperienced judge Bernard Martin, had been far quieter, but certainly, she thought, as she glanced around at the men in bowlers and caps puffing on cigarettes and cigars, no less filled with winkers, even customers forward enough to put their hands on her skirts as she waited on their tables. "No," she shouted back. "They didn't smoke so much back then, nor did they keep their hats on." But she pressed his hand under the table to show that she understood his meaning. She may have finally risen to the rank of "madame le professeur," but she hadn't always been. She was the daughter of a blacksmith, the niece of hardworking cooks, a former waitress. A girl with her past, he seemed to be saying, should find comfort in a place like this. He was telling her to relax, not to worry about what she had become.

Within minutes, the red-haired Colette appeared and thumped two beers on the table. Clarie watched as the foam floated precariously back and forth, dripping white cascades along the sides of the glasses. Without a word, the waitress grabbed the end of her already wet and spotted apron, and wiped the table before turning her back. This time it was Clarie who raised her eyebrows in amusement. Then she took the stein by its handle and lifted it up. "To your new career," she said. "To the Labor Exchange," he responded with clink. The stalwart Colette arrived again and plunked two sandwiches on their table. A long sausage peeked out invitingly from each end of their half baguettes. Clarie was starving. As she was about to take her first bite, she spotted a man in a flat bowler and jacket waving at them. When he caught Bernard's attention, he walked over to greet her husband.

"Maître Martin," he said, extending his hand toward Bernard.

"Joseph, good to see you here," said Bernard as he got up and introduced Joseph Tilyer, head of the carpenter's union, to Clarie.

When she extended her hand, the short, squat sandy-haired man reached down to kiss rather than shake it, tickling her ever so slightly with his bushy mustache and scratchy unshaved chin. "Ah yes," he said, when he straightened up, "the professor."

Clarie blushed as his eyes roved over her. He was sizing her up.

"Bourgeois girls, high school, no? What of teaching workers' children?" he muttered, his mouth so close she could smell his cigarettes and see his yellowing teeth.

"Monsieur Tilyer, it would be my greatest wish that all children, workers or not, boys or girls, could go to high school." Clarie could have bitten her tongue. She sounded so prim.

"Well said." Tilyer's smile was much too sardonic for her taste. "But for now," he said, speaking louder, "I'm sending my kids to classes at the Bourse, so that they can learn a thing or two about unions and workers' rights." Before Clarie could muster a response, he turned to Bernard and clapped him on the arm. "And you're going to help teach them. Our professor," he paused, "for certain things that the workers can't teach themselves, of course. Like bourgeois law." He said this last phrase as if he had just bitten into a sour lemon.

A baby began to scream at the next table and, with all the shouts and shushing, Clarie could not discern how Bernard was responding, or if he had even heard what the rude union boss had said to her. She watched as he nodded at something the carpenter was telling him and offered his hand before the man took his leave. While she was still feeling the sting of Tilyer's disapproval, Bernard seemed quite pleased. Sipping her beer, she determined not to worry about whether her husband fit in to his new position. He had obviously just entered another man's world as far removed from her as the courthouse had been. It was childish, but, perhaps because of what she had become, a respectable bourgeois mother and teacher, she felt left out. And, more, unfairly judged by a stranger. She had worked very hard, believed in what she did. Clarie felt angry, and at the same time a little sad, because she could not help wondering if, in becoming who she thought she wanted to be, she had not left something important behind.

Suddenly the pianist struck a loud chord and ran a glissando. When the café quieted down, he got up and, with a sweep of his hand, presented Marie Rossignol. A petite middle-aged woman made a dramatic entrance on the center of the little stage. Her raven black hair was cut into a sharply angled bob and her satiny purple dress swayed above her ankles. Hands folded in front of her, the singer turned slowly and, with piercing dark eyes and resolutely closed scarlet lips, demanded the attention of everyone in the room.

"I've been told," she announced, "that we have a special guest, a new supporter of our cause, born and raised in Lille. Let's sing this song for him."

Bernard leaned over to Clarie and whispered, "Tilyer knows I'm from the north, so he requested something for me." Still tense from her exchange with the carpenter, Clarie nodded and gave Bernard a tight smile. The pianist played a few measures and paused. The singer lifted her head and raised her folded hands to her chest. A surprisingly stirring voice issued from her bird-like body. She began slowly:

They were from the same village
And loved each other tenderly
To unite themselves in marriage
They had vowed with great solemnity
The lad worked with such energy
As he followed his father into the mines
She became a weaver in a factory
They lived with honor all through that time

"Sing with me, now," the singer interjected. And a few voices joined her in a chorus.

She was young and beautiful
He was strong and full of worth
Everyone remembers them
The Fiancés of the North

Marie Rossignol put up her hand, for silence. Spreading her arms she sang about the fiancés' pure love and how they marched for their rights on the Workers' Holiday. After another chorus joined by more of the audience, she opened her eyes wide and signaled a halt to the piano. She began the next lines in a harsh whisper which slowly rose to a tragic crescendo:

The dawn that day shone bright and clear
As flowers bloomed on the First of May

The day that put all France in tears
Because of the great calamity
In the square near the church in the crowd
They stood tall at the front of the line
Then shots rang forth and the blood flowed out
And the two of them lay there dying

She began singing again, louder and stronger:

Oh massacre so sinister
That all will cry henceforth
O'er the tomb where they're fore'er interred
The Fiancés of the North

She waved her hand, and shouted "Now!" and most of the room responded, some with beer steins pounding on the wooden tables and others lifted by emotion to their feet:

She was young and beautiful
He was strong and full of worth
Everyone remembers them
The Fiancés of the North

Clarie was mesmerized by the passion of the performer. Still, she glanced at Bernard from time to time to observe his reactions. She thought she saw tears forming in his eyes. He leaned forward as if he were about to stand and join the singing. But this was not him, at least not yet. She had never seen him show his emotions in public. He did clap with those who clamored and whistled as Marie Rossignol bowed.

"The Fourmies massacre," he shouted to Clarie above the din. "In 1891. This is their song." Having some vague memory of the event, in which workers peacefully marching for their rights had been shot by government troops, she nodded. Bernard joined the applause again.

"Maître Martin." Tilyer appeared at Bernard's side. A weary-looking woman and two towheaded boys dragged behind him. "I hope you enjoyed that." He pointed to the pianist and singer conferring. "It's going to be mushy love songs from here on in, and we gotta get home. Work tomorrow. Even the wife, you know."

"Thanks for this," Bernard said, gesturing with his head toward the stage.

"Eh, maître," the carpenter said as he clapped Bernard's arm again, "it will be such a victory when we finally have a living wage and the eight-hour day they were striking for at Fourmies." Bernard took the man's hand eagerly, shaking it in agreement.

Although she was happy that Tilyer was ignoring her, Clarie hung on his every word. If she were still living at home in Arles, her father would have taught her this worker's song and what it meant. But in 1891 she was hard at work, far from home, studying for her degree.

Tilyer did not bother to introduce Bernard or her to his wife before he led them out the door. He seemed very much in command of his family. And utterly sure of the rightness of his ideas.

Clarie slathered her sausage with hot mustard as if that would bring some taste back into her mouth. The room was quieter now. Some couples, men and women, and women together, began to dance to the singer's sentimental love songs. Through the smoky haze, they all looked tired and sad, sagging with drink or the day's labors. At least it was quiet enough so she wouldn't have to shout. "You told them about the people you knew in Lille, the weavers and the miners?"

"I mentioned it, yes, to let them know that I had long been aware of how hard life was for workers and why they need unions."

"Did you tell them about Merckx?" She sucked in a breath. Merckx was Bernard's oldest friend, a fanatical anarchist, who had been shot and killed outside of Aix as he was trying to flee from the army. She wondered if Bernard had decided to tell them about his role in Merckx's attempted escape, since he was no longer a judge who had broken a "bourgeois law," since he wanted so much to be a man among the men at the Labor Exchange.

"Oh, no, never." He seemed shocked by the question. "You are the only one who will ever know." He took her hand and kissed it. "My brave, loyal girl."

No longer brave, she thought. Just busy and tired. But at least she was a wife, sharing her dear husband's darkest, most dangerous secrets. "We must go soon," she said, taking another sip from her stein. "I work tomorrow too."

He raised his glass again, as if to say "Eat up and enjoy," even as he signaled his consent to her request to depart. She sat back, determined to demonstrate her enjoyment on the day of Bernard's unexpected triumph. And then she thought of the perfect way to cap off the evening. "You know," she said, leaning across the table, "Papa is going to be so proud of you." Her papa, the dear "old red" down in Arles, the man Bernard loved as a second father. Yes, he would be proud. The thought of Giuseppe Falchetti made Bernard smile broadly as they lifted their glasses for their final toast.

Once outside the café, they discovered it had rained. A delightful breeze broke the early summer heat, and the wet cobblestones, cleansed by the downpour, glistened under the gas lights.

"Ah, fresh air," Bernard sighed.

"Yes," she murmured as she linked her arms in his. Getting away from the smoke and crowds in the café enlivened Clarie, reminding her that she, too, had some news that day. First, though, she decided to tease her husband a bit. "Are there any women at the Labor Exchange, or is it all men?"

"I don't think you liked Joseph Tilyer. He's a little gruff. But a good man."

Oh, really, Clarie thought as she fingered the fringe on her fanciest shawl. Someone had made this. And undoubtedly it had been a woman. "Seriously," she said. "Are there women?"

Martin waited until after they crossed a street glittering with puddles to answer. "Not that many," he conceded. "Our women unionists come from factories, like the big sugar factory. A few seamstresses. But most women sew at home or work in small sweatshops or. . . ."

"Are maids and charwomen," Clarie murmured. "I met one today," she began. "A woman who works at our school. An Italian immigrant. She told me a terrible story about her daughters." Clarie hesitated to say the worst. "She thinks someone has kidnapped and killed one of them."

By the time she finished telling Francesca's story, they had arrived at the end of the rue Rodier. They strolled in silence for a few moments, before Bernard paused in front of their building. Clarie assumed that he did not want his voice to echo in the courtyard. He tried to reassure Clarie by reminding her of the many wayward girls he had seen in his chambers and in the Paris courts. It was much, much more likely that they were runaways, he explained, than victims of kidnapping or murder. Or girls, innocent enough, trying to have some fun and not finding their way back home. If the sisters were together, he assured her, they were probably safe. He embraced her and kissed her lightly on the cheek. "Next week," he counseled as he held her by her shoulders and looked into her eyes, "seek this Francesca out. I'll bet you'll find that her daughters have returned."

5

MAURA HATED LIVING WITH THE Russian girls. Hated, hated, hated it. She punctuated her indignation with greater and greater force as she pumped the water from the public faucet in the rue de l'Arbalète. Living with the Russians was every bit as bad as living with her mother. Every one of them *chose* Maura to take out the night soil pail in the morning, clean it, pump water in the other bucket and carry it up the stairs. Why her? With her mother it was those pleading eyes, trying to make you feel guilty, and her complaining about spending all night scrubbing on her hands and knees. With the Russians it was even worse. They had had a *meeting* about it! Maura had been *delegated* to do the water-carrying, *if she was willing*. She was the strongest, they had told her, and they had to get ready for school and for their exams. Well, she'd show them, she vowed, as she carried the heavy sloshing bucket up the stairs in one hand and the empty disgusting one in the other. She'd be working before they knew it, and out of there. Then who would they "elect" to carry their water?

By the time she reached the third floor, the hardest part had passed, and so had some of her ire. She pounded on the door and called out her name. Vera, the tall blond one, opened it and stepped aside, inviting Maura into a room that was as drab and depressing as the one she and Angela had left behind on the other side of Paris: one bed shared by the two Russian girls, one table, one little chest of drawers, one pot-belly stove for cooking and heating. Their shawls and cloaks hung on nails protruding from a scaly greenish gray wall. Across from it, two shelves held a few dented pots and pans, and their bread and lard, provisions that could never be high enough to keep away the bugs and mice. *Pouah!*

The only thing that was really different was what they hung on the walls. At home, Maura's mother had nailed a picture of the sad-eyed Virgin Mary, with a crown of thorns circling her heart, over her bed. Right beside a crucifix. They gave Maura the creeps. Who needed to see all that suffering when you lived it every day?

Over the Russians' bed there were three watercolors of distant places, beautiful places they had left behind. Maura plopped down on the bed next to Angela, who, like the good girl she was, had already folded up the blanket the two of them had slept on. Maura twisted her mouth to one side of her face and shook her head. She could not understand why rich people chose to live like poor people. Maybe all Russians were crazy. Except, Maura sighed, as she watched Vera and Lidia, washing up, sharing the water they had poured into the basin, they didn't seem crazy.

Maura scuffed her shoe along the rough wooden floor. She knew in her heart that Vera and Lidia weren't really so bad. As soon as they were done studying on the first night, they had spent a long time talking to her and Angela, trying to figure out how to keep them away from the police. In fact, she mused, they were like Pyotr. They looked in your eyes when they asked questions, as if they cared about your answers. They had even gotten her to tell them her most secret ambition, something she had not even dared to tell Angela. And they were smart. They were going to be doctors. They knew things. They knew people. On Sunday, two days after she and Angela had shown up, Vera brought them new identity cards, from "a friend." Vera and Lidia even knew the best way out of the city, in case she and Angela had to flee. Still they couldn't stay with the Russian girls forever. It was Wednesday. It had already been five nights. *Where was Pyotr?*

Armed with her notebooks, Vera bent down to give Maura and Angela a kiss good-bye. Lidia, the short, dark one, didn't even have to bend. "We'll be back by dinner," she said, "right after our classes. Don't let anyone in except Pyotr. And if you are nervous, you can watch the street from the window. Remember the back door down the hall. You can make it out of here before the police get up the stairs."

Angela reached to give her a hug. "Thank you," she whispered.

As soon as the Russians had left, Maura got up, put her hands on her hips, and stood before her sister. "We've got to get out of here."

"We can't." Angela shook her head. The bruises on her face were barely perceptible in the thin light. No one would give her a second look now. Still she resisted leaving the room. "We can't go back home," she said in a quiet voice. "We have to wait for Pyotr."

Impatient, Maura began to pace back and forth over the small space in front of the bed. "We can't keep sleeping on the floor with the mice." *At least at home they had a mattress.* "We can't keep eating their food. We can't hide here forever."

"We can give them money, some of what you stole from Monsieur Barbereau."

"Monsieur Barbereau," Maura repeated sarcastically. How could she call that bastard monsieur? "We didn't steal it. It was ours. He owed it to us. I'm sure," she added less confidently. "Anyway, he's dead. You can't steal from a dead man."

Angela got up and took Maura by the shoulders. "Of course you can, and we did."

"Okay, so that's done. Nothing we can do about it." Maura turned toward the window and bit her lip. Angela wasn't the only one who had nightmares about that bastard's bloody skull. And the squishy thuds as Pyotr hit him twice from behind with the iron poker. And the moans, until his body stopped twitching. And the blood dripping from the side of his ugly mouth. Maura closed her eyes and held herself tight to keep from shivering. The morning's black bread lurched in her stomach. *It was done. He's dead. Nothing to do about it except go on living.* She wanted to shout "Stop being a ninny. What about us?" She swirled back to face her sister.

"You know," Maura said, trying another tack, "being Russians and anarchists, Vera and Lidia could be dangerous. The police could be watching *them.*" Maura made her eyes large, as though she really believed in this made-up peril. "Maybe there's a bomb right under the bed," she said, carrying on the act by lunging forward.

Angela stopped her before she could pull the blanket out and begin searching. "Maura, don't be silly. They told us that they don't believe in violence anymore. That it didn't work. That they have to find another way."

"Oh sure, your lover, the anarchist, doesn't believe in violence, that's why he crushed Barbereau's skull."

"Quiet!" Angela slapped Maura on the cheek. And then began to cry. "I'm sorry, I'm sorry," she sobbed as she fell down onto the bed. "I just can't stand to think about it. And Pyotr is not my lover. How could you say such a thing?"

Well, he wants to be, Maura thought resentfully as she rubbed her stinging cheek. She was glad that Angela was suffering more than she from that slap. Angela, Angelina, the little angel. The one everyone loves most. Well, where would they be if she, Maura, hadn't thought to cover the little angel's mouth after Barbereau fell to the floor like an angry stuck bull. If she hadn't thought to say out loud for anyone who might be listening through the windows in their courtyard, "Oh, thank God, you stopped hitting my sister." If she hadn't given Pyotr a sign to bar the door until they figured out what to do. She was the strong one, the smart one. Her chest heaved up and down. She felt like crying too, but she wasn't going to give in.

"All right, all right, so they're not violent. They've done nothing wrong. But haven't they told us, just like Pyotr did, about police spies everywhere? Didn't they say sometimes they think they are being followed?"

"We must wait for Pyotr," Angela insisted.

Maura rolled her eyes and let out a loud sigh, hoping to convey all her impatient disgust with her ever-obedient, docile sister. Well, she, Maura, had to do something.

She turned to the table and opened the book where Vera had hidden her new identity card. She smiled, admiring it. The Russians had let her choose a new name and a new age. She was no longer Maura Lucia Laurenzano, age 17, abandoned daughter of Luigi, the accordionist, and unloved child of Francesca, the charwoman. She was no longer the "dark one," the "Moor" who had aroused the suspicions of her tall blond father the very day she was born. No longer the one to blame. She raised the card to her lips and kissed it. She had become Albertine Hélène LeChevalier, age 20, ready and able to fulfill her ambition. The Russians had tried to talk her into calling herself something more common. But she wanted to sound more high-born. What she hadn't told them was that LeChevalier, the knight, was in honor of Pyotr.

She wrinkled the card a little, like they had told her, to make it seem worn, and pressed it out over the heavy medical book with the palm of her hand. Reaching down under the table, she pulled out one of the bundles Angela and she had brought with them on that fatal night. She paused when she glimpsed Pyotr's clothes reverently folded on top of hers. She would have lifted his shirt and breathed in his scent, if Angela had not been watching. Then, almost crying out in frustration, she retied the heavy sack and pushed it back in place. Why hadn't she thought: Maura Laurenzano didn't own anything suitable for an Albertine.

Clenching her teeth, she straightened up and went to the chest of drawers, yanking them open and searching.

"What are you doing?" Angela jumped off the bed to stop her.

"Looking for something nice to wear."

"You can't take their clothes."

"I'm only *borrowing* them. And besides, they liked the shirtwaist blouses we brought with us. We can trade. I'll leave them all here." Only she had had the presence of mind to grab a few of the stiff cotton garments they had slaved over.

"Maura!" Angela stood behind her, breathing down her neck.

"Angela," Maura said, keeping her back to her sister, refusing to argue, "I'm going to look for a job."

"You can't. Someone might—"

"Don't worry. I'm not going to cross the river. I know what I'm doing," she said as she pulled out an ice-blue blouse that was soft and silky. She laid it on top of the dresser and kept looking until she found a matching satin bag that she could hang from her wrist, and a brooch of emerald stones. She held the blouse up to her chest and smiled. When she had asked Vera and Lidia, ever so casually, if they had been to one of the grand department stores, they admitted that they had gone to the Bon Marché, to try to understand why some people succumbed to their desire for *things*, rather than yearning for freedom and equality. How had they gotten there, Maura had asked, even more casually. And they explained how you could walk, for a long way, or take the omnibus. Because she had been smart enough to go through the dead Barbereau's pockets before they put the stones in them, Maura had money for the omnibus.

"Maura, you can't do this. Not without permission," Angela pleaded.

"If they come back before me, let them choose one of the shirtwaists," Maura sniffed with a put-on hauteur, rehearsing for her new role in life.

Then she proceeded to change from her frayed floral blouse, pin up her hair, and attach the brooch, even though the Russians, being who they were, willing to be poor, willing to be spinsters, did not have a looking glass in their room.

Maura wended her way up toward the Place du Panthéon. She knew nothing about the massive gray building that loomed in her path except that it held the tombs of famous people. She couldn't imagine why anyone cared. Seeing one dead man had been quite enough for her. That gloomy mood lifted as she approached her destination. Even before she circled around to the front of the building, she heard the joyful hubbub of youth and privilege. A few handsome young men in straw hats sprawled along the low steps of the Panthéon, enjoying the sun, reading, talking, and laughing. The ornate, columned façade hovered over a broad street dotted with lively cafés spilling outdoors and tinkling with dishes and silver. Since the omnibus was not in sight yet, Maura had time to observe what it was like to be a student in the famous Latin Quarter. She peered into dusty old shops where law books or medical books or history books were piled high, all the way up to the ceiling. Enough to give you a headache, she thought, turning toward the open street. She pressed on her growling stomach as she passed a woman selling fried potatoes from a cart. This smell and the aroma of coffee were so tempting. But she couldn't. She had to keep her gloves clean and be sure to drip nothing on Vera's blouse.

Maura wrinkled her brow as she observed three women sitting by themselves in a café. They were probably either foreigners or *grisettes*, the working-class girls who befriended students in order to be treated to a good time. She'd never be a grisette, giving herself over to someone else for a pittance. Nor would she want to become depressingly earnest, like Vera or Lidia. Ordinary Frenchwomen did not go to the Sorbonne or Law School or any other university in Paris. And yet. Maura paused to stare down at a pimply-faced boy poring over his books at a table. Maybe that wasn't right. As far as she could see, *he* was quite ordinary, and yet *he* was probably studying to be a lawyer or a doctor or . . . someone else rich. Men were so lucky.

Just then an omnibus pulled by three bay horses rounded the corner, and she hurried to the stop. She paid full fare to sit inside rather than climb the curving ladder to the open air at the top. She was not going to take the chance of mussing her hair or her outfit, even though there was hardly a breeze. The day had already turned sultry. A gentleman got up and offered his seat. After nodding solemnly as she took it, she made it her business to ignore him and stare out the window. They rumbled through the broad Boulevards Saint-Michel and Saint-Germain, both crowded with students and loungers, enjoying themselves at canopied cafés or window-shopping under leafy trees. It was so pretty here. Not at all like the crooked, stinking, treeless street where Maura lived with her mother and sister. She sighed. She had seldom left her old neighborhood.

But one such rare journey had served as a revelation. Maura's mother had dragged her reluctant daughters to the central city to read the job notices posted at Saint-Eustache. She had hoped to find better positions for all of them. As a special treat, she decided to show Angela and Maura the windows of La Samaritaine, a grand new department store. Even though the sign said "free entry," Maura's mother had been too backward to walk in, and Angela had been too shy. Maura smiled, remembering how she had left them behind to enter a shiny new world, illuminated by electricity and filled with luxury. Spellbinding light fell from the ceiling in clusters of flowery glass chandeliers. Maura strolled under their magic through rows and rows of beautiful things: jewelry cascading down toward counters, scarves fluttering in a rainbow of colors, dresses and blouses and skirts and cloaks parading everywhere she looked. When she reached to touch one of the scarves, a clerk, a girl not much older than she, waved her away.

That's when Maura noticed them, the clerks, in crisp new dresses, standing behind the counters, living in this clean, bright world. At the very moment that she realized they were looking down their noses at her, she decided that someday she would become one of them.

"Albertine LeChevalier," she whispered. She needed to get used to that name and learn how to stick *her* nose up in the air. "I am Albertine."

"Excuse me?" a man beside her said.

Maura gasped; she hadn't meant for anyone to hear. "Nothing." She shook her head and was about to look away again, until she realized that she did not know exactly where to get off the bus. "Do you know the stop for the Bon Marché?" she asked.

"Are you going shopping there?"

She lifted her hand to straighten her glove. The little blue satin sack hung prettily from her wrist. "Yes," she said. She knew that the Bon Marché was even grander than La Samaritaine. It was the kind of place in which an Albertine might well spend a few happy hours.

He smiled through tobacco-colored teeth. He was well dressed, but old, at least forty. She could see glimmers of flinty gray in his mustache and beard, and smell the lingering odor of his cigarettes. She needed to be careful. She was relieved when he told her that he'd love to take her there himself, but he had business to conduct across the river. "However," he said, "it's only two more stops after this. You'll see. You can't miss it." Then, the stranger stood up to get off the bus. As he left, he tipped his bowler and chuckled. Was he laughing because he knew that she was not the type of woman who could afford the Bon Marché? Maura straightened herself up and turned back to the window. Albertine would show them all.

The man was right. You couldn't miss the grandest emporium of them all. Especially since almost every other woman on the omnibus got off at the stop across from it. Maura hopped off last, into an atmosphere abuzz with the excited voices of shoppers, the shouts of drivers and haulers, and the snorting of horses. She stood gaping, while others pushed past her to cross a broad intersection made perilous by moving carriages, omnibuses, bicycle riders, and boys pushing delivery carts filled with goods. Although she had never seen a palace, Maura was sure that no duke or king or czar could have built anything more magnificent than a store that took up an entire city block. The windows shone like jewels. Each corner was crowned by a dome that reminded her of the Russian church in one of Vera's watercolors. Maura took a deep breath. To work in such a place, with so many people, so many things! No mother, no garlic-breathing lecherous boss, no sister to tell her what to do. How wonderful it would be. Before attempting the hazardous crossing that would lead to the fulfillment of her dreams, Maura squinted and watched to see how the other women got into this marvel. Then she saw it, the most magnificent crown of all over the grand entrance in the middle of one side of the building. Biting down on her lip, and glancing from side to side, she ventured forward.

Entering the store, she reminded herself to keep her spine erect and her chin ever-so-slightly in the air. Still, she could not keep from gasping. Was this a palace? Or was it a cathedral in the throes of some grand ceremony? Four floors above her, skylights streamed the noon-day sun along the central aisle. On either side, a circular staircase led up to galleries lining the second, third and fourth floors. Murmurs and sighs of delight flowed from top to bottom, like a chorus of cherubim singing and thrumming their wings. She processed slowly, like a bride. Not a bride saying her vows at the local wineshop, as so many of her neighbors had done, but a princess-bride joining her handsome groom in front of a bishop. *Albertine,* she thought, *I am Albertine Hélène LeChevalier.*

Midway through the aisle she decided to examine the merchandise and lightly ran a finger over a man's striped silk cravat.

"May I help you?" said a suave masculine voice.

She paused for one tasteful second before replying, "I am looking for the ladies' things."

"Lingerie, dresses, scarves, linens, what—?"

"Lingerie," she interjected quickly and bowed her head as if she were the kind of girl who blushed at the very thought of referring to her under and night wear.

"Second floor, in the gallery to the left. A lady will help you when you get there."

The speaker was clean-shaven and younger than the man on the bus. And rather handsome, all tucked into his dark blue suit. She peered around him. She hadn't noticed before that all the clerks on the main floor seemed to be men in suits just like his. But she didn't let this bother her. He had said "a lady" would help her upstairs. "Thank you."

"You've not been to our store before? Do you know about the outdoor concerts?"

She pressed her lips together and shook her head. "No. My first time."

"A moment." He went behind the counter and handed her a brochure.

"Every Sunday during the summer. Right in front of the grand entrance."

A concert every week! The Bon Marché was even more magnificent than she could have imagined.

"Thank you," she said again, as she delicately relieved him of the program, making sure not to touch the man's hand with her glove. Then with a solemn nod and a slight, gracious smile, she lifted the side of her skirt and sauntered toward the staircase.

By the time she got to the top, she was out of breath. Nervousness. She stood by the rail to calm herself and then launched into an enormous room hung with satin nightgowns arrayed in a myriad of the palest, most beautiful colors. Whoever bought them, she thought, does not live where it is too hot or too cold. Everything in their life must be just right. Someday I will have a room like that.

"May I help you?"

There was a coldness in the voice that put Maura on guard.

"I am wondering where I can inquire about a position." *Inquire, position*, that sounded just right, just so "Albertine" to Maura's ears. On the other hand, the woman in front of her didn't appear to be an "Albertine" at all. She was dressed in a broadcloth navy blue shirtwaist dress that made her look like a schoolmarm.

"Really." The witch had the nerve to arch her eyebrows.

"Really," Maura responded.

"Very well, come with me." The haughty clerk's brisk walk created a breeze which made some of the gowns ebb and flow as she moved. Maura's heart began to pound. *Albertine*, she whispered to herself.

At the back of the huge, high-ceilinged room, a much older woman, in the same dress, sat at a desk, writing. "Madame Vergennes, this young woman wants to inquire about a place in our department."

Without even looking up, this Mme Vergennes murmured, "Did you tell her you need to have a great deal of selling experience and be very good at numbers to work at the Bon Marché?"

"I know a great deal about shirtwaists," Maura blurted out before she realized that this was not a very "Albertine" thing to say. She should have talked about her schooling, made it sound much better than it was.

Her outburst caught the woman's attention. She lifted her head and peered through her pince-nez. "Shirtwaists?"

Maura stayed utterly still as the woman surveyed her from head to toe. "Yes, I sold them in a nice shop on the Boulevard Rochechouart." Maura squeezed her eyes shut and cringed. Albertine would not have been merely a clerk, nor would she have worked near Maura's old neighborhood on one of the outer boulevards. She would have gone to a high school, a good one. But it was done, said. Maura forced herself to meet the woman's eyes.

"Hmmm. The Boulevard Rochechouart. Is that near where you live?"

"Yes." Maura could feel the sweat sprouting under her arms. She hoped it was not staining Vera's blouse.

"I see." Mme Vergennes glanced beyond Maura's shoulder. "Mademoiselle Henri, you may go back to your post."

Maura heard the feet and skirt shuffle behind her.

"Your name?"

Maura noted that the woman's eyes were the same color as Vera's blouse, only their iciness pierced through you rather than covered you. She felt exposed and, even in the heat, chilled. If this woman was a schoolmarm, she was the sternest one ever, worse than the nuns that had frequently struck Maura's knuckles with a ruler.

"Albertine Hélène LeChevalier," Maura whispered.

"Age?"

"Twenty." Maura could not keep her chest from heaving.

"May I see your identity card?" The woman held out her hand, which looked hardened and strong.

Maura reached in her sack and handed over the false identity card. The woman's silence was worse than her questions. She held the card in her two hands glancing between it and Maura's face for what seemed an eternity, as if she were deciding what to do next, as if she were going to call the police or find someone to throw Maura out of the store. Finally, Mme Vergennes handed back the card.

"Come with me."

Going down the aisle toward the door was torture. The witchy Mademoiselle Henri and another clerk watched, cupping their hands over their faces as they whispered and giggled. Maura's face was burning, but she held her head high, never letting on that she noticed their scorn.

Mme Vergennes led Maura around the second floor gallery into another magnificent room. But this one was not filled with merchandise. Rather it had a few tables and benches, and walls covered with paintings above shelves and shelves of leather-bound books.

"Sit here." Mme Vergennes took a place on a bench.

Having no other choice, Maura followed her command.

"Where did you get that card?" the woman demanded. She had taken her glasses from her nose, leaving them to hang by a black cord over her chest.

It did not matter that Maura's mind was a jumble, for she dare not say anything. She almost stopped breathing.

"You are not Albertine LeChevalier, are you?"

Although her mouth fell open, Maura still could not make a sound.

Mme Vergennes sighed and rubbed the reddened spots left by the pince-nez on the bridge of her nose. When she looked at Maura again, her eyes seemed sad rather than angry. "This is dangerous, you know. The people who do this sort of thing. I hope you are not connected with them, criminals, anarchists."

Maura squeezed her hands together and bowed her head. "No," she mumbled, "no," biting down hard on her lip.

"Good. You are young. You are an innocent girl. You've never committed a crime, have you?"

The morning's meager breakfast roiled in Maura's stomach. Was watching a man die, carrying his body through the streets, and throwing it into a basin a crime? Somehow Maura was sure it must be a very serious one. Fortunately, she got out another denial.

"You don't steal. You do not sell your body."

"No, no, no." This was easier because it was true.

"Then, my child," the woman placed a hand gently over Maura's, "you must beware. There are so many people out there who will want to take advantage of you. You need to find honest work. And maybe someday you can come here and join our family. We are a family of sorts, you know, and I am in charge of selecting and looking after our girls." She paused. "You should come back only after you've proven your worth and are willing to tell the truth about who you are."

When Maura did not answer, the woman withdrew her hand. "Do you see all of this?" she asked. "It is our reading room. For our clients *and* for our employees. There are so many benefits here, a lunch room, a pension, but you must earn it, and it is hard work. Yet, I believe, it is the best such job in all of France."

The worst part of being humiliated was that the woman was being kind. Maura could not hold back the tears. "Go back to your neighborhood," Mme Vergennes told her. "Try to get a position in a shop. Be diligent and hardworking. Learn how to calculate quickly and accurately. And, then, we shall see, in a few years." She paused before standing up over the chastened Maura. "I must get back."

Not until she was sure that Mme Vergennes had left the library did Maura dare look up. She couldn't bear the thought that she had so easily been caught in a lie, that she'd let her hopes be dashed without a struggle. She wanted to scream. To tear up the stupid identity card. To rend Vera's silky blouse. She swiped her cheeks and nose with her glove and sleeve, and sniffled until she was sure that she had stopped driveling. As the breaths came into her body, her chest expanded, filling her with angry energy. She fled to the staircase and, with her hand on the rail, raced down to the first floor. *What did these people know about being poor? What did oh-so-proper Mme Vergennes know about crime, real crime? She had never lifted and pulled a bleeding, dead body. She could not possibly know what real trouble felt like.* Maura did, and felt the weight of it now more than ever. Lowering her eyes to avoid any encounter with the courtly salesman, she hurried to the grand entrance. Once outside, she crossed her arms over her chest and kept her eyes to the sidewalk as she got as far away from the Bon Marché as she could. She had to think. She had to find a way out.

After about fifteen minutes of ignoring strangers and skirting past carriages, she found herself at a gate of the Luxembourg Gardens, the park the Russian girls had described when they talked about their foray to the Bon Marché. Shrugging her shoulders, Maura decided to go in. Perhaps she'd find a bench, shade, some consolation for her terrible day. She was hungry too, and as soon as she saw a woman selling fried potatoes she knew she had to have them. Her gloved fingers ran over the money in the thin silk sack. Barbereau's money. Maura resisted the shiver that the thought of his rigid, dead body always sent through her. She set her chin resolutely forward. The money was hers now. She took off her gloves and shoved them into the little sack, digging out a few coins. She bought a cone of *frites* and gobbled them up as she stood by the stand, as if eating them fast would chase away her fears. When she realized that she'd hardly tasted her rare treat, she bought another cone and munched on them more slowly as she strolled, trying to look as if she fit in.

The labyrinth of stony paths led her past men in top hats, nannies pushing strollers, and lovers communing on benches. Had she been in a better frame of mind, she might have tried to guess whether these couples were having a tryst, or even sat down by them just to be annoying. But what was the joy in that? In any of this?

The gardens of brilliantly colored flowers didn't give Maura much pleasure either, at least not until she remembered Lidia's complaint, that every French garden looked like a regiment of soldiers on parade. That image brought a smile to Maura's lips, and so did the memory of Lidia's vehemence. Flowers, she had insisted, should be free, allowed to grow wild, not made to stand at attention in carefully pruned and groomed rows.

If only she could believe the way Pyotr, Lidia and Vera did, Maura thought as she ate the last of her frites. The Russians proclaimed that everyone should and eventually *would* be free: free to live, to learn, to earn, to love. Maura felt too poor to believe in these dreams. And too aware that you could love someone who did not love you.

Maura sank into a metal chair by a pair of grandmothers in big feathered hats knitting baby clothes and exchanging judgments on passersby. She closed her eyes, blocking them out. Mme Vergennes had told her to come back when she was willing to reveal who she really was. But who was Maura Laurenzano, really? A shirt finisher with high ambitions? An accomplice to a murder? A bad sister, a worse daughter? Why would she ever want to tell anyone who she was?

Suddenly a little boy in breeches bumped into her. "Felix!" his nanny scolded, "not so fast, we'll get to the show in time."

"Rude," clucked one grandmother, and Maura could not agree more. The stupid nanny, all decked out in her black-and-white uniform, hadn't even offered an apology.

"You would think," said the other old woman, "that they could offer more elevating entertainments than Punch and Judy."

Maura straightened up. A puppet show. Watching Punch and Judy hit each other might be just the thing to get her mind off her troubles. She crushed the greasy paper that had held her potatoes and dropped it under the chair, before getting up to follow the nanny and the rambunctious boy.

But she never got to the puppet theater in the park. As mothers and nursemaids began to congregate with their charges toward the children's playground, Maura heard an organ grinder playing a familiar Italian song. Heart pounding, she followed the music. What if she was about to find her tall, handsome father? As she rounded a bend she saw that the musician was stout and mustachioed, wearing the kind of silly alpine hat her tall, blond father never wore. She scurried out of sight before a little girl holding out a cup for donations spotted her. Of course, it wasn't her father, just as that little girl was not Maura, but seeing the accordionist and the child evoked the old sadness.

There were signs everywhere warning her against stepping on the grass, so Maura leaned against a pole and let the memories float in her mind. Her father always claimed to hate singing in the street. Like many poor Italian children of his generation, he had been practically sold by his impoverished parents to be apprenticed as an "accordion boy." Maura remembered the bitterness in his voice when he talked about being torn from his mother and native village in the Italian mountains. He spent his childhood on the streets of French cities, playing and begging, being beaten by his master and hounded by the authorities. Abandoned in Paris, he only survived because he was rescued by a kind Polish immigrant who taught him how to lay bricks.

He had been happy, he said, for just a little while. But once he had family to support, he took up his accordion again, every Sunday, this time enlisting his own daughters to hold out the begging cups. He'd claimed that Angela made the most money because of her blond curls. He hardly noticed that Maura was the one who listened and learned all the songs, who felt his unhappiness every time he talked about his faraway home. Her favorite songs were his favorites, sad ballads that he sang at their table after he had drunk a good deal of wine. She began to hum:

Vado di notte come fa la luna
I wander through the night like the moon
Vado cercando lo mio innamorato
Searching to find my true love
Ritrovai la Morte acerba et dura

Instead I found mocking, cruel Death
Mi disse: "Non cercar, l'ho sotterato"
Who told me, "Don't look anymore, I've buried him."

When Maura was a child, she had always loved the notion of wandering like the moon. Back then, sitting on the floor, watching her father, she hadn't known death or abandonment. Now she did. And the haunting melody, with its eerie lyrics, suddenly made her uneasy. She needed to get back. What if they had found the body? What if something had happened to Pyotr? Or to Angela? She searched for someone, anyone, who could tell her how to get to the Panthéon.

6

The police came for the Russian girls that afternoon.

Maura spotted the black van before she got to her street. She knew it was a police wagon because of the breathing slits slashed along its windowless side. For an instant, she thought of turning back and running. But she had to know what was happening. What if they had found Angela? Maura glanced at the driver, who sat smoking a cigarette, reins in hand, as indifferent and impassive as the horses he commanded. Heart pounding, she walked by as if she had no interest in his presence, as if she were completely innocent.

When she rounded the corner onto the rue de l'Arbelète, she heard the shouting. A score of men and women had gathered in front of the dank wineshop across from her building. For one insane, hopeful moment, she imagined the police were there to quell a drunken brawl. Then she understood what they were saying, and she knew. "Foreigners!" "Anarchists!" "Killers!" "Bombers!" An old crone, screaming with righteous anger, stepped in front of the crowd and pointed toward the entrance to Maura's building. Vera and Lidia stumbled out, their hands tied behind their backs. They were being poked and prodded with rifles by three uniformed men. Despite their ill treatment and the curses being flung at them, they held their heads high.

Maura flattened herself against a wall. She felt as if someone had grabbed her by the throat and was squeezing the life out of her. Was there some mistake? Had they really come for her and Angela? Maura froze in place as the frightening entourage approached. She almost cried out when she heard footsteps scurrying behind her. A toothless old woman jostled her, trying to get a better view. "Looks like those foreigners are at it again," the woman crowed to her companion, a man in a blue worker's smock, carrying a street sweeper's broom. The man grinned and shrugged his shoulders, enjoying the spectacle. Much to Maura's relief, they ignored her.

As the police and their prisoners got closer and closer to the corner, Maura caught Vera's eye. Instinctively she reached for the brooch she had "borrowed" from the Russian girl. Vera shook her head ever so slightly. She wasn't worried about jewelry or borrowed clothes. She had a more urgent message to convey: "Act like you don't know us."

"What are you looking at?" one of the policemen said as he struck the tall Russian girl in the ribs with the butt of his rifle.

She gasped with pain, but refused to bend. "I'm looking at the poor people of Paris. Those you oppress," she said loud enough for all to hear.

Maura's finger nails clawed into the wall. Bullies! She wanted to run up and slap the vicious brute. But she could do nothing. The police might have found Barbereau. They wouldn't care that Pyotr didn't mean to do it, that he was only saving Angela. They'd say that she and Angela helped murder the bastard, and then, and then, they'd happily let go of the Russian girls and drag her and Angela all the way to the guillotine.

The toothless old woman stepped forward and spit on Lidia. Not knowing what to do, Maura glanced at Vera, who again signaled with a slight shake of head, *do nothing*. Some of wineshop habitués trailed the terrible procession through the narrow street, hooting and shaking their fists. Sweating with fear and from the relentless heat of the waning afternoon, Maura wound her way past them toward her building. Angela, she had to find Angela. *Maman*, she bit her lip, the plea came unbidden into her mind. *Maman*. Oh, to be home again. Oh, to be back to the way things were, as miserable as they were.

"I hope you weren't part of their plots."

The stocky concierge, heightened by her clogs, stepped in front of Maura, blocking her entrance to the building. Every concierge that Maura had ever known was nosy, controlling the comings and goings of tenants and resenting the cleaning up they had to do. Maura had always done her best to steer clear of them. This one was not about to let her pass.

"You heard what I said, missy. I know you are up there with them."

"What did they do?" Maura tried to sound innocent, even as she played the part of Judas. Her mind ran with questions. *Why take the Russians away now? Have they found Barbereau's body? Or have the police decided to round up all anarchists and foreigners?* Maura shuddered. Either way, she was in danger. The French suspected Italians of all kinds of crimes and plots too.

"Another bomb."

"Bomb?" This time Maura did not have to feign her innocence or alarm.

"Yeah, over near Montmartre. Some Russian." She cackled with glee. "Blew him up instead of anyone else. Served him right. At least that's what the police told me."

"A Russian," Maura whispered. *Pyotr!* But she daren't ask more, daren't admit that she knew a Russian boy. Or that she loved one. "I must find my sister," she mumbled. "Please," she pleaded. "We haven't done anything wrong," she lied.

"I want you gone by tomorrow, you hear?" the woman said as she stepped aside.

Maura could feel the concierge's eyes boring into her back as she tried to walk up the stairs like a normal person. But her feet were leaden, as if already weighed down with the chains of a condemned prisoner. Still she persisted, one foot in front of the other, up all three flights, hoping against hope that Angela would be in the room waiting for her. They had to figure out what to do.

As soon as she saw the wide-open door, she knew that her sister would not be there. Still she was shocked to see the destruction: books and pictures flung on the floor, clothes torn off their hooks and out of drawers, the bed mattress upended and slashed. Even Angela and Maura's poor possessions had been strewn about and trampled on.

Everything was going wrong. Everything! Frustrated and scared, Maura pulled the mattress back into place and flung herself upon the bed. She hid her head in her arms, trying to push the day and all its terrible events out of her mind. She didn't know how long she had lain there before she felt a hand gently shaking her shoulder.

"Maura."

Angela. Maura sat up and embraced her sister. "What happened?" she asked.

"I don't know. I ran. Vera and Lidia told me to hide and not come back for a while. Do you think all this," Angela grimaced as she looked about the room, "all this is because of us?"

Maura shook her head.

"If it is," Angela continued, "then we need to go to the police. We need to confess. We can't let—"

"Stop it. Stop talking nonsense." Maura put her hand over Angela's mouth and peered into her eyes. "We *can't* go to the police. They'll send us to the guillotine, and Pyotr too." *Pyotr! Was he even alive?* "Listen," she said more calmly, "Vera and Lidia were arrested because they are anarchists. Maybe there is another roundup."

Maura let go of Angela and told her what she had found out. When Angela heard there was a possibility that a Russian had been killed, she rose from the bed and began picking up and folding the scattered clothes, one by one, placing them on the table.

"It may not be Pyotr, you know. Maybe it's just a rumor," Maura offered.

Still Angela lifted and folded, flattening each blouse and skirt without saying a word. This was no good. They had decisions to make.

"We have to find out for sure. You stay here," Maura ordered. "Fix things up for when Vera and Lidia come back." Maura swallowed hard, suppressing her own doubts about whether the Russian girls would ever be allowed to come back. "I'll go and see if I can find out if anything really happened near Montmartre."

"Don't leave me!" Angela suddenly came to life and grabbed Maura's arm.

Maura patted her hand. "Don't worry. I'm only going to look for a newspaper. Surely the late editions will have something. And, if not, we'll know it was all lies. That will be good, don't you think?" she added, searching for some way to reassure her sister.

Angela nodded and turned away, surveying the destruction before once again picking and folding and smoothing out Vera and Lidia's things, her movements slow, deliberate and futile. Maura feared that if she stayed, watching, one more minute, she'd be immobilized by the cloud of despair that had enveloped her sister. She had to get out.

When she reached the bottom of the stairs, she waited until she could slip unnoticed past the lodge in the courtyard where the concierge lived. Once on the street, she ran to the nearest market square, hoping to find a newspaper hawker. A small crowd had already gathered. She heard the word "bomb" and pushed her way through, holding up one of Barbereau's smallest coins and wresting a copy of *Le Petit Parisien* from the seller's hands. Then she hurried to the old church on the square, yanked at its door, and went in. Her hard breathing filled her with the familiar smell of burning tallow as she scanned the interior to see if she was safe. Only a few people were there. A woman was showing a little girl how to light a candle at a side altar. Two others, on the opposite side of the church, knelt in front of thatched chairs, reciting their beads. A hatless man, near the front, sat immobile, staring up at the painted ceiling. No priest, no nosy nuns. Maura sat down, panting. Vera's blouse was pasted to her skin. It was a relief to be in the dark, cool vastness of the ancient building.

Maura mumbled a prayer. *Please, God, not Pyotr.* If she had not been so close to tears, she might have laughed. Within the last hour, she had called out to her mother, and now she expected God to hear her. *How desperate can you get?* Her mother didn't love her, and Maura certainly did not expect God to answer her prayer. She was on her own. Her eyes fell on the newspaper clutched in her damp hands. The headline screamed ANARCHIST BOMB IN THE GOUTTE-D'OR! Maura gasped. Her neighborhood. Pyotr's neighborhood. She forced herself to read on:

Early this morning a bomb exploded in the Goutte-d'Or Quartier, disturbing those going about their daily lives, and waking others from a peaceful sleep.

"One moment I saw a man across the street hauling his cart, then I heard a boom, and his arm fell on the ground right in front of me," said laundress Marie Riboyet. "I've never seen anything like it. An arm flying in the air, with a bloody stump. The cart going up in flames."

Maura covered her mouth with her hand to keep from crying out. An arm? What about his body? His heart? His beautiful head. Her chest heaved; it couldn't be Pyotr. It just couldn't.

Mme Riboyet still had the assassin's blood on her forehead when the police arrived. After answering their questions, she went on about her business, to the washhouse, planning to scrub extra hard, she told this reporter, to get the dead man's spattered blood out of the sheets in her basket.

She claimed she did not know the dead porter, but the police soon discovered his identity, setting off an alarm that anarchist terror once again is about to strike the capital.

Police Inspector Alain Jobert traced the cart back to its owner, the dry goods merchant Jacques Landière. He told the police that the driver of the cart was one Pyotr Ivanovich Balenov, a Russian "student."

Maura bit her lip, fighting back a moan. *No! No! No! Pyotr. Dear Pyotr!* She blinked away the tears blurring her vision.

> *"I never had any trouble with him before," Landière said. "He was quiet, always so obedient. Did everything I asked him to."*
>
> *Jeannette Blacas, the concierge of the building where the anarchist lived, told a different story. "I never trusted him. I saw him in the café giving speeches about the poor," she snorted, as she sucked on her pipe. "Our poor can take care of themselves. They don't need the likes of foreigners."*
>
> *A Parisian concierge can't be fooled. The police searched the monster's place in the barracks room he shared with other poor carters, looking for explosives, maps and incendiary pamphlets. Little did they know that the crucial evidence had already arrived at the nearby precinct. A pneumatic letter dated 6 A.M. revealed the fiend's plans to destroy part of our city's fashion district. "Bourgeois of Paris. Your Springtime is over," it said in big block letters. "I will put your Grand Boulevards to flames." It was signed, "The Russian."*
>
> *What did he mean by "our Springtime"? Did he plan to throw the bomb into the grand department store Au Printemps? How many innocent women and children would have suffered and died if the anarchist had been able to carry out his diabolical plot? Can we forget the bomb that Emile Henry threw in the Terminus Café three years ago? Or that the President of France was assassinated by an Italian anarchist? Or this very May, how the Charity Bazaar fire engulfed our city's fairest wives, mothers, and daughters with horrifying, annihilating swiftness? That tragedy was an accident, an Act of God. This would have been an Act of Terrorism. Only the diligence of the police and our citizens can keep us safe from another outbreak of anarchist violence.*
>
> *The police are continuing their investigation across Paris, looking for explosives and rounding up associates.*
>
> *Parisians! Be on alert! The bombs may be going off again!*

Maura slapped the paper on the chair next to her. *It's not true. Not true!* Pyotr would never hurt women and children. Hadn't he saved Angela from the real monster? She shook her head. No, no, no. She pressed her lips together in an attempt to muffle her sobs. Not true!

Just then she spotted the priest sauntering down the aisle, getting ready to lock up the church for the night. She folded the paper and bowed her head, holding it to her breast.

"My child, is something wrong?" He had frizzy gray hair and a big belly, like most priests do. She certainly wasn't going to talk to him. What good was God when mocking, cruel Death had won again?

"Nothing is wrong," she murmured to the cassocked figure hovering near her. She got up and fled.

She found Angela sitting by the table, staring at Pyotr's folded shirt.

"Angela," she said quietly, "it was him."

Her sister nodded and closed her eyes.

Maura went down on one knee by her sister's side and put her arm around her waist. "I'm sure he didn't do it. Pyotr didn't believe in bombing."

"I know," Angela whispered; "he was so gentle." She pulled away and began to sob.

Maura sat back against the bed. It was more than his gentleness. She knew what he believed in. Despite Angela's warnings, she used to sneak out before her mother came back from work at night. She'd go to the shabby café where he ate supper with his comrades and stand at the back, listening raptly as he argued against anyone who drunkenly claimed that a bomb or a gun might shake up the bourgeoisie. Patiently, he'd remind them of the destruction that violence had wrought in France and, worse, in his native land, where the bombings and assassinations had only made life harder and crueler for everyone. Then, emboldened by wine, Pyotr would proclaim his faith in the liberation of man's "better nature."

Closing her eyes, Maura tried to recapture Pyotr in those memories. How his face was illuminated by the candle on the wooden table in that dark café. How it reminded her of the gentle living Christ on her mother's favorite holy card. She tried to recall his voice, so sweet, so slow and careful because of his accent. In his new world there would be no Church or State, no rich or poor, no oppressed peasants or workers or women. Everyone would work. Everyone would have a good life.

Tears rolled down Maura's cheeks. She had loved him because he was so good, because he made her want to be good. Yet part of her always held back from believing him, because she knew that some people were bad. Now he was dead. Now everyone was going to blame him and Vera and Lidia for something they would not dream of doing—hurting other people. *It was so unfair!* Maura stood up, clenching her fists and her teeth.

She paced as useless questions drove her back and forth in front of the bed. Who'd want to kill Pyotr? And why? Pyotr had always warned them about the *agents provocateurs*, policemen in disguise, who would say and do terrible things so they could blame and persecute the anarchists. Is that what happened? Or, Maura paused, had someone seen them with Barbereau? Someone who wanted to take revenge. Like the man on the pier, the one Pyotr claimed was a friend. Maura glanced at Angela. The one who had made her sister recoil. Who was he?

If Angela hadn't been so inert, staring, one arm in her lap, the other on the table, Maura would have asked her to tell everything she knew about him right then and there. Instead, she continued to pace until she saw Angela's fingers play lightly over Pyotr's shirt. As if her touch would bring him back to life. When nothing was going to bring him back. He'd never be whole again. Maura grabbed the shirt and smothered her face in it, breathing the last traces of the boy she had loved. She ignored Angela's shocked stare as she thrust the shirt back to her. Then Maura dropped into the rickety chair across the table from her sister. They sat there, silent, until it grew so dark they could barely see each other.

Finally, Angela got up and hugged Maura, telling her they needed to get some sleep. They spent the still, humid night on the Russians' bed, holding each other and crying.

7

THE MORNING THE BOMB WENT off in the Goutte-d'Or district, Bernard Martin was a kilometer away, defending a mason before the industrial council. The mason, Jacques Leroux, sat uncomfortably in a cane-backed chair, pleading his case. His arm was in a dirty, ragged sling, and his face was swollen and discolored. He had taken a terrible fall. Still, without Martin, the council board most likely would have judged him to be negligent in his work habits and made him pay for the builder's broken ladder, the bricks which came crashing down upon him, and the time lost finding a substitute. The odds were clearly against men like Leroux when five of the seven mediators sitting behind the great table were industrialists, wearing suits and frock coats, and only two, more humbly attired, had ever worked with their own hands.

As Martin made his arguments, calling the builder's claims for compensation outrageous, citing the latest laws, and eliciting civil, logical testimony from his defendant, he grew more and more confident. He was changing the odds in favor of the working man, if only because he was "Maître Martin," a real lawyer, a fact that clearly impressed the board. Elation filled him as he waited for the verdict. Martin was doing the job the men at the Labor Exchange had hired him to do, wringing every bit of justice he could from a legal system stacked against them. When the council decided in favor of Leroux, it was almost an anti-climax.

Five minutes later, after handshakes all around, Leroux limped beside Martin as they walked out of the council building. When they got a block away, Martin felt free to say some of the things he could not say in front of the businessmen, for fear of alienating them.

"If we work together, elect the right politicians, there will come a time," he promised, "when the builders will have to pay *you* and other injured workers compensation, instead of covering their faults by blaming the men they exploit for everything that goes wrong. Someday there will be real justice for all."

Leroux bowed his head, not answering.

"You'll be all right for awhile?" Martin asked, fearing that he had been insensitive to Leroux's situation. He was still so new at this. "The mutual funds will get you through, I hope. Thank God for the union, no?"

Leroux nodded, then mumbled, "I don't vote, sir. I wait for the day when the workers will run everything themselves and not count on the. . . "

Martin filled in the word that Leroux hesitated to say, "The bourgeoisie."

The mason nodded again, not wanting to look at the man he might have just insulted, for what could be more bourgeois than a lawyer?

Martin slapped him on the back in good humor. "Two different paths, huh? We'll see which one gets everyone their rights." Leroux's anarchism was the kind that Martin admired and supported, based not on terrorist tactics coming from the fringe of the movement, but on solidarity, self-education, and unions.

Leroux looked up at him, almost grateful. "Thank you, Maître Martin; the union president told us that the Labor Exchange would be better off if we hired our own windbag to compete with their windbags, and I can see—" The man broke off again. This time, the insult had been even more pointed. "I didn't mean. . . "

Martin laughed. "Listen, you want to see windbags, lucky we didn't have to go to the civil court at the Palais de Justice. I would have had to wear one of those black gowns, and you would have seen scores of lawyers and judges flying around the marble halls like a plague of crows cawing their own self-importance. I liked this much better."

When they reached the canals, Leroux stuck out his uninjured hand. "Thank you, Maître Martin, I'm going to take the tram home now."

Martin took the calloused hand gladly. "We made the case," he said. "Do you have need of tram fare?"

This time the smile on the mason's face was genuine. "No, sir, I think I can find a brother who will let me on for free."

Martin nodded. Workers, Anarchists, Socialists. The mason would only be breaking a minor law, yet it was something Martin would not dream of doing. He was in their clubhouse, but not really of their club.

After a wave good-bye, he walked along the canals for a while, which, despite the poverty of the surrounding neighborhood, glistened like jewels under the late morning sun. He loosened his dampened cravat to catch a bit of a breeze before turning down the street that led to the grand Place de la République. He stuck his hands in his pockets, strolling past the hawkers and shoppers. He *was* floating a little and couldn't keep from smiling like a fool as he imagined relating his first victory to Clarie. "He called me a windbag, and that almost took the wind out of my sails, I can tell you," he would say, and her beautiful almond-shaped brown eyes would shine. She'd smile at his *bon mot* and be so pleased for him. Happy that he was happy. Rejuvenated. He had certainly dealt with more important cases as a judge, solving murders, keeping the peace where violence threatened to erupt. But now it was different. He felt part of something, a movement forward, progress in bettering the human condition, not just cleaning up its messes.

A bent-over, toothless man, mumbling a plea, almost fell into Martin. The old beggar's desperation and the unwashed odor that reeked from his filthy clothes vividly reminded Martin of how far he had come and why. After a moment's hesitation, he pulled a coin out of his pocket and dropped it in the man's gnarled hand. Martin had been brought up to believe in charity. The altar-boy son of a pious widow, he believed everything the Church taught him until he encountered the true face and smell of poverty. Merckx. It always came back to Merckx, his oldest boyhood friend. The towheaded thirteen-year-old schoolmate who hated the priests and led Martin through the tottering wooden tenements of Lille to his large family's two miserable rooms. Martin would never forget watching Merckx's father coughing up blood mixed with the coal black dirt of the mines, or observing how the women of the family had been misshapen by years of 14-hour days in the humid, clanging woolen mills. Mills owned by Lille's leading and proudly "charitable" families. It was Merckx who taught Martin that charity without justice or equality was cruel and ineffective. When Martin became a judge, how Merckx had mocked his belief that the state could bring justice! He chose to live by the sword and died an anarchist with four bullet holes in him. *Well, Jean-Jacques*, Martin said in his mind, without really believing that his friend could hear him, *I may have finally found the path I can travel on.*

He wound his way toward his new office tucked into the third floor of the Bourse du Travail, the Labor Exchange's massive new building. He shared the floor with a warren of offices dedicated to union organizing, dispersing mutual funds to the injured and out-of-work, and providing job referrals and financial aid to craftsmen new to the city. The municipal government of Paris had authorized the construction of the building during a radical moment in its history. Ostensibly, it gave workers a place to meet, to learn, and to celebrate. But the inhabitants of the Bourse were well aware that the "gift" also allowed the government to keep an eye on their activities and had been given in the hope that unions would encourage their members to become stalwart supporters of the Republic. But many, like Tilyer, the tough head of the Carpenters' Union, believed the Republic was run by and for the bourgeoisie and were determined to subvert any attempts to control them. Because of the anarchist or socialist leanings of those he worked with, Martin was painfully aware that his chosen path would not always be easy. Still, when he entered the Place de la République he was quite shocked to see it obstructed by an armed force.

The Bourse lay only a few paces from the square, on the rue du Château-d'Eau. That street was now closed, blocked off by gendarmes holding bayoneted rifles. Martin stopped to take stock. At this time of day, the Place de la République was usually the habitat of lingering lovers, idle strollers, or office clerks eating their lunches. Now he observed clusters of laborers in shirts and caps, talking quietly and pointing. He walked over to the nearest group of about half a dozen men.

"What's going on?" he asked. At first no one responded. They didn't know him, and he did not recognize any of them from his first few days at the Exchange. Finally, one said, "They came out of there." He gestured with his head to the northern edge of the square, adding, "and went over there," raising his chin toward the rue du Château-d'Eau. Not much of an answer. In fact no answer at all beyond what Martin could see with his own eyes. Instead, it was an uncomfortable reminder that Martin, in his suit and cravat, could easily be seen as the enemy, an upholder of the state, and that the state had made its power quite evident by headquartering the gendarmerie on the square that was named after Martin's beloved Republic. The state police station was only a stone's throw from the Bourse du Travail, ready to quell any workers' uprising.

Realizing he was unwelcome, Martin strode away from the group and went up to the uniformed men. He chose to address one of the youngest, a skinny lad with barely enough fur over his lip to be called a mustache. "Let me through," Martin demanded. "I work at the Bourse."

"No sir, we cannot. No entry." The soldier's Adam's apple bobbed up and down as he gulped and stared straight ahead. His accent indicated that he was probably a country boy, finding himself in the big city with no idea of what he might be facing.

"I said, let me through. I am a lawyer at the Exchange." The soldier, already red in the face and perspiring from the heat, seemed about to cave in. But instead, he thrust his rifle diagonally across Martin's chest and repeated, louder this time, "No entry."

At that instant, Martin recognized fully what he had given up. Had he been a judge, the little provincial would not have had the nerve to physically try to push him around. Martin was trying to decide what to do next, when a voice behind the line of soldiers boomed out, "Maître Martin, I assume." The voice emerged from a suit, a bowler and a cigar, held tight between thick lips topped with a ginger-colored mustache. A very real, mature and bushy one. A police detective or, as some of the union men might say, a *flic*. *Funny how, when you cross to the "other side," the workers' side,* Martin thought, *you can smell one a mile away.*

"Inspector Alain Jobert," the man confirmed, taking the stub out of his mouth. "We've been waiting for you." There was a sardonic gleam in his blue eyes.

"What's this about?" Martin demanded.

"Come inside out of the sun." The inspector stretched out a thick arm and nodded at the gendarme to let Martin through. "After what happened this morning, we're all going to have to keep cooler heads," he said as Martin caught up to him.

Martin had known many inspectors in his role as a judge. The competent and the incompetent, the good and the bad, even the very good and the very bad. As they walked toward the multi-doored entrance to the Bourse, Martin wondered how long it would take him to figure out what kind he was dealing with now. The only thing he was sure of, as he followed Jobert's bull-like back into the Bourse, was the man's physical strength.

"What happened?" Martin asked once they were inside the cool interior of the Bourse's high-ceilinged, stone-arched entryway.

"A bomb. This morning. Goutte-d'Or district. Anarchist." The inspector was as laconic as the workingmen, but much more informative. Frighteningly informative.

Martin, very conscious of whose side he must be on, persisted, "So what are you doing here?"

"Searching for bombs, guns, inflammatory pamphlets. We've been at it for over an hour."

"Do you have any proof that the bomber came from the Exchange?" Even as Martin said the words, he realized that as a judge he might have been asking the same question with a very different intent: to command the police to do exactly what they were doing, invade the workers' organization in search of evidence. "Do you have a warrant? Who authorized—"

"Yes, yes, signed and sealed," Jobert interrupted, before taking a piece of paper out of his pocket and unfolding and showing it to Martin.

Martin pushed it away. The perspiration earned on that sunny once-victorious day was prickling into an icy chill and fear as he finally allowed the momentousness of the inspector's revelations to sink in. *A bomb*. Could it be beginning again, the anarchist violence that had held the capital in its grip for years? What about Clarie? And Jean-Luc? What about the Exchange? Would the government close it down? Everything could be lost.

"Come," the inspector laid an unwelcome hand on Martin's back, "let's go in here and talk." He gestured straight ahead to the auditorium where the Exchange held its speeches and entertainments. "We've already searched under all the seats and the lectern," Jobert commented as he opened the door for a benumbed Martin to enter.

They sat on one of the benches in the back of the large hexagonal hall. Martin untied his cravat and ripped it from his neck. He held it in his hands, trying to slow his breathing and empty his mind of violent images, readying himself to do the job for which the Exchange had hired him.

Jobert took off his hat and crossed his legs, as relaxed as if he were going to see one of the performances put on in the hall. "Tell me, Maître Martin, exactly what you, as a member of the Paris Bar, do in this building."

"I defend the workers when they are in trouble, and, eventually, I will teach. I don't see that this has anything to do—"

"Teach, here?" Jobert seemed to find this a preposterous idea.

"Yes." Martin clenched his jaw. "Teach them about the law."

When the police inspector gave out a snort, Martin added, "You know what they told me when they hired me? That instead of their kids being forced to recite their catechism in school, they should have been learning something a little more relevant for their lives, like how the law works against them."

"Humph. Godless. I'm not surprised," Jobert responded, a frown of distaste replacing his smirk. "Maître Martin, what else do you know of this place and the men who are in charge?"

Martin shrugged. "I've only been here a few days, spending most of my time in the library, orienting myself."

Jobert raised his eyebrows to show his skepticism that an educated man, a lawyer, would be studying in a workers' library. But Martin had already learned a great deal. The library on the second floor contained not only the expected ideological tracts, which he mostly ignored, but also volumes of statistics and inquiries on the condition of the working class. The sight of men poring over the research painstakingly gathered by their leaders had won Martin's admiration and, he thought, as he straightened up to face the inspector, assured his loyalty.

Jobert flicked a bit of ash on the floor and sucked long on his cigar before changing the subject. "I want you to know that I went through your office myself. I didn't want my men to make a mess of things."

Martin was tempted to express outrage, but he held himself back in order to take advantage of Jobert's insinuation that the two of them had something in common, as "professional men." He desperately wanted to know more about what had happened. "Was anyone hurt today?" he began.

"Only the bomber, a Russian émigré. Young man, about twenty."

"He died?"

"Oh, yes. It was quite a blast."

"Then how did you identify him?"

"Ha!" Jobert gave out contented sigh. "He made it easy for us. An hour after it happened, we got a note at the precinct. From him! Taking credit for setting off the bomb on the Grand Boulevards." Jobert waited to go on until Martin met his eyes. "Lucky he didn't get there, wouldn't you say? Think of all the women and children he could have killed—shoppers, but also seamstresses and department store clerks. Presumably your kind of people. Workers. Or your own wife or mother could have been there, having a day out. So if you know anything. . . ."

"I don't. And I don't believe anyone else here does," Martin insisted and hoped to God that it was true.

"Well, if you find out anything—"

"I'm not a *mouchard*, I'm not going to be one of your informants."

Jobert smiled. "You must know yourself from your days as a judge that police spies can be very useful and so important to keeping order."

They already knew that about him, that he had been a judge. Martin wanted very much to wipe that grin off Jobert's ruddy face. "Well," Martin began, "if your mouchards are so useful, why didn't you know the bomb was coming? Or is there a possibility that one of your own spies set it off, so that the police could invade the workers' lawful organizations?"

This attempt at offense seemed to fall wide of the mark. Jobert scowled and shook his head. "Please, Maître Martin, let's not make wild accusations. As for our agents, whom you seem to disdain," he continued with a shrug, "they are, as you must know, crucial to the maintenance of law and order. But they can't be everywhere. There are hundreds of cafés and wineshops where potentially dangerous characters hang out, thousands of street corners in Paris. Apparently the bomber had made some fine little speeches. Too bad you never got to hear any of them."

"Do you know whether or not the alleged bomber called himself a nihilist?" Martin asked. "Do you have any idea who his associates were? Since we serve mostly Frenchmen here, there's no reason to believe—"

"Maître Martin," Jobert was polite enough to blow a mouthful of sweet, acrid smoke in the air before leaning toward him. "You are no longer a judge. No longer the one asking the questions. Let me pose a few to you. Are all the unions in compliance with the law of 1884? Does each union have an accurate, available list of all its members? What really goes on here at all the little meetings and study groups and cultural nights?"

Martin crossed his arms and stayed mum. He didn't yet know the answers to all of these questions; and even if he did, he had no intention of reporting infractions to a police inspector.

But Jobert was not through. "When some poor yokel comes here from the country looking for a job, does he simply come out of this building with a piece of paper that introduces him to an employer, or does he also come out with a head full of inflammatory crap about exploitation and revolution?" There was no smile crinkling those blue eyes as he concluded, "This place has only been open for ten years. We shut it down once, and if we don't feel you people are willing to help us stop the terrorists, I'm sure we can find a lot of reasons to shut it down again."

This little speech was intended to knock every last bit of wind out of Martin's sails. Instead, it fortified his determination to defend the Labor Exchange with his last breath if necessary. He had seen no indications of nihilism, the worst kind of anarchism, in his dealing with the union men, heard no one talk of loving violence for its own sake.

"I am sure our men will cooperate with you," Martin said, keeping a chill distance in his voice. "Just as I am sure you will treat them with respect. No brutality. If you have anyone else to question, I want to be there."

Jobert got up, put his hands on his hips, and stretched his back, his cigar sticking out from his lips at a triumphant angle. He took the stub out of his mouth and breathed deeply. "All right, then. I think we can agree on what our goal is. Time for lunch. Want to join me?"

Just like that! As if they were going to become collaborators. Martin wanted no part of it. "Thank you," he said, "I think I'll go up to my office and see what you've done with it."

"Very well, my men need a break. But we'll be back by one." With that, the inspector put on his hat and left. Martin did not move until he heard one of the wooden doors close behind him. The only thing left of the inspector was the trailing aroma of his cigar and the dread he had planted in Martin's soul.

It has to be an isolated incident, some Russian craziness, Martin told himself. *Or even the police trying to root out foreign agitators. It could not have come from here*. At that moment, he did not know which he feared more: the threat of violence in the city or that his dream of doing good, useful work would end.

He sat on the bench for a few minutes, letting the sun beam down on him through the skylight that covered the great hall. When he got to his feet, he walked down into the well of the auditorium and looked up toward the top of the room at the names and symbols of the trades. Butchers and bakers, carpenters and masons, glassmakers and painters. Crafts, thirty-odd in all, running in one line along the entire perimeter of the room. They had made everything in this place, just as they had made the world. With their own hands. Work that deserved respect, lives that warranted justice and dignity. Martin was not about to give up their cause without a fight.

8

Clarie looked up startled when the clock over the fireplace struck nine. If she hadn't been so absorbed in reading her students' essays, she might have been more worried. Jean-Luc was already asleep, and Rose had gone to her room on the fourth floor of their apartment building. Bernard had not yet come home. He had never been so late before.

Suddenly she heard the key in the lock. She put her pencil down on her desk and hurried to the door.

"Sorry I'm late," Bernard said as he entered the foyer. "It's been quite a day."

After he took off his bowler and placed it on the little table by the door, she reached to push a wave of his gray-flecked hair from his damp forehead. "You look vexed," she said, and smiled, even though she realized at that moment that *she* was a little vexed. Was this going to happen often because of his work at the Labor Exchange?

Bernard gave a short, bitter laugh as he let her help him off with his suit jacket and began to loosen his cravat. "More than vexed, I fear. Worried. And getting over being more than a little scared."

"Why, what happened?" She took a step back to get a better look at him. His expression was pained, creased with fatigue. His shoulders slumped. "Are you all right?"

"I'm fine," he said. "The worst is over now. Let's sit for a moment."

Clarie's pulse quickened as she went into the living room and sat down on the edge of one of the flowered chairs that stood at an angle to the small, round table that held their reading lamp. Martin took his usual seat opposite her.

"You've heard, I assume, about the bombing," he began.

"Oh, my God!" Clarie gasped. "Did someone bomb the Labor Exchange?" She clapped her hand on her heart to keep it from leaping out of her chest.

"No, no." Bernard shook his head as he reached for her. "Nothing like that."

"But you said—"

"No reason to worry about me or the Exchange, or you and Jean-Luc," he said. "Darling, please, listen for a moment." He kissed her hand before letting it go.

She settled back into her seat, unable to stop trembling while he explained that a Russian had been killed in the Goutte-d'Or, a neighborhood not far from where they lived, but poorer, and with a bad reputation. Apparently the slain man sent a note to the police warning of an explosion he had hoped to set off in a department store on the Grand Boulevards.

"He called himself an anarchist," Martin continued, "like so many of our members do. That's why the police were all over the Labor Exchange today, asking questions, threatening."

"Did they threaten you?" Clarie could not take the worry out of her voice.

"No, not me. But they were a little rough with a few of the union men. I insisted on sitting in on some of the questioning." He paused. "For two reasons. To make sure that the men were treated fairly, and to make sure that none of them were involved. Because if they were—" Bernard frowned and pressed his lips together, "I wouldn't want to be there. I made it clear when I took the position that I had no tolerance for violence. A strike, yes. Even a general strike, yes. I could honestly tell them that I believed in the rights of the workers to use all non-violent means. But bombs? Killing innocent people? Never."

Clarie recognized the vehemence behind these remarks as a sign of a hurt that would never quite go away: Bernard's role in the death of his childhood friend Merckx, an anarchist who had never abjured violence. "And you're sure?" she asked quietly. It would be terrible if Bernard already felt betrayed by the men who had hired him and made promises to him.

"Oh, yes. While the police were searching the place, I talked to some of the men. They knew nothing about the Russian, who was only a carter, not a union member, or someone they had helped to hire at the Exchange. Apparently, according to the police inspector, he was some kind of intellectual, maybe a student. But we checked through our records, and he hadn't come to study at the Exchange's library or, as far as anyone knew, attended any of our lectures." Bernard relaxed back into his chair. "In fact, the biggest danger for us—you and me—" he said, with a weary sigh, "is that the authorities would close down the Exchange. Then what would we do?"

Clarie knew exactly what they would do: rely on her salary again. She knew how hard this would be on Bernard, on his pride. Until a year ago he had been the main support of the family. And that's what he wanted to be, even if he believed in her right to work. No matter what happened, they'd get by. She was sure of it. But, rather than say any of this, she kept her own counsel. She nodded, encouraging Bernard to continue.

"That's why I stayed and talked with the inspector after the other police had left. I gave him my word that I had heard no one talk about bombs, that I would make sure that everyone understands the laws and tries to follow them." Bernard shrugged. "Of course, some of our more militant members might have a slightly different view of things. But I'm not their nanny, only their lawyer. And today they got their money's worth. The inspector said he would not recommend any actions against us. So I'm fairly sure they won't shut us down like they did a few years ago."

"That must be a relief," Clarie said, glad to hear the pride in his voice at having protected the Labor Exchange. Happy that her family was safe and secure for the time being. "But what about—"

"The bomber. The police, who have their spies everywhere, think it was an isolated incident. No reason to panic."

"Well, then." After taking in so much, Clarie couldn't bear to sit still any longer. She got up and kissed Bernard on the cheek. "Good work, Maître Martin!"

"So good you can give solace to a starving man?" Bernard said as he stood up and patted his stomach.

"Of course." The hunger of her hard-working man earned him another kiss. "I'll warm up your supper."

"And I'll go look in on Jean-Luc."

Clarie watched as her dear, tired husband ambled into their child's bedroom. She took a breath and stretched her own weary back before going into the kitchen. As she lit a match under the pot and adjusted the flame, she tried to repress the dangers that lurked in what Bernard had told her. A bomb had gone off. And that explosion almost changed their lives once again. Her brow furrowed as she reminded herself of all the reasons why taking the position at the Labor Exchange had been the right thing for Bernard to do. He'd been a good judge, but hated prosecuting those less fortunate than himself. He'd often told her that the people who lived in the world of the truly poor were only one illness, one accident, one crime away from starvation, death, or imprisonment, and he wanted to dedicate his life to helping them avoid these disasters. But he'd also just told her he had come close to losing this new job. Did throwing in his lot with the poor mean that Bernard's well-being would also be as precarious?

9

LATE THE NEXT AFTERNOON, THE teachers' meeting began in a hubbub. Mlles. Calin, Veroux and Geraud, being single, lived together, and had picked up a newspaper on the way back to their dormitory. Obviously they had spent a good deal of the night talking about the dangers of Paris.

"Can you imagine," Fanny Calin exclaimed, "our tram passes right by the neighborhood where the bomb went off!"

"But you, my dear, were not on it when it happened," Mme Roubinovitch, the *directrice*, commented icily. She rapped her knuckles on the table. "Let's proceed, shall we?"

Clarie lowered her head to hide her grin. *That should put an end to it.* The long table in Mme Roubinovitch's office was more crowded than usual, since both the professors—those teachers who had been trained at Sèvres—and the various arts instructors attended the meeting dedicated to deciding which students would receive the year's prizes. In the heat, Clarie could already feel a clammy dampness spreading under her blouse. Only the slightest breeze accompanied the sun streaming in through the windows.

Fortunately, the first part of the agenda did not take up much time. Mme Roubinovitch opened with the obligatory caution about how they were walking a fine line between pleasing the parents and rewarding the girls, on the one hand, and not encouraging unseemly pride in their female students, on the other. Clarie had heard this speech many times before. Everyone knew that public boys' high schools ended the year with grand ceremonies, featuring important government officials wearing patriotic red, white and blue sashes across their chests. This year, Mme Roubinovitch had enlisted the mayors of the ninth and tenth arrondissements, who administered the neighborhoods in which most of the students lived, and a minor official from the Ministry of Education. Not as grand as the best boys' schools could offer, but something.

At Mme Roubinovitch's urging, they quickly agreed upon the music that would be played or sung, and which students would be allowed to demonstrate their talents. They had no difficulty deciding upon the prizes for excellence in art, mathematics, science, German and English. Then came the more difficult choices that most concerned Clarie, the history and French prizes, and the awards that involved every teacher in the school, the prizes for morality and virtue.

When Clarie voiced her hope they might find a way to reward as many students as possible, she got a swift rebuttal from Mme Roubinovitch. "Our girls must learn to accept what comes to them, and not take shining or not shining in front of others too seriously. Life will bring many disappointments." Clarie should have known her principal would insist upon their responsibility to make young women think, and not cater to their feelings. With a nod, Clarie acceded to Mme Roubinovitch's view and was rewarded by a smile so maternal in its affection, it made her blush with pleasure. How she loved her principal, how they all did.

As Clarie was recovering from this swell of emotion, her friend Emilie Franchet, who taught French, leaped into the breach by nominating her choices for the literature prize, an essay on Mme de Sévigné and on the poet for whom the school was named, Alphonse Lamartine. Clarie, in turn, described her choices for history, papers on the rule of Louis XIV and the heroism of Joan of Arc. She bit her lip as she waited for questions. When none came, she sat back with a sigh. She had done well. They were moving along.

Mme Roubinovitch herself taught the courses on philosophy and morality, and kept track of the students' delinquencies, which, at the Lycée Lamartine, were slight and very few. The director expected no objection to her judgments. But when she announced that a Jewish student, Rachel Cahlmann, would get the award for moral example, Annette Girardet, sitting at the end of the table, raised her hand. "I need to say something about Mlle Cahlmann," she said. The gasp was almost audible. Mme Girardet was merely an *adjunct instructor* who taught *fancy sewing* in the late afternoon to the daughters of widowers or working mothers.

"Yes?" Although Mme Roubinovitch got her surname from her husband, a doctor born in Russia, she carried it well. She had an exotic, almost Slavic face with dark eyes and full lips. At first Clarie had thought that she was an Israelite, but she wasn't. She was, even more than most of her staff, a professed Catholic. But she had stood up against the parents who threatened to boycott the school because of the number of Jewish students who attended. And she had won. Clarie glanced across the table at her friend Emilie. They both raised their eyebrows and did their best not to smile. The frown that greeted the sewing teacher's objection was something neither of them had experienced, or wanted to.

"She only stays because of her younger sister, and the fact that she has to wait for her father to accompany them home. She talks too much." By now Annette Girardet's voice was quivering. She took a breath and went on. "Lately, she's been talking about this book, which claims that the traitor Dreyfus is not really a traitor. It was written by another Israelite."

"So our Rachel has her own ideas about things." Mme Roubinovitch pressed her lips together and gave the sewing teacher a piercing look.

"I just thought you should know, Mme Director."

"Thank you," Mme Roubinovitch responded, as she turned toward the others. "Any other objections?"

Clarie felt a little sorry for poor Annette Girardet, consigned to teach the so-called womanly arts, and outranked by those who had attended Sèvres and had gained the broadening worldview it offered. But there was no way to come to her aid, not without displaying the one quality that Mme Roubinovitch had criticized Clarie for, being too tender-hearted. So she silently took stock as the meeting came to a close. Looking around at the other professors, she felt a surge of pride. They belonged to a rare breed—educated, intellectual working women—and they served under a principal whose strength and independence she greatly admired. It had been a hard year, but a good one. She had succeeded in her first year at one of the best schools in Paris. And now, as Mme Roubinovitch asked if there were any other matters to discuss, it was almost over.

"Well, then, we are done," she announced, rising from her chair. "I'll let you go, before we all melt. I'll see those monitoring the preliminary examinations tomorrow morning; otherwise, I'll see everyone at three sharp on Saturday afternoon for the graduation ceremony," Mme Roubinovitch said before marching to her huge desk, which was covered with budgets and reports.

Clarie sprang to her feet. She had only to give Emilie a special hug good-bye and Mme Girardet a sympathetic pat on the back. Then, if she could slip by the eager Mlles. Calin, Veroux and Geraud on her way to her room, she'd avoid talking about the bombing. She didn't want to think any more about the violence that had struck too close to home.

Clarie ran down the stairs with the minimum of dignity required of a successful, full-time professor at a Parisian lycée. She felt like cheering, like a student being let out for the summer. Soon her days were going to be so much freer! She'd play with Jean-Luc, make dinners, read all the books she'd been meaning to read.

Her mood evaporated as soon as she swung open the door and entered her classroom. The charwoman, Francesca, sat at a student desk near the door at the back of the room, waiting for her. Clarie grimaced. She had been so busy, so preoccupied that she'd almost forgotten about her. "Francesca, I pray that your daughters have come home," she said with a mixture of hope and apology in her voice.

"They have," the woman answered gravely, "this morning."

This should have been good news, but as she rose to her feet, Francesca couldn't seem to control the tiny tremors agitating her lips and clasped hands.

"They're all right, I hope," Clarie said, even as her mind raced to all the terrible things that could happen to young women wandering the city alone. "And you're all right, too," she added, searching to understand why Francesca looked so distressed.

"It's not me. It's my girls. I told them about you. Told them you were kind, married to a lawyer. Angela, at least, thought you could help."

"If they're in trouble," Clarie explained, "I'm not the one to talk to. Neither is my husband. I do know that down at the Palais de Justice there are lawyers who accept cases—" Clarie hesitated as she searched for the right words, "from those who cannot pay the usual fees." These were the cases Bernard had been assigned to for the past year, as part of his apprenticeship to the Paris Bar.

"It's not that kind of trouble. They're afraid. They think someone killed their friend and might try to kill them."

A murder? Last time it was kidnapping and beating, now murder? Stunned, Clarie leaned against the wall. This was insane. Or perhaps it was Francesca who was a little crazy, or even lying. "Surely, if someone you know has been murdered, you must go to the police." When Francesca stood staring at her, not responding, Clarie recalled their first conversation and the Italian woman's claim that the police would never help an Italian immigrant. Clarie shook her head. As a wife and teacher, with a reputation to protect, as the mother of a young child, she could not let herself be drawn into Francesca's problems. "I'm sorry, I must go," she said finally. "I'm expected at home."

As Clarie started toward the front of the room, Francesca broke her silence and began to plead. "I don't know what to do. They've been crying all day. And they're scared." Francesca's words tumbled out faster and with more urgency. "Per favore, please, just talk to them. I brought them here and hid them in the basement. I promised them."

Just talk to them. Despite her misgivings, Clarie stopped. According to Francesca, her daughters were the same age as her students. Perhaps there was something she could say to them, or at least find out how much truth there was to what Francesca was telling her. She stood for a moment, all too aware of the charwoman behind her. Clarie turned. "Very well," she said, shrugging her shoulders. "Bring them here. And remember I have to leave soon." Francesca made a slight, grateful bow of her head before limping out of the room.

Clarie thrust a few papers into her brown leather bag and began to pace in front of her desk. She'd find out if there was really a threat, give advice, just as she would to her own students. And that would be the end of it.

When the three of them knocked on the door and entered the room, Clarie saw at once that no one would have mistaken Francesca's daughters for her eager, crisply uniformed students. Their faces were worn and puffy from crying, and their long floral dresses were faded and rumpled. Still they were a striking pair, if only because they were so different. The almost ethereally blond Angela timidly approached the front of the room, while the tall, dark one, Maura, hung back. Francesca quietly closed the door behind them. She had obviously taken the precaution of making sure no one had seen them lurking about. This made Clarie even more wary.

"Can you tell me who was killed?" she asked, trying to keep the suspicion out of her voice.

"Pyotr. Pyotr Ivanovich," whispered Angela. "And he's been accused of terrible things. We need to find a way to prove that he was innocent."

Clarie's mouth fell open. "The bomber? The anarchist? That was your friend?" She did not even try to hide her alarm.

"He was a very good friend. So gentle, he would not hurt anyone." Angela's hands were clasped in front, as if in prayer. Watching her, Clarie recalled her first conversation with Francesca. Angela was the angel, the beauty, the innocent one, and so obviously her mother's favorite. In the sunlight beaming into the closed, stifling room, the wisps of hair escaping from the topknot she had wound on her head shone like spun gold. Her eyes were an astonishing shade of blue. She was pretty, pretty enough to be in a fairy tale. But she could also be lying.

Clarie lifted her chin toward Maura. "And what do you think?"

Maura crossed her arms in front of her chest and answered, "Pyotr was a good man. The best we have ever known. He did not believe in violence." Her tone was as defiant as her stance, and for that reason, and the fact that she wasn't her mother's favorite, Clarie's heart went out to her. In Maura, Clarie saw something of her own younger self. She, too, had been tall for her age, tawny-skinned, saddled with thick, unruly black hair—and angry. She hadn't understood why God had allowed her mother to die. Maura's father had left her. Did she love him as much as Clarie had loved her mother? Was there anyone loving and sheltering her in the way that Clarie's father, aunt and uncle had coddled and protected her, easing her pain, helping her to grow up?

"How well did you know him? What makes you think he did not intend to plant a bomb?" The least she could do was make them understand how skeptical people would be about their version of things.

Angela hastened to answer her. "We knew him for a year. He lived next to our building. Sometimes he carried the work up the stairs for our boss and down for us. Our sewing work, the shirts we finished." Her lips trembled as she added, "He used to sit and talk with us. To tell us about his homeland. How people had believed in assassinations, in throwing bombs.

How much worse it made things. If he had bread or a bit of cheese, he'd share it with us. He had a beautiful soul. He would never hurt anyone."

Clarie's contemplated the two girls. It was obvious from the tears they had shed that their relationship with the Russian boy had hardly been casual. Angela, at least, must have been in love with him. Yet presumably they had tried to run away. Or was it that they had planned to run away with him, an anarchist, a would-be assassin? No, Clarie thought, she would have nothing to do with this.

"If you feel he is innocent, then you must go to the police," she said finally. What else could she say?

"You know they won't believe people like us!" Maura spit out.

"Maura, the professor is trying to help us," Francesca hissed.

The dark-haired girl responded by scowling, crossing her arms even tighter, and staring at the ceiling. Although her demeanor was extremely rude, Clarie understood her frustration. The police *were* unlikely to believe anything two girls, especially two infatuated girls, had to say. Francesca had been wrong to bring them here, to hide them in the dusty, spidery cellar for God knows how long, in the futile hope that Clarie could do anything for them.

"Please, you must understand," Angela sat down on a chair in the first row as if her knees had become weak from fear, "someone killed him."

"Who?" Clarie asked, before she could stop herself from being drawn in any further.

"Maybe the police," Maura cried. "Although people like you probably believe that they would not break their own laws."

Clarie shook her head. The girl was going too far. What could Maura Laurenzano possibly know about people like her? If Angela hadn't spoken she would have turned her back on the lot. But the older girl did speak.

"Maybe someone who saw us with Monsieur Barbereau," Angela's chest began to heave, "someone who—"

"That's right. Monsieur Barbereau," Maura blurted out, interrupting her sister. "Our boss. He's the one who did it. He was jealous. He beat Angela because she didn't want to marry him."

Angela gasped as her sister spoke and let out a long moan. She covered her mouth and began to sob, rocking back and forth.

Clarie walked over to her. "He hurt you, didn't he?" she said gently. "Your mother told me."

Angela nodded, as her fingers quivered over her temple and cheek. Clarie took a closer look. The yellowing marks were barely perceptible, but Clarie had no trouble imagining what they would have looked like days ago, black and blue and purple. "How long has this been going on?" she asked.

"Months," Angela whispered and refused to meet her eyes.

She's ashamed, Clarie thought as stepped back, her heart swelling with pity, *ashamed of what he's done to her.* No matter what her relationship with the young anarchist had been, Angela's suffering was real. No one should have to live with such brutality. "If you go back home, will you be safe?" Clarie asked. "Is there somewhere else you can go? Someone to protect you?"

"Nothing for *you* to worry about," Maura said. She marched over to her older sister, put a protective arm around her, and told her she didn't have to say anything else. Maura glowered at Clarie, undoubtedly hating her because she was so useless.

Really, the girl was impossible. Clarie strode back to her desk and began to fasten the belts on her schoolbag with hard, swift motions until she gained enough composure to tell them she would talk to her husband to see if anything could be done to bring Barbereau to justice.

By this time, Maura had already led her sister halfway to the door. "Maman," she ordered, "it's time to go." Offering Clarie an apologetic nod, Francesca got up to follow her daughters. The girls did not look back as they left.

Clarie sighed and closed her eyes. In this room, she was accustomed to young women obeying and adoring her. Perhaps that's why she had reacted too quickly to Maura's youthful resentments. What mattered is that a girl had been horribly abused. This time Bernard would have to listen to her story.

10

Clarie did not bring up the plight of the Italian girls until after supper. By the time she came out of Jean-Luc's room, Bernard had settled into his chair, holding the staid *Le Temps* angled into the circle of light thrown by the kerosene lamp. In his pin-striped shirt and suspenders, one leg crossed over the other, he looked so dear, as engrossed as a child at serious play. She went over to him, bent down and kissed him on his forehead.

"And what is this about?" he asked, obviously pleased.

"I want to talk to you for a moment, ask your advice."

Bernard straightened the newspaper and folded it on his lap. "A problem at school?" His blue-gray eyes were kind. He'd always shown a keen interest in her teaching and colleagues.

"Nothing like that." She sat down across from him and laid one hand on the reading table as she leaned toward him. "It's the Italian girls, the charwoman's daughters. Remember, I told you about them."

"Are they still missing?"

"No, they're back. I actually saw them today."

"Really. And?" He raised his eyebrows, his curiosity aroused.

"Francesca brought them to my classroom. They came to seek my advice. But I'm not sure how I can help them." She cleared her throat, hesitating to say something that might alarm Martin. "It turns out they knew the anarchist who was killed. They don't think he planted the bomb."

"The Russian anarchist." Martin sat up, displeasure overshadowing his curiosity. "If they were at all involved—"

"Don't worry. They insisted that he didn't do anything wrong, that he couldn't."

"And you believed them?"

Clarie withdrew her hand from the table. There was something in Bernard's tone that she did not like, an assumption she had been gullible. "Actually, I didn't know what to believe. They seemed intent on wanting to prove him innocent. They described him as gentle and generous. They said he would never plot to hurt anyone."

Bernard shook his head. "That proves nothing, except that he was clever and the girls were naïve. Or perhaps they are being clever, too."

"I don't think so." Heat flushed her cheeks.

"In any case," Bernard went on, seemingly unaware of her pique, "whether he did it or not is a matter for the police and for the courts."

"For men and for judges," she responded rather too tartly.

"Yes, my dear," his smile broadened into a grin. "Not for a beautiful wife and mother. Besides," he said, becoming serious again, "if the Russian didn't do it, who did? Did they have any ideas about that?"

"They thought it could be police." She paused. When Bernard pressed his lips together without responding, she realized that this accusation was not as wild as she had thought. She had to wonder why he didn't mention this suspicion to her last night.

"Or," Clarie continued, "they thought it might be their boss. *The man who beats one of them*," she emphasized. She had no desire to get involved with anarchists, or the police. She simply wanted to enlist Bernard to help her rescue Angela. "The older daughter is still very frightened of this Monsieur Barbereau," she added.

Bernard straightened up, alert. "Barbereau? Marcel Barbereau?"

"Perhaps." She could not imagine why her husband would know that name. Or be alarmed.

"That can't be." He rattled the paper open and turned to the second page. "It says right here, a body they found floating in the Basin yesterday morning has been identified as that of Marcel Barbereau, and he had been in the water for several days. If it's the same man, he can't still be threatening the girls. Nor could he have planted the bomb."

Clarie slumped back in her seat. Her eyes roved over the floral pattern of the carpet. *A bomb, a drowning. No, first a drowning, then a bomb?* Both connected to the girls. "How do they know," she murmured, "that he didn't die after the bombing?"

"They seem sure, by this account. They do have their ways of estimating how long someone has been in the water."

Of course Bernard, who had prosecuted many criminals, knew all the gruesome details of investigations at the morgue. Clarie did not even want to imagine what happens to a body left in the water for several days. "You think it was the same Barbereau?" She had to know for sure.

"They say he ran sweatshops in the Goutte-d'Or district."

Clarie fell silent. *It had to be him.* She could feel Bernard scrutinizing her.

"Clarie, they think the man was murdered. Perhaps he was another victim of the Russian. Or those girls, for all we know. *Do not get involved with these people.*"

This was an order. An emphatic order. Bernard had never given her an order before. She didn't like it. But the worst part was that he might be right. Especially if Maura Laurenzano had deliberately lied to her. Clasping her hands together, Clarie stood up. She'd been a fool. She didn't face Bernard as she started walking past him to her desk. "I've still got some work to do to get ready for the preliminary examinations tomorrow."

He stood up, caught her with one arm and held her in an embrace. He put his finger under her chin until she was willing to meet his eyes. "I never want anything to happen to you. You're not used to dealing with criminals and deceivers, and you shouldn't have to. You should enjoy your summer, relax, spend time with Jean-Luc. You've earned a rest," he said as he planted a kiss on her forehead.

All very sweet. She kissed him on the cheek before striding over to her desk, where, instead of reading her students' essays, she stared into space. She was angry. At Francesca, at Maura and Angela, even, not quite fairly, at Bernard. She tapped her pencil, thinking about how Emilie would often talk about her and her teacher husband "having words." At least, Clarie thought sardonically, Emilie wasn't married to an ex-judge who knew so much more than she about the world. *Words.* Angela's pleas, Maura's lies, her dear husband's solicitous warnings. Clarie had words going through her mind all right: used, lied to, and patronized.

11

THE NEXT MORNING CLARIE RESOLVED to forget about Francesca and her daughters. She had her own girls and her position to think about. Six of her students, among those whom Mme Roubinovitch liked to refer to as the sharp ones or "the needles," had signed up to take the preliminary written examination that was the first step to becoming a teacher. As the professor of the most advanced history classes, Clarie had prepared them for the humanities-and-classics section and was to monitor the three-hour test. If they passed, they would go on to take their orals before a panel of lycée and University professors. If they were successful at that stage, they would either receive an elementary school certificate or be invited to apply to the teachers' college at Sèvres.

At exactly 8:45 that Wednesday, Clarie stood holding the exam questions close to her chest as her students, in their black pinafores and starched white collars, fluttered in, twittering and nervous. Her pulse quickened as she watched them. Since this was a city-wide examination, to be graded by men at the University, the results would be as much an evaluation of the female faculty at the Lycée Lamartine—of their training, their intelligence, their *seriousness*—as of their students' knowledge. Her girls had to do well, for everyone's sake.

"Please sit far apart," Clarie ordered. She smiled as they settled in. She moved from girl to girl distributing the test booklets. When she returned to the front, she clapped her hands for attention. "You have three hours," she told them. "And, if you feel you can't answer the first question, go on to the second. If you can't answer the second, try the third. Or," she demonstrated in the most exaggerated way, "just take a deep breath." This produced the relaxing giggles she had hoped for. She looked at her watch. "Time," she said. In unison, their heads, all uniformly pinned up in topknots, bent over the papers.

These were her *Alphonsines*, as all the lycée's students proudly called themselves in honor of the school's namesake, the poet Alphonse Lamartine. Or rather, those laboring before her represented a particular portion of Alphonsines, among the smartest, but also among the least well off. At Lamartine, only the daughters of shopkeepers or teachers had to find a dignified path toward making their own way. The others, even the other "needles," were not here. Many of her seniors had been withdrawn from afternoon classes in order to stay home with their mothers, to learn to pour tea, have visitors and make social calls. All with the goal of guaranteeing that they would enter an appropriate marriage. Clarie sighed. No matter where they ended up, she would miss all of them.

She opened her book, Mme de La Fayette's *The Princess of Cleves*, a classic she had been intending to reread for a long time, but she could not concentrate. Her heart was with her girls, scribbling away, or staring into space, or even doing two things absolutely disallowed during the school year—chewing on their nails or pencils. She certainly had no intention of censuring them now, when they were under so much pressure.

She'd never forget all the anxieties and uncertainties she had suffered through. In her day there had been no lycées. Instead she had been educated by the nuns in Arles and, after leaving school, had had to study on her own for a long time to qualify. She smiled as she thought of her father, traveling with her to Nîmes to take the written examinations. When she finally passed, after two tries, he even took her on the long train ride north, to Paris, where she had stood alone before five men charged with enforcing the stiff standards of the new women's education. It had been quite an adventure, and she had been so nervous that she held her hands behind her back to keep them from shaking. If it hadn't been for the most indulgent of all fathers, she would never have made it.

At least, she thought, as she observed their bowed heads, it was easier for her Alphonsines. They were, in a sense, at home, part of a proud corps. The black-and-white uniforms, which set them apart from everyone else in the neighborhood, guaranteed that once inside the walls of the school, social differences did not matter. They were all part of the little meritocratic republic governed by the redoubtable Marie Roubinovitch. Clarie fingered the fringe on her bookmark. Even with these advantages, she feared for her test takers. There were so few teaching posts for women. Most of them would probably end up in shops or as clerks in offices or at one of the big department stores. All she could do for them now was to nod encouragement, which she did, each time a head popped up and gave her an anxious glance.

When the sun crept in, heating up the room, Clarie got up to fling open the windows and let in some air. Unfortunately, fat, lazy flies accompanied the breeze, buzzing and pestering her girls through the rest of the morning. Every fifteen minutes, Clarie wrote the time in big block letters on the blackboard, letting the test-takers know how long they had. At noon, the last two stragglers, wilted and exhausted but still offering a smile to a favorite teacher, laid their booklets on her desk. Clarie's own starched collar was damp with sweat. She was more than ready to go home, to lunch and to her son.

The door creaked open as she was stacking her papers. She turned to face someone she had managed with great effort to put out of her mind, Francesca Laurenzano.

"Francesca," she said warily. "I didn't expect you at this time."

"Professoressa, I came to apologize." The charwoman limped toward the front of the room.

"Oh." Feeling again the sting of last night's contretemps with Bernard, Clarie was careful not to be too welcoming.

"I made Maura write a note." The woman held out a folded piece of paper.

Clarie walked over to get it, before retreating behind her desk.

"I would have made her come, to apologize, but she's afraid," Francesca explained, her head bowed, not meeting Clarie's eyes. "She and Angela hid when the police came last night asking about Monsieur Barbereau. Please forgive me and my daughters. I would've never allowed them to say something so bad about the dead."

Speaking ill of the dead is hardly the issue, Clarie thought as she unfolded the paper. It read, in round, legible script: *I am sorry that I said Barbereau might have killed Pieter. I did not know that he was dead*. Clarie refolded the paper, her cheeks blotched with anger. This was hardly an apology, certainly not very polite, and quite possibly a lie. "There was no reason for you to have troubled yourself. Perhaps you, too, could have just sent a note."

"Maura was so good in school," Francesca said.

A comment so seemingly irrelevant that it left Clarie stunned into silence until the Italian woman added, with touching eagerness, "See how well she can write," and Clarie realized that, of course, Francesca could not.

Clarie sat down and buried her head in her hands. Even if the daughters had lied, there was no evidence that Francesca had tried to deceive her. She must try to be kind.

By the time she looked up again, Francesca had sunk into a wooden chair in the front row, her hands folded in her lap, staring down. The only true way to help was to be honest and realistic. "Francesca," she said gently, "do you think that your daughters could have been involved in Marcel Barbereau's death?"

The charwoman's mouth fell open slightly, and she began to shake her head, back and forth, slowly and mechanically. Clarie understood almost immediately that Francesca was not attempting to deny the implied accusation. Not at all. Rather she was making one last effort to vanquish the fear that must have been haunting her since the police started asking questions, the fear Clarie had made more real by speaking it aloud. Francesca's face shriveled into a mask of pain, the pain of resignation, the pain of coming to grips with her worse nightmares, the pain of knowing her daughters could be in terrible trouble, and the ultimate and worst pain of all, which she cried out: "I can't lose my babies."

For Clarie, who had lost a child, this was a cry she could not ignore. "We don't know yet if they were involved," she said more gently. "Perhaps they're just afraid of the police after what happened to their friend."

Francesca shook her head, ignoring Clarie's offer of hope. "It's my fault. When their father left me, I made them work. They wanted to stay in school. I couldn't do anything else, don't you see?" she said, looking at Clarie, pleading.

"Of course not," Clarie soothed. "It's terrible that things are so difficult for so many." *How vapid, what mush,* she thought as she got up and approached the charwoman. Clarie sat down and placed her hand over Francesca's. She breathed in the scent of hard work and anxieties, the sharp, musty smell reminiscent of the forge, of her own Italian father and the other men who worked there. "Your girls may not be involved," she repeated. "And if they are accused, there is help. My husband assured me that you can go to the Palais de Justice and ask for a lawyer." Of course, Clarie thought, as she struggled to keep her demeanor calm, this is not at all what Bernard had said. He had told her, in no uncertain terms, not to get involved. And she wouldn't. Not after today. Not after she gave the only help a woman in her position was capable of, words of sympathy and advice.

"Come now." Clarie placed her arm around Francesca's shoulder. "You told me your girls were good, hard-working. I'm sure they'll be all right."

Francesca nodded, although she didn't look at all convinced.

After a moment, Clarie got up. "I'm so sorry these terrible things are happening. But," Clarie swallowed hard, knowing that once again she had so little to offer, "I have some work to do." She tried to lighten the mood by adding, "We're all getting ready for the fuss and commotion of graduation."

It took some effort for Francesca to stand up. She pushed against the desk with both arms, slowly unbending her back, as if she carried the weight of Atlas on her shoulders. She sniffled and reached into her apron pocket to pull out a handkerchief. Clarie had seen it all before, a week ago. It pained her to realize how hard Francesca's life must have been and would forever be. She went back to her desk and thumped her papers against it, straightening their edges. She could not bear to watch Francesca leave.

12

How can she keep on doing it? Maura thought, as she watched her mother hobble through the courtyard on her way to the lycée. How can she bear to get down on her hands and knees to clean up for their damned graduation? Maura turned from the window of their fifth-floor room and stared at the crucifix over her mother's bed. She claimed that Jesus and the Virgin Mary helped her. Helped her to be a slave, Maura silently countered. And if she didn't watch out, she'd become one too.

Quickly, now that she was sure her mother was gone, Maura squatted down and removed a loosened floorboard.

"What are you doing?" Angela glanced up from the table where she was darning stockings.

"Getting the money."

"You have more?" Angela got up to get a better look. "You must give it to Maman. There's not much work at the school during the summer. You know how worried she gets."

"No," Maura said as she pulled up Vera's torn and dirty blue satin sack. "I'm only moving the money because I've read in the papers that the police look under the floor for stolen goods."

"Do you think they'll really come back?" Angela whispered, clutching the stockings in her hand.

Maura shrugged, then went over to the wall, grabbed her best dress, and looped it over her arm. She didn't want to talk about the police coming again, although she worried about it all the time and had come up with a story that would save her and Angela. She'd tell them that Pyotr killed Barbereau, that they tried to stop him, that they were so afraid of the Russian boy they ran away, that he was the one who took the money so he could use it to— Maura bit down hard on her lip to keep the shameful words from slipping out. She stood for a moment and stared at the sack of coins in her right hand. To blame it all on Pyotr. To become a Judas. But, she rationalized, as she dropped her arm, if she lied, just a little, they'd survive, she and Angela. After all, hadn't Pyotr struck the fatal blows to save Angela? He'd want her to survive. He would! Relieved to have worked it all out, Maura settled into one of the room's two rickety chairs and began to tear at the threads that hemmed her cotton floral dress.

"Maura, you must give the money to Maman," Angela said, grabbing at Maura's arm. Maura shook her off and picked up the scissors to hasten her work.

"Maura!"

"What if we need to escape? What if we need it later?" She looked up at Angela. "Besides, Maman will ask where we got it. Are you going to tell her, like you almost told that schoolteacher? Are you?" Tears blurred her eyes, making it impossible for her to see what she was doing. Maura thrust the dress down on the rough wooden table, almost toppling the kerosene lamp. This was crazy. Every time she and Angela argued, they both began to cry. They were so scared.

When she stopped her sniffling, she swiped her sleeve across her eyes and nose, and placed the dress on her lap again. Angela sank into the chair across from her.

"We can't tell anyone," Maura continued quietly. "I am, after all, doing my part, promising to work for that witch Mme Guyot."

"She's not a witch."

Maura sighed and picked up the needle. Leave it to Angela to defend the mean, pious laundress. Of course, Maura thought as she stabbed the needle into the hem of her dress, since Angela never snuck away into the local wineshop at night, she didn't get to hear how hard Fanny Guyot worked her "girls." So hard that they had to console themselves with drink. Everybody's favorite, Angela, didn't have to contemplate slaving under the hissing steam machine in the boiling heat of summer. She didn't have to worry about skinning her hands on the scrub board, straining her arms to beat the clothes, getting burned by splattered bleach, exhausting herself wringing out sheets, listening to Mme Guyot giving orders all day long. Not Angela. It was bad enough when Maura had helped her mother wash their things. Now to be at the district laundry all day, every day, sweating like a pig. Maura knew how hard it was going to be.

Angela leaned toward Maura. "I'll do it, you know. I told Maman I'd do it instead of you."

In and out Maura pushed and pulled the thread, fitting the coins in the fold of her dress.

"I will," Angela insisted.

"As you know," Maura said, punching the needle in again, "Mme Guyot doesn't want you. She wants me because I am strong."

"But you're too smart to be stuck in the laundry. You should find a job in a shop. Like you wanted."

Sometimes it made Maura even angrier at her sister when she said nice things and tried to defend her. Maura made a show of concentrating on her sewing.

"Maura—"

"No! You find a job as a seamstress, just as Maman said. I'll work at the laundry and while I'm there, I'll look for this Marie Riboyet and her bloody sheets. Maybe I can get out of her what she saw. Maybe I can find out who killed Pyotr. Or maybe you can tell me. Can't you remember anything else about the man you met near the Basin?"

Maura had asked that question a hundred times, and gotten the same answer: he was tall; he was in the shadows; he had a raspy voice; there was something scary about him. This time Angela did not even bother to respond. She slumped back in the chair, as if she realized she'd never win an argument with her sister.

Maura shrugged in frustration and pressed her lips together as she concentrated on her sewing. She did not like having the police after her. She did not want to be a slave forever. She planned to use every minute she was sweating it out at the laundry to work out her escape.

13

Clarie had one last academic duty: the fuss and commotion of the Graduation and Prize-Giving Ceremony. That Saturday afternoon was the only time the outward trappings of wealth and status were allowed to breach the walls of the Lycée Lamartine. The colors and shapes of social distinction flowed through the gates in a flood of masculine top hats and bowlers, and gigantic showy feminine chapeaux. Before the ceremony, Clarie stood in the reception line greeting the parents. The fathers doffed their hats, while most of the mothers offered their long-gloved bejeweled hands. The artificial birds and flowers of their monstrously expensive headwear wagged at her approvingly as she spoke to them about their daughters, carefully walking the fine line between being truthful and gratifying parental egos. A tedious but necessary duty, for the new republican schools for girls needed support, and tuition.

At last, it was time for the ceremony to begin. The teachers, hatless, in the modest high-necked attire appropriate to their calling, ascended to the stage set up in the school's large cobble-stoned courtyard. They were followed by the two district mayors and an official from the Ministry of Education. Two of the men proudly wore a Legion of Honor medal on their lapels. Fortunately, only one of them was scheduled to speak.

The sun bore down on the stage as the dignitary from the Ministry began his oration. At first Clarie's attention was focused on the five rows just below the stage, her Alphonsines in all their black-and-white uniformity. Today was their time to celebrate. Although their youthful high spirits delighted her, Clarie had to hide her amusement at their raised eyebrows, furtive glances, and rolling eyes. By now, any of them could have given the assistant minister's speech. It was that predictable.

And, as the words droned into Clarie's consciousness, that irritating. There was something about pompous men telling women who they are and what they should be that roused the rebel in Clarie. When, for the third and, she hoped, the last time, he praised the Lycée Lamartine for preparing its students to become the "true companions" of republican men, she almost groaned. She lowered her head to hide her frown. If only she could ask him who was training young men to become the true companions of women. She was certain that the Ministry of Education never thought to address that question.

The tacit message was, of course, "better here than with the nuns," where aristocrats and other anti-Republicans sent their daughters to learn how to listen to priests instead of husbands. Clarie shifted in her chair ever so slightly. Surely professors at Lamartine were more than an antidote to Catholic sisters who didn't have nearly their education. She longed to scratch the prickly itch under her collar, anything to rub away her irritation. Instead, she reset her face in an attitude of polite interest, as a woman, the "true companion of a republican husband," should when a man was holding forth. When he went on to flatter the audience as the backbone of the great Third Republic, she took a closer look at the crowd. While he praised "the honest business and professional men united in upholding the traditions of the Great French Revolution," Clarie saw only snobbishness and division: the bankers and richer merchants sitting apart from the shopkeepers, and Christian parents quite successfully segregating themselves from the Israelites. She could tell by the hats. Birds of a feather, she thought ironically.

His Republic, his backbone. Clarie examined her fingers, turning her wedding ring, calming herself. Was she any better, any less hypocritical? She knew full well who was not yet part of the Alphonsine republic she was so proud of. Francesca's words came back to her: *Maura was such a good student. I had to take her out of school.* Neither the august representative of the nation nor the women sitting under those enormous hats thought about the daughters who spent hours in dank apartments making the artificial flowers that adorned them or stitching their silk and satin dresses together. Or sewing the buttons on Clarie's own neat, pristine shirtwaist. This last thought humbled and saddened her, evoking Maura's glowering, skeptical demeanor. As Clarie joined in the polite applause that signaled an end to the dignitary's speech, she found herself longing for a time when she would be able to offer the mothers and daughters of the poor more than words of advice and sympathy.

II

Wednesday, 7 July 1897

1

"ENOUGH!" EMILIE ANNOUNCED AS SHE hit the last chord. Clarie laughed and clapped. She had requested Schumann's *Scenes from Childhood* because she loved their gay simplicity. Besides, as she'd told Emilie, what could better accompany the scene of their two boys playing together on the floor. For Jean-Luc, still in his toddler gown, Emilie's five-year-old son, who was decked out in a snow-white sailor shirt and short pants, was a veritable hero. Clarie sighed as she watched little Robert save her son's tower of wooden blocks from toppling. The afternoon was all too soon coming to its inevitable bitter-sweet end. Emilie's family was leaving for Normandy the very next morning.

Clarie had sought out Emilie Franchet her first day at the Lycée Lamartine. When she thought about it later, she had to admit she'd chosen Emilie because she was short and rather plain, and not as stern-looking as the other veteran teachers. When she introduced herself, and

Emilie smiled, Clarie immediately recognized she could not possibly be alone in her attraction. One forgot that Emilie's hair was a straight mousy brown and perpetually coming out of the pins, that she barely reached Clarie's chin, that her cheeks were covered with the tiny pockmarks of adolescence. The amused glimmer in her brown eyes said it all: life could be fun. Even French grammar, which was Emilie's own particular burden to teach, could be fun! This is why her students loved her as much as her colleagues.

As Clarie and Emilie grew closer during the year, they often regretted that they had not been at Sèvres at the same time. How they could have explored Paris together! Studied for their exams, encouraged each other before each nerve-racking oral. But then, they always conceded, they had a lifetime. Just not this summer, Clarie thought ruefully.

"You must, must come to visit," Emilie said, as if reading her thoughts.

"No, not with Bernard's new position, we can't really leave."

Another crash sounded from the bedroom, where Emilie's mother and a maid were busily packing up for the journey to Normandy.

Emilie threw up her hands. "I'd better go see."

Jean-Luc ran up to Clarie and pulled on her skirt. He wasn't used to so much commotion. Emilie's boy, Robert, continued twirling his top, unperturbed. A modicum of chaos was all part of a life lived with a grandmother, a maid, a nanny, and two exuberant, working parents.

Clarie picked up her boy and swayed back and forth with him in her arms. "As soon as Madame Franchet is ready, *we* are going to the park to see if the ice cream cart is there and if the man will play a nice song for us." This time it was her son's turn to clap his hands. "Choco, Maman, choco."

"Chocolate," she agreed, putting him back on the floor and watching as he toddled toward his blocks. He was growing so fast.

"All right," Emilie continued the conversation as if she had not been interrupted, "you and Jean-Luc will come to visit. Has your little boy ever been to the sea? Has he ever traveled on the train?"

Before Clarie could demur again, Emilie added, "Jean-Luc and Robert are like cousins. They are each other's family in Paris."

"If I go anywhere this summer—"

"Oh, that's right. Arles. Your doting Italian papa. All those half-brothers and their big families. The veritable southern clan," Emilie exclaimed in mock horror. During their lunch hours and their walks home together, she and Clarie had often marveled at how different their upbringings had been, yet how immediately they had become attached to each other. Emilie's father had been a rich banker, her mother from an old merchant family. Neither could keep themselves from indulging their only child, even if that meant she would refuse an appropriate marriage and insist on becoming a teacher. Even if, in the last year of her father's life, she married a teacher, every bit as clever and sardonic as she. But, of course, quite poor. Emilie always insisted she had been thoroughly spoiled, while Clarie countered that the only way to spoil a child, or anyone, for that matter, is not to love them.

"If you go to Arles I'll be so jealous, but I'll just have to accept it," Emilie conceded, putting on a playful pout.

"What's this I hear?" Emilie's short, plump mother peeked into the parlor. "Arles in the summer, when we have my dear late husband's huge estate on the coast. Oh no, my dear. Impossible. Look at those little boys." And, of course, being a grandmother she did pause to admire Robert and Jean-Luc. "You both should have more of them. Forget this teaching. Forget everything except coming," she said, her voice rising to a crescendo as she threw up her hands echoing Emilie's exasperated gestures. Then once again she disappeared into the bedroom. Even on a day filled with domestic duties, Emilie's mother wore a rose and cream silk dress and wound her white hair in a fantastic cluster of curls around her face. Somehow she had raised a daughter who cared not a whit for fashion or show, but one who demonstrably shared her ebullient and generous spirit.

"Oh, dear Emilie, I'm going to miss you. Can you come to the Square d'Anvers with us?" Anything to prolong this perfect, carefree day.

Clarie's invitation brought little Robert to his feet, running to his mother. "They're getting ice cream. I want some too!"

"And why not," she said, lifting her son's chin with her finger and peering into his eyes. "Besides," she commented to Clarie, "Mother likes to organize. Let's play hooky."

Emilie lived in one of the elegant new apartments in a quiet, narrow street behind the administration building of the Paris Gas Company. The gas works themselves had been moved to the northern suburbs, much to the relief of the old, and new, inhabitants of the district. Just in time, Emilie would say, to provide her with a bright new home near her school. In the winter, if both of them worked late, Emilie and Clarie often walked part-way home together, separating near the gild-edged, iron-wrought gates of the Company. If they were really late, they'd see lamplighters leaving the building, heading out to illuminate the city.

This time, reaching the rue Condorcet, they turned away from the Gas Company and in the direction of Clarie's apartment. Each of them held on to her boy's hand to keep them away from shoppers, bustling by on sidewalks, and the carriages clomping through the street. Emilie and Robert took the lead, and Jean-Luc proudly followed in the footsteps of his big friend. Over the traffic, Clarie heard the stream of questions that Robert babbled to his mother. Where are we going? What kind of ice cream can I have? Why doesn't Jean-Luc wear short pants? Are we going to see Papa?

The little park in Square d'Anvers bordered the College Rollin, one of the biggest boys' high schools in Paris. And, indeed, Robert's father, Edgar Franchet, did teach there. As for Jean-Luc, Emilie patiently told her son that by the end of the summer his little friend would be in britches. For his part, Jean-Luc, who had to struggle to keep up, was silenced by his friend's loquacity. When they came to a halt at the rue Turgot, Clarie tousled her boy's hair, imagining the day he would be able to talk and walk as fast as his friend, and even go to the College Rollin.

When Robert crossed the street ahead of Clarie and Jean-Luc, he began to swivel his head, searching, and finally pointed his finger toward Montmartre. "Look. Look on top of the hill. There's the abom . . . abom . . . abominer." Clarie immediately knew what the boy was referring to. The rue Turgot cut through the dense neighborhood at just the right angle to give a spectacular uphill view of the unfinished Sacré-Coeur Basilica.

"Shhh," Emilie bent down to shush her boy and took him by the arm. Then she turned back to Clarie. "I believe he is truly his father's son," she said, with a resigned shake of her head.

Amused by little Robert's attempt to repeat Edgar Franchet's words, Clarie picked up Jean-Luc to show him what had made his friend so excited. The four of them huddled at the corner of the rues Turgot and Condorcet, waiting for a few matrons, who might well be a shocked by a five-year-old's loud condemnation of a church, to pass them by.

"Now, dear," Emilie said to her son, when they were alone, "we all know that churches should be only about love and charity, not about condemning others. But we needn't talk so loud about what we believe." Clarie listened with interest to this lesson of maternal moderation, knowing that at some point she'd probably have to give the same admonition to her own son. Bernard also complained bitterly about having to witness the construction of the gleaming white edifice from his neighborhood. For all left-leaning republicans, all socialists, all anarchists, the rising national basilica was truly an "abomination" because its builders proclaimed its purpose to be retribution for the sins of those who had revolted during the Paris Commune. Men like Bernard Martin and Edgar Franchet thought of it in quite the opposite way: that it was an ugly representation of the sins of the bourgeoisie who had crushed and killed the rebellion of 1871.

"I see it every day at this corner," Clarie said, shaking her head. The fact that it was so white, so high, so expensive and so ornately Byzantine made it particularly galling. "I'll tell you what," she said, changing the mood. "Of course well-behaved children are not supposed to give offence, but that doesn't mean we can't march right down this street to the park to show that we're not afraid of any old church. May Robert lead?" she raised her eyebrows to Emilie, who nodded her agreement. When his mother let go of him, the five-year-old straightened up and held his arms in the slightly bent pose of a toy soldier. Then, humming a military song, he led them all up the quiet street. Clarie and Emilie laughed together at the way in which Jean-Luc tried joyfully to imitate his friend.

Half an hour later, spilled chocolate ice cream and drowsy-making sunshine were getting to Jean-Luc. "Definitely time for his nap," Clarie announced as she picked up her sleepy son.

"We'll walk with you."

Clarie gratefully recognized Emilie's offer as a way of prolonging the day. The rue Rodier formed part of a triangle with the rue Turgot, and the two streets met across from the Square d'Anvers. Clarie would only have to carry her load for half of a long block and up three flights of stairs, where Rose would employ her usual magic to get "her Luca" to take his afternoon nap.

Clarie and Emilie strolled slowly. Because they were chatting intensely, getting in their last words before parting, it was Robert who noticed a post boy, dressed in a blue uniform with a leather bag strapped across his chest, coming up the street toward them.

"Look Maman, someone is getting a 'a little blue'!" Robert exclaimed.

"Yes, dear," Emilie said, as she barely looked up. "His grandmother," she explained to Clarie, "sent him a pneumatic letter while she was out shopping, then she came home and described all the tubes, and how fast the paper had traveled, and how he got a message from the Bon Marché within the hour. My mother," she shook her head, "she spoils him, as she spoiled me."

Clarie was once again about to disagree with Emilie's assessment, when the boy stopped in front of her building and rang the bell. The concierge answered almost immediately and then looked up to see her. "There's Madame Martin now," Mme Peyroud told the letter carrier as she pointed to Clarie.

"It's for you, it's for you, Madame Martin," Robert sang, dancing around her. The excitement even brought Jean-Luc out of his stupor. "For you," he echoed.

There was a big difference between a boy, for fun, getting a "little blue," as the Parisians affectionately dubbed their pneumatic letters, and one sent to an adult. Although Clarie tried to hide her alarm, Emilie sensed it, and offered to take Jean-Luc.

Trying to ward off anxiety, Clarie relinquished her son to her friend and took the letter from the post boy. It was from the *économe*, the lycée's accountant.

"Perhaps they're going to offer you a raise," Emilie commented as she glanced at the envelope.

"Or fire me," a feeble joke. School was over and done with for the summer. She couldn't imagine why an administrator was sending her an urgent message. She carefully ripped open the envelope.

> *Madame Martin, I regret to tell you that one of our family has met a terrible tragedy. Yesterday, after working in a seamstress's establishment in the Sentier district, a daughter of Francesca Laurenzano was stabbed and killed. A friend of Madame Laurenzano came to my office today to report the tragedy and to say that Francesca would not be working for a while. She also said that Francesca particularly mentioned you as someone who had been kind and who should know what has befallen her. I hope you do not find this news too disturbing. Yours, Berthe Sauvaget*

Clarie gasped and covered her mouth.

"What does it say? What does it say?" Robert eagerly asked.

"Shush, Robert, I'm sure this is adult business," Emilie said. "May I?" she asked concerned.

Clarie reached for Jean-Luc, who had fallen asleep, and gave Emilie the message. She clutched her son to her and kissed him on his forehead. She had to hide the clamoring in her chest.

"Did you know this Francesca?" Emilie asked, puzzled.

"I spoke to her once or twice. She cleaned my classroom." Despite all her efforts, Clarie heard her voice falter.

"This is terrible, of course. . . ." Emilie handed the note back to Clarie. "You're all right? I could stay."

"No, no." Clarie had never told Emilie about her encounters with Francesca and her daughters. Some instinct had held her back from telling anyone except Bernard. That instinct had only become stronger when she learned the Laurenzano girls had a connection with the dead Russian anarchist.

"You're sure?" Emilie's brow wrinkled with concern.

"Yes, yes. I know you must go, dear Emilie." Clarie's eyes glistened with tears provoked by far more than their parting. "Sorry the day had to end like this."

"Me, too," Emilie answered as she gave Clarie a kiss on each cheek. "Good-bye, my dearest friend."

Clarie forced a smile. Robert, like the little gentleman he was trained to be, reached up to kiss her too.

"Have a beautiful summer, sweet Robert," Clarie managed to say to him, "and when you come back, you'll see how big Jean-Luc will be."

Clarie watched as Emilie and her son waved good-bye. Then she hurried through the courtyard to the stairs, away from the eyes of her concierge. Inside the darkened entryway, she began to gulp for air, but made herself be quiet so as not to disturb Jean-Luc. She pressed her hand over her mouth, smothering a sob. The question that pierced her, that would haunt her, was whether she could have done something to prevent the death of a young woman. For now she had to find the strength to get up the stairs, ask Rose to put Jean-Luc down for his nap, say she was tired, retreat to her bedroom, and decide what to do.

2

"WHERE IS ANGELA? WHERE IS my girl?" After Francesca Laurenzano woke up to the realization that her daughter had not returned during the night, she spent the dawn hours imploring Jesus, the Virgin Mary and Maura to tell her where her older daughter had gone.

Maura didn't know. All night she had tossed and turned on her mattress, growing more and more afraid. *Where is Angela?* Were they cursed? Were they all in danger? Barbereau, Pyotr, now Angela? When her mother *again* dropped to her knees and raised clasped hands up toward the crucifix over her bed, Maura could stand it no longer.

"I'm not going to the laundry today until I find her," she said. "Don't worry, Maman, I'll bring her home."

Francesca reached to the bed to hoist herself up. "How can you? You told me that you didn't know where she is."

"Maybe she's staying with those nice girls in the Latin Quarter," Maura offered, fully aware that Lidia and Vera were either in prison or on a train back to Russia. "Look," she saw, reaching in her skirt pocket, "I have money enough for an omnibus in case I have to cross the river." Barbereau's money. The few coins she had not sewn into the hem of her dress. Her hand trembled as she showed them to her mother. She was as shaky as she had been the night they dragged the bastard's body to the Basin. She made a fist, squeezing the coins into the palm of her hand. What was Barbereau's death going to cost them? Someone had already killed Pyotr. She had to think. Stay calm. Get away from her mother's praying and weeping. And find Angela.

"You should tell Madame Guyot—"

"This is more important than the nasty old laundry. I'm going right now." Maura was afraid if she stayed, she'd tell her mother what she planned to do: Go to the morgue. Make sure her sister wasn't there. After that, she'd search every sweatshop and alley in the Sentier—the garment district where Angela had set out to work the day before.

Before her mother could object, Maura rushed out of the room, down the stairs, through the courtyard, toward the nearest omnibus stop. If it went to the Ile de la Cité, she'd take it.

As she hurried through familiar streets, she couldn't help thinking about how she had once imagined that going to the morgue, where unidentified bodies were displayed free of charge, might be entertaining. She loved reading the descriptions and seeing the pictures in the cheap dailies: strangled babies dressed like dolls, murder victims nakedly revealing their wounds, wretched suicides rescued from the Seine in various stages of decomposition. She'd never dreamed that her first foray would be to look for her own sister.

On the bus, she clung to a pole for support, silently repeating over and over again, "It can't be true. It can't be true." The city passed by in a blur. She barely noticed the other passengers. At least she remembered to get off as soon as they crossed the river near the Notre Dame Cathedral. The morgue, a massive low stone building, sat on a broad street behind the great church. A crowd had already gathered for the day's viewings.

Maura frantically tried to push her way toward the front of the line. "I have to see, I have to see," she shouted. A few refused to give up their place, muttering against her, but others recognizing her as a person of great interest—someone who could actually identify a victim—stepped aside. She heard curious murmurs. One middle-aged woman in a ridiculous hat was even bold enough to inquire, "Who do you think is in there, dearie? Your mother? Your lover?"

Disdaining to answer, Maura kept jostling until, panting hard, she got to the front of the line close to the entrance. The people ahead of her were moving with agonizing slowness into the vast viewing hall.

"Do you think she knows who 'the angel' is?" someone whispered behind her.

Maura gasped and turned. "What angel?"

"A beautiful blond creature," a short, earnest working girl, in a red-and-white-striped cotton blouse, answered. "It was in the *faits divers* this morning. That's why there's such a crowd today."

Even if Maura had wanted to answer them, to tell them to mind their own business, she couldn't. Her heart had jumped into her throat, blocking her from saying anything. She could hardly breathe and would have stumbled if she hadn't been in a crowd.

"Let her through," the same girl shouted. "She knows the blond angel."

Maura tried to move her legs as she was being pushed forward. Was she going to regret everything she had ever done in her life? She'd always loved the *faits divers*. Any time she could afford a newspaper, she'd devour the little paragraphs that, as they days went by, eventually grew into the big stories everyone talked about, the infamous murders with full-page illustrations in the Sunday editions. Now would there be pictures of Angela? Out of the side of her eye, she saw a policeman approach. He grabbed her by her elbow and, shoving everyone else aside, led her through the door into the viewing hall. Whispers, like stinging buzzing insects, swirled around her: "She knows one of the victims."

And then she was there, in front of the glass window that ran all the way up to the high ceiling. At first she could not bear to look at the bodies, twelve of them, laid out in two rows, each occupying a marble slab. Instead, her eyes roved past them to the wall behind the corpses. To aid identification, clothes were hung on two rows of six hooks. Angela's best plaid dress, the dress she put on for her first day of work, was there, right in the middle of the lower row. Maura wrested her arm from the uniformed man and spread her hands over the glass. Her breathing made a fog between her and the refrigerated bodies. She wanted the fog to last forever. She didn't want to see. The policeman wiped the glass with his handkerchief and her eyes fell upon her sister, naked except for her private parts, her breasts exposed and the blackened wound above her heart evident to all.

"No! No! No!" she heard her voice but it came from somewhere else, somewhere above or below or behind her. She wanted to be there, somewhere else, where the No was real, not Angela's dead body. "No!"

"You know her?" the policeman grasped her shoulder.

"She's my sister," she sobbed and clapped her hand over her mouth.

And then she heard a chorus behind her, "The blond angel's sister."

"We need to talk to you, and after that, you'll have to get your mother to identify her and bring money to transport her if you don't want her buried in a pauper's grave," the nasty policeman said.

"Money, we have no money," Maura said. Burial, a priest, no, who could afford that? "My mother has no money, and I'm just a laundress," she whispered. All the dreams and schemes that had fueled Maura's hopes seemed to evaporate as she stared at her sister. All she could utter from the benumbed places that held her heart and mind were a few bare, necessary truths.

A hush filled the hall. Somehow Maura sensed that everyone was hanging on her every word. They were the audience to her tragedy.

This is what they all had come for. To gawk and stare at her during her darkest hour.

Someone said, "Oh, look at her, those dark curls peeping out of the bun on top of her head, it's like Rose Red and Snow White, the two poor beautiful sisters in the fairy tale."

Another called out, "Was she really an angel?"

Maura didn't like the uniformed man holding on to her. She didn't want to talk to him. What if he knew about Barbereau? Some instinct broke through her paralysis and told her the crowd could help.

"Yes," she turned, shaking off her captor, "she was an angel. Angela, Angelina, the little angel. I am Maura. My mother is a poor widow." Her chest was heaving in turbulent waves. *Rescue me. I don't want to talk to the police. I don't want my sister to be dead.*

"They can't bury an angel in a pauper's grave," a woman dressed in silks said, and others murmured their agreement. "Here," the same wealthy woman unfolded a lace-trimmed handkerchief and held it in the air. "Let's take up a collection for Rose Red and Snow White. For the Angel and her dark-haired sister. For a proper Catholic burial," she ended with a flourish.

The policeman's hand tightened around Maura's shoulder as if she could get through the crowd and flee, when all she could do was watch and wait, knowing that for the moment, she was the center of their attention, the object of their charity.

She lowered her eyes. For isn't that what one should do when you have just seen your dead sister? She folded her hands. Help me, help me now, were the only words running through her mind. Help get me out of here.

The policeman cleared his throat and loosened his grip, raising her hopes, for no single man could thwart the emotions of those filling the stifling hall. But he was clever. He shouted his good will. "Do gather the money and we will send her home to her mother to arrange a burial. For now, I will take her to a quiet place to ask a few questions. You can leave your generous donations at the door. We all want to find the murderer of the Angel, don't we?"

"Yes," someone yelled, and again a murmur of assent fluttered through the crowd.

"This way, mademoiselle," the policeman said to Maura, loud enough for those around to hear. "Come quickly. And you'll be on your way soon."

Angry that he had foiled her feeble attempt to escape, Maura tried to yank her arm away. Instead of letting go, he growled in her ear, "If you don't want to get into big trouble, come with me quietly." Maybe he knew she was clever too.

He led her through a door near the exit into a small room with a table and two chairs. A man smoking a cigar was waiting for them. He got up and tipped his bowler. "Inspector Jobert." He was ginger-haired and mustached, broad as a wall, fitted like a fat sausage into his beige summer suit. "And who are you?" he asked, as he gestured with his hand for her to take a seat.

An inspector. Why an inspector? Maura tried to resist the policeman pushing behind her.

"Come, come," he urged. "No use trying to stall. Better to tell the truth."

The odor of something far stronger than the soap and bleach of the laundry seeped into the room and mingled with the aroma of the inspector's cigar. Nausea lurched up from Maura's stomach.

"Sit her down before she faints," the man called Jobert ordered. Maura felt herself being pressed into a chair.

"Once again," Jobert said, peering into her face. "Who are you?"

"Maura, Maura Laurenzano." She felt her lips moving and heard the sound of her words.

"Good!" he said, as he reached into his pocket and slapped an identity card on the table. "Angela's sister."

Maura's eyes moved from his satisfied ruddy sneer to the card on the table. Angela's identity card.

"You knew!" Her heart began to pound. They had trapped her, here in the smells, by the dead bodies. Trapped. But why? Did they know she'd been involved in a murder? No longer able to hold her fear and nausea down, she bent over and threw up on the floor. When she was able to sit upright, she covered her face with her hands, trying to block everything out. She heard the door open and close.

When she looked up she saw Jobert scrutinizing her. "Not quite as strong or as clever as you thought you were, huh? Well, we're used to that here."

The door opened again behind her.

"Ah, give the young lady the wet towel to wipe herself off."

She hated being grateful, but she was. She wiped her face and arms, and ran the towel down her dress. She rolled it up and laid it on the table with her hands over it. She needed its coolness. But the policeman took it away from her and slapped it on the floor, over her vomit.

"You know," the inspector said as he leaned across the table toward her, "it would have been much easier if you had not run away when we came to investigate Barbereau's murder. Maybe if you had chosen to talk to me then instead of hiding, your sister would still be alive."

"Don't say that!" Maura jumped up. "Never say that! We were afraid, that's all." How could he possibly blame her for Angela's death? How could she live without Angela? Why had she let Angela go alone to work? Hadn't they always done everything together? Why had she even dreamed of running away alone, without her sister?

Putting his elbow on the table, Jobert turned away from her and took a few long draws on his cigar. She stared at his rosy, well-fed profile. He was demonstrating his calm, his control. And her vulnerability. She hated him.

Finally, after blowing a ring of smoke in the air, he said, "Your sister played a dangerous game, being the lover of both Barbereau and the Russian anarchist."

"She was not their lover!" Maura shouted. "Cover her up right now. She was always modest. She's not a show."

"Well, she was someone's lover. We've done the full examination, you know."

"He violated her! And beat her. She did not love him!"

"Which one is that?"

"Barbereau," she whispered, realizing her outburst had led her into a trap.

"And that's why you killed him."

Maura fell into the chair, silent. "No," she lied. "We did not kill him."

"Not your Russian friend?"

She shook head. She would say no more. They could beat her. They could keep her here forever, surrounded by that sickening smell and dead bodies. She crossed her arms. She would say no more.

Jobert tried. He told her about all the gossip spread by the concierges in Maura's neighborhood and his interviews with the other seamstresses that Barbereau had hired and tried to seduce. He told her that he suspected both her and Angela of sympathy with Pyotr Ivanovich's violent brand of anarchism.

"Lies," she shouted out against this libel, forgetting her pledge not to speak. And then she crossed her arms, waiting for their tortures.

"You don't want to accuse the Russian? He's dead, you know. It wouldn't hurt him."

Some instinct of self-preservation stilled her tongue. No, she would not betray Pyotr by saying he had killed Barbereau and frightened her and Angela into hiding. She had invented that lie to protect her sister. And now Angela was dead. *Angela is dead.* The three words reverberated in her brain. Angela is dead. She began to sob, and the tears came in torrents. Finally, somehow, gasping for air, she stopped. She wiped the tears and snot from her face with her sleeve, ready to be defiant again.

Jobert was close enough for her to see the wart on the side of his ruddy nose and smell his cigar-laden breath. "Don't you see a connection?" he asked. "Barbereau, the Russian, your sister? Doesn't it make you a little afraid?"

Although she was sitting very still, Maura felt like someone was pressing hard against her, squeezing the air out of her chest. She could not feel her arms and legs. Her mouth fell open. It as was if all her lies were coming back to haunt her. When they were in the Russian girls' room, hadn't she tried to scare Angela by saying they might be in danger? And now, it might actually be true. What if the person who had killed Pyotr had killed Angela and would eventually try to kill her? Because of Barbereau. Or what if the police were involved already, killing Pyotr to prove he was dangerous, and then. . . . It was too confusing. Too scary.

"We can help you, you know."

She didn't believe him. Even though he seemed to be able to see right through her, she didn't believe a word he said. Why should he help her, except to help her into the Saint-Lazare Prison for the rest of her life? Or to the guillotine. No! She'd tell them nothing.

The door opened again, a man in a long white smock. "It's hot out there," he remarked to Jobert. "We'd better get this done before noon."

The inspector nodded and gestured that the man should talk to Maura. The attendant bent over and gave her a list. "Go home," he explained, "get your mother to come back to identify the body, sign a certificate, have someone inform a priest, and try to arrange for a burial for tomorrow."

As if she were stupid and wouldn't remember or could not read. Or as if the man had dealt with many shocked souls before. She nodded and picked up the piece of paper. "I understand that a collection has been taken up for the burial," the man in the white coat continued. "Officer Olivier has it. We're going to dress her now." He said it just like that. "We're going to dress her." Angela's dead body.

When Maura walked into the hall, she paused to see the huge green curtains drawn to a close over the exhibition window. Hot tears streaked her cheeks again. Behind that curtain someone was yanking Angela's cold rigid arms into useless bloody clothes. Holding Maura more gently this time, Officer Olivier led her out of the exit door, which was at the opposite end of the building from the entrance. She was grateful for his authority now, for no one tried to stop her or talk to her. He walked her to the bus stop, waited until he saw the bay horses approaching, then handed her the tied-up, lace-trimmed handkerchief, once belonging to the silk-dressed woman. In parting, he admonished her to bring her mother back as soon as possible.

3

CLARIE STARED OUT HER BEDROOM window, watching the first shadows encroach upon the quiet, sunlit courtyard. What could she have done? She was a wife, a mother, a teacher, so busy, so . . . what? She realized she had been clutching her hands so hard, they were almost numb. She let them go and began to pace around the bed. Wasn't she, above all, a human being? Wasn't she a mother who had lost a child? Yet even in the worst of times, she had never been as alone or as destitute as Francesca seemed to be. As her steps quickened, a growing frustration surged into Clarie's sadness. She wasn't useless. She didn't want to be useless. Clarie paused. What had Bernard often said? That for the poor a death was more than a tragedy, it was a catastrophe, a hand lost to the labors that made survival possible, an unsanctified burial in a pauper's grave. She *could* do something.

She pulled open the drawer that held her chemises and blouses and searched underneath for the envelope containing the secret savings which she used to buy little surprises for Rose and Jean-Luc. She spilled its contents onto the dresser. Only two five-franc notes and a few coins. She put the bills in her pocket and replaced the coins. Then, because she was unaccustomed to telling lies, she took a deep breath before going to talk to Rose.

"Madame Clarie, are you all right?" Rose came out of the kitchen as soon as she heard Clarie enter the parlor. Her eyes searched Clarie's face.

"Oh, yes, just a bit tired. And I realized that I need to pick up something from the school. Do you think Jean-Luc will sleep for another hour?"

"He's no problem, our little Luca. If he's awake," Rose shrugged, "he can help me in the kitchen."

"Thank you," Clarie said as she put on her gloves and smiled, a smile she feared could hardly seem real. "It may take a while."

Without having any clear idea of what she was going to do, Clarie hurried down the steps and out of the building, striding quickly through the streets that had become so familiar to her. She had to reach the school before Berthe Sauvaget left. She was panting when she arrived at the lycée. She wiped her hot, damp brow with a handkerchief before ringing the bell. When the économe opened the door to the empty school, Clarie almost lost heart. How was she going to explain herself?

Fortunately Mme Sauvaget spoke first. "Oh, Madame Martin, I so feared that you would find the news upsetting. But I promised that I would tell you. I wasn't aware that you knew Francesca."

"I encountered her one evening when I was working late. I'm surprised she remembered my name." Clarie bit her lip, before again heeding the instinct that kept her from telling the entire truth. "I thought if I had her address, I could send her a note of sympathy."

"Of course, come with me," Berthe Sauvaget said with the cheery efficiency that allowed her to keep the school's complicated accounts in order.

Clarie followed the short, wide, bustling bookkeeper up the stairs. As they crossed through the second floor, Clarie glanced anxiously toward the principal's office. Much to her relief, the door was closed. She dreaded the possibility of running into Mme Roubinovitch, who might well ask penetrating questions about why she was there. Mme Sauvaget, a much less formidable administrator, was quite happy to accommodate Clarie without pressing her. As soon as they got to her office, Mme Sauvaget searched through the notebooks lined up on the shelves behind her desk until she found the one containing the accounts for maintenance. "Just a moment, just a moment," she mumbled, as she shuffled through the pages before giving out an "ah" and triumphantly announcing, "here it is. I can remember her saying it was just on the other side of the hospital when we all worried about her getting here on time." Then Mme Sauvaget wrote the address on a piece of paper and handed it to Clarie.

She murmured her thanks and hurried down the hall and out of the school. Once the big wooden doors had closed behind her, Clarie examined the address. If Francesca truly lived just beyond the new Lariboisière Hospital, her apartment wasn't far away. Yet it was over a line that Clarie hardly ever crossed, on the other side of the so-called outer boulevards. So-called, Clarie thought ruefully, because they weren't outer at all. Not since the expansion of the city in the 1860s. Yet, even though the linked, wide commercial streets coursed through outdated boundaries, they had not lost their capacity to divide one Paris from another. On one side, Clarie's side, commerce and relative comfort reigned; on the other, factories, poverty and slums. She stood, hesitating as late afternoon shoppers hurried past her. *They'll need the money now*, she told herself. And *she* needed to know which girl had been killed, and why.

The surest, though perhaps not the shortest, way to reach Francesca's neighborhood was to retrace some of her steps and then follow the rue du Faubourg Poissonnière to its northern end. This led Clarie to a jumble of broad streets rattling with carriages, carts, omnibuses and cabs going to and from the nearby railroad station. It was a perilous crossing, and a relief to arrive at the relative quiet of the boulevard in front of the massive Lariboisière Hospital. Clarie followed its thick gray walls, hoping to encounter a winged-hat nursing sister who might guide her to the rue Goutte-d'Or. She did not want to ask any of the men in worn overalls and smocks, who eyed her every time she paused to look around. Finally she approached a woman carrying a laundry basket on her head.

"You can go back to that corner to the rue Caplat," the woman pointed, gracefully balancing her basket with her one strong bare arm, "or maybe they live near the laundry all the way back to Islettes or," she turned the other way, in the direction that Clarie had been walking, thought for a moment, and shook her head, "too confusing for the likes of you, I fear."

Clarie had an idea that by "the likes of her" the laundress meant a bourgeois lady out of place and nervous. She was about to thank her and take her leave, when the woman asked, "You ain't here about those Laurenzano girls, are you?"

"Yes, yes, I am," Clarie answered, surprised yet relieved that she had found someone who might help her find their apartment.

"I had a feeling." The woman sighed and put her basket on the sidewalk. "One of 'em was supposed to be working for me this morning, but took off to the morgue. Found Angela there, naked as the day she was born just about."

"Angela," Clarie whispered.

"Yeah, the pretty blond one. When Francesca heard, she went a little crazy, so someone came to get me at the washhouse. We live in the same building, see. I'm goin' there soon as I get these delivered. I already got the priest for tomorrow to do a mass. And then off to the cemetery." The woman twisted her mouth down and shook her head again.

"Can they bury her so quickly?"

"Gotta, in this heat. That's what the police said when they brought the body up. Hope she lasts the night."

The image of Angela's decaying body sent tremors through Clarie's chest. She was tempted to give the laundress the money and scurry back to her own neighborhood. She did not feel ready to confront the terrible human realities of Angela's murder.

"Me and Francesca are the only real church-goers in the whole place. So I gotta help."

Clarie perceived kindness in that hard, reddened face. She glanced at the laundress's swollen hands, her torn cotton dress darkened by perspiration. Even as her own resolutions were fading, Clarie realized that nothing or no one could be more real or human than this big-boned gray-haired woman, who spent her days scrubbing and ironing to survive and still found the time, and the will, to help her neighbor.

"Perhaps I can do something—"

"A few sous would be good," the woman said, a little too sharply, then added, "and I'm sure Francesca would be honored to see you."

Given her hesitations about coming, Clarie did not feel she deserved any honor. It was humbling to acknowledge that the laundress had so easily jumped to the conclusion that Clarie was capable of nothing more than sympathy and a little charity. That she could not understand or be of any real use in their hard, poverty-stricken lives. Even knowing she was unlikely to prove them wrong, Clarie resolved to go on.

After thanking the woman for her help, Clarie retraced her steps to the rue Caplat, which led to the Goutte-d'Or, where among the low one- and two-story buildings she would find the five-story tenement where the Laurenzanos lived. Once she got there, the laundress said, she'd find someone to tell her how to get through the courtyard and up the stairs to the right room.

A courtyard and stairs like my own building, Clarie thought, reassuring herself as she walked quickly through the unfamiliar streets. But of course the tenement on the rue Goutte-d'Or was nothing like the apartment house on the rue Rodier. The pavement that led to it was cracked and uneven, spattered with garbage, and lined with stores and shops so dank and dark that without their signs, Clarie would have had no idea of their functions. Fortunately, there was no mistaking the tenement hovering over low wooden and brick buildings.

The large courtyard was unguarded and open; still Clarie hesitated to enter, for it wasn't as deserted as hers would be the hour before the men of the rue Rodier began to arrive from their shops and offices. Half-naked children were all about, yelling and running, dodging a few scrawny, scratching hens and a large indolent dog that lay in the middle of the yard, as if drugged by the waning sun. Clarie heard the hissing and pounding of tools and machinery and realized that the entire first floor was occupied by small workshops. The windows above her fluttered with hung clothes and sheets. She took a few wary steps in and caught the fetid smell, worse even than in the street. She lifted her skirt ever so slightly over the uneven cobblestones searching for the odor's source. She soon found it, for some of the children made a game of jumping over the drain that led from the middle of the apartments to the street. She began breathing through her mouth, as she looked for the concierge's lodge. A tugging on her skirt almost made her jump. Her assailant was a dear little towheaded boy or girl. "Hello, lady," it said, then ran away giggling. Suddenly everything seemed to stop as the other children noticed her.

"Lady, lady," one of them yelled, "come to give us something?" "Me first," said another, taller boy as he ran up to Clarie.

"You stop that, stop that right now, you ragamuffins. Let her alone."

Clarie gave out a sigh of relief. Only a concierge would yell with such authority. She turned to find a small, wrinkled woman in a loose, dark striped dress and slippers.

"You here about those Laurenzano girls?" she asked before Clarie could explain herself. "You a reporter or something?"

"No, a teacher. In the school where Francesca works."

"Humpf. Well, they already got the pauper's coffin upstairs. Don't know why they bothered. They're going to have to carry it down before it gets all smelly. What a lot."

When Clarie could find no response for her harsh judgments, the woman went on, "Eh, the washerwoman will help 'em. She's strong as an ox."

"Where—"

"Five floors up that staircase," the concierge said as she gestured toward one of the doorless openings at the back of the courtyard. "And watch your step."

Clarie was relieved to enter the obscure passageway out of sight of the children, the concierge and whoever else might have been watching through the windows. In the hall, the smell was no better, but at least it mingled with the odors of cooking. She climbed the uneven, unlighted stairs at a crawl, clinging to the wobbly banister. Once she almost slipped on what might have been a potato peel. After a dozen more careful steps, she panicked, fearing that she would not be able to keep track of the floors. Then she remembered that the fifth floor would be at the top where the staircase ended. A few inhabitants of the building kept their doors opened as they worked. Clarie was grateful for every bit of light they threw in her path, even as she tried to pass unnoticed. Finally she came to the fifth floor, and a door opened to a room dominated by a simple, wooden coffin.

She heard weeping, approached and knocked on the doorframe. Someone told her to come in.

Maura sat on the bed, holding on to her mother, whose sobs had reached out into the hallway. The coffin lay between them and the single table in the room.

"Maman, look who's here," Maura said shaking her mother. "It's that teacher."

"Oh, oh," Francesca stuttered as she wiped her eyes with a handkerchief.

"Please, don't trouble yourself," Clarie said, taking another step into the room. "I've only come to express my deepest sympathies."

But of course Francesca, whose life had been one long trail of humbling experiences, did trouble herself for this unexpected guest. She rose from her bed and came over to Clarie.

"Do you want to see my baby?" she asked in voice hoarse with tears. "Someone stabbed her."

My baby. Someone stabbed her. There was no way to respond to the sadness and horror of those words, so Clarie merely nodded and moved around to look into the coffin. Someone had combed Angela's hair so it framed her face with soft curls. They had placed a cross around her neck and posed her hands together as if in prayer. As angelic and obedient as the girl Clarie had seen sitting in the first row of her classroom. It was tragic, and a little grotesque. The perfectly posed girl had been murdered. It took all of Clarie's strength not to gasp or cry out.

"They did that in the morgue," Maura said. "And they refrigerated her."

Clarie had already learned that Francesca's younger daughter was not given to piety. And that the girl did not like her. Still Clarie was shocked by her bluntness. Or was it strength? When Clarie looked up at Maura, she saw that her face, too, was red and swollen. Maura quickly lowered her eyes, as if to deny Clarie any window into her emotions.

"Professoressa, why? Why kill my little girl?" Francesca cried.

"I don't know," Clarie murmured. "I don't know." When she saw the poor woman's shoulders begin to shudder again, Clarie reached over and put her arms around her. "I'm so sorry," she whispered as the weeping began again. When it subsided, Clarie reached in her pocket and pulled out the franc notes. "Here," she said, urging the bills into Francesca's hand. "Something for the funeral."

"Oh no, professoressa, that's too much. We already have money collected from the people at the morgue. We can bury her at Batignolles, in a real grave."

Maura had gotten up to see what "too much" was, and when a slight glimmer of approval showed in her eyes, Clarie imagined that ten francs was probably more than a week's wages for the kind of work that Maura and her mother did.

"No, take it, please; it's from all of us," she lied, knowing that Francesca was too caught in the web of grief to remember that very few people were at the lycée. "And I will come again, next week, to see that you are all right," Clarie said, striving to find a graceful way to flee this unbearably mournful place.

"Yes, of course, your baby, you must go," Francesca mumbled, as if remembering that Clarie was a personage who had a busy, important life somewhere, and that this important person, too, was a mother. "Maura," she said, "take a candle, show Madame Martin down the stairs and to the hospital."

Clarie bowed her head and grimaced. In spite of her grieving, Francesca had calculated how far Clarie would need an escort to feel comfortable walking in her neighborhood. She was about to demur, when she saw that Maura had gone to the cupboard and taken out a candle. The girl seemed eager to leave.

The two made a silent descent down the rickety staircase. When they reached the bottom, Maura snuffed out the candle with her finger and shoved it in the pocket of her apron. The children in the courtyard did not harass them; they didn't dare. They just stood and stared as a striding Maura led Clarie out of the courtyard. Because she was so conscious of the unevenness of the dirty sidewalk, Clarie had trouble keeping up with Maura as she marched through the streets to the edge of the huge hospital. When they got to the corner, Maura swirled around to face Clarie. Although Clarie longed to reach out to try to comfort the girl, she didn't dare. Not only because she knew that Maura was suspicious of her and her motives, but because something in the girl reminded Clarie of her younger self, and of the days right after her own mother's death when she resisted all efforts to touch or console her. So Clarie stood and waited for Maura to say what was on her mind.

"I'm glad you brought the money for my mother. She will need it. Also, you should come and see her, as you promised. After the funeral, I'm leaving," Maura said, her voice a matter-of-fact monotone which didn't allow for any response. "I'm not going to let him kill me too."

"Who?" Clarie cried out. "Tell me—"

But Maura had already turned away and was striding away from her. "I don't know yet," she yelled.

"You mustn't leave your mother alone," Clarie called. This time Maura refused to respond, leaving Clarie to stare at her proud, upright figure as she disappeared around the corner.

With a sigh of exasperation, Clarie began to walk as fast as she could along the long gray wall that enclosed the hospital. As soon as she reached the busy intersection where the La Chapelle boulevard became Rochechouart, she knew her way, a blessedly short way, back to her apartment. Because it was late, she hurried past the gaudy commerce that had made Montmartre and its foothills the destination of pleasure-seekers from all over Paris. She never paid any attention to the risqué posters advertising the dancehalls and café-concerts because this was not her world. Nor did she want it to be. Yet she felt more at home here than only a few blocks away, among the tenements that housed the Laurenzanos and the laundress.

Not for the first time did she wonder where the daughter of an immigrant blacksmith had gone, the one who grew up surrounded by the blood-like smell of hot iron and the grunts of burly, blackened, laboring men. Or, and perhaps this was more troublesome, where had Bernard's "brave girl" gone? The girl who had, without question, kept his darkest, most dangerous secret. The nineteen-year-old who, in the early days of their love, when she hadn't felt sufficiently trusted and respected, got up from a park bench and walked away from her young judge, forever! Despite her sad perplexity at what she seemed to have become, Clarie caught herself smiling as she imagined Bernard watching *her* on that sunny afternoon over a decade ago. Undoubtedly she had been every bit as exasperating as Maura Laurenzano.

But—and this brought Clarie up short—she had never been in mortal danger.

Her headlong rush home brought her to the gates of the Square d'Anvers. She peered through the wrought-iron fence at the world she had left merely hours ago. A world of nannies and bourgeois mothers and happy, safe, well-fed children. Before meeting the Laurenzanos, Clarie had known violence only through the experiences that Bernard had brought home from the courthouse. Now she had seen a corpse, a beautiful girl laid out like a grotesque doll. A victim of murder. Clarie grimaced and grasped the iron bars of the fence. What made Maura believe that Angela's killer would be after her? Did she really have to abandon her grief-stricken mother? Three deaths, perhaps even three murders. And a killer on the loose. Clarie shook her head. Even as her heart ached for the mother who had lost her precious child, it was all beyond her ken.

At dinner that night, Clarie told Bernard about Emilie and little Robert, being careful to make it clear that she was not at all disappointed to be spending the summer in Paris. Although she was, a little. But that was such a small thing, compared to. . . . She tried to hide her distraction while her husband and son ate, talked and enjoyed each other. She could not get Francesca's question out of her mind. *Why*? Why was such a good, hard-working woman assaulted by abandonment and tragedy? Why do some mothers' children die? Why is life so unfair? She knew she had to wait for the right moment to talk to Bernard about these sad, unanswerable questions.

Later that night, after she had put Jean-Luc to bed, Clarie returned to the parlor and stood, hesitating, in front of Bernard.

"Is something wrong?" he asked as he set his newspaper in his lap. "I noticed you weren't always with us at dinner."

"Oh." She sat in the chair beside their reading lamp. "I'm sorry—"

"No, no. If you'd like to take Jean-Luc to Normandy for a week or go home to Arles—"

"It's not that," she cut him off, eager to get it over and done with. "It's Francesca again. It wasn't in the newspaper?"

Bernard shook his head, waiting, the expression on his face not entirely pleased.

"Her daughter Angela was stabbed and killed."

"The murder in the garment district?" His mouth fell slightly agape, as he shook his head. "I'm not sure they knew who—"

"It's her." Clarie moistened her lips, before going on. She was utterly aware that Bernard did not want her to get involved any further with the Laurenzanos. "I got a note about it from school and went to Francesca's to offer my sympathy." Before Bernard could voice his disapproval, Clarie added, "It's so sad. For Francesca and the other girl, who actually seems to believe that she is in danger. I can't understand how this could be happening to them, or what they can do."

Bernard pursed his lips. "As I've said before, the girl must go to the police."

"But if they don't believe her, and she doesn't trust them?"

"Clarie, darling," Bernard said as he straightened up in his chair, "there is something very fishy about all of this. First their boss, then their friend, who was obviously a violent anarchist, and now one of them. Who knows what they were plotting and why. And if the girl is innocent," he spoke again more slowly, "one has to assume she would want to go to the police."

Clarie sank back, chagrined. Bernard was looking at this like a judge or a lawyer, not like a mother. Not like a witness to a terrible tragedy. A tragedy that could get even worse. Yet his questions made sense. Why Barbereau? Why the Russian boy? Why Angela?

"You don't think," she murmured, "that the police had anything to do with the Russian boy's death?"

Bernard sighed, as if he were reluctant to teach a lesson in the way his world worked. "I would hate to believe it, but the Paris police have been known to go to great lengths to root out people they consider to be dangerous. They could have planted the bomb without intending to hurt anyone. But I doubt it."

"And Angela?"

"No, an innocent young girl, no." He shook his head and rattled his newspaper as if he wanted to end the discussion without any disagreement.

"You're probably right about contacting the police," she said, getting up and planting a kiss on the brow she had just troubled. "That's what I'll tell Francesca if I happen to see her again. And now," she said, letting her lips curve slightly upward to hide her discontent at his perfectly husbandly response, "I've got some clearing up to do."

4

*A*NGELA FLOATS DOWN THE *B*OULEVARD *Saint-Germain. Overhead, a canopy of tender green leaves gently sways with her every move. Glimmers of sun wink through the branches and spin her hair into gold. She wears a gauzy white dress that flutters down to her pink satin shoes. Students in straw hats and elegant women streaming out of the Bon Marché stop to stare. Suddenly she begins to run, graceful as a ballerina, past the students and the shoppers, past tightly corseted ladies and top-hatted gentlemen. She runs, until breathless and panting, she reaches the gilded gates of the Luxembourg Gardens.*

Handsome as a prince, Pyotr stands there waiting. The sleeves of his shirt billow in the breeze. They stretch out their arms to grasp each others' hands. Lidia and Vera shower Angela and Pyotr with fresh blossoms. The students and gentlemen invite the ladies from the Bon Marché to dance. Everyone is dancing.

Round and round, faster and faster. Too fast. Pyotr and Angela cannot stop. They whirl out of the park, onto the docks, too close to the water. Stop them, stop! They'll fall in. But they don't. Still dancing at arm's length like innocent children, they circle back to the darkness and safety of the warehouses. They see, they want to see, only each other until . . . a tall, thin man creeps out of the shadows. Angela lets go of Pyotr. She can't bear to look at the stranger. But Pyotr, brave Pyotr, holds out his hand. Angela backs away, toward the water, her lips contort into one sound, No! No! No! No!

"Will you shut up down there, we need our sleep!"

Maura woke up with a start. She huddled in the blanket, pulling it tight to quell her trembling. She had come down to the courtyard because she could not bear to sleep in the same room as her sister's corpse. And somehow, through the foul smells and her grief, she had snatched a few moments' sleep. If only she could reach up and snatch the dream, too, and make it end differently. For a moment, Pyotr and Angela had still been alive, the Russian girls had been free, and she was not alone. Maura struggled to her feet and stumbled out of the courtyard, away from the loathsome, fetid drain. She searched the sky for the first signs of dawn, wishing the night to be over. But the only light she saw was the yellowish flickering cast by the street's single gas lamp.

Still shaking, Maura leaned against the wall of the tenement. Although the uneven cobbles dug into her bare feet, she did not move for a long time. She had to think about the dream, she had to understand why it made her so sad and so afraid. She closed her eyes trying to recapture the happy images. Angela, Pyotr, the Russian girls. Instead what she saw was the long, thin shadow of the stranger who suddenly appeared at the La Villette Basin. Her eyes shot open and her heart began to pound. Had he seen her hiding behind the wheel of the cart when Pyotr went to comfort Angela? Pyotr had said he was a friend and took his hand. But Angela had shrunk away from him. Why? Is he someone who would murder them because of what they had done to Barbereau?

Maura held her breath, not wanting to make a sound, alert to anything that moved around her. She heard nothing but the trickle of the tenement's drain running into the sewer. When she let go, the sound of her breathing seemed to reverberate in the street. She couldn't stay here. She had to get to safety.

She turned and ran across the courtyard toward the entrance to her staircase. Even in the unlit hallway she knew the way by heart, as long as she mounted the stairs slowly, feeling them under her feet, careful not to trip on the old, tattered blanket. Finally she reached the door to the room that she shared with her mother and Angela's dead body. She didn't want to sleep by the coffin. Still shaking, she sank to the floor of the hallway.

A few hours later, the sound of footsteps and the roving light of ascending candles woke Maura up. She got to her feet and looked down the staircase. It was the laundress, Mme Guyot, accompanied by two men that Maura did not know. Maura closed her eyes and grimaced. It was time.

"Such a sad day," the washerwoman said as she haltingly reached the top of the stairs. "You've been waiting for us?"

"No," Maura mumbled as she turned the knob to let the laundress into the room. Maman was already awake, praying over the coffin.

"It's time, dear," Mme Guyot said. "The priest will only give us an early mass."

"No, no," Maura's mother moaned. "Not yet."

"Yes, dear." Mme Guyot, displaying the strength that years at the washhouse had given her, lifted Maura's mother to her feet. The laundress took one last look at Angela, then she set the candle on the floor and lowered the lid of the simple pine coffin that the municipality provided for the very poor. Sighing, she reached in her apron for a black cloth which she unfolded and draped over the rough, splintery box.

"I've hired two men with a dray that brings the barrels to the wineshop. They'll take her to the church and then out to the graveyard."

Arms and fingers outstretched, Maura flattened herself against the wall by the door. She felt glued to it, afraid to move, afraid that her legs would give out. This was it! Angela was dead. Angela was going into the ground. Maura bit her lip and almost fell upon her mother. They hugged each other, crying. Then Maman put the palms of her hands under Maura's chin and held up her head. "It's only the two of us now. Our sweet Angela is gone."

Maura could hardly bear to look into her mother's eyes, which were usually sharply and darkly disapproving of something she had done or said. Now they were swollen, dull, awash with tears.

"Come now. It's got to be done."

The laundress. Why didn't she shut up! Why didn't she. . . . But Maura knew that she was right. They had to do it.

"Come, Maman, come. We must." She put her arms around her mother's thin shoulders, supporting her. "We have a priest." That should please her mother. Because of what Maura had done at the morgue, getting people on her side, they could afford a priest. Maura swallowed hard and said words she barely believed: "And he is going to send Angela to heaven."

Mme Guyot nodded her approval of Maura's words before barking to Jacques and Marcel, to come in and take the coffin down the stairs. She took the candle that one of them had been holding. "You take care of your mother now," she said before leaving the room.

Maura took her mother by the hand and gently led her out the door. "Hold on to the railing, Maman," she ordered, sure that her mother's knees were every bit as shaky as her own.

Step-by-step they went down the stairs, following the candles lofted by the laundress who walked behind the men carrying the coffin. Maura felt more tender toward her mother than she had for a long time, as if her mother were a child who had to be watched and guarded so she would not stumble. When they reached the door to the courtyard, the sky was streaked with the portents of a hot, sunny day. The laundress, though, did not blow out the two candles. Maura sensed that Mme Guyot meant to give Angela a proper funeral procession, or at least as proper as they could afford. A few men coming into the courtyard to open their workshops took off their caps when they saw the coffin. The concierge, ever alert, crossed herself before puckering her lips in disgust.

Maura wanted to slap the pious, hypocritical witch, but she had something more important to do. She had to hold up her mother, who seemed to grow smaller with each step. "Can you make it to the church?" she asked. "Or do you want to ride on the dray?"

In reply, Francesca Laurenzano straightened up and clenched her jaw. "I will walk," she said, "and carry a candle." She freed herself from Maura, showing that she, too, was determined to give her daughter a proper procession. She stepped up to the laundress and together, each holding a burning taper, they followed the dray.

Maura walked behind, head bowed as they wound their way to the ancient church that served their neighborhood. Even though her thoughts should be with the body in the coffin, she could not forget the dream and was alert to everything happening in the streets. They were almost as empty as the night she and Pyotr had dragged Barbereau's body to the Basin. The owners of the wineshop and the creamery and the bakery paused from opening their shops and lowered their heads respectfully as the funereal dray passed. Maura was grateful, as she had never been grateful before, for their familiar presence. Their watchfulness served as a kind of protection—at least for the moment.

The priest at Saint-Bernard mumbled through the Latin mass, going as fast as he could. Maura glanced at her mother, who was hanging on his every word, waiting for the consolation that he was in too much of a hurry to give. Maman deserved more. Angela deserved more. *If we were rich or important. . . .* As soon as those angry words came into her mind, Maura felt guilty. She shouldn't have angry thoughts now. Her dead sister lay in the church's middle aisle in a coffin so close to Maura, she could reach out and touch it. She was kneeling in a beautiful holy place, echoing with grand, ancient words. How could she feel anything but sadness and awe? Maura bowed her head and tried to pray, remembering that once she had prayed, had believed. When the priest swung the censer over the coffin, releasing the smoke of burning incense, Maura's eyes stung with new tears. Not only for Angela or Pyotr or her mother. But for herself, her sinful self.

She clasped her hands together so tightly, her knuckles turned white. If she believed in heaven for Angela, what about Pyotr? He always said he would honor no church until a church learned to honor the poor. Would he. . . . No, he could not go to hell. She shook her head and almost spoke her denial aloud. He could not be eternally damned. She would pray and pray and pray. He had to be in heaven with Angela. If there was a heaven. If? Maura bit down hard on her lip, as if that would still her sinful doubts. Nevertheless, a sob broke through the dam in her throat. What good could the prayers of someone like her do? She was so confused, so alone.

After the priest sprinkled holy water over the coffin, ending the ceremony, the two haulers picked up the wooden box, carried it out of the church, and tied it to the dray. Mme Guyot was too busy to make the long trip to the Batignolles cemetery. The men signaled for Maura and her mother to get in. Then they mounted the drivers' seat and urged their mangy old horse forward. They, too, were in a hurry.

Weighed down by an almost unbearable heaviness in her chest, Maura flattened her hands on the wine-stained floor of the wagon and leaned against the coffin. Swaying to the rhythm of the horse as it clopped through the cobbled streets, she repeated to herself over and over again, *This can't be happening, this can't be happening.* She closed her eyes, hoping to recapture the dream, when Pyotr and Angela were alive and beautiful, when the Russian girls were free and safe. But the dream would not come back. She was stuck in a nightmare. The wagon reeked with the acid smell of cheap wine. When she opened her eyes again, she saw humble men and women on their way to work take off their caps or make the sign of the cross as the dray passed by. The further they went toward the graveyard, which lay outside the city walls, the grayer everything became. Looking out at the hodgepodge of factories, forges, depots, and low hovels, Maura felt as if she were suffocating. The rough dray that transported Angela's body to the grave seemed to be taking Maura on another kind of journey, foreshadowing the rest of her life: days filled with the gray pain of hard, dull labor and nights punctuated only by the queasy pleasures of cheap red wine.

5

When the dawn peeked through the thinly curtained window, Maura, numb with fatigue and grief, quietly slid off her mother's bed. For the first time in her memory, she had lain with her mother because they both needed to be close. Now Maura needed to get away. She did not want to wake Maman; she did not want to talk. She tiptoed over to the hooks that held their clothes. She chose her oldest, most tattered skirt and blouse. Today, at least, she would go to the laundry, because she could not think of anything else to do. It was as if all her hopes and dreams had been drained out of her on the way to Angela's grave. Or, worse, that she had seen what little her life could hold. With a sigh, she pulled up her thin black stockings, then picked up the clogs she had disdained to wear for many years. At least, in the washhouse, being surrounded by the women, she would be safe.

After a last glance at her mother, Maura left the room and padded down the stairs to wait for Mme Guyot. Maura slipped past the laundress's two-room apartment on the second floor, where she lived alone, having thrown out her feckless husband. To Maura's mother, the washerwoman's two rooms and little laundry business had seemed like the most that anyone could wish for, an undreamed-of attainment of prosperity and comfort. That was until she saw Barbereau's three-room flat and believed all his promises. That he would marry Angela. That he would buy them a sewing machine. How could she have been so gullible? When Maura got to the courtyard, she leaned against the wall and thrust her feet into her clogs. Why were such terrible things happening to them? Was it because of her mother's ambitions? Pyotr's dreams of a better world? A stranger's murderous revenge?

Shivering, she surveyed the courtyard to make sure no one was lurking. At first she looked for anyone who was out of place; but when she realized that she truly was alone, she raised her skirt and relieved herself in the drain that ran into the gutter. She had forgotten to do even this before coming downstairs. What was happening to her?

She didn't have to wait long before the workmen started to come to open their shops and Mme Guyot descended from the stairs, ready to pick up her loads.

"Good," she said, as soon as she saw Maura. "We have a lot today. And it's payday. Of course, you know I can't pay you for yesterday. I even lost half a day myself," she explained, as if she were expecting an argument from Maura.

But arguing was the furthest thing from Maura's mind. She merely nodded, then mumbled, "I can help you with the pick-ups, if you'd like." Mme Guyot's strength would surely protect her. And, God knows, the washwoman would do all the talking.

It took them almost an hour to solicit all of Mme Guyot's usual customers. By the time they circled back to the rue Goutte-d'Or, the washhouse, which lay at the end of the street, was ready for business. The engine on the roof was loudly pumping steam into the three gray zinc water tanks that jutted up from the laundry's roof. The tanks shared the upper level of the laundry with a drying room surrounded by slitted walls. The door to the vast washing shed below stood wide open. On any other day, Maura would have resented every step she took toward the drumming rhythm that echoed her sweated labors of beating and scrubbing. But not today. Today entering the hot, humid shed promised some comfort. By this time, she was eager to get away from Mme Guyot who had kept harping on about "poor Francesca" and "dear sweet Angela." And she was tired of looking over her shoulder for a policeman or a murderer. At least listening to the other women shouting their stories to each other above the racket would give her something else to think about.

Maura already knew the routine. Mme Guyot commanded four zinc washtubs along the long central aisle of the glassed-in shed, three for her "girls" and one across the way, strategically located to keep an eye on them. She paid for the beaters, the scrub boards, the soap, the bicarbonate, the bleach, and the hot water, which only arrived at the final stage, for it cost one sou per bucket. Because of the steam engine, damp vapors pervaded the washhouse, fogging the ceiling-high windows, its only source of light, and adding a layer of moisture to the sweat and splashing water that doused the laundresses as they worked. Within the first few minutes of arrival, all the women hiked up their skirts and rolled their sleeves up to their shoulders. By midday lunch break, the heat would be unbearable.

As soon as they entered the washhouse, Mme Guyot went over to her two other girls and insisted that Maura take the tub between them. "Cheer her up, she's had a bad turn, poor dear," she told them before going to buy bleach and soap from the booth by the door.

Maura knew little about Mimi and Yvette, except that they loudly complained in the local wineshop about their boss being a slave driver. During Maura's first days at the laundry they had ignored her, because she had so little "experience" in a place where love, sex and men were the major topics of enthusiastically bawdy conversation. Yet the two girls were not much older than she, perhaps, at most, nineteen or twenty. Both of them displayed the strong arms so necessary to their trade, but the resemblance ended there. Mimi was short, buxom and blond. Not as blond as Angela, a kind of dirty blond with hair so fine that it often strayed from the bun she wore on top of her head. She had soft brown eyes and a lovely full mouth. Yvette was taller, with crinkly red hair and freckles all up and down her arms as well as on her face, which was a bit crooked, because she had already lost some of her teeth.

It was Yvette who spoke first, leaning toward Maura. "'Twas your sister, no? The dead girl. How horrible."

From the glimmer in Yvette's cat-like gray eyes Maura sensed that she was more excited and curious than horrified. Maura nodded and pressed her lips together. She did not want to talk about Angela.

"Hey, Yve, we're supposed to cheer her up, didn't you hear?" Mimi shouted above the growing din echoing through the shed. "Let's tell her what happened last night."

As Maura listened, she realized that what happened last night was probably no different from the night before that, or before that. An encounter with the neighborhood men, drinks solicited and consumed, hands searching all over their bodies at the darkest spot in the street.

"We stick together just in case," Yvette assured Maura. "You can't trust 'em to always treat you nice, like the *ladies* we are," she said with a hoot, as she beat the shirt she was washing with a special abandon.

"And you have to be careful about the married ones. See Colette over there, talking to Mme Guyot, she almost had acid thrown in her face by a jealous wife. Lucky she ran," Mimi added.

Maura glanced across the aisle. She had heard cautionary tales about acid-throwing in the neighborhood for jealousy or revenge. But she had never known anyone who was actually involved. How scary. She bent her head over the scrub board. The water grew grayer and grayer as she worked. Part of her longed to be back in the calm idealistic atmosphere of the Russian girls' room. But another part of her was enjoying the stories and the titillating possibility of attracting the admiration and largesse of strange men.

When the bell rang for lunch, Maura realized she had forgotten that too. But Yvette and Mimi convinced her that she could share their bread, sausages and rough red wine as they continued to recount their many adventures together. Huddled in their little circle, in the relative quiet of the noon hour, Yvette confided, "You know, Coupeau's wineshop is only for in-between days. On paydays, like tonight, we usually go to Montmartre."

Maura nodded, waiting to hear more, until Mimi, brushing away one of Maura's errant curls, commented, "With that hair and your green eyes, I bet you could have some fun there too."

"Oh, I'm not sure." Once the opportunity to join them really presented itself, Maura felt a little afraid. Going outside the neighborhood at night was something she and Angela had never done. She picked up the bottle and took a swig. "I'll think about it," she said, after a hard swallow and a coughing fit. She did not want to seem to be a prig.

"You do that," Yvette said as she gave Maura a pat on the back.

And, indeed, Maura did think about going with her new friends all afternoon as they scrubbed and rinsed, then, together, wrung out the sheets and hung them in the drying room on the second floor. Since leaving school at the age of thirteen, Maura hadn't had any friends her age, except for Angela. The more she considered the invitation, the more she reasoned that she deserved to go out with some of the money she was earning. She'd divide it in three. Some for Maman, some to save for the day that she would apply to be a shop clerk, and some . . . for herself! After all, her mother still had some of the money Maura had collected in the morgue, plus the ten francs that that teacher had given to her. And Maura could not bear the thought of spending another night alone with her mother in their room. *Let Mme Guyot stay with Maman, I have to be able to go out sometime, I'm young, I'm not dead yet.* The "yet," which had become so palpable since yesterday's nightmare, reverberated in her mind. She decided to go. She wanted to be free.

The plan was simple. Wait until ten o'clock, for that's when things really get started. Wear your best clothes, and meet outside the courtyard of the Goutte-d'Or tenement.

When Maura arrived home with cheese and a loaf of dark bread, her mother was still in bed. After urging her to eat, Maura told her that she was going out. "Do you want me to get Mme Guyot to stay with you?" she asked. She was relieved when her mother, who had barely spoken, shook her head. Maura did not want to have to explain to the laundress where she was going, or who she was going with.

"Be careful," Maman said as she got up from the table to hold Maura's face in her hands. "I can't lose you too."

"I'm only going into the neighborhood to be with some girls," Maura lied. "Just to get out."

When her mother nodded and started toward the bed, Maura sensed her resignation to all that had happened and all that might befall her: her slavish labors at the school, the loss of a husband, the death of a daughter, being left with only the wild, unfavored one. Maura frowned and turned away. She hated the way her mother passively accepted her fate. *I'll never be like that,* she thought as she kicked her clogs across the floor and began to change her clothes.

Yvette and Mimi were already waiting when Maura slipped out of the courtyard. They linked their arms in hers and escorted her to the nearest gas lamp. "Let's take a look at you," Mimi said as she examined Maura. In that light, Maura saw that both of her friends had painted their faces. "Here, you need some more color," Yvette said as she reached into the little sack hanging from her wrist and took out a small bottle of rouge. She stuck her long finger in it and smeared it on Maura's lips and rubbed a little on her cheeks. "Rose Red!" she said, which almost brought Maura to her knees in a faint. It's what they had called her in the morgue. She didn't like being painted. She didn't like being called some fairytale name. Most of all, she didn't want to be reminded of Angela's dead body.

"Now, what's wrong with you?" Mimi asked, a look of shocked disapproval on her face. "Don't you want to have some fun?"

"Yes, of course," Maura blurted out before they could ask any more questions. "Let's go."

They headed off toward the big hospital, the deadest part of the outer boulevards, then on to Rochechouart, which was alive with noisy food venders in the streets. Maura wanted to stop for an ice and listen to a street singer who was passionately performing a love song. The bird-like woman stood next to an organ grinder, while a little boy tried to sell her lyrics to passers-by. But Yvette and Mimi did not want to pause. "Really, this is nothing," Yvette confided, still gripping Maura's arm. "Wait until we get to the Moulin Rouge. There are *famous* singers there, and we can get in for free." A few blocks later, Maura understood. If Rochechouart at nighttime seemed bright and inviting, the next boulevard, Clichy, was even more *electric*.

Taxis and omnibuses along the broad street seemed to be continually disgorging men in top hats and women in fancy satins and silks. More enchanting than the people were the lights. A myriad of colors flashed down one side of the street as far as the eye could see. Toward the end of the street, the bright red blades of the faux windmill, for which the Moulin Rouge was named, slowly rotated over its crimson entrance. Maura had seen the posters for this famous cabaret pasted on the sides of buildings and kiosks. And now she was here!

They lined up to get in. The ticket-taker seemed to know Yvette and Mimi and gave them a nod which was neither approving nor disapproving as far as Maura could tell. "Why are we free?" she whispered as she watched gentlemen in top hats pay a fee.

"Because we're young and pretty," said Yvette, who was the least pretty among them, "and men will pay too much for our drinks. Let's find a table so we can see the cancan."

The cancan! Maura had seen signs advertising the scandalous dance. She pressed her hand against her heart. It was really happening. She was having fun. They squeezed through the crowd to a table next to the dance floor where a few couples waltzed to the music played by a small orchestra. Maura squinted to see if there was anyone she knew. The men all seemed rich, but not all the women were smartly dressed. She glanced at Yvette, who was using her long neck to survey who was coming in. "Oh good, there are three of them," she yelled to Mimi above the music as she gave a wave. "They'll be so glad we brought Maura."

Maura screwed her head around to see who Yvette was talking about. Three oldish men in top hats with beards and whiskers approached their table. "Meet Maura," Yvette shouted as she jumped to her feet.

The shortest, portliest and most white-haired of the men peered into Maura's face and smiled.

Maura didn't like his false-teethed grin nor the way his boozy tobacco odor poured over her.

"Maura," the man's syrupy voice lingered over her name. "How nice to see you."

Maura inched ever so slightly away from him as he sat down next to her.

"This is Ralph," said Yvette gesturing toward the man next to Maura, "and Jim, from England," the man next to her, "and?" she looked toward the last man, who remained standing.

"Charles, a business associate from Bordeaux on his way to London," Jim-from-England answered.

"Oh, Charles. Then we must show you around," Mimi said as she patted the seat next to her. Jim-from-England seemed quite happy taking a place next to Yvette.

Maura's heart began to pound when Ralph put his hand around her waist and began to grope up to her breast. This wasn't like in the local wineshop, where if someone did you wrong, you could complain to all the neighbors. It was more like the Latin Quarter. Like the grisettes, who gave their favors to the students in return for a meal or a good time. Like the girls she swore she would never be. How could she have been so stupid?

Maura turned her attention to the dance floor, even as she could feel Ralph's beard touching the back of her neck. She was a laundress now, not a home-bound seamstress, and definitely not a respectable shop clerk. A laundress, and this is how laundresses "had fun." A tear trickled down her cheek. If she left, if she was cold, what would Mimi and Yvette think of her? How could she work with them? She examined her fingers as Ralph blew on the soft hairs that she had not been able to pin into her bun. She clenched her teeth and closed her eyes.

"I think we have a shy one here," Ralph proclaimed. "Let's all loosen up. Bock or champagne, ladies?"

"Champagne," Yvette and Mimi called out. "Champagne before the cancan, and afterwards we'll dance!" Yvette added.

"And will you show your knickers too?"

Without looking Maura could tell from his accent that it was Jim who had spoken.

"Maybe." Mimi in a singsong voice.

"Why not?" Yvette's husky tones.

Ralph pulled Maura closer to him.

She was about to jump out of her chair when wild shouts erupted from behind the dance floor. Eight women in big feathered hats streamed out, swishing their red skirts back and forth and kicking their legs high into the air, revealing thigh-high black stockings held up by black satin garters, and ruffled white chemises and knickers. Soon everyone around her was clapping to the raucous rhythm of the dance. In the whirl of color and noise there was no place for Maura to go. She pressed her hands on her skirt. She was not going to show her knickers to anyone.

Somehow in the din, champagne arrived at the table, and Ralph set a glass in front of Maura. Hand trembling, she reached for it and took a sip. She had heard champagne was delicious but could go to your head. At any other time, she might have liked the way the tiny bubbles tickled her nose, but tonight they felt like pinpricks. What was she doing here?

"Drink up," Ralph whispered in her ear, too close.

"I think I have to go," she said in response.

"And why is that?"

"My sister just died, and I must be with my mother." She hated using Angela's death as an excuse, but she could not think of anything else. Except she did not want the old man's hand creeping up her body.

"Oh, really?" His voice was skeptical. "Then why are you here?"

"I don't know."

"I could take you to heaven or hell, and take the fear of death out of you." Again in her ear.

"No!" What was this horrible man talking about?

She heard him chuckle. "I was talking about the cafés, the famous cafés; don't you want to see them?"

She shook her head.

"Jim," he yelled across the table, "it's a special night with our new friends, Charles and Maura. Let's drink up and go to Heaven and Hell."

"Heaven and Hell! We've never been!" cried Yvette.

"Quick, quick," Mimi exclaimed, as she drained her glass. "Charles," she turned to him and gave him a hug, "how exciting, on your first night!"

The cancan had stopped and patrons were once again advancing toward the dance floor. Ralph threw some bills on the table, and the six of them pushed their way out. Maura went along, hoping that when they got outside she could plan her escape.

They strolled, arms linked, back in the direction of Goutte-d'Or. When Maura had been told they were going to the Moulin Rouge, she had been too excited to take note of all the signs and entrances along the way; now she could not avoid the bizarre façades that electrified the boul' Clichy. Their first stop was an entrance, flanked by black velvet mourning curtains, to something called the Café of Nothingness. "We can drink 'the microbes of death' here," Jim announced. "It's very delicious."

"No," Maura backed away. She didn't want to have anything to do with death.

"Or we can go into the cave of death, very exciting," the tall Englishman continued undeterred, "and you don't know where you'll end up."

"Not that one!" Yvette decided. Although Jim was holding on to her, she managed to bend toward Maura and whisper, "These places are much more expensive. Everyone must pay, even girls. But they'll pay for us, I'm sure."

Ralph pulled her away from her friend. "Would you prefer Heaven?" he asked.

"Heaven, yes, Heaven," said Jim leading the little parade to the gaudy white entrance of the Café of Heaven, "Let's take a look."

Maura did not want to take a look, but she wasn't sure how to get away without making a fuss.

Jim tipped the ticket-taker, a burly man dressed as an angel, promising to come back to pay full admission if they decided to stay. The six of them crowded into the entrance. "Here," Jim said, directing his remarks to Charles, "you can drink 'the ambrosia of the gods' served by angels and listen to heavenly music."

The music didn't sound heavenly to Maura. It sounded morbid. Like the worst, lowest grumblings of a church organ. The big dining room was all shiny white with gauzy curtains and waiters wearing body-length wings. Her chest began to heave. She didn't want to think about death or heaven.

"Which do you like best?" Charles asked Jim. "If I'm going to catch the train to London tomorrow, I should only go to one."

"Ralph, don't you think—" Jim was tall enough to look over everyone toward the white-whiskered man and wink.

"Definitely," Ralph said as he tightened his grip on Maura's arm.

"Then, let's go to Hell!" Jim cried. "All red and black with devils all about," he said in a dramatic voice before planting a kiss on Yvette's red mouth, "and you can watch bodies disintegrate in the fire and become skeletons!"

"Ohhh," Mimi excitedly clapped her two little fists together over her amble chest. "Let's do it, please, please!"

"Yes, let's!" Charles agreed.

Meanwhile Ralph's hand gripped Maura's arm, pulling her to the entrance next to the Café of Heaven. She would not have had the strength to resist him if her worst nightmare hadn't loomed up in front of her. The entrance to the Café of Hell was the huge open mouth of a hideous devil with blazing crimson eyes. While others eagerly went under the fang-like teeth, Maura held back. A short man dressed like a devil emerged yelling, "Enter and be damned. We want more of you to roast!"

"I can't," she pleaded and tried to wrench her arm away.

"My little girl. I've paid for the champagne and I'm going to pay for this. Don't you think I deserve something in return?"

She kept pulling away.

"Listen to me. There's a policeman only a block away, watching over things. What if I told him you were flirting with me, trying to get me to spend my money. You know what they do with unlicensed whores? They send them straight to Saint-Lazare where they examine them for diseases before throwing them into the cells."

"No," Maura cried desperately. "I've never—" She'd heard of girls from the neighborhood being picked up just for looking at a strange man. It could happen. She would not let it happen to her.

"I know you've *never*. That's exactly what makes you so interesting."

The bastard. Suddenly anger overtook her fear and she reached down and bit his hand hard.

Shocked, he let go to give her a slap, which resounded across her painted cheek and threw her almost to the ground.

"Hey, hey there, mister, why are you treating a girl like that?" Two men in caps, rough blue muslin shirts and brown vests, stepped in between her and Ralph.

"She's a whore. She tried to steal my wallet. Didn't you see?"

"Dirty bourgeois, we saw nothing of the sort!" The smaller of the two men shook his fist at Ralph in a threatening manner.

"I'm calling the police. I'll tell them you're all in league together. Help me," Ralph called to the devilish imp who guarded the door to the cabaret.

"Let's go, quick. We can't win a battle with the bourgeois and the cops, not in this crowd," the bigger man said as he grabbed Maura's hand. The three of them took off, threading through the top-hatted crowd until they reached a side street, taking them up the hill. With both men holding on to her, Maura ran as fast as she could, away from Ralph, away from the police, along the dark, narrow streets above the boulevards. Finally, they stopped, all three of them panting. "I think it's safe to go down now," the bigger man pronounced, and led them to the far end of Rochechouart, where they melted into the crowd around the singer, who was still performing her passionate love songs.

When they were breathing more steadily, the taller man introduced himself as Gilbert and his friend as Léon.

The younger man was skinny and pimply faced, and still had a firm hold on Maura's hand, even after Gilbert had let go.

"I can't stand when they treat our girls like that. But you should know better," the older, bigger Gilbert said.

"I've never done this before, I was with two other girls," Maura tried to explain away her mortification.

"And that paint. Sure to get the cops looking," Gilbert continued, making Maura's face, which was already hot from her flight, burn even redder.

"It's not mine, it's—" She closed her eyes and stopped. Why should she blame anyone else? She was the one who had been stupid.

"I kinda like it," said Léon as he peered directly at Maura and emitted a strong odor of cheese and beer.

Maura ripped her hand away. After Ralph, was she going to have to contend with him?

"Where do you live?" asked Gilbert.

Under the gas lamp she could see that he was a handsome man, perhaps in his twenties. Clean-shaven and, it would seem, serious, like Pyotr. Still, she didn't know if she should tell him.

"C'mon," he urged. "We're not going to hurt you. We just want to make sure you get home. We don't like the rich bastards hurting our girls just 'cause they can get away with it."

"Goutte-d'Or." She had to trust them. What if Ralph came after her? Or the police? Or Angela's killer?

Gilbert considered for a moment, then nodded. "It's not too far out of our way. What do you say, Léon?"

"Sure."

She wished the skinny boy would stop looking at her with such big eyes. At the same time, she wished Gilbert would find something in her that met his approval. Instead he was involved in surveying the crowd around him. When approached, he even paid the poor little musician's assistant half a sou for a sheet of the singer's music. *He must be a good man, generous and kind, like*—the name Pyotr almost brought tears to her eyes. No one would ever be Pyotr, ever again. She bent her head, waiting. Finally, Gilbert gave the command to move along.

As they walked, Gilbert told Maura that he and Léon lived on the other side of the Montmartre hill because they worked at a forge on the rue Marcadet. Gilbert was a journeyman, his comrade an apprentice. *A blacksmith*. No wonder Maura could feel his strength and steadiness. She hoped he would ask more about her, but they continued in silence until they reached the tenement.

"Well, here it is," Maura managed a smile. "I guess it's good-bye."

"Not yet," declared Léon, who grabbed her and planted a malodorous kiss on her lips.

She shoved his hand away as it moved up toward her breasts.

"Léon, stop. Do you want to be as contemptible as those bourgeois bastards, taking advantage—"

"Don't we deserve a little—"

Gilbert yanked his friend away from Maura. "Here." He handed her the singer's lyrics. "I don't like love songs. You can have this."

Maura limply accepted the sheet of paper. She fell back against the wall, feeling worse than she had after Ralph's slap. She wondered if

Gilbert would have paid more attention to her if she had been like Angela, pretty and sweet. But, of course, Angela would have never gone off with Mimi and Yvette.

Maura blinked back tears as her two saviors ambled off, back up toward the Montmartre hill. "Thank you," she called. But she wasn't even sure if they heard her. Clutching the piece of paper in her hands, she slowly ascended the all-too-familiar steps to her room. When she got there, she reached into what little water was left in the basin and tried to wash the rouge off her face. Then she lay down beside her mother, staring at the ceiling. She kept going over in her mind how stupid she had been. She was not like Yvette and Mimi. And she didn't want to be. She wished that Pyotr and Angela were still here. They would comfort her and teach her how to be good.

6

"I've been thinking about it," Bernard said between sips of his morning *café au lait*; "perhaps it would be a good idea if you and Jean-Luc went to Normandy for part of the summer."

"Thinking about it?" Clarie looked up, surprised. "I didn't think we could really afford—"

"Train fare? Surely we can, for you and little Luca. And when you get there, you'll be the guests of the Franchets."

"And you?"

"Rose can take care of me."

In their tiny kitchen, Rose heard everything as she bustled around getting the baguettes sliced and the *confiture* on the table. She never joined in the Martins' conversations unless invited to, and seemed grateful to be concentrating on buttering Jean-Luc's bread.

Clarie placed her bowl of coffee gently on the table and, raising one eyebrow, gave her husband a skeptical look. "Is this about our conversation two nights ago? Are you afraid that I am going to do something 'foolish'?" *Like visit Francesca again.*

"Oh, no, I was just—"

"Mmmm," Clarie twisted her mouth into a smile.

"Really, you know how hot it was last summer in the city. Think of how good it will be for Jean-Luc. As you said yourself, Robert is like a cousin to him. The fresh air. The sea."

By this time, Clarie had folded her arms and was gazing at her husband, who had picked up his bowl to drink, but also, she suspected, to hide his face.

"You're not afraid that Emilie will be a bad influence on me?" She could not resist tweaking him.

"Of course not!" He looked genuinely shocked.

"You know what Emilie says?" She paused to let the rapier possibilities of her friend's wit sink in. "She says that our republican husbands love to talk about how they believe in women's rights, but somehow they still believe they are more rational, more capable, and, shall we say," she let her eyes roam over the ceiling as if searching for the right words, "less foolish than we are."

"Perhaps Emilie has gone to too many women's rights conventions," Bernard said dryly. The blade had found its mark.

"And perhaps not," Clarie responded.

Bernard wiped his mouth with his napkin. "Still something to think about," he mumbled as he rose. "I have to go to work."

Clarie got up, too, and put her hands on his shoulders. "Darling," she said, "let's scrimp and save this summer, and go to Arles together in August to see Papa. It will make him so happy, you can tell him all the wonderful things you are doing, and we can give Rose a real vacation from all of us."

It took less than a moment for Bernard to accept the truce. He always said that he could not resist Clarie's almond-shaped brown eyes. "We'll talk about it tomorrow when we have all the time in the world to decide. For now," he said, before kissing the tip of her long, slightly upturned nose, "I have to get to work."

"All the time in the world" meant Sunday, a day that Clarie had come to treasure more than ever since her arrival in Paris with a child, a demanding teaching post, and a husband desperately looking for a position. Sundays were even better now, for Bernard had found his place and was as happy as she had ever seen him. Sundays meant letting Rose enjoy the day off, going to the bakery to get their own bread, strolling to the Square Montholon playground with Luca in Bernard's arms, buying a treat from the ice cream man, picking up a roast chicken for dinner, reading, laughing, enjoying each other. On Sundays Paris always looked brighter. There was less hustle and bustle, fewer people and carriages hurrying from one place to another as if their life depended on it, more time to see the city with the wonderment of a child.

That Sunday, Clarie sighed with contentment as they headed home after the park. She listened as Bernard and Luca tried to decide what they should buy to have with their cold chicken. Tomatoes were not yet ready, but strawberries were still available. Clarie listened with pleasure as Bernard tried to teach their son about the seasons.

"Summer is the hot time of year," she explained to Jean-Luc, whose head was bobbing over his father's shoulder. "Don't you feel hot?"

"No," her boy shook his sweaty head. When they stopped at a corner, she smoothed away some of the dark curls from his drowsy damp brow before kissing his sticky little hand.

"Or tired, after all that swinging?" she asked.

"No!"

She walked a little forward to catch Bernard's attention. "I think it's time. You take Luca and I'll do the shopping."

"No!"

She and Bernard both laughed. Luca was getting to an age when it was harder and harder to hide their intentions from him.

"And when you wake up, my boy," Bernard said to console him, "we'll have chicken *and* strawberries." Bernard picked up the pace as they approached the rue Condorcet. "Wave to your Maman," he said, before leaving Clarie behind to do the marketing.

She watched as "her two men" started back to the apartment. *Chicken and strawberries*. Bernard was in a good mood. While Luca was sleeping, they'd talk about going to Arles in August, and Clarie planned to broach the subject of inviting his mother to Paris for a week in July. Free from schoolwork, Clarie was fully prepared to host the sometimes difficult Adèle Martin. If Bernard balked, she'd remind him that family was important and how helpful his mother had been when Henri-Joseph died.

Those last words always brought her up short, making her gasp as if someone had pulled a rope around her throat. *We have Jean-Luc now; he is thriving*. After standing stock-still, in the midst of jostling shoppers, she exhorted herself forward. She had to get to the *rôtisserie* before the early Sunday closings.

By the time she got there, people were packed tight in the stifling shop. After purchasing one of the last chickens, Clarie stepped, triumphant and relieved, into the street. At least here, despite the afternoon heat, she could breathe. She was approaching a cart selling fruit when she heard the news hawker.

"Who killed the Angel of Anarchy? Is Paris Under Threat? Read about the Angel of Death in today's *Petit Parisien*." The boy, who could not have been much more than ten, strode through the rue Condorcet, shouting at the top of his lungs and waving a newspaper.

"Madam?" the farmer, who had spotted Clarie surveying his produce, tried to get her attention.

"Oh, sorry, not now, maybe later," she murmured, staring as the boy passed them. Sunday was the day when the cheap Paris dailies printed their illustrated editions. She had to see the picture. She needed to know if they were talking about Angela. Squinting toward the picture he was holding up, Clarie followed the hawker, who had attracted a small crowd. She did not have to push through them to recognize the subject of the tabloid drawing: Angela Laurenzano as she had seen her in the coffin, as the morgue had dressed her, in white, like an angel.

Clarie didn't want anyone to see her buying the scandal sheet, yet she had to know what they were saying about the Laurenzanos. She pretended to be examining the dresses in a store window until she heard the throng around the newsboy dissipate. When the shouts and footsteps died down, she turned back toward the street.

"Garçon!" she called, trying to catch him before he got away.

"Yes, lady?" The boy stopped. She saw that his face was grimy and bruised. Who had done this to him? Did he have to sell a certain number of papers to go home safe, or was he apprenticed to a cruel printer? Is this how Angela had looked after a night spent with Barbereau? Clarie took in breath. She knew so little about the city's life outside her family and the school.

"A paper," she managed.

"Five centimes, it's the Sunday special."

Her trembling fingers searched for a sou in the sack hanging from her wrist. She wanted to get the transaction over with as quickly as possible.

"There," she dropped the coin into his hand. Without even a thank-you, he thrust a copy of the Sunday *Petit Parisien Illustré* into hers.

She tucked the paper in her basket and headed up the rue Turgot as fast as she could without attracting attention. *I'll tell Bernard the stores were crowded. I'll say I met one of the teachers on the way home. I'll*—She could hardly believe that she was already spinning a camouflage of lies around the simple act of buying a newspaper. But in her heart, she knew it was not so simple. Bernard was so set against her having anything to do with the Laurenzanos.

Aware of the fluttering in her chest, Clarie took special care to cross the wide street to the Square d'Anvers. When she reached the little park, she plopped down on an unoccupied bench, grateful for the meager shade offered by a young tree. She wiped her damp forehead with the back of her gloved hand before summoning the courage to look at Angela's picture again. The headline read ANGEL OF DEATH.

With trembling fingers, Clarie turned from the full-page illustration to get to the story.

> *Paris has been deceived! The police have been deceived! Angela Maria Laurenzano was neither an innocent angel nor an accidental victim of a senseless cruel crime, but the deceiving lover of two men recently murdered on the Paris streets. Evidence is mounting that she plotted with the dead anarchist Pyotr Ivanovich Balenov to kill and rob her boss, the deceased Marcel Barbereau, who was fished out of the Basin de la Villette ten days ago. We must also assume that the Russian, his angelic-looking lover and their dastardly accomplices plotted to set off a bomb on one of the capital's fashionable boulevards. Instead, as we know, the bomb killed him before he could cart it out of the Goutte-d'Or quarter.*

Clarie let the opened newspaper drop in her lap and stared into space, trying to conjure up her first meeting with Francesca's daughters. She did not want to believe that Angela had willfully practiced deception, that she had had two lovers, that she was a terrorist. She pictured Angela sitting in the front row of the classroom, innocent and afraid, obedient to her mother's wishes to seek Clarie's help. Or so it seemed. Clarie had seen the traces of bruises on Angela's face. She knew the girl had been beaten. Yet as time passed she had become more and more certain that Francesca's daughters had not told the entire truth about Marcel Barbereau's death or about their relationship with the Russian anarchist. Were they really terrorists, or just girls in trouble? Terrible trouble. But, if that were the case, why would anyone kill Angela?

Thinking, *reasoning* calmed Clarie down. She bent over the article, scouring it for some proof, some logic. She found very little, even though, according to the newspaper, the police thought they had all the answers. An inspector Alain Jobert asserted that the deaths of Marcel

Barbereau, Pyotr Balenov and Angela Laurenzano could not be "mere coincidence." He hypothesized that Angela had been killed by a *"fellow violent anarchist, who was afraid her loyalty to their cause perished in the explosion that killed her Russian lover."* The article concluded with the inspector's clever turn of phrase. *"If Angela Laurenzano was the weak link in the plots, then her sister, Maura Laurenzano, has become the missing link."* The police had searched yesterday and not been able to find her.

Brow furrowed, Clarie fell back against the bench. Maura, missing? She had really taken off, and poor Francesca was left with two daughters gone and no idea of what they had gotten themselves into. Clarie's heart ached for her, but she didn't know what to do. Or what or who to believe. Bernard said the union anarchists he worked with had abjured violence, if only because the terrorists and their associates had been persecuted, rooted out by the police years ago. And yet the police inspector claimed the Laurenzano girls might have been part of a gang. Clarie's every instinct cried out against this. At least some of what she had heard and seen at their first meeting had to be true. Both girls had sworn that Pyotr was gentle and would never have planted a bomb. They had told her about Barbereau's cruelties. Maura, especially, was sure that no one in authority, including Clarie, would help or believe them. Clarie grimaced as she once again acknowledged the possibility that Maura's scornful attitude toward her was justified. The girl perceived Clarie as someone with neither the will nor the power to help them. Bitter Maura, clever Maura had managed to penetrate Clarie's soul. She pitied Francesca, as a mother, but she was beginning to realize that Maura was the one she could not forget, a girl with intelligence and determination. A girl who desperately wanted to live and strive. A girl worth saving.

Numbly, she rose from the bench. She folded the paper with quiet, deliberate motions before putting it in the basket. Strawberries: she had to find strawberries.

Fifteen minutes later, having tracked down one of the last farmer's carts near the square, Clarie hurried into her building. She paused before climbing the stairs, and retreated. The concierge kept her cleaning supplies under the staircase. She would enjoy a copy of the illustrated paper. Clarie folded the journal and placed it near a bucket and mop. There was no reason to disturb her Sunday with Bernard, she reasoned. He'd find out about the accusations against Angela soon enough. By tomorrow, the tabloids would be pasted on walls and hanging from every kiosk. She was not really keeping any secrets from him.

7

THE SHARP WHISTLE PIERCED THROUGH the courtyard, rousing Maura from a restless sleep. Her head was heavy and aching. After last night, she had no idea how she was going to face Yvette and Mimi at the wash-house. She had been so stupid.

The second whistle tore through her torpor. It was a signal. Except for the concierge and a few other nosy biddies, the inhabitants of the tenement hated and feared the police, and did everything to protect each other from "the law."

Maura sprang to the window. An early-arriving carpenter from one of the workshops in the courtyard watched near the entrance as two uniformed policemen and the stocky inspector who had questioned her at the morgue came in. She had to hide. She raced into the hall and began violently to rattle the door next to hers. If the deaf mute was awake, she prayed that he would see the movement of the door. If not, she would rip it open with her own arms.

She almost fainted with relief when gnarled old Monsieur Gaston answered. Frantically she drew him to his window where they could see the last policeman entering the staircase below. She pointed to herself and then under his bed. He nodded. He understood. It was the only place to hide. Like Maman and Maura, he lived in one small room.

Maura crawled shaking under his narrow bed, careful to avoid the chamber pot near her feet. As she flattened herself out on the dusty, rough floor, she found another reason for regret. How often she had made fun of the deaf-mute's animal grunts and moans. She had always thought him stupid, even when he shared his extra bread with her mother. Now she had to hope that he was smart enough to fool the police. She pressed her lips together, determined not to make a sound. She heard the police thunder up the rickety stairs and begin to pound on her mother's door. When her mother answered, their shouts and threats reverberated through the thin wall, but Maura could not make out the words. After a few minutes, the voices died down. She heard the table and bed screeching on the wood floor, the sounds of a search. Then more threats. Then steps coming to Monsieur Gaston's door. Since he could not hear, he did not move from his table, where he sat eating his morning bread.

More and different steps up the staircase. Maura grimaced with the effort of trying to make out what the sounds meant.

"What are you doing?" It was Mme Guyot. "This poor woman is still in mourning!" *Did they have Maman? Were they hurting her?* Maura's first instinct was to go to her rescue. When her foot almost tumbled the chamber pot, she stopped. She had to be rational. *She* was the one in real danger.

"And that poor man in there is deaf. He can't hear you," Mme Guyot continued just outside the door. For the first time in her life, Maura felt admiration for the big, raw-boned laundress, who showed no fear, even of the police.

"Madame, this is none of your—"

"It is. Francesca Laurenzano is my friend, an honest woman."

The idiot policeman kept on knocking, and Maura was sure that even if she suppressed her breathing, her thumping heart would give her away.

"Here, let me," Mme Guyot said. Maura heard the door shifting back and forth. Through the ragged edges of Monsieur Gaston's covers, she saw his carpet slippers amble toward it. They were soon joined by four shoes, good shoes, pushing themselves forward into the room.

Maura recognized the inspector's voice as he shouted, "Have you seen Maura Laurenzano?"

The tailor inched himself in front of the bed and sat down, his legs and feet well-positioned to block the policeman's view of everything underneath except the chamber pot. The deaf-mute responded with his version of a mumbling denial.

The inspector, obviously exasperated, told one of his men to get "that woman." "Maybe she can get him to talk."

Mme Guyot's clogs tramped into the room. Maura imagined her making signs and motions, toward the room next door, the room where a policeman must be standing guard over Maman.

All at once Monsieur Gaston began to grunt and moan even louder. From the way the bed was shaking she knew that he was waving his arms and pointing, employing the same gesticulations that had inspired all the kids in the tenement, including Maura, to make fun of him.

"What is he saying?" the inspector asked angrily.

"He's afraid, I think. He doesn't know what you are talking about," Mme Guyot said.

But the tailor went on and on, louder and louder, shaking the bed harder and harder. It was like an earthquake coming down on Maura.

"Can't he answer a simple question?" The inspector's voice rose higher.

"He can't hear, he can't speak. He's a poor tailor who barely feeds himself."

Maura didn't have to see Mme Guyot to know that she had crossed her arms, waiting for the inspector to come to his senses and stop berating the old man. After all, didn't he understand that this was Monsieur Gaston's attempt to communicate? Or—as Maura listened, hardly breathing, a tentative grin spreading across her face—was this the deaf-mute's attempt *not* to communicate, to make everyone so disgusted they would just leave him alone? She pressed her fingernails into her palms contritely. She would never make fun of him again.

When the well-shod feet and the clogs left the room, Maura sensed the deaf-mute's calm return to his seat by the window. She heard the shuffling rearrangement of Monsieur Gaston's table and then a sigh. Time to get to work. Maura understood. She and Angela had always started working on the shirtwaists early in the morning, as close to the window as possible, afraid to waste even a moment of free light.

Maura did not know how long she lay there, breathing in the smell of Monsieur Gaston's pungent, unwashed bedding, in constant fear that a rat or mouse would crawl out of a hole to torment her. She kept an ear to the floor in the hope of hearing the policemen's progress through the building. But she heard nothing except the tenement waking up: sleepy voices heading out to work or, through the window, the grinding and sawing tools of the men who labored in the shops around the courtyard.

Finally, Monsieur Gaston knocked on the floor by the bed and waved his hand. She crawled out, and he took her by the sleeve of her nightgown and led her to the window to show her that the policemen were leaving.

Her chest began to heave as she slapped the dust off her nightgown. She had to pee, to cry out, anything. She had held everything in under the bed. "I must go see my Maman," she told Monsieur Gaston. And then she almost laughed at herself. She pointed to her chest and to the wall that separated their rooms. He nodded.

"Thank you, thank you," she said as tears came rolling down her cheeks. "Thank you." She kissed him on both cheeks, bringing a smile to his face, the first real smile she had ever seen from him. She took his hand, but he waved her off, pointing to her mother's room.

Wiping her nose on the sleeve of her gown, Maura quickly padded out of the room in her bare feet and knocked on her mother's door. "Maman, it's me. Maura."

The door flew up and her mother grabbed her, holding her tight. "I can't lose you!" she cried.

"Don't worry, Maman, everything is going to be all right," Maura said as she untangled herself from her mother's embrace. She brushed a kiss on her mother's forehead, remembering how she loved those gentle reassuring kisses that Maman used to give her when she was a little girl.

Suddenly her mother drew away from her. "What have you done?" she cried, breaking the mood.

"What do you mean?" Fear thudded in Maura's chest. Had they told her mother about her role in disposing of Barbereau's body?

"Look at this," her mother stretched out an arm. "Look what they did." She stepped aside, forcing Maura to take in the destruction. Clothes on the floor, pots and pans swept from the shelf, even the chamber pot kicked from under the bed, lying on its side. "They were searching for dynamite, for stolen money. They said that you and Angela plotted with that boy to blow people up, that you murdered Barbereau because he was a boss."

"It's not true." Although part of it was, of course. But Pyotr had only hit Barbereau because he was beating Angela. He had not meant to kill him.

"They said you were anarchists, violent. Like the Italian who killed the French president three years ago."

"Maman, it's not true." And once more Maura felt the urge, the impossible urge to tell everyone about the real Pyotr, how good and kind he was. "Let me—" She pointed to the chamber pot, righted it, then lifted her gown and peed. "I'll take it down later," she said as she stood up.

"Don't worry about that. Tell me what you've done," her mother demanded.

"Nothing, Maman, nothing bad, really bad. We'd never hurt people. It's Barbereau who was hurting Angela."

"I don't want to hear about that," Maura's mother cried and covered her ears. "I don't want to know what he did to her, my poor baby."

The warm opening in Maura's heart froze and closed a little. Whose fault was it that Angela had gotten involved with that bastard, made to have sex with him, take his blows? And why care about what had happened to Angela, who was dead, when Maura was standing in front of her mother, alive and in trouble? But instead of embracing her again, Francesca turned, held out her arms, hands clasped, toward the crucifix over her bed. "Oh, sweet Jesus, what have I done, what have I done to deserve this?"

"Nothing, Maman, nothing," Maura muttered as she went over to the window to make sure that none of the police were still about.

"All I've done is try to put bread on the table, and now my little girl is gone and the police are accusing me." Her mother's pleas to the inert cross continued.

"Maman, don't worry, the police know you are innocent." How could they not? How could anyone believe that pious Francesca Laurenzano would break a law?

Maura's mother bowed her head and turned back to her daughter. "Are you going to the laundry today? It's Saturday. Mme Guyot's busiest time."

"No." Maura shook her head. "The police are probably going there right now. And besides," she put her hand over her belly, "I don't feel well." As proof, she sidled past her mother and plopped down on the bed, folding her knees against her chest. Even if the police weren't there, she wasn't going to face Yvette or Mimi. She had to figure out what to do next.

"Then I'll go."

If her mother expected Maura to object, to save her from the bruising labors of that horrible place, she was mistaken. Something had hardened again between them. If she insisted on being the martyr, so be it, Maura thought. Besides, if Maura came up with a plan, it would be better for her mother if she didn't know anything about it. Maman should go.

Maura lay curled up, waiting and watching through half-opened eyes as her mother dressed. The tears welled up again. She didn't want to be angry with Maman, and she didn't want her mother to be angry with her. She longed more than ever for Pyotr and Angela. They had loved her. When they corrected her, told her things she had done wrong or thought wrong, they had done it gently. They wanted her to be better. Like them. Instead, here she was, again, fighting with the only person left in the entire world who cared about her.

After her mother left the room, Maura rolled over to face the cracked ceiling, letting the tears trail down her cheeks onto the thin pillow. The past was past. She was alone. If she wanted to survive, she'd have to stop feeling sorry for herself and do something. The police could come back any time.

She pushed herself up. Her only chance was to leave. Hide somehow. From the police, from a killer. She began picking up the clothes to pack when she spotted Pyotr's pants, vest and shirt. Of course. A disguise.

She threw Pyotr's clothes on a chair and began flipping through the rest of the debris on the floor. Finding her flowered dress, she anxiously ran her fingers over the hem. The money was still there. She tossed the dress on a chair and began searching for something to carry it in. Slithering out beneath her mother's shawl was a string bag large enough to hold everything she'd need. Finally, she came across the box that held the tools of her former trade.

She snatched the small cotton bag inside and poured the needles, thread and buttons on the table. She grabbed the scissors and went to the mirror by the window. She pulled tight on one of her curls and hacked it off, and continued hacking until all of her black locks fell to the floor, until she looked like a boy. Then she scooped up her hair and stuffed it into the bag that had held her needles and thread. She'd sell it later. She picked up Pyotr's shirt. Until that moment her pulse had been racing.

Now she held Pyotr's shirt up to her face, slowly, reverentially hoping to breathe in what was left of his smell and his spirit. She decided then, she'd call herself Pierre, French for Pyotr.

After putting on his clothes, she whirled around to think of what else she'd need. Protection. She reached for the scissors. Paused. Would a boy carry scissors? No, he'd carry a knife. With all the dexterity that sewing hems and buttons had taught her, she worked for a desperate five minutes to unscrew the blades, leaving one on the table and stuffing the other in the string bag with her dress and some underclothes.

She should have run out immediately. But she had to look again, at the table where she and Angela had worked, at her mother's bed and her mother's cross and picture of the Virgin, at the clothes flung about, the stove, the collection of cracked dishes and utensils. Trying to be strong and logical, she reached up and took a spoon in case she found something to eat. As she tucked it into the string bag, she pressed her lips together to keep from sobbing. Poor Angela. Poor Maman. It would be too cruel to leave without a word, as if she were angry or imprisoned or dead.

Dropping the string bag on the bed, Maura went out into hall and moved the door back and forth until Monsieur Gaston answered. She pantomimed that she needed paper and pencil, which he kept for the moments when his hand gestures failed. With a frowning expression of concern, he pointed to her hair and touched her cheek lightly. Then he led her to his table, where she sat down and wrote a note to her mother.

8

Maura tipped Pyotr's cap over her eyes and lowered her head, clutching the bundle of clothes to her chest as she hurried out of the courtyard. She did not want the children to take any notice of her. With only one sideways glance toward her past, she turned in the opposite direction from the laundry. She slung the bag over her shoulder and began to sway and strut, trying to appear nonchalant, like a confident young man going forth to meet his future. But Maura couldn't keep up the act for long, because she couldn't keep her heart from pounding or her eyes from roving side to side, searching for a policeman or a tall thin shadow. Walking faster and faster, urgently, as if the sun-heated cobblestones were burning through the thin soles of her shoes, she reached the end of her neighborhood, the railroad tracks to the Gare du Nord.

Her forehead was already trickling with nervous sweat. She wiped her face off with her sleeve before heading up a street that ran parallel to the tracks toward the outskirts of the city. She desperately needed work and a place to stay. If she could find Gilbert's forge, she would beg him to hire her. She'd do anything: haul coals, sweep the floors, run for provisions. Maybe, after she explained about the police and the killer, he would even help her find a room and help her stay safe. Maybe. Her steps slowed as repeating the plan reminded her of its obvious flaw. The handsome Gilbert had been kind last night, but he might not be so kind today. Fighting back discouragement, she followed the street to its end in front of the huge warehouses serving freight trains going to the two train stations.

She sheltered her eyes from the hot noonday sun as she watched workers in smocks carrying and hauling huge crates and wine barrels. Back and forth they went, bringing goods to wagons hitched to restless snorting horses or into the vast, mute storehouses. In the horizon far beyond the railroad yard, plumes of smoke and fire rose from the tall chimneys of suburban factories. Maura covered her mouth as anxiety constricted her throat. It was all so dusty and gray, a world meant for men with strong arms and callused hands. How would she ever fit in? A self-pitying sob escaped through her splayed fingers. Life was so unfair. Somewhere a girl her age, in a pristine white shirt and navy blue skirt, was standing in a department store amidst a rainbow of luxuries. To serve fashionable women in a bright, clean place, was that really too much to wish for? She pulled at a strand of her cropped hair. What had she done? How had she gotten into this mess? Retreating a few steps, she pressed her lips together and nodded to herself. I'll find a way, someday I'll find a way, she whispered.

First, she had to find the forge. The only thing she knew was that it was on the rue Marcadet. Turning her back on the railroad yard, she slipped into the first shop she encountered. The proprietor gave her directions and called her "son." Her spirits lifted. She was not far away from the right street and her disguise was working.

Although the eastern end of the rue Marcadet was every bit as grim and industrial as the warehouse area, as the street curved up toward the northern slope of Montmartre, it reminded her more and more of the Goutte-d'Or. There were men talking and smoking in clusters, and women out shopping; tenements and humble hotels, as well as workshops and cheap clothing stores. The smell of fresh baked bread wafted out of a boulangerie and the shouts of a farmer selling lettuce and spinach from a cart echoed down the street. Finally, after several blocks, she heard hammering and glimpsed flames leaping from an open hearth. As she neared the forge, she caught the intense, blood-like smell of hot iron.

With the roaring fire, the shouting and the pounding, there was no reason to enter the open shop on tiptoe. Yet Maura, suddenly shy, approached cautiously. She longed to be noticed, recognized, and welcomed. Instead, Gilbert, pasted with soot, was fully focused on shaping a lump of glowing hot metal, which a shorter man held steady over the anvil with long tongs. Nearer the kiln she recognized the gawky figure of Léon, who was bent over, pumping air into a tube. "More, until it's high," Gilbert yelled as his strong arms brought the hammer down again and again. Maura crept closer. Without even looking up, Gilbert shouted, "We have no work. Sorry. Go away."

"It's me, Maura, from last night," she called out, then put down her bundle and waited.

Gilbert barely glanced at her as he turned toward the furnace and announced that Léon could stop. He resumed hammering and said, a little quieter this time, "Sorry, the boss says we're full up."

Maura wasn't sure he had heard her say her name. He didn't seem to recognize her in Pyotr's clothes. She drew a bit closer, only to have him wave her away, so intent on his pounding that he didn't even look up. She clenched her jaw. She'd almost given herself away to someone who couldn't take the time to remember her. Suddenly, Léon emerged from behind the fire. Still holding the bellows, he approached, smiling his jagged-toothed smile. The flames threw orange waves across his smudged face. Maura stumbled backward. She didn't like the devilish look the fire gave the nasty boy, nor the heat from the forge, nor the way Gilbert just went about his business, ignoring her. She didn't like any of it. She shouldered her bag once more. She wanted to shout, "Don't you see, I still need help," but she swallowed the cry and hurried back to the street.

Maura wandered in a sullen daze until she reached a crossroads, a steep street leading up and down Montmartre. She glanced toward the top of the hill, where they were building a big church; where cabarets, every bit as famous as the Moulin Rouge, promised pleasure and forgetfulness. She shook her head. She would not go near those places, not for a long time, not with their Ralphs and his dirty-minded companions. But where should she go? If she kept on the rue Marcadet, she had no idea where she'd end up. At least she knew what lay below. Escape. The walls of the city and the Saint-Ouen Gate. She had passed through it on the saddest day of her life, when they buried Angela.

She began zigzagging north and west, through city streets and past pocket vineyards, in a hurry now, eager to leave the city and all its perils behind her. Maybe she should visit Angela's grave. Sit by it and talk to her. Or maybe she'd find the paupers' cemetery where criminals and the unknown poor, where Pyotr, had been buried. Or perhaps she'd just keep on walking until she reached the next town, Saint-Ouen, which she had glimpsed from the funeral dray. She didn't stop her headlong march toward the fortress walls until she had to wait for the passing of the *petite ceinture*, the "little belt" train that circled the city. Maura stared as a few of the well-dressed passengers waved at her. She didn't wave back. Why should she, when she'd never have a life like that, with lots of money and nothing to do? Disgusted with the rich, with herself, with everything, she crossed over the tracks and continued walking along the walls.

When she reached the Saint-Ouen Gate, she came to another halt. Men in uniform! She clutched her bag to her chest and flattened herself against the gray stone wall, watching. Two officers approached a guard house. They took over for the man who was stopping wagons, carts and pedestrians as they entered the city. She let out a sigh of relief. Of course, they were collecting taxes and tariffs. They didn't care about who or what left Paris, only what came in. Besides, she was no longer Maura Laurenzano, a fugitive. She was a boy. An ordinary runaway.

Swinging her string bag back over her shoulder, she strode out of the wide opening onto a field sparsely covered with grass. She was not alone. Others, perhaps on the lookout for cheap food or drink, sat around in groups, enjoying the sun. She squinted, trying to get her bearings. The town of Saint-Ouen loomed about a kilometer away directly in front of her, its skyline punctuated by a church steeple and smoking factories. It was not a welcoming sight. Tired, discouraged and hungry, she wasn't ready for graveyards either.

Maura followed her nose and a cluster of people to a man selling sausages from a cart. She had heard that everything cost less outside the city walls, and she got a long baguette filled with greasy meat for only a sou. When she asked for water to wash it down, the seller shrugged and offered a bottle of cheap red wine. Grabbing it by its neck, Maura hunted for a spot near the fortress walls where she could settle on the hard dirt, little softened by the scarce, browning grass. She wanted to be alone. She wanted to be out of the sun. She wanted . . . as she tore the meat and the bread with her teeth, she wasn't sure what she wanted. In the courtyard of her tenement, she had seen others drink themselves into oblivion. She, too, wanted to be numbed. The wine, though raw and sour, was cool enough to quench her thirst.

But the sun was hot and impossible to escape. By the time she finished half the bottle, the ground beneath her began to sway and lurch. Nausea engulfed her. The world was spinning. She had to find a way to keep perfectly still. She pulled her flowered dress half-way out of the sack and draped the skirt over her face to block out the light. Gently, ever so gently, she lowered her head, using the rest of her possessions as a pillow. Mercifully, after what seemed an eternity, she fell asleep.

"*Garçon, garçon.*" Someone was poking at Maura with a stick, calling her a boy. She threw the dress aside and focused her blurry eyes on a frail white-haired old man.

"Stop that!" she yelled. "Get away from me!" She was trying to sound forceful, but her voice came out in a whimper.

"Oh, garçon, I wondered if you wanted to sell that pretty rag."

"That's not a rag, it's my—" Maura stopped herself before she said "my dress." She was a boy. Boys didn't wear dresses. "It's not for sale."

She wanted nothing more than to lie, still, on the ground; but she sat up, placing one hand firmly on her dress while she felt around the hem for the coins she'd sewn into it. She stuffed the dress back into the bag, before surveying her surroundings. The field was almost deserted. The sun had dipped. Hours had passed. And she still felt like she was on a rolling sea, her stomach churning inside of her.

"Are you alone, my boy? Was that your mother's dress?"

He was still bent over her, watching her. Although he spoke with an accent like her mother's, the simplicity, even stupidity, of his expression and the slightness of his frame reminded Maura of the deaf-mute Monsieur Gaston. "I'm fine. Leave me be," she said, sticking out her lower lip to show she meant business.

But instead of leaving, the old bones, with some effort, sat down beside her and pointed to the overturned bottle of red wine. "If you are drinking that, you are not fine, young man. And you do not look fine. Are you running away?"

Maura's head and mouth felt fuzzy. She had no desire to argue, or even talk. Besides, her life was none of his affair. At least he was not scary. She had the feeling that she could knock him down with one solid punch.

"You can't stay here, you know," the old man persisted. "Not at night. Thieves and robbers gather here after dark. They'll hit you over the head for a few sous."

Although he was clean and didn't smell, his clothes looked liked they had belonged to someone else a long time ago. How did she know he wasn't a thief? "What are you?" Maura sniffed, as she held everything she owned close to her chest.

"A ragpicker," he sighed. "An honest old ragpicker, who, at your age, was also a runaway, a twelve-year-old runaway, who would not have survived if—"

"So all you are is an old ragpicker!" she interrupted. "What makes you so proud?" *There*, Maura thought, *that should send him on his way.*

But instead of getting angry or insulted, the old man smiled, baring a mouth of yellowing small teeth, only a few of which were missing. "Does it matter what you do, as long as you are free and honest and love your fellow human beings?"

Maura stared at the old man. That was exactly the kind of thing that Pyotr used to say when he talked about the "dignity" of workers and the poor.

"See here," he said, pointing to a small oval brass medal pinned on his vest, "I'm registered. Everyone trusts me. Everyone knows Nico."

"I don't," Maura said. After squinting at the name and the number on the piece of metal he bore on his chest, she groaned and lay down again, her head on her bag. She did not want to talk to anyone. Especially not a ragpicker with a ragpicker badge.

"Do you have a place to stay? A family?"

"I'm going to Saint-Ouen."

He shook his head as if he did not believe her. "There are desperate people there too. It's not a good place for a boy alone."

Worse for a girl alone. Maura wished she didn't feel so sick.

"I am getting old. Other pickers have families to help. I'm all alone. You can stay with me, at least tonight. I have some bread left. That will help make you feel better. You can use my bed while I am out picking. Then maybe you will decide to help me."

Maura closed her eyes, trying to think through the throbbing in her head. She hated it when people tried to be kind. She hated talk about dignity and being free and loving your fellow human beings. Stupid words, stupid! Because that is not how the world worked. Because somewhere deep down Maura suspected that Pyotr's eloquent words had gotten him killed. Because, despite their stupidity, those very words had made her love him, trust him. And now, because before the sun was going down, she might have to trust someone who talked like him—even as she resolved to keep the scissors blade in her hand while she slept.

"Come," he said, struggling to his feet. He offered a hand so papery and thin, it was almost translucent.

Refusing his help, Maura got up and brushed herself off. She was glad to see that she was taller than him.

"Do you have a name, my boy?"

"Pierre," Maura muttered, turning away as she tried out Pyotr's French name. "Pierre," she whispered to herself. That's all she was going to tell this Nico. She wished he would stop talking.

He nodded and, alternating steps with the rhythm of his walking stick, started toward the Saint-Ouen Gate back into the city.

"I can't go there," she said, remembering the uniformed men.

"You are in trouble, my son, I can see it. Most runaways are running from something. I know. I did. Don't be afraid, all the men know Nico, they'll let you through."

Maura stopped and gazed out in the dimming light, calculating her choices. One way led to Angela's grave; another to a town with smoking factories; the other to warehouses, the gasworks and trains coming into the city. If she didn't go back inside the walls now, how long would she be exiled from everything she had ever known? Maura nodded, and followed the ragpicker, staying a little behind, in case she had to flee. Her heart was pounding so hard that she almost forgot her throbbing head and wobbly stomach.

When she heard the officer in the guard post greet Nico by name, she drew closer. After a short exchange, Nico introduced her as "my new helper" and waved her forward. Head bowed, she reminded herself to walk slowly, as if there were nothing to fear.

"We all live close to the walls, but I don't live with the other ragpickers," Nico explained. "They are mostly families or groups of runaways like you. And it can smell terrible, especially in the morning when everyone returns to divide their finds. Ever since I found a widow's wedding ring in the garbage, she has let me stay in a shed by her vineyard. She trusts me to watch over things. And even lets me take eggs from her chicken coop once a week and water from the well."

Maura had trouble understanding his pride about living in a shed until they passed through a street of one- and two-room hovels, made of wood and tin, huddled up against each other. The stones, where there were cobbles, were so uneven and loose, they had to step carefully in order not to trip. Low mounds of stinking debris were strewn in front of the shacks. A strange quiet pervaded, and except for a goat and a rabbit, a few toddling naked babies, and children playing in the dirt, there was no one about. "Shhhh," Nico whispered. "The pickers are still getting their sleep. Old men don't need so much sleep," he said pointing to himself. The odors were making Maura gag. She swore she'd never sink as low as these people.

Mercifully, after a few blocks, they reached a vineyard. Nico paused and stretched out his arms. "This is it. We must have beauty in our life, don't you agree?"

Maura snorted. The vines looked spindly and dry to her. She could not imagine anything beautiful coming out of this place. The clothes and the women on the Boulevard Saint-Germain and in the Bon Marché, they were beautiful. Yet ahead of them, the hut Nico called home glistened in the sunset. When they drew near, Maura saw that he had adorned his shed with the faces of decorated tin boxes, the kind containing fancy biscuits and candies. He had pounded this colorful display into the plain graying wood that comprised the outside of the shed. There was also a real window. Beauty! Maura humphed to herself.

The door was a moth-eaten floral rug. He held it aside for her to enter. In the shadows she could make out a narrow bed pushed against the wall opposite the window, two chairs and a table in the middle, and a big basket of the kind, she presumed, ragpickers used to ply their trade. When Nico slid around her, struck a match, and lit the four candles that sat upon the table, she gasped. Instead of being bare and drab, most of the walls were covered with pieces of cloth, shiny and dull, hundreds of them, in stripes and flowers and every imaginable color. She had to smile. How Lidia, the anarchist student, would have loved the wildness, the chaos of it all. And, in its way, it was beautiful.

"You like it?" he asked. "This is why I so wanted the dress. I sell most of my rags and bones to the ragpicker mistress. But if I find something really pretty, I always keep a piece for myself."

The candlelight illuminated his eager smile. But Maura was not willing to concede any admiration. Not yet. She sank into one of the two wooden chairs. The memory of Lidia made her sad. Lidia, Vera, Pyotr, Angela, all gone. She peered at her companion, taking in his pallor, his white whiskers, and his cloudy dark eyes. His life had to be sad and lonely. The realization pierced her, if only because she had learned that very morning, lonely old men were worthy of more than scorn and ridicule. The opening in her heart frightened her. "It's nice here," she finally said. "Perhaps I'll give you a piece of my mother's dress later."

"Good!" He opened a tin, a banged-up version of a fancy cake box, and took out some bread. "Eat," he said. "It will help." Then he dipped a cup into a bucket of water beside the table, and placed it before her. She sipped some water and munched on the bread, which did offer some comfort. "You can use my bed until I come back. Then I must sleep for a while. And now," he said, getting up from his chair, "I must go. It takes me longer than the others to get to my territory." Maura watched as he strapped the basket to his back and took up his stick. She marveled that he could carry the basket, let alone fill it. "Blow out the candles before you sleep," he admonished her. Then he smiled again. "Don't worry. You'll be safe. No one knows you're here."

As soon as she was sure he had gone, Maura got up to watch his progress from the window. *You'll be safe,* she repeated to herself. Maybe. But she felt like a prisoner. She paced around the table, scrutinizing the familiar objects of poverty: the hooks on the walls holding old clothes, the single cupboard with its motley collection of dishes and pots, the little stove that heated and cooked, the narrow bed. She blew out the candles, grabbed the bread and plopped down on the bed, chewing, fighting back tears, waiting for night to fall.

At dawn, Maura woke to a familiar song. "*Vado di notte come fa la luna*. I wander through the night like the moon. *Vado cercando lo mio inamorato*. Searching to find my true love."

She sat up. "Why are you singing that?" she shouted. "Who are you?"

"Nico, Domenico Scarpaci. Your friend. You are in my house. What is wrong?"

Coming out of sleep's dense fog, Maura realized where she was. She fell back on the bed. Her head was heavy, but not in pain. Not like yesterday. Oh God, yesterday! "Please don't sing it again," she said.

"You know it?"

She nodded. "My father used to sing it," she whispered, as if that would explain everything she hated about that song, as if she would ever tell anyone that she had recited the verse about a dead, lost lover just hours before she learned that Pyotr had been killed.

"I used to sing it to my dear Jeanne, God be with her. Did your father sing in the streets?"

Maura closed her eyes. "Yes."

"And you?"

"When I was very little. Before he left us."

"Then it must be sad for you."

She curled up toward the wall. She didn't want to say any more. She needed to be left alone.

But she was not alone. Behind her she heard Nico rustling around the shed, putting things on the table and moving the chairs.

"Pierre," he called.

She didn't answer, because at first, she didn't recognize herself in the name.

"Pierre?"

She rolled over. Seeing Nico standing at the table, she remembered that he needed the bed in the daytime after his night work. She sat up and, out of habit, reached to smooth the unruly curls that were no longer there.

"Look, I got some fresh bread and a piece of fruit and a nice newspaper with a pretty picture on it."

Still blurry-eyed, Maura got up and took the few steps necessary to pull out a chair. He wanted to have a regular breakfast with her! She sat down and stared at a hunk of dense, dark bread.

"I thought you could read to me from the newspaper while I go to sleep."

With a heavy sigh, she picked up the paper, unfolded it, and gasped. The pretty picture was her sister's corpse. She dropped the newspaper as if it were on fire. It called Angela an *Angel of Death*. An instant later, she grabbed it and began to read. Angela, Pyotr, evil killers. "It's not true! None of it!"

"My child." Nico got up to see what was troubling her.

"It isn't true, I tell you." Maura was sobbing. She slid the dish away to make room for her head, and buried her face in her arms on the table. Her whole body shook, convulsing with an explosive combustion of sorrow and anger. She did not know how much time had passed before she felt two hands on her shoulders. Nico's papery thin hands felt warm and strong as they pressed and released in a rhythmic effort to comfort.

When she had quieted down, he gave her one of his "pretty rags." "I washed it in the well," he said. "You can wipe your face."

Although he did not ask, Maura could tell from the questioning look in his dark brown eyes that he wanted to know why she was crying. And she needed to tell him, to tell someone. She started at the beginning, telling him about working with her sister twelve hours a day in their little room, about the man who brought the shirts and tried to seduce Angela, about the way he beat and raped her, and about the iron rod that Pyotr used to stop him. They hadn't meant to kill him, she explained, only to stop him from hurting Angela again, to make him understand that they were not his slaves. And then, without admitting her love for

Pyotr, she told of his death and Angela's murder. "She was too gentle to hurt anyone. Too good. Not like me. That's why Barbereau made promises to her and my mother that he never intended to keep. I tried to tell them." Maura shook her head. "I tried."

Nico had pulled up a chair beside her as he listened. He reached out for her hand. "Yes, my Maurina, you tried to protect your sister. You are a good, strong girl."

Maurina. Her father used to call her Maurina, "his little dark one." When he still loved her. Before he left. She gazed at Nico's kind face. He believed she was good. That what she had done was right.

"You can stay here," he said, "as long as you like. Help me if you wish, until you know what you must do. You will be safe."

Maura took her hand away and bowed her head, making a fist. The newspaper had ignited something inside her. She didn't want only to be safe. She wanted the truth to be known. As Pyotr would have said, she wanted justice.

9

On Tuesday, as soon as she put Jean-Luc down for his morning nap, Clarie told Rose that she was going for a walk until lunch. This was not exactly true. She intended to walk, but only after perusing the headlines of the newspapers that covered the sides of the kiosk at the Square d'Anvers. She had to know if Maura was still missing.

Yesterday's newspapers had reported nothing new, even though *L'Intransigeant* had promised to reveal "The Secrets of Angela's Violent Longings." Today she could not resist buying one of the most popular tabloids, *Le Petit Journal*, because of its alluring headline, "The Russian Anarchist's Women." After giving the man inside the kiosk a few centimes, Clarie quickly folded the paper in her gloved hands and headed through the wrought-iron gates into the small rectangular park. She sat down on an isolated bench under one of the trees that lined each side of the square. It was a beautiful July day. The flowers bordering the grassy central oval were in full bloom. The sun was shining. She was doing nothing wrong. Why, then, did she feel guilty?

Clarie frowned. It was not in her nature to keep secrets, even innocent ones, from Rose or from Bernard. But, since their contretemps at Saturday's breakfast, Bernard had been strangely silent on the subject of the Laurenzanos, even though he must have encountered headlines about them at every street corner. Perhaps he was saying nothing because he did not want to provoke another disagreement. Or—and this made her smile—perhaps he thought it would hurt or embarrass her if he cited evidence that he had been right after all, that Francesca's daughters were criminal or dangerous. Bernard Martin, the judge and the lawyer, had no compunction about going after miscreants, using their words against them. But this was not his way with those he loved. With her and Rose, with her father and his mother, he was the soul of kindness and discretion.

Clarie sighed and opened the newspaper. If Maura remained missing, it would be up to Clarie to bring the issue of Francesca and her daughter back into the Martin household.

Le Petit Journal's account did not immediately deal with the supposed love affair between Angela and the dead boy. It began by linking him to two Russian medical students who had been held for two weeks in the notorious Saint-Lazare Prison for fallen women. Despite persistent questioning, they continued to deny any part in bombing plots. Clarie laid the paper down and slumped back against the bench. *How terrible,* she thought. *How alone the Russian girls must feel.* They were only a year or two older than Clarie's students and yet the authorities saw fit to jail them with prostitutes and interrogate them over and over again. Bernard had told her how brutal the police could be when they were looking for "answers." Clarie stared at a man, whistling complacently as he passed. Was anyone standing up for these girls? Or were they being ignored and scorned because they were foreign, because they were accused of violence, because they dared to enter a male profession? The reporter implied that the two young women were particularly suspicious because they had had the audacity to travel unescorted to Paris to study at the University.

Prickling with irritation, Clarie picked up the newspaper again. Where were all those Republican men with their high-flown rhetoric about equality and justice when it came to these girls? Sometimes she thought Emilie was right: women needed their own party, their own advocates. Clarie shook her head, trying to vanquish her frustration and focus on her search for news about Maura and her mother. There was nothing she could hope to do for anyone else at this point.

Unfortunately, the second half of the story merely repeated the same unproven lurid speculations about Angela and the Russian bomber: that they had formed a love triangle with Barbereau in order to trap and kill him. Clarie refused to believe this version of events. When the reporter concluded with the stock, meaningless line, "the police are continuing their investigations," Clarie slapped the paper down in her lap.

She should have known better. *Le Petit Journal* was one of the scores of dailies that fed a gullible public's appetite for titillation and scandal. These papers didn't care about truth or justice. They were all part of the Paris "noise": hawkers hectoring you at every step, advertisements for bawdy entertainments screaming from every blank wall, the crowds at the morgue, the wax museum that specialized in recreating the scenes of horrific crimes . . . and in the last few days, Clarie had bought into it by expecting that a sensation-mongering tabloid would tell her what she needed to know.

The angry shame of that brought Clarie to her feet. Francesca and Maura were not sensations, they were human beings. She whirled around, looking for a gentleman with a watch, then heard a single bell toll from a nearby church. Eleven-thirty. She stood calculating for a moment. She was closer to the Goutte-d'Or now than she had been when she walked from the lycée. There was only one way to know what was really happening to Francesca and Maura. She left the paper on the bench, knowing that some bored nanny would gratefully pick it up, and resolutely strode down the gravel alley of the park toward the Boulevard Rochechouart.

She walked with such purpose that she did not feel the fear or self-consciousness that had stalked her first sojourn to the Goutte-d'Or. The vulgar shops, the hawkers, the gentlemen tipping their hats all passed in a blur. She only paused for breath at the huge, busy intersections. When she got to the hospital, her steps slowed. The memory of her last encounter with Maura came back with powerful clarity. She saw again that wild-haired, wild-eyed girl and felt her sullen anger. Clarie heard her voice, too, shouting that she was not going to let herself be killed. Maura Laurenzano, so irritating and self-centered. So much like Clarie had been at her age, when she blamed the world for her mother's death. Was Maura really in danger? Clarie picked up the pace. Entering the tenement courtyard, she paid no attention to the shouting children or loitering workmen. She passed through quickly to the dark staircase. Clinging to the railing and ignoring the pervasive odor of garbage and urine, she climbed to the top.

The door was half-open. Clarie heard drone-like humming. She knocked.

"Come in."

Recognizing Francesca's voice, Clarie stepped inside. The charwoman was sitting on a chair by the table under the meager light coming from the window. When she saw Clarie, she dropped her sewing on the table and stood up.

"Madame Martin!"

"Are you all right?" Clarie peered into Francesca's face as she approached.

"Yes, yes," Francesca answered in the same monotonous tone as her song. The fact that she needed her hand to steady herself as she sank back into the wooden chair belied her words. She did not look well at all. Her features seemed blurred. Because Clarie had lost her own child, she recognized the dull resignation that offered temporary respite between waves of agonizing grief. Clarie sat down and reached for the charwoman's hand.

"Are you sure you are all right?" Clarie asked, still peering into Francesca's face.

"Yes, I think so." Francesca pulled away to take up her sewing and, Clarie sensed, to lower her head and move her worn face out of sight.

"I'm sorry. I must be intruding," Clarie said.

"Of course not."

Of course not, Clarie thought bitterly. *I am her "better," how could a humble charwoman dare imply that I am intruding.* Clarie hated this unfairness, this wall between them. At least Maura, as irritating as she was, knew not to put Clarie on a pedestal. To show that she did not intend to stay and bother Francesca with unwelcome expressions of sympathy, Clarie got up. "I only came to see how you were, and to see if Maura has returned. We both want your girl to be safe."

"Maura, yes, Maura," Francesca said, as if saying the name through a dark, echoing tunnel. Then, emerging, she brightened up. "I'm sure she is safe. We don't have to worry."

"We don't?" The doubt slipped out before Clarie could stop herself. In her mind's eye, she saw images of the Russian girls in the Saint-Lazare Prison and Angela's bloodless, dead body. "That's good," she quickly recovered. "You know where she is then?" Clarie paused, hoping for an answer. When none came, she added, "You don't have to tell me, I just wanted to make sure that she's all right."

"Oh, she is, I can show you." Francesca searched for a piece of paper under the jumble of socks and yarn on the table. "Mme Guyot read this to me. She is safe, I know she is."

Clarie hesitated to take the paper.

"Please, can you read it to me? I'd like hearing it again. You'll see, she's all right."

Clarie could not refuse the eager urgency in Francesca's voice. "Thank you," she said, offering a weak smile as she glanced at the note, written in bold penciled strokes. She swallowed hard and began:

Dearest Maman,

I must leave you for a while. I don't want you to worry. And I don't want you to believe all the bad things the police are saying about me and Angela and Pieter.

I am not afraid! But I do think the man who killed our Angela might come to look for me. So I am going away to find a job somewhere else. I'll come back when the police find Angela's killer.

Most important, don't worry! You always said I was the strong one and knew how to take care of myself. And I will. And when I come back, I will take care of you too.

Love, Maura

P.S. If the police don't find Angela's killer, I will! I promise you!

Clarie barely managed to get through the postscript, which could only be a piece of desperate bravado. There was no way that Maura could find her sister's killer. And if she tried, she would be in more danger than ever.

"You see?" prodded Francesca.

"Yes." Now it was Clarie emerging from some dark place.

"She'll be all right, my Maura. She's the strong one." Suddenly Francesca's voice cracked. "And she'll come back, she promised. She won't leave me alone." She grimaced as her head bowed even lower over her sewing, revealing bald streaks amid the gray in her hair.

"Is there anything you need?" Clarie asked as she looked around the room, trying to find something, some way, to help. She glanced at the paltry collection of pots and dishes on the shelf, the clothes hanging from hooks, and at the sewing materials on the table.

"What happened to the scissors?" There was only one blade.

Francesca shrugged. "I found them that way after Maura left."

Clarie stared at the single blade. Suddenly alert, she scrutinized the room with more care. She'd never have noticed if her suspicions hadn't been aroused. A lock of hair, dark like her own, dark like Maura's, on the floor. What was that girl up to? Clarie imagined Maura hacking off her curls. She must have also unscrewed the scissors. Did she actually believe that a scissors blade would shield her from all the dangers facing a young woman in Paris? Or was she planning some craziness, some crime of her own?

Determined to hide her concern, Clarie said casually, "Work must be very slow at the school in the summer. So if you—"

"Yes, we only do one day a week," Francesca interrupted, "but I am helping Fanny—Mme Guyot—at the laundry too. I'll manage until, until . . . my girl comes back." She looked away again, refusing to meet Clarie's eyes.

Convinced she was only intruding, Clarie said, "I must go. But, please, Francesca, if you need anything or hear any news about Maura, you can leave a message at the school. Promise me you'll do that."

"Yes, thank you." The words were those required by politeness. But Francesca did not rise as her guest took her leave. Clarie knew, she remembered, the crushing burden of grief and anxiety that left one immobile, wanting only to be left alone. She went out quietly, leaving the door ajar as she had found it. Sadness weighed her down as she descended the staircase and started the walk home. But her frustration pushed her forward in equal measure. Francesca, Maura, the Russian girls. They were all so alone. They could not depend upon the authorities. Indeed, they perceived the police as their enemies. And despite everything Bernard had argued, the Laurenzanos might be right. There must be something else someone could do.

That someone appeared, as if by magic, only hours later. Clarie and Rose were each holding Jean-Luc's hand as they walked through the Square d'Anvers. The joy of watching her boy push his chubby legs as fast as they could go toward the ice cream cart drove Clarie's worries away. Rose, too, was laughing. It was the hottest time of day, but a lovely time of day. The park was filled with nannies or mothers with their charges hoping to catch a breeze. It was a peaceful world of women and children, suspended in leisure until the men came home, a world that Clarie, who had put on her new straw boater, could only enjoy during summer vacation.

"Come, Rose, have something," she urged as they approached the head of the line. Ice cream was Rose's weakness, and it always gave Clarie pleasure to see the woman who had become almost a grandmother to Jean-Luc allowing herself a treat.

Rose was deciding between strawberry and chocolate when Clarie heard the hawker. "Just out, *L'Echo de Paris*, Séverine defends the anarchists! Says they are innocent." Clarie had vowed just that morning to block out all the Paris "noise," but she turned sharply at the words "anarchist" and "innocent."

"Can you hold on to Jean-Luc for a moment?" she asked Rose, "and here, for the ice cream." She placed a coin in Rose's free hand. If she was going to catch the hawker before he moved, she didn't have time for explanations or secrets. Grabbing the side of her skirt, Clarie maneuvered through the little crowd to get to the newsboy.

He was bigger and older than some, and ruder. As she paid for her paper, he shouted, "The lady wants the latest news. What about you?"

Embarrassed by the attention, Clarie lowered her head, so that the brim of her straw hat hid her eyes, and hastened back to find Rose and Jean-Luc. She led them to a shady spot on the side of the square. She sat there, talking to Jean-Luc, using her handkerchief to wipe the chocolate dribbles from his mouth, smiling with Rose, and *waiting*, ever conscious of the folded newspaper on the bench beside her. She would read it after they returned to the apartment and Jean-Luc was safely settled, playing at her feet. Clarie refused to hurry this moment, of peace and of summer, even as part of her mind kept retreating to a darker place. Finally, Rose declared that she had to start dinner, and they headed home.

While Rose was busy in the kitchen, Clarie took out Jean-Luc's blocks and played with him for a few minutes, until he began to concentrate on his building projects. Only then did Clarie open the newspaper. She had the vaguest notion that Séverine was a well-known writer. The article quickly revealed her political sentiments.

The Russians, Séverine contended, Pyotr Balenov as well as the girls in prison, were unlikely perpetrators of the crimes of which they were accused. It was much more likely that the bomb had been set off by an agent provocateur acting for the police. As for the "Angel of the Goutte-d'Or," what could she, a poor young seamstress, know of assassinations and bombs? Wasn't there ample proof that her boss had exploited her? Yet instead of protecting the poor and the weak, the press and the police were carrying on a war against them and foreigners, and "woe be unto anyone living in France who was *both* poor and foreign!"

Clarie clutched the paper, thinking, *yes, yes, yes,* until she got to Séverine's last paragraph, which asserted that *even if* the Russians and Angela were guilty of plotting violent crimes, "they had a right to fight the hell of exploitation with a fire of their own making." She concluded, "I will always, no matter what, stand on the side of the poor."

Always. No matter what. Coming from a woman. Clarie was shocked.

"Papa!" Jean-Luc heard the familiar sound of his father's key in the door.

Clarie placed the newspaper on the fireplace, picked up her son, and went to the door. Bernard greeted them with the usual kisses. When he set his bowler on the little table in the foyer, he noticed a letter. "From Singer," he said, examining the envelope.

"Oh, I forgot." And, indeed, with all that had been going on, she had forgotten that Bernard's former colleague had just written him. "What do you think it's about?"

"We'll know very soon, after I ask Luca here what he's been doing today."

Bernard took Jean-Luc from her and nestled his face for a moment in the boy's neck.Jean-Luc still pointed more than he talked. He was eager to show Bernard his block house and little soldiers, but not ready to relinquish his father's arms. Bernard followed the boy's gestures into the parlor and sat down with his son in his lap. "Let's read the letter together," he said, letting Jean-Luc help to tear the envelope.

Clarie settled into the other chair beside the reading lamp. She relished any news from the Singers. Noémie had been so kind after the death of Henri-Joseph and such a wonderful guide during the early weeks after Jean-Luc's birth.

"Any more children?" she asked.

Bernard, who had been skimming the letter, laughed. "No, I think they are going to stop at four, and they're growing fast." He furrowed his brow as he continued to read, nodded, murmured "Oh yes," and handed the letter to Clarie.

"As you'll see, everyone is fine. But he brings up something I've been meaning to talk about with you."

"Yes?" Despite the squirming of Jean-Luc, who was reaching for Bernard's beard, her husband had that serious, judicial look on his face.

"There's a mounting campaign to reopen the Dreyfus case. Do you remember it?"

"Of course." The Jewish officer had been found guilty of treason while they were in Nancy. There had been a terrible upsurge of anti-Israelite sentiment and violence, even a small riot on their street a few weeks after Henri-Joseph died. "And," Clarie quickly moved away from that past, "I remember, during our last faculty meeting, a teacher mentioned that one of the students had brought up a book about his case."

"Probably Bernard-Lazare."

"You know it?" Clarie should have guessed. Since the Nancy murders and his close friendship with Singer, Bernard had taken a particular interest in the Israelites.

"Here, son." Bernard gave Jean-Luc another kiss before setting him on his feet, where he swayed between his father's legs, humming to himself. Over what Clarie considered the loveliest music in the world, Bernard continued. "I've been following the new developments in all the papers. On my own, really. The men at the Labor Exchange consider this a rather bourgeois affair. Upper-class officer, the army. But for me—and, of course, for Singer—it is a matter of justice. The man who is languishing on Devil's Island might well be innocent."

Clarie's mind immediately conjured up an image of the isolated, imprisoned Russian girls.

"I didn't want to put an extra burden on you, but I've been thinking of attending some meetings this week. And now with Singer's urging," Bernard said, gesturing toward the letter Clarie held in her hand, "I've even more reason. He wants a full report of what's going on in Paris. This means I'll miss a few of our dinners together."

A matter of justice. Clarie mused over these words before responding. "Of course, you must go. But there is something I need to show you, too." She walked over the fireplace and picked up *L'Echo de Paris*. "Do you know anything about a woman reporter named Séverine?"

"Séverine! She's quite notorious."

"Notorious? Really?" Once again, with teaching duties, the household, and Jean-Luc, Clarie felt she was missing out on things she should know.

"She published a newspaper with an old anarchist Communard. She's had more than one husband. Left her children with one of them. Then she was caught with her lover—or so they say—in a public restroom. When there was a mining strike, she, a woman, went down into the mine to report 'first-hand' on the conditions—"

"But surely that's a good thing," Clarie interrupted, "standing up for the workers."

"Yes, but a woman."

"Why not?" *Why not, indeed.* Clarie was not about to defend Séverine's relationships with her husbands or lovers, although had she been a man. . . .

"Well," Bernard said with a wry smile, "more recently her fame has come from columns begging alms for the poor during the winter. They earned her the nickname 'pity on wheels.'"

"I take it you don't like her or her work," Clarie commented dryly.

"Well, she did raise quite a bit of money for charity," Bernard conceded. "Anyway, what about her?"

Clarie brought the article over to Bernard. "She asserts that the bomb Angela Laurenzano's friend is accused of planting was actually the work of an agent provocateur."

"Hmmm." Bernard hardly glanced at the article before handing it back to her. "She'll always say she's on the side of the poorest, most despised people. That's her brand of anarchism."

"But isn't that what you're doing? Seeking justice for poor workers?"

"Yes, as long as they stand up for themselves and *don't commit violent crimes*. We're building unions, institutions. That's the way to go."

There was so much more Clarie could have said. Wasn't beating and abusing a young girl, practically a child, a violent crime? What about women who sewed alone in their rooms for hour after hour for a pittance, with no unions to protect them, no one to be on their side? But she didn't say any of this. It was almost dinner time, and she did not want to revisit a futile disagreement in front of Jean-Luc. Besides, if the authorities had every legal right to hold the Russian girls and Francesca would not go to the police in search of Maura, there was little that Bernard could do, even if he wanted to. Clarie sighed and got up to put the paper back on the fireplace. Behind her she heard Bernard talking to Jean-Luc about how they were all going to see plays and hear music at the Labor Exchange to celebrate Bastille Day. She opened the *L'Echo de Paris* again and stared at Séverine's byline, wondering what kind of woman would stand up so courageously against common opinion.

10

Maura tried to help Nico. Really tried, although she found picking through the stinking refuse of Paris thoroughly disgusting.

On Sunday night, she carried the lamp as Nico scoured his assigned territory in the eighth arrondissement, where the city conscientiously collected garbage from rich mansions and apartment houses. Since it was a wealthy and relatively clean neighborhood, it was much less profitable than poorer districts, like the Goutte-d'Or, where municipal collections were less regular and fastidious, and whole families of ragpickers scavenged for rags, bones, fat, metal, cork, and glass to sell and, if they were lucky, some discarded food for their shanty-households.

Maura learned about the territories and routines quickly because there was little to learn, except how nauseating and humiliating life could be. Ragpickers could not begin work before ten p.m. and had to be off the streets by four in the morning, lest they offend the eyes and noses of their fellow citizens. And so before every dawn, this army of malodorous souls returned to their hovels, where they sorted their spoils into piles to be sold to a master ragpicker, an enterprising man or woman who had made it to the top of the heap. Whatever they could not sell or consume was strewn, in rotting mounds of filth, along the cobbled road outside their shanties, making Maura grateful she shared Nico's oasis by the vineyard. She at least had the consolation of knowing that after the revolting task of cleaning, sorting, and selling, she'd be able to wash in the well water and sleep on the pallet that Nico had fashioned for her on the packed earth floor of his shed. She might have found the routine almost bearable, if it hadn't been for Mme Florent.

In their northern district, this loud, fat harridan in turban and pantaloons was the Queen of Garbage, the General of the Scavenging Army, the High Priestess of Just Rewards. Except she was neither royal nor pious nor just. Standing on one side of Mme Florent's huge receiving tent, Maura quickly perceived that the ragpicker mistress had favorites among the pushing and yelling men and women eager to get their pay. With those who brought the biggest piles, she carried on a bantering bidding war, which always ended up in her favor. With the old and the weak, like Nico, she was stingier and nasty. She even threatened that if he and "his new helper" didn't do better, she might not do business with him anymore.

"Does she always talk to you that way?" Maura asked as soon as they were out of the hearing of others.

"She is not a nice woman."

"She doesn't have to be that mean." Maura hated seeing the kind old man treated that way.

Nico shrugged.

Maura continued to press. "That quivering piece of flesh stands on that platform! Her helpers do all the dirty work. She's got a purse full of money. She only pays you for what you bring. What difference is it to her how much you collect?"

"I believe," Nico said patiently, "that she wants to become richer than she already is. Besides, what do I need? Only to eat, to wash, to sleep, to keep warm in the winter."

Clenching her fists, Maura strode ahead of her companion. She wasn't sure what made her angrier, the uncalled-for spitefulness of the ragpicker mistress or the resignation of the old man. Resigned, like her mother. Except, Maura slowed down, he was so peaceful, not a martyr like Maman, always asking for your pity. Maura did not understand Nico, but she could not forsake him either. She stopped, closed her eyes and waited for him to catch up. Offering a lopsided smile to show she had calmed down, she lifted the basket from his shoulders and strapped it on hers. They trudged the rest of the way, across the vineyard, in silence.

Her quiet demeanor during their washing up and preparing for bed apparently made the soft-hearted Nico believe that she was sad and in need of consolation. "The first days are the hardest," he told her. "I remember. It can break your spirit, this work. But you are strong. And you'll soon be going back to your mother."

These words did make her sad. She hadn't realized how much she would miss Maman. But she couldn't go home, not as long as the police were after her and there was a killer lurking about. "How did you become a ragpicker?" she asked. She wanted to think about something else.

"That is a story."

"Tell me," she said, as she lay down on the rag-and-straw mat he had set on the floor for her. She moved the bag packed with her belongings under head, using it as a pillow.

Nico pulled a dark cloth across the window above her head. He limped to his bed and lay down with a sigh that seemed to say that there was an aching heart inside his old aching bones. "You want to hear?"

"Yes."

"It might put you to sleep."

Maura smiled. That's what she had been thinking, remembering her father's bedtime tales. She hadn't realized his story would be all too familiar.

When Nico was only six years old, a man had come to his Italian village, offering to teach the skills of a musician to young boys and girls. Nico's father signed a contract with the man and told his son that he would be coming home in a few years, after he earned enough to pay for his training. Nico was sent to Marseilles where another *padrone* took over, teaching him to beg and to play the violin. If he didn't make enough money by the end of the day, he was beaten and not given his dinner. Eventually the padrone taught him the concertina. As Nicoletto, he became somewhat famous in the streets and parks of the port city, and made a great deal of money for the padrone. But the beatings did not stop, so he ran away. "Like you," Nico said to Maura, "I had to run. I was twelve."

"Did you ever get to go home?"

"No, I never saw my mother or father again."

"That's what my father used to say," she whispered. "He was abandoned in Paris because they said he was getting too old and too big to beg." She stared at the rag-covered ceiling, wondering if her father had ever found his way back to his native village.

"A man who had often brought his children to see me play," Nico continued, "found me wandering in the streets. When I told him that I was afraid of being caught, he took me with him on a trip to Paris and asked his brother, who ran a restaurant, to take me in. For years, I was afraid to show my face. I worked hard in the kitchen, washing and cleaning. It was the kindness of these two men that saved me."

"Then what happened, how—"

The sigh was even heavier than before.

"Gradually I learned to cook, and one day when I was sent to buy meat, I met my sweet, dear Jeanne. I thought my loneliness was over. She owned a shop. We sold beautiful sausages hanging from the ceiling. She taught me to make them. She was so kind. She liked to laugh. But she got a cancer. Oh, how my dear one suffered! After she died, her relatives took back the shop and told me to leave. I called her my wife, because she was my love for many years, but we never married, never had children. And in the end, I was only an old Italian who no one wanted."

Maura rolled over. She shouldn't have asked him to tell his story. She already knew how unfair life was. Pyotr and Angela were dead, and everyone thought that they were violent criminals.

"Maura? Maurina?"

"Yes."

"I do still have my concertina. I used to play it for my Jeanne. It made her happy. I can play it for you tomorrow."

"All right," she said, although she wasn't sure what tomorrow meant in the world of night-time ragpicking. Was it when they woke at dusk or when they went to bed in the daytime? A piece of straw poked through a rag and tickled her nose. She brushed it aside as she tried not to think about Nico's story. Part of him was happy, she told herself, the part that loved the patches of beauty that he wove into his tattered life: music, color, the vineyard, the well, a fresh egg or two every week. She could feel from the way he talked to her that, because she was a companion, because he thought of her as someone like the boy he had been, a young person in need, she, too, brought him some happiness. Comforted by that thought, she closed her eyes, determined to stay at least for a while.

The next day their collections were even sparser. Unable to bear seeing Nico humiliated again, Maura offered one of the treasures she had brought from home, her hair to sell to a wigmaker. At first he refused, but Maura insisted. Yet even this bounty provoked a reproof from the harridan. "At last," Mme Florent said, as she held up the little string bag bursting with Maura's black curls, "something worth buying. Too bad I can't give the old limper a full price, since I've been giving him charity for months." And with that, to laughs of derision from her helpers, she dismissed him with a ten sous, only half a franc.

Maura was fuming. She knew the hair must be worth much more, a good meal for the two of them at the very least. If she could, she would have snatched it back. Instead, she grabbed Nico's basket, strapped it on her shoulders, and hurried through the crowded ragpickers' neighborhood. She pushed her way through the street as men, women and children scurried over the mounds in front of their doors like a colony of ants, gathering scraps for their bedtime meal. By the time Nico caught up with her, she had pulled up the bucket of water from the vineyard's well, and was washing her hands and face.

"I'm sorry about your beautiful hair," he said, putting a gentle hand on her shoulder.

"I thought at least we could get something good to eat." She had squandered part of herself. It was silly, but she was almost in tears because they had sold her hair for a pittance.

"We will eat well today," Nico assured her. "Today is the day of the anarchists' soup kitchen."

"I don't care."

"It will make you feel better." His cloudy, dark brown eyes grew large as he tried to convince her. "They sing and make good speeches. They say that everyone should eat well and be free, that we don't need governments or churches to tell us what to do. They say all work has dignity, even this, as long as we help each other."

"I know that!" Hadn't she told him about Pyotr?

"Come," he urged. "You know I like to wander a bit and think of different things."

"Like a better world?" she asked sarcastically. When was that going to happen?

"Yes, Maurina, a better world. Come, my child. You'll feel happier."

If she hadn't been so hungry, she would have never agreed. But, then, she would have never found a way to tell the truth about Pyotr and Angela.

The anarchists distributed soup in a dusty field which lay somewhere between the ragpickers' quartier and Nico's territory. As Maura and Nico, empty tin bowls in hand, lined up for their soup, a man accompanied by an organ grinder sang revolutionary songs. They were meant to inspire, but Maura tried to ignore the music until she heard the words "She was young and beautiful. He was strong and full of worth. Everyone remembers them. The Fiancés of the North." She liked the words and the melody.

"Do you know that song?" she asked Nico.

"Oh, yes," he said. "It really happened. Two young lovers killed by soldiers because they were marching for freedom."

It had really happened. It was true. Two pure, young lovers, like Pyotr and Angela.

Maura settled down next to Nico under a scrawny tree. Listening to speeches was the price a few score bedraggled men, women and children paid for their "free" meal.

Today the speakers complained about tomorrow, Bastille Day, a holiday which should honor "the people" who rose up against the King, the Queen and the rich. Instead, they said, the so-called Republic was showing its true colors by parading its military power down the Champs-Elysées. "Down with the army! Down with the rich!" they cried. "Let us make our own celebration!"

They announced a parade through the entire arrondissement, ending in soup and bread for all.

As the speeches droned on above her, Maura slowly chewed on the pieces of potato and gristle in her greasy soup. She remembered the musicians on the Boulevard Rochechouart selling copies of their songs to the crowd. Maybe there was a better way for her and Nico to make money. A way for them to tell the truth about Pyotr and Angela. Nico could play. She could sing. She'd use the money sewed into her dress to buy pencil and paper, and Nico, who knew about selling rags for paper, would get a printer to make hundreds of copies. If the Fiancé of the North was "strong and full of worth," wasn't Pyotr more, a Russian Prince? Maura's dear sister, Angela, was not only young and beautiful, she was an Angel from the Goutte-d'Or. Everyone in Paris knew the Goutte-d'Or. Nico would help because he believed her, because he loved music, because he liked to talk to everyone about things like justice and dignity. They'd start right away, tomorrow, Bastille Day, near the parade. And maybe eventually they'd persuade the world to find the real killer.

11

The morning after Bastille Day, Clarie sat down to write a letter. It was not an easy task. Even to begin "Dear Madame Séverine" seemed oddly intimate. Yet that is what Clarie decided to do. She wasn't sure how else to address the famous writer, and she had to assume that someone so notorious enjoyed being referred to by her first name. Of course, it was only polite that Clarie go on to introduce herself, which she did, as "a teacher at the Lycée Lamartine, who has come to know Francesca Laurenzano, a charwoman at the school and the mother of the dead girl, Angela." Clarie held her pen aloft. She had reached the very point of the letter, recruiting Séverine to search for Maura.

"I very much admired your defense of the Russian girls being held at the Saint-Lazare Prison." That was true, honest. "I know that you have often defended those who are among the poorest and most despised." True again. "And I also know that you are famous for your ability to carry out investigations." Actually, that is what Bernard had told Clarie, in a rather dismissive way. "This makes me hopeful that once you learn about the plight of Francesca Laurenzano, you will widen your interest in this case to include the search for her younger daughter, Maura, who may be in danger." There.

Clarie went on to describe Francesca's poverty and the circumstances, as far as she knew them, of Maura's disappearance. After closing with the usual respectful flourish required by gentility, she sealed the letter in an envelope, addressed it to the offices of *L'Echo de Paris*, and announced to Rose that she was going to the post office. If all went well, someone else would be taking up the case of the missing girl.

The next day Clarie made her way to the kiosk at the Square d'Anvers several times to peruse the headlines, even though she knew that there was little chance that anything new would be reported. She was about to try again on Saturday morning when the doorbell rang.

"I'll get it, Rose," she called, since she was near the foyer. When Clarie swung open the door, she saw a young boy with a mail bag strapped across his chest. A pneumatic letter carrier.

"Madame Martin?"

"Yes." Clarie flushed as her heart contracted in her chest. The last time she had received a "little blue," it had brought news of Angela's death. Could something terrible have happened to Maura or Francesca? Or Bernard? The boy thrust a thin light blue letter toward her, and before she recovered enough to thank him, he turned and ran down the stairs. The return address was simple: Séverine.

Gazing at the envelope as she retreated into the parlor, Clarie almost ran into Rose, who had come out of the kitchen.

"Madame Clarie, a letter?" Rose asked, as she wiped her hands on her apron.

"Just something from the school," Clarie murmured. This was not the time for confidences, not until she knew what was in the pneu.

"Then I'll go back to Luca, while you read it," Rose responded, before returning to the kitchen where Jean-Luc was taking his time finishing his breakfast. Clarie, for the hundredth time that year, whispered a prayer of gratitude for having someone as devoted and discreet as Rose in her home. Then she sank into an armchair and tore open the fragile envelope. The script, in purple ink, was bold, the contents brief.

"Dear Madame Martin, I am home from 11 to 2 today. 14 Boulevard Montmartre, 4th floor. I hope to see you. Séverine."

Clarie's mouth gaped open as the hand holding the letter dropped into her lap. This Séverine expected that she, a teacher and wife and mother, would, just like that, drop everything and come to visit a notorious, divorced woman. This was outrageous. Or was it? Clarie picked up the all-too-brief message again. Séverine was not refusing Clarie's request to help find Maura. In fact, by her invitation, she seemed to be stating her willingness to get involved. Clarie got up and began to pace back and forth over the floral carpet in front of the armchairs. If she accepted, what terrible thing could happen? And if it meant that Maura would be safely returned to Francesca? Clarie stopped and folded her arms, fortifying herself. Yes. She'd take Luca to the park, read to him, put him down for his nap, and, if she still had the nerve, she'd do it.

Hours later, Clarie was examining a short, gray homespun jacket wondering whether she should put it on, despite the fact that the day was already beastly hot. Pressing her lips together, she decided against it. Her shirtwaist dress was teacherly and prim enough to express her utter respectability. She thrust the jacket back into the armoire and picked up her straw hat. She pinned it with more force and decisiveness than necessary in her hair, which was pulled back in a neat chignon. She took a look in the mirror. It was now or never. Another white lie delivered to the faithful Rose, and she would be on her way.

After rushing down the stairs and out of the entryway, Clarie turned and started her journey down the familiar rue Rodier. The Boulevard Montmartre was a short link in the chain of so-called "Grand

Boulevards," the new wide thoroughfares that formed a semicircle around the center of Paris. Threading her way through the crowded street, she reflected on how rarely she spent time in the fashionable districts of shops and arcades. She tried for a few minutes to think of what she was doing as an excursion. But as she waited for the traffic of cabs and omnibuses to slow on the rue de Maubeuge, she had to acknowledge that to consider this an "excursion" was to ignore the obvious.

Her chest fluttered so hard, she felt as if a wild bird inside her was throwing itself against a cage. She was visiting a woman, but it felt like an assignation. Aware of her growing anxiety, she entered the cross section with utmost care. She hardly looked from side to side as she wound her way down to the boulevards. She repeated in her mind, like a calming mantra, the question she had asked just hours ago: What terrible thing could happen?

So intent had she become that she was startled when she reached the boulevards. At first, she had trouble getting her bearings. It was as if she had walked onto a stage, the theatrical spectacle of Paris high life. Men in top hats and women in silk dresses strolled, peering into shop windows or scrutinizing each other. The inviting aroma of coffee and the murmur of conversation and tinkle of plates and silverware rose from the outdoor cafés dotting the boulevard in every direction. Tender green-leaved trees lined the broad sidewalks, lending a freshness to the summer's air. Even the horse hooves sounded more genteel on the wooden cobbles, and the gas lamps rising in the middle of the broad avenue performed the act of dividing the chaotic traffic with balletic grace.

She had to search for addresses because they were obscured by the commercial establishments on the ground and the bannered names of newspapers, manufacturers and political associations inhabiting the floors above. Keeping careful track, she was suddenly inhibited by a ragged line of people of all ages and social classes chattering in English and French. The big signs and display told her that they were waiting to get into Paris's famous wax museum. She shuddered. The Musée

Grévin was as notorious for its lifelike dioramas of torture and infamous crimes as for its promise to offer a peek into the private lives of prominent Parisians. After noting the address, number 10, she hurried past the double-doored entrance emblazoned with the museum's name. She was close. Taking the temporary respite provided by an empty wall, she stood and shaded her eyes to survey the balconies jutting from almost every building. She could not imagine what it was like to live amidst all this hubbub. It was so alien to her that she might have lost heart if she had not heard a female voice cutting through the cries of cabmen and the rumble of omnibuses. "Hallo down there!" Clarie craned her neck and saw an exceedingly blond woman waving at her. "Madame Martin, come up!" she shouted with no more self-consciousness than if she had been in a country village.

Clarie responded with a reluctant wave. There was no going back. At number 14, the door to the courtyard clicked open automatically, for, according to a sign near the main entrance, the building served a number of businesses, including the anti-Semitic newspaper, *La Libre Parole*. This gave Clarie another reason to shudder. She remembered the hatred that newspaper had fomented during the anti-Israelite riots in Nancy, and couldn't believe it was still thriving, still beating the drums against Dreyfus, and against people like the Singers. She climbed past the thrumming of the printing presses on the second floor and muffled mahogany-enclosed residences on the third.

When she arrived out of breath on the fourth floor, she caused quite a stir. Behind the door marked "Madame Séverine," barking, yipping, and shouting broke out. "Sit! Quiet!" Clarie heard, and finally, "dear Augustine, do take our rambunctious Rip into the kitchen." Clarie was raising her arm to knock, when the door flew open and a woman stood before her, holding a puggish mutt in her arms.

Clarie knew at once that this was Séverine, for no servant would greet you in a florid silk gown and felt slippers.

"Madame Martin, please come in," the woman said as she stood aside to let Clarie into the foyer.

"Thank you. I'm pleased you could see me," Clarie murmured as she was led into a room that looked more like a greenhouse, or a menagerie, or even a museum, than a parlor. Palm trees and cacti filled every corner. Fresh flowers sprung from vases on the coffee table and desk. Besides what sounded like at least two dogs howling, as if imprisoned behind a door, and the pooch being held and petted in Séverine's arms, there was a bird, a beady-eyed blue-and-green parrot giving out occasional squawks from a cage suspended on a tall stand. Newspapers lay in piles on the floor by the desk, which was laden with books and papers, and pens and pencils, gathered like soldiers ready for action, by the inkpot. In addition to all this, there was an embellished version of the usual: a few floral-patterned sitting chairs, a sofa bursting with pillows and covered with a chintz of bright gold, green and crimson stripes overlaid with a fleur de lis pattern. Finally, covering the walls and spreading onto almost every available surface, a myriad of photographs, lithographs and paintings. The most impressive of these was a gigantic portrait of a handsome, bearded man hanging above the sofa. Not only was the painting in a gilded frame, there was also a velvet curtain edging the top and sides, as if it were a memorial.

"That's Jules Vallès, the great Communard and anarchist, the man who taught me everything I know about the newspaper business, and about life, real life," Séverine said, seemingly aware of Clarie's bewilderment.

"He was one of those who had been exiled after 1871?" Clarie asked, as she stared at the commanding face of the anarchist.

"Oh, yes. Exiled and persecuted, but never cowed nor defeated. I do so miss him." After expelling a mournful sigh, she changed the mood by pointing, with a certain pride, to a small painting on the side wall. "That's me. By Renoir, a few years ago. He made my hair darker than it was even then." She smiled ruefully as if recognizing that she was not as pretty—or prettified—as the picture, although she certainly was striking. Of medium height, she had lively periwinkle eyes and a startling fringe of tight, almost white curls around her face. "As for all of this," she spread out her free arm, "I like to be surrounded by living things, my greenery and my beasts. So necessary in the city, don't you think?"

Clarie did not know what to answer. Her "living things" were neither animals nor plants, they were Jean-Luc, Bernard and Rose. And she certainly would have never dreamed of abandoning her children, even to the best of fathers.

"My roses, too, are necessary," Séverine continued undaunted by Clarie's silence. "When I was cutting them, I admit, I was hoping you would come."

"Thank you. And I am hoping that you can help." There, she had said it. That's why she was here and for no other reason.

"Please sit," Séverine said, gesturing toward one of the chairs.

Clarie settled on the edge of a seat, near the cage, which gave off a slightly gamey odor. She pressed her gloved hands together, wondering how to begin.

Séverine sat down on the sofa and gave her panting pet a kiss on his forehead before setting him down beside her. After a few strokes on his back, the mutt laid his head on her lap and sighed in peaceful surrender. "There now," she smiled at Clarie. Before her guest could speak, she called out toward the closed door, "Dear Augustine, chocolate and biscuits, and no more dogs."

"Oh no, I really can't stay." Clarie almost leaped out of her chair.

"But it's to celebrate your coming. That's why I'm allowing myself a second cup for the day."

"I—"

The bird gave out a terrible shriek before Clarie could formulate another excuse.

"Monsieur de Coco Bleu, be quiet, so I can talk to our guest," Séverine said in a sharp voice, although it was obvious she was not angry. "Go on," she said to Clarie. "Tell me everything you know about Angela and Maura Laurenzano." She picked up a small notebook and pencil that Clarie had not noticed on the coffee table, and waited.

Haltingly at first, and then in a rush, as though relieved to be able to confess her involvement and her fears for Maura, Clarie talked while Séverine took notes. Just as she was describing her last visit to the Goutte-d'Or, the kitchen door opened, and a tall, older woman in a striped cotton dress and apron entered with a silver tray. She placed it on the crowded coffee table in front of the sofa.

"Oh, dear Augustine, thank you," Séverine said, and she reached up to clasp the woman's hand. "This is my housekeeper, Augustine, who has been with me for many, many years," she said to Clarie, and to her housekeeper, "And this is Madame Martin, who has come to see me about a very interesting case."

"So I hear." The voice was a little gruff. She gave Clarie a nod before leaving the room with the declaration that she'd "better get back to the pooches."

That brief exchange warmed Clarie to Séverine, for she recognized that the two women were as close as she and Rose. If not closer. She could not imagine Rose ever daring to be gruff with her. Despite her initial bewilderment, Clarie found herself enjoying Séverine's and Augustine's verdant little realm. With their "beasts," they were like a family, an unusual one, but a family nevertheless.

"Madame Martin," Séverine asked as she poured the chocolate, "do you think the Laurenzano girls were telling you the truth about the Russian anarchist and what the three of them had done?"

Clarie picked up a thin flowered cup and took a sip. Bernard had asked the same question, in a very different way, with the presumption that they probably had been deceiving her. "I think Angela was truthful in what she said, but that she didn't tell everything she could have," Clarie responded, remembering how Maura had cut her sister off as soon as the name Barbereau came up. She frowned. "I think the other one lied about what happened to their boss. But to protect herself and to protect her sister." Clarie took another sip, giving herself a moment to think while Séverine divided a biscuit between herself and the dog.

"This may sound odd, but although Maura lied, in a way I felt she was more truly honest than her sister or her mother, because she sees the world as it is and is willing to confront its unfairness. A liar who sees through to the truth and acts on it."

"Not odd at all," Séverine said, as she flicked some crumbs off her robe; "it sounds like the girl is poor, young and defiant. A struggler and a survivor. We must find her."

We? "I was hoping," Clarie ventured, "that you might be able to use your contacts among the lower classes, the press and the police to help find Maura. I'm sure you know better than I where to look for a runaway girl."

"But you know what she looks like."

Clarie placed her cup back on the tray. "Really, I can't. I have a child and a husband and—"

"Oh, husbands!" Séverine threw up her hands.

Clarie was shocked. She had never heard anyone use the word so dismissively. "My husband is a good man," she said, feeling her face redden as she shrunk back into the chair. "He is working for the Labor Exchange, and he goes to meetings to get justice for Dreyfus." *Things that Séverine certainly should appreciate and honor.*

"My dear, it is not men I object to." Séverine's eyebrows arched expectantly, as if she was certain that Clarie, like all of Paris, knew that she had taken on many lovers. "It's when they become *husbands* with all the laws and customs on their side. That's when one has to learn how to deal with them and their presumption of authority."

Clarie wrinkled her brow. "I don't see how I can get involved any more than I have been." I can't search for a fugitive runaway, she thought, and I cannot join forces with a woman of such scandalous reputation. Yet at the same time, here she was enjoying that woman's hospitality and asking her to save Maura Laurenzano.

"Really?" Séverine picked up her cup and took a drink, never taking her eyes off Clarie. They were no longer twinkling and friendly; they seemed to be piercing through Clarie's mind, reading its confusion.

"What I like about your husband already is you, that you are the kind of woman we are counting on to show what women can do. Teachers have always led the way. How can we forget that Louise Michel was a teacher before she became a revolutionary?"

"Red Louise," famed, exiled Communard, the beloved heroine of socialists and anarchists alike. Clarie shook her head. "I'm not like that."

"Perhaps because no one has suggested it to you," Séverine said, placing her cup in its saucer.

"The violence. I could never sanction it."

"Oh, my dear, you must know that most of the men and women who call themselves anarchists these days have rejected violence. And besides, I'm not saying we should foment revolution, I'm only suggesting that together we might find this lost girl."

"Yes, I know," Clarie whispered. This time instead of blushing for Bernard, she blushed for herself. *What terrible thing could happen?* The risk of hurting her reputation seemed a small thing compared to having seen Angela, a beautiful young woman, transformed into a pallidly green corpse. Or the fear that the same thing could happen to Maura. But Clarie didn't like dealing with violence and murder. Or arguing with Bernard. She had to think. She got up from the chair. "I must go. I'm sorry. My son. . . ."

"Of course." Séverine also rose from her seat.

Clarie held out her hand, to say good-bye and thank her hostess. "Will you please let me know if you find out anything," she asked, even as she feared that her cowardly reluctance to help forfeited her right to make any demands.

"Yes," Séverine said, softening her demeanor. "As long as you promise me you'll think about what I said. You've got some fight in you, I know it. Just like that girl, Maura."

Like Maura? Clarie had more than once had the same thought. But she was not about to reveal it. Not now. Not when opening her heart more could lead her to do something foolish.

Tail wagging, the little mutt followed Séverine and Clarie to the foyer, and the parrot, freed from human restraint, began to squawk. When the door closed behind her, Clarie sighed with relief. She'd done it. She'd gotten someone else involved and willing to help.

12

IF CLARIE HAD ANY WORRIES about how she was going to keep her visit to Séverine secret, they vanished as soon as Bernard walked in the door, for he was eager to convey his own news. After kissing Clarie and Jean-Luc, he asked them to guess who was coming to town.

"Your mother?" Clarie could not suppress a slight grimace. It was too early; she wasn't prepared for the outings and the shopping.

"Noooo."

"No?"

"David. David Singer. He sent a telegram to the Exchange asking us to join him for dinner Sunday evening at the Hôtel de l'Europe."

"Tomorrow! How lovely." Clarie was genuinely pleased, for Bernard, who had not developed any close friendships since his arrival in Paris, and for herself. "I don't suppose Noémie and the children will be with him."

"Unfortunately no. He's coming for an important meeting about the Dreyfus case on Monday night. He wants me to go with him. But, of course, he also wants to see you and Luca."

"Of course." She jiggled Jean-Luc on her hip. "Uncle David. Won't that be nice?" And nice it was to have a special occasion to take her mind off the Laurenzanos and the things she wasn't telling her husband.

On Sunday afternoon, Clarie and Bernard, after consultations with Rose and Jean-Luc, decided that the evening dinner with David Singer offered the perfect occasion to put their Luca in short pants for the first time. "You'll be a big boy, and Uncle David will be so proud of you," Clarie said as she knelt down and gave her son a hug.

"Maman!" Jean-Luc objected.

She was pressing too hard, because it was so hard to let go. The next thing you knew, they would be cutting his curls, and he really would be a boy. No longer a baby. She looked up at Bernard, who smiled down at them from his chair. He reached over and clasped Clarie's shoulder. "Your eyes are so beautiful when they have tears in them, but there's no need to be sad."

"Yes, it's silly," she said as she got to her feet. *And foolish.* At moments like these, she felt there was no reason in the world to care about anything except her little family. She gave Bernard's hand a tug before going to get Luca's short pants. Tonight after dinner, after putting Luca to bed, she resolved to tell Bernard that she had met the notorious Séverine and assure him that nothing more would come of it.

As it turned out, their dinner with David Singer inspired a very different kind of resolve. It began splendidly. As always, David was impeccably dressed, so much so that Clarie half-expected that some day he would walk in swinging a silver-knobbed cane to complete the image of almost dandified fashionableness. His frock coat, vest, trousers and top hat were all of a matching luxurious ash-gray. His silk ebony cravat drooped slightly down over his immaculately white shirt, while his equally black, waxed mustache curved up, forming two sharp points on his clean-shaven face. Yet despite the elegance of his appearance and of the restaurant he had chosen, his first reaction was to grab Jean-Luc from Bernard's arms and swing him in the air.

"Such a handsome lad you are," he kept saying.

Watching, Clarie almost laughed with pleasure. It was David's heartfelt joy in children and absolute devotion to family that gave her such deep affection for a man who could easily seem excessively formal. And, of course, there was his loyalty to her and Bernard.

Once he relinquished Jean-Luc to his father, David kissed Clarie on both cheeks, tickling her with his stiff mustache, before telling her how beautiful and elegant she looked. Then he led them to a reserved table in an alcove of the vast restaurant and announced that he had ordered dinner. "I hope you don't mind, but I know you have to get the little one home, and we have so much to catch up on," he said as he pulled out a chair for Clarie. Of course she didn't mind. He had arranged for Clarie to sit beside Jean-Luc, while he and Bernard sat across from them on the other side of the square table. "I want to drink both of you in with my eyes all evening," he explained to her.

Clarie blushed, knowing that her worn crimson silk dress was far from elegant. She knew, too, that David's flattery came from a reflex she always found a bit discomfiting, his need to demonstrate, even in the most intimate circles, that he was a well brought-up man of means. She presumed, or at least Bernard had explained, that part of this need derived from being an Israelite, always having to prove himself to others. The meal was yet another aspect of this. As she worked her way through the fish, the beef and the cheeses served by over-solicitous tuxedoed waiters, Clarie found herself wishing that David hadn't gone to such expense and could be more relaxed. This is why she was at first relieved when the wine, ordered particularly to go with each course, began to have an effect on him.

While the men were drinking their brandy and Clarie was trying to get Jean-Luc to eat his chocolate ice cream without smearing his new outfit, she heard David declare, in a voice that rose ever so slightly above the polite murmur of the restaurant, "I tell you, this is going to be the cause of our time."

For an instant, the chiming of crystal and the sound of silver on plates stopped at the tables near them. David closed his eyes, bit down on his lower lip, and waited. When the murmurs resumed again, he added, "Don't you agree?"

"Yes," Bernard said mildly, "but I don't know how you are going to get the working man involved. For him, it's a battle among two factions of the bourgeoisie."

"That's short-sighted. Justice for one is justice for all."

Clarie reached for a napkin. If the chocolate got on Jean-Luc's little blue shirt, she and Rose would have a devil of a time getting it out.

"Yes, but they have their priorities. Shorter hours. Decent wages."

Jean-Luc's legs began to wave petulantly: "More, more."

"Just a little more. We don't want to get a tummy-ache. Let me give it to you," Clarie said as she picked up the spoon.

"Can't you educate them, as a man of law?" This was David. The two of them were going on and on as if they were at some grand hostess's formal dinner and had just removed themselves to the library with all the other men to drink brandy and smoke cigars.

"*They* are educating *me*."

How often had she heard Bernard tell her this. The workers educating him, him educating the workers. Well, she thought, as she carefully measured out an unspillable bit of ice cream, at least neither of them smokes cigars.

"Ah, Maître Martin, still much too modest," exclaimed David, as he reached over to slap Bernard on the back.

Just then, Jean-Luc bubbled some of the ice cream out of his lips.

Oh, husbands! As soon as Clarie thought those words, she felt better. She even felt like laughing as she wiped Jean-Luc's mouth and put him on her lap. What would Emilie think when she told her about her encounter with Séverine? Oh, husbands, indeed. Fortunately, the discussion was reaching its grand conclusion. She whispered in Jean-Luc's ear that they would be going soon.

"Yes," by now David was speaking almost in a hissing whisper, "but the defense of one man, a man of a despised race, gets to the heart of what the Republic should be. Do we want it to be only the bulwark of the Army and the Church, or does it stand for every man?"

And women, Clarie thought as she bounced Jean-Luc on her knee. *Does the Republic stand for women?*

Bernard lifted his glass and clinked against the one that David was holding aloft. "Let's agree. Both struggles are important. I'll do what I can."

"And women?" The words slipped out.

"Do you mean," said David, turning his attention to Clarie, "are any women involved in fighting for Dreyfus? Certainly his wife has written letters pleading for his release," David said in a matter-of-fact way, as if this matter of fact was exactly as it should be.

"To men, she wrote letters pleading to men, like a good wife," Clarie blurted out before she realized that the wine had also had its effect on her. She hadn't really been thinking about Dreyfus at all. She had been thinking of exploited women, beaten women, lost girls, *that cause*.

"Right or wrong," Bernard said, as he got up to take Jean-Luc from Clarie's lap, "men have the power to change things."

13

SÉVERINE'S SECOND "PNEU" ARRIVED ON Monday. Rose scurried to answer the bell because Clarie had just put Jean-Luc down for his afternoon nap. This time, Clarie did not even bother to offer an explanation as she tore open the envelope, fervently hoping that it would contain good news. Instead it proffered another invitation. "I have learned a great deal since our last meeting. I will be at the café at the corner of Rodier and Trudaine from 8 to 8:30 tonight. Please meet me there. S."

Stunned by Séverine's assumption that she would saunter out at night by herself, Clarie sank into a chair and stared at the fireplace.

"Is it bad news, Madame Clarie?"

"No, Rose. Nothing like that."

A look somewhere between puzzlement and dismay shadowed across Rose's face. Clarie closed her eyes. Surely, given her increasingly mysterious coming and goings, Rose sensed something was amiss. For the first time, Clarie feared that her faithful companion, the almost-grandmother of her child, might suspect the worst, that Clarie was betraying her marriage. Horrified by this possibility, Clarie tried to calm her racing pulse by analyzing what betrayal could mean under these circumstances. To act seemed like a betrayal of Bernard. But, if she did not act, would she be betraying something inside herself? And if she confided in Rose, would she not be putting her in an impossible position? Séverine had been clever. She knew the café was a mere half-block from Clarie's apartment. Barely an unescorted walk for a respectable woman.

"It's a friend," Clarie finally said. "She wants to discuss something with me tonight. She wrote that she finds my advice helpful." She looked directly at Rose, as if to prove the veracity of her words. "Monsieur Martin is going to a meeting after work, so if you could stay with Jean-Luc. . . ."

"Of course, Madame Clarie."

Longing to escape Rose's gaze, Clarie got up and walked to her desk. "I think I'll try to read a chapter or two, while Luca is sleeping."

"And I'd better get to the washing up," Rose said as she headed toward the kitchen.

Clarie put her hand on her desk, thankful her back was turned as Rose left the room. She stared at her bookshelf for a moment, before picking out a treatise on morality, a text from her days at the teachers' college. She opened the book, but didn't bother reading. She knew what it would say. It was as if the maxim "To do one's duty is the goal of life" had been branded with a holy fire onto the cover and into her memory. How earnestly all of them, the would-be teachers of a new generation of girls, had talked of duty. Duty to family, duty to students, duty to the Republic, duty to others. Yet no one had ever spoken of anarchists, or lost girls.

At eight o'clock that evening, Clarie did not hesitate to put on the short broadcloth jacket over her prim shirtwaist. The more covered, the more protected she felt, from the eyes of neighbors, the curiosity of the concierge, and the perplexed glances of her beloved Rose. She tiptoed through the parlor as if not wanting to awaken Jean-Luc, but really as a way of not having to explain herself again to the woman who was caring for her child. When she arrived at the café across from the Square d'Anvers, she spotted Séverine immediately. She had taken an outside table under the gas jet which lit the entrance. She stood up to greet Clarie.

"I was afraid you wouldn't come."

"I almost didn't. I can't do this. It's only because—"

"Your husband is at a meeting. I know. The Society for the Rights of Man convenes only a few doors from me."

"You knew that." Clarie did not even try to hide the chill in her voice. She didn't like being manipulated.

"Yes. If *he* is spending the evening answering a moral call to duty, is there any reason why *you* should not?"

"And what duty would that be?" At least Séverine had dressed in a respectable manner. A collar as high as Clarie's, a dark blue jacket veiling her rather buxom figure, her showy white-blond curls subdued by a small hat.

"What duty? Helping a poor mother find her lost daughter. Rescuing two innocent imprisoned girls from the hands of brutal authority."

Clarie sank into one of the wrought-iron chairs in front of Séverine's table. "I don't see how I—"

"Come with me tonight. That's all I ask," Séverine said as she sat down. "Perhaps you will see Maura. At least you will have a chance to listen, and to know what the anarchists are doing."

Anarchists? "No, I can't—" It wasn't only the impropriety that stopped Clarie. It was the idea of doing something dangerous and foolish. What if the *Petit Parisien* had been right? What if it was the anarchists who had killed Angela? What if—

"My dear, I'm not drawing you into some kind of secret meeting," Séverine said, almost as if she had been reading Clarie's mind. "I'm only asking you to come with me to a poor man's café, where this Pyotr, the Russian boy who was killed, used to hold forth."

Clarie kept shaking her head. "You said you had found something," she insisted. Her voice trembled between a childish sense of betrayal and full-grown anger.

"Yes, I have found out some things." Perhaps in response to Clarie's querulousness, Séverine began to sound impatient. "I know where the anarchists who are Pyotr's friends meet. I know that Maura used to go to the café to listen. Perhaps she goes there now for solace. You've seen her. You'd be able to pick her out. And," Séverine paused, "there's this." She picked up a piece of paper that lay near her cup of coffee. "Someone is defending the Russian anarchist. One of my sources saw a young boy and an old Italian street musician going around and singing a song that claims Angela and Pyotr are innocent."

"A boy?" Clarie's lips parted. *Who?* The sisters had only mentioned one boy, the Russian. But, of course, he could have had an entire coterie following his example.

Séverine handed Clarie a printed page. "They are selling these for a centime."

Clarie took the paper and held it up to the flickering, yellow light. When she saw the title, "Pieter's Song," she gasped. That odd spelling; it was like Maura's.

Pieter a boy from Tzarist Russia
Loved mankind with all his heart
He came to Paris with but one hope
In the workers' struggle to take his part.
He knew the way of the bourgeois state
Was to turn all men against each other
He said we were born to cooperate
Not to compete with one another

Why can't we all be free
To work with joy and dignity

To earn our bread and all we need
To live, to love, to play, to breathe?

Clarie exhaled slowly. So far, these lines could have been written by anyone sympathetic to anarchism.

Our blond-haired boy, this Russian Prince
Of goodness and gentility
In Paris his fair Princess met
An angel raised in poverty
A beauty barely more than a child
Our Angela of the Goutte-d'Or
So innocent and sweetly mild
She'd never loved a man before.

This time the chorus began "All *they wanted* was to be free. . . ." Of course, because Pyotr and Angela were dead. The person who wrote this must have known and loved them. Clarie's breathing quickened as her suspicions—and hopes—mounted. *Maura.* She traced the next verses with a white-gloved finger.

So often our girls tender and poor
Get bosses who dare to want more and more
And when she refused to be his whore
A rain of cruel blows our Angela bore.

In her mind's eye, Clarie saw the faded bruises on Angela's cheeks, the scissors and single lock of dark hair on the floor. It had to be Maura.

The kindest of men could not bear to see
This haughty bourgeois brutality.
So Pieter helped his angel to flee
And taught her what a new world could be.

Clarie's relief that Maura was alive was fast turning to chagrin. Did she really believe that masquerading as a boy would keep her safe from the police or a killer? She was about to say something when Séverine reached over and pointed to the last stanzas. "This is what's going to get the authorities up in arms."

But this earthly world they will never see
For both of them are dead
Killed by a monster that still goes free
And they are blamed instead.
The police, the press, the men who rule,
Why do they blacken Pieter's name?
Why do they say a sweet young girl
Would want to bomb, to kill, to maim?

Why do they tell these dreadful lies?
Why do they innocents defame?
Because it is their evil spies
Who lie and bomb and kill and maim.

It ended with a bravado flourish, so characteristic of the girl that Clarie had come to know: *BOTH CHORUSES SHOULD BE SUNG IN OUR STREETS 100 TIMES!!*

"Well?" Séverine gazed intently at her companion.

Clarie let the sheet of paper droop toward the table. "It's Maura," she said, furrowing her brow. "She's parading around as a boy. When I went to her apartment I saw broken scissors and a lock of her hair on the floor. She cut it off to go around in disguise, and presumably has made the scissors into a kind of weapon." Clarie shook her head. "Foolish girl."

"Very good, my dear," Séverine said as she retrieved the song from Clarie. "I read a certain love sickness in all this and thought it might be her, but needed confirmation."

"Do you think the police already know?" Clarie wasn't sure whether or not she hoped they did. At least, if they caught Maura, she would be safe.

"The police. Oh yes. Either they know now or will eventually," Séverine said, with a shrug. "They've got their eyes out for anyone fomenting subversion. After all, there's been one bomb explosion and two murders."

"Two?"

"Barbereau and Angela Laurenzano."

"Maura and Angela insisted, as this song does, that their friend Pyotr was murdered too," Clarie murmured, staring at the red-checked tablecloth.

"Three, then."

Three murders. If the man has killed more than once, what's to stop him? "Maura is making herself a target, trying to flush him out."

"Oh, yes. The girl's in danger, no doubt about that."

Séverine said these words so dispassionately, so authoritatively, while Clarie's head teemed with frightening possibilities. "Do you really think it's wise to depend on the information you're getting from the anarchists?" Clarie asked. "The *Petit Parisien* said the killer could be someone from a terrorist cell."

"No, no, no." Again, with such authority. "That's exactly why I want you to come with me. To show you that the anarchists are not fomenting this violence. And to help find Maura. That is, if you still want to find her. . . ."

Clarie's eyes roved over the lines and blocks of the tablecloth. It was no longer the lock of Maura's dark hair that she was seeing in her mind's eye, but Angela's pallid corpse. "So now, he has reason to kill Maura. But why kill Angela in the first case?"

"We don't know. That's why we investigate." Séverine tugged at Clarie's hand. "Come with me. Tonight. If you see Maura, we can find a way to help her. If not, you'll see that the anarchists are good men who," she picked up the song, "only want 'to work with joy and dignity,' 'to live, to love, to play, to breathe'—free." She scrutinized the sheet as if an idea had just struck her. "This is really quite good. I think I will try to get it published. I'll call it 'Requiem for an Anarchist' by an anonymous street singer."

At first Clarie was repelled by this sudden shift in Séverine's tone. She wanted to grab the page and demand that the reporter not use Maura for her own gain. But almost at the same time, Clarie realized that she was seeing, tonight, who Séverine really was. She was making no effort to cover up the infamous journalist that Bernard disdained, the writer who uncompromisingly pursued her radical causes and her stories, and had no compunction about inserting herself into them. Ironically, this willing revelation of her ambitions made Clarie decide to trust her. After all, the fact that Séverine had more than one motive for wanting to find Maura, gave her all the more reason to pursue the search until she succeeded. Could Clarie do so much less?

"All right," Clarie whispered, "I'll go with you. But I can't take very long," she insisted. "I've got to be back before Bernard returns." Clarie was still a wife and mother. For Bernard to arrive home while she was still gone would be shocking.

Séverine understood and promised that as soon as "their mission" was over, she would hire a cab and drop Clarie off at a corner so that no one would see her descending from the carriage.

They took the now-familiar path past the Square d'Anvers, onto the Boulevard Rochechouart, and along part of the wall surrounding the great hospital. They walked rapidly, Clarie with lowered eyes and Séverine, chin jutting forward with proud insouciance, both of them signaling that no man's flirtation and gaze would stop them. Intent on getting it over with, Clarie did not bother to observe their route. There was no reason to remember the direction of the narrow, curving, sewage-infested cobbled streets. She would never return to them. She was only here to find Maura.

At last they got to the café, which was nothing like the working-class establishment that Bernard had taken her to. There, gas jets lit up the interior and exterior, and a piano gaily pounded out music. There had been room for dancing, and a multitude of tables big and small. But this café, hardly bigger than Clarie's parlor, was lit only by the candles standing on a high wooden bar and on five or six equally shabby long, low tables. The nearest of these barely left enough room for Clarie and Séverine to enter and stand by the door. A hush fell as more and more of the drinkers noticed their presence.

"Please don't let us disturb you," Séverine said in a loud voice, breaking the silence. "We are here to hear what you have to say. I am Séverine, the reporter." She waited for those who recognized her name to give approving nods. "And this is a teacher." Another dramatic pause. "Like our own Louise Michel." By this time everyone was nodding. Clarie avoided their eyes. Her shoes lightly stuck to a floor made tacky by spilled drink mixed with ashes. The café reeked with the sour odor of hard-worked bodies, and cheap tobacco and alcohol.

"We were about to read from the Bible," one of the men called out.

Clarie looked up, startled. A Bible at an anarchists' café?

"And what Bible would that be?" Séverine retorted with confidence, obviously pleased at having been recognized.

"Anything by the man who said 'Property is Theft'!" he retorted, to the laughter and clapping of his table.

"Proudhon," Séverine whispered to Clarie.

Clarie had heard the name, but she certainly had not read him. She stood up straight, not wanting to touch the wall, which she feared might be crawling with vermin.

The short stocky man waved his arm as he declared "I dedicate this reading to our bourgeois state." This drew even more hoots and hollers. He cleared his throat, held the book near a candle, and read: "'To be governed is to be watched over, inspected, spied on, directed, legislated at, regulated, docketed, indoctrinated, preached at, controlled, assessed, weighed, censored, ordered about, by men who have neither the right nor the knowledge nor the virtue.'"

"Hear! Hear!" someone shouted.

"'To be governed means to be, at each operation, at each transaction, at each movement, noted, registered, controlled, taxed, stamped, measured, valued, assessed, patented, licensed, authorized, endorsed, admonished, hampered, reformed, rebuked,' and finally," the reader said, spreading out his arms, "'arrested.'"

When the cheers died down, the brawny bartender, whose damp opened shirt revealed a hairy chest, turned to Clarie and Séverine. "What is it that you want with us?"

Séverine ignored the suspicious edge in his voice. "We are looking for Maura Laurenzano. She is missing. She is the sister of the dead girl, Angela. We understand she used to come here to listen to the Russian, Pyotr Ivanovich Balenov. Have any of you seen her?"

There was a general shaking of heads. Those who were bored, or already too drunk to care, began to lift their glasses.

"Have any of you heard 'Pieter's Song'? Do you know where the street singers are?"

"I've seen them," an old toothless man raised his hand. "At the Anarchist Soup Kitchen. It's a good song."

"Thank you," Séverine responded. "Anyone else?"

"Along the rue Marcadet, at dinner time, near a big café." This from one of the rough-looking women in a striped dress.

"Good!" Séverine said.

Clarie clasped her hands together and pressed them against her queasy stomach. These were not places where she wanted to go looking for the girl.

"And do you know where they live?"

Those who were not drinking either shook their heads or just stared at Séverine.

"I want to defend the young Russian anarchist women being so wrongly held at Saint-Lazare. I want to prove that they are not violent.

Did Pyotr ever talk of violence? Do you believe that he planted the bomb that went off in his cart?" Clarie heard pride in Séverine's bold assertions of her intentions and her capabilities.

"That girl who was moonin' after him, is that the one you're lookin' for?" asked the bartender, wiping his counter with a dirty cloth.

"Yes!" Séverine said, almost rising to her toes.

"Ain't been here."

Clarie grimaced. He had raised her hopes, too. She had been scanning the room, looking for Maura. There were only a few women dispersed among the men, none of them as young or as innocent as the Laurenzano girl.

"Then let's return to my last question. Pyotr, was he violent?" Séverine persisted.

Clarie shifted from one foot to another, longing for an answer that would prove Maura and Angela had been telling the truth.

"Nah, but he should have been," one drunk retorted. "It would have done us all more good."

"No!" one of the younger men shouted. "He saw what violence had done in his homeland. He always spoke of peaceful ways to get our freedom. Isn't that right?"

"Yeah. Yeah." The answer and the nodding came from a few patrons, who slammed their glasses on the tables in agreement.

"Well, I'll tell you what I think," a tall man standing amid the shadows and smoke at the back of the room said: "I think he was fooling us."

"What!" someone yelled in surprise.

"Yes, I think Pyotr Ivanovich was a true revolutionary, as we all should be, and that he knew how to build a bomb and was going to kill those bourgeois ladies in the fashion district. Just like those women who died in the Charity Bazaar fire. We didn't do it. But we could do the next one."

Suddenly all eyes were on Séverine and Clarie, two bourgeois ladies. Clarie closed her eyes. She prayed that her jacket was covering her enough to hide her heaving chest. She didn't belong here. This was all such a bad, foolish idea.

"Thank you!" Séverine said, showing no signs of shock or fright. "I will do my best to defend the Russian girls. And if any of you see the singers, contact me at *Le Petit Parisien* or *L'Echo de Paris*." Then, she linked her arm in Clarie's and led her out the doorway.

"That was terrible," Clarie said as soon as they were a block from the café. "To want to repeat something like the Charity Bazaar fire." Over a hundred upper-class girls and women had been burnt alive as they tried to flee a wall of fire rolling across the pretty displays they had set up for their annual charity fair.

"You know that was an accident. Or, as some say, God's punishment of *someone* for *something*."

Clarie noted the sarcasm in Séverine's response. "Of course, I know that." It had been in the papers for days. A movie projector had erupted into flames just as the Bazaar was getting under way. Clarie shuddered at the ironic horror of it. A machine promising the newest of pleasures causing the most ancient of nightmares—a storm of hellfire—to rain down upon the poor, screaming women.

Séverine shook her head as she pulled Clarie along. "That one could want something like that to happen again." The irritation directed at Clarie had become anger aimed at the man who had spoken with such cold hatred.

"But don't you see, some of these people are violent."

Séverine stopped and grabbed Clarie's other arm. "No, my dear," she said, forcing Clarie to look her in the eye, "that's not what I see at all. What I see are agents provocateurs. Two of them. But why two? Unless one is a police spy and the other a madman."

"Police spies," Clarie whispered. As in Maura's song, lying, hoping to provoke, in order to arrest. Or a madman on the loose.

Séverine began pulling Clarie along again. "I'd better get you home."

14

Martin had reason to worry. He put down his pencil and closed the books he had been perusing in the Labor Exchange's library. To keep his newly created position at the Bourse, he had to prove himself useful. But he didn't want merely to *prove* himself useful, he wanted to *be* useful. He glanced across the table at a youth mouthing each word of a newspaper article. It was workers like him that Martin wanted to help, to elevate, to enlighten. This is why he was here.

Martin yawned and rubbed his eyes. He was preparing a course on labor law and trying to figure out the best way to explain the snarl of regulations that limited worker freedoms. The class was scheduled to begin next week, and he desperately hoped someone would show up for it. As he picked up his bowler to go out for a reinvigorating walk, he was all too conscious of the fact that what he was doing, taking a few minutes for rest and refreshment, was a right none of the union men or women legally held. Not yet. Engrossed in how they might produce legislation for that right, he almost ran into the Bourse's reception clerk.

"Maître Martin!"

"Yes."

"This message has come for you." The man handed Martin a pneumatic letter.

"Thank you," Martin murmured as he scanned the thin blue envelope in vain for a return address. It wasn't from Clarie. Nothing terrible had happened at home. He pocketed it to read later.

The clerk stood aside to let Martin go first, then both of them took the stairs down toward the Exchange's main entrance. The clerk returned to his post, while Martin headed out into the sunshine. As he strolled toward the Place de la République he debated whether to stop at the corner café for a cup of coffee. No, he'd rather a bench under a tree. After he crossed the street to the square, he reached in his pocket, pulled out the pneu, and tore the envelope open. When he saw who the letter was from, he thanked God he had not attempted to read it at the Exchange.

"Maître Martin, I write as a matter of professional courtesy. Please meet me at the Café Madeleine, between three and four this afternoon. I have a serious matter to discuss with you. Jobert."

Martin was tempted to tear up the letter and forget it. He could see no good reason to meet in private with a police inspector. Yet he read it again and shook his head at the way, in these very few lines, Jobert had managed to put his considerable cunning on display. The appointment hour, since it was already almost three, did not give Martin much time to think about what to do. The place was easy to get to by omnibus, *and* it was posh, unlikely to be frequented by anyone from the unions. At the same time, the message conveyed a sense of urgency, without telling Martin anything. He closed his hand in a fist. If Jobert expected that he, Martin, would become a police spy or some other appendage of the government, just because he had once been a judge, because he had once worked for the state, well, then he needed to stop these suppositions once and for all.

Martin beat a hasty retreat to the Bourse to tell the receptionist that he was off to work at the Law Library of the Palais de Justice and would be in early tomorrow. Then, cursing the police inspector who had turned him into a deceiver, Martin set out for the omnibus.

Martin had to thread through a throng of tables serving contented well-dressed customers before he spotted Jobert, enjoying his cigar, at the back of the café, pointedly far from the windows. When he saw Martin, he jumped up to greet him and extended a hammy-pink hand. Martin did not take it. "Why am I here?" he demanded.

"Sit down," Jobert said, responding to Martin's rudeness with his own.

"I don't think that will be necessary."

Jobert peered at him and sucked on his cigar. As in their first meeting, the inspector's blue eyes conveyed an irritating superiority, as if he possessed some secret knowledge. And again, even more loathsomely, he proved that he did. After blowing out a cloud of his sweet-smelling smoke, he declared "I think you may want to sit down when I tell you what your wife has been up to."

"I don't see what business that is of yours—"

"Consorting with loose women, anarchists."

Martin dropped into the chair. "What do you mean? What loose women? What proof do you have?" The questions tumbled in rapid fire, bullets aimed at Jobert's impudence. Martin took off his bowler and placed it on the table.

"Séverine. You've heard of her, I presume. Close friend of the old, dead Communards. Divorcée. Child abandoner. Always skirting the law, if you'll excuse my *bon mot* for that thing she tends to lift for any man who comes along." Jobert chuckled, enjoying his own joke.

"And a good investigative journalist who doesn't let the police get away with their abuses." Why in God's name had Martin blurted out a defense of a woman he disdained? Unless, having shot blanks at Jobert, he had no choice but to send up his own smokescreen. He was still getting over the shock that Clarie had come to the attention of the Paris police. He was grateful, at least, for the relative coolness of the cavernous café and the uninterrupted low conversations surrounding them.

Jobert ran his tongue over his upper lip, almost touching his bushy gingery mustache. Finding some speck, he reached up and picked off a bit of the cigar's debris. He was in no hurry. Martin got the annoying feeling that he was enjoying himself. Finally, leaning forward, the inspector said, quietly, "I am doing this as a professional courtesy. No matter what side we are on, I trust we are both men of the law. It's not only that your wife is stepping out. She may also be putting herself in danger."

"What do you mean? How do you know all this?"

Jobert stretched back, as if to get a better look at Martin. His hand rested on the table, with the last of the burning cigar jutting up through his fingers. "As you well know, we keep some of our own men in strategic places. One of them, a good man, had gotten on to this Russian anarchist, Pyotr Balenov, only a few days before his demise. This man was at this stinking little working-class café last night when your wife appeared on the scene with the so-called journalist." Jobert crushed his stub into an ashtray and waited.

"Your man, an agent provocateur."

Jobert pursed his lips and nodded. "If that is what you insist on calling him."

"Yes, a police agent who tries to provoke a few fanatics to commit some violent crime so that you can prosecute anyone who calls himself an anarchist, even good union men."

"A man who protects the public. Upholds the laws. . . . Anyway," the smile was sardonic, "we're not talking about the Labor Exchange now. We're talking about your wife. Do you know what she was doing there?"

"No." That's all Martin intended to say about Clarie. No.

"Well, here's what I'm getting at. Generally, I think of these places as being filled with fools, but occasionally we spot someone who is really, seriously dangerous. That night after my man delivered the usual, shall we say, provoking declaration, some idiot went even further. He stood at the back wall and talked all sorts of bombast about wanting to set off a major explosion to kill a lot of people. That's when your wife and her 'friend' took off. But not until everyone had a good look at them."

Just like that. "How do you know it was her?" Martin demanded.

"My man followed her. Easy enough to do. Although the cab gave him a bit of a run for his money. She was even clever enough to be dropped off at the corner so that none of the neighbors would see her getting out of the carriage. After that it was a walk in the park, so to speak, to follow her to your place."

"Do you mean to say, he chose to follow some innocent woman, whoever she may be, rather than the man who was making all the threats?"

"Maître Martin," Jobert drawled. "Please. Changing the subject will not change the fact that you had better talk to your wife."

Martin had to restrain himself from grabbing Jobert's suit jacket by the collar and shaking him. "I repeat, why was your agent following an innocent woman instead of that man?"

Jobert shrugged. "Until last night, there was no particular need to follow him. He seems to have become something of a fixture at that café. According to the bartender, he started coming around a few months ago, claiming that the side of his face was burned by an eruption of flames while he was shoveling coal at the gas works. But we doubt it. My man says he is too skinny, too refined to be a stoker. But it was a good story. Industrial accidents. Isn't that one of the things you and your union men bleat about all the time? It certainly got the sympathy of the young Russian." Jobert screwed his mouth to one side and peered into Martin's face with those irritatingly knowing eyes. "He may be crazy *and* violent."

Clarie in danger. Clarie associating with a loose woman. Clarie, Clarie, Clarie. What are you doing?

Taking advantage of Martin's stunned silence, Jobert reached into his vest and took out a new cigar and his "little guillotine."

"And you don't know who he is?"

"Not yet. Doesn't seem to be from the neighborhood. Of course," Jobert said, as he carefully aimed one end of the cigar into the hole of the guillotine and chopped off the cap, "maybe he's from yours."

The complacency with which Jobert insinuated that this fanatic might be near enough to put Clarie in danger filled Martin with loathing. He bolted out of his chair. "Is that all?"

"Mmm," Jobert nodded as he struck a match and puffed on his cigar until the fire caught. Then he waved his hand to put out the flame. "All for now," he said, taking the cigar out of his mouth. "Talk to your wife."

If Jobert expected a response, Martin made sure that he would be sorely disappointed. He grabbed his bowler and wove his way out of the café as fast as he could.

Reaching the street did not offer much relief. He wanted to walk. To work off the tension. But he realized that pushing his way through the gawking, chattering, window-shopping crowds on the Grand Boulevards would only frustrate him. After almost being hit by a motor car as he neared the Place de l'Opera, he boarded a tram. Even that moved too slowly. Hanging on to a strap, Martin lowered and shook his head. He had to talk to Clarie. No, he had to confront his wife. What did she think she was doing? He tried to calm down. He tried to tell himself that perhaps she wasn't the woman that the police agent had seen. But a quick reprise of the last few days routed this hope. She didn't just come upon this Séverine's article by accident. She had to be looking for it, and she had to buy it, and, then, read it, before showing it to him. Or, worse, she had to have had some secret connection with that woman before the article came out. Sweat sprouted under the lining of his bowler and into his shirt. How had this gotten by him? What in God's name was Clarie up to? He had never been so humiliated. Being told by a police inspector to "talk to your wife."

He jumped off as the tram slowed at the Square Montholon and wound his way home, along the same route they took on their peaceful Sundays. He was so angry that everything around him was a blur. How could she?

When he got to the apartment, he ran through the entrance and courtyard to their stairway and took the steps two at a time. Chest heaving, he forced himself to catch his breath before, with trembling fingers, he took out his key and opened the door.

Clarie was in her chair, reading to Jean-Luc. When she first looked up, there was a smile on her face, before it turned white. "Bernard, you're home early. This is a surprise."

"Not as big a surprise as the one I just had. Talking to a police inspector." Martin barely got these words out through his clenched teeth. "Where is Rose?"

"I don't know . . . I suppose. . . ."

"Rose," he called. "Rose."

They stared at each other for a moment before their maid came scurrying out of the kitchen. "Yes, Monsieur Martin. Oh, you're home."

"Would you mind taking Jean-Luc into the kitchen with you for a few minutes? I need to talk to my wife."

Clarie got up, kissed her son, and handed him to Rose without once taking her eyes off Martin. "Your wife?" she said, even before the door had closed to the kitchen.

"Yes, my wife." Unable to stand still, he began to pace. "How could you?"

"How could I what?"

"You know what. I knew it was true as soon as I came in and mentioned the police."

"I have a right—"

"To what? To consort with that woman? Go where you want? Even if it's dangerous? You are a mother." His hands had become hard fists; his heart was pounding.

"I was in no danger. I'm here, aren't I?"

This was a weak defense, and Martin was sure that she knew it. He knew, too, that he should try to regain his composure. But he was angry. And he could see that whatever remorse she had, should have had, had turned into anger. "How long have you known that woman? When did all this start?" he demanded.

"A few days ago. After that column. I went to see her, because she, at least, was willing to help."

"Help? With those Laurenzano girls? You have no idea what they were involved in." There was terrible buzzing in his ears, a sign that his anger was mounting, a sign that he should try to calm down.

"I think I have a better idea than you." Each word came out distinctly, defiantly.

"Listen, Clarie, my love," he pleaded, "you may be putting yourself in danger, or at least taking up the wrong cause. That boy was carrying a bomb. Those girls probably knew it. One of them was murdered, for God's sake, murdered, probably by one of their own gang."

"I don't believe it."

It was the cold calm of her declaration that drove him mad, mad enough to say it. "I forbid you to consort with that woman. I forbid you to have any more to do with those girls."

"You *forbid* me?"

Suddenly Clarie's beautiful, passionate face dissolved before his eyes, the buzzing got louder, and his heart was pounding. It was frightening until he realized that his vision was dimmed by tears—of frustration and sorrow. They had never been so angry at each other before. They had to stop. "I'm sorry. I shouldn't have said that. I'm just trying to reason with you."

"Reason?" Her tone was defiant, incredulous.

He took out a handkerchief to wipe the sweat from his brow, hoping Clarie would not notice that he was also wiping his tears away. "Yes, reason." He looked down at the crumpled white cloth in his hand.

"Did I try to reason you out of helping your friend Merckx, even when you were breaking the law? No, I comforted you, I helped you, I kept your secret. And you loved me for it. You called me your strong, brave girl. And now, what am I, your *wife*?"

"Quiet. Rose."

"Oh, don't be silly. She's not listening. And if she were, she'd never betray us."

Martin put his handkerchief in his pocket and continued more quietly. "What happened to Merckx happened a long time ago. And there's a difference. He was my oldest friend. And I was young and foolish." She knew how important his childhood friend had been to him and how guilty he felt for trying and failing to help him escape from the army.

"You wouldn't do it again?"

Do what again? Get Merckx shot dead? The room fell so silent, Martin heard the clock ticking over the fireplace.

"I'm sorry," she whispered, as if she finally understood the cruelty of using what had happened to Merckx against him.

"You don't know these people," he retorted. He was so hurt.

"But I know from you about justice. How we should seek it. How we should understand what it means to be poor." The fire in her almond-shaped brown eyes had been almost completely extinguished. She was the one who was pleading now.

"Justice is my profession," he said, still smarting. Another blunder, which reignited her defiance.

"Your profession. Your sense of justice. For men, for workers, for Jewish army officers. Girls are beaten every day, by their bosses, by their husbands, by their lovers, and you always found their trials rather 'sordid.' Perhaps I have a different sense of justice: for mothers who have lost their children, for girls lost in the world." Her voice was steely, and her gaze never wavered from his face. *Mothers who have lost their children. Clarie and their dear, dead Henri-Joseph.* They had to stop. They could not continue to thrust and probe until they laid bare their deepest wounds. Even though he wanted nothing more in the world than to convince Clarie that his concern was for her, her safety, her well-being, the ground they were treading was too treacherous. He dare not say another word.

Clarie relented and offered a meager conciliation. "In any case, you needn't worry. I do not plan to see 'that woman' again. But I will insist on my right to see Francesca if I think I can help her." When Martin did not respond, she raised her hand toward the kitchen. "I'm going to get my son and read to him."

"And I'm," Martin stuttered, not knowing exactly what to say, "I'm going for a walk until dinner." He went out the foyer and closed the door quietly behind him. They'd talk more when both of them were calm.

15

All during the night and through to the next morning, Clarie played the argument over and over again in her head. She wished she had been more conciliatory, even admitted she was wrong. But admitting she was wrong would have required her to know *how* she had been wrong. Although she hadn't lied to Bernard about seeing Séverine, she was well aware that not telling was a form of lying. But what crime against marriage and society had she actually committed? Had it been wrong to seek out Séverine, to meet her one night, even to go to that wretched café? What sins, except the sin of doing something, anything, that had nothing to do with her child or her profession or Bernard. "Hah," a quiet troubled retort escaped from Clarie's lips as she pictured yesterday's confrontation. It was obvious why she hadn't told him. He would have tried to keep her from doing what she thought was right.

Clarie pulled out a piece of stationery from her desk drawer. She wanted their lives to return to normal. Inviting Bernard's mother to come as soon as possible would be a first step. Then he would see that Clarie intended to put Séverine and all her ideas aside for the time being. No police, no "consorting with loose women," no anarchists. Clarie slumped back in her chair. Normal. What did that mean for her?

"Maman!" Jean-Luc came running out of the kitchen.

"Darling," Clarie answered as she reached down and scooped up her son.

"Did you drink all your milk?"

Jean-Luc pursed his lips, puffed out his chubby cheeks, and nodded, trying hard to put on a serious mien. Rose, who had followed him into the parlor, rubbed his back and said, "Yes, our Luca was a very good boy." Then she stepped back and looked at Clarie. "Is everything all right, Madame Clarie?" she asked. Undoubtedly she had heard the shouting and noted the silences at last night's dinner.

"Yes, Rose. I'm going to write Monsieur Martin's mother today. I expect she will be here soon. You think we can be ready?" Clarie said, hoping to insert some levity into the morning. Adèle Martin was a very demanding personage.

"Of course," Rose bowed her head. The humor had fallen flat.

"Well, then, this is Luca's time to go to the park. We," Clarie said as she bounced her son in her lap, "are going to go on the swings and, if we are lucky, we'll meet some new friends." She gently nuzzled her nose against his, as he reached for her ear.

"Good, enjoy yourselves," Rose said as she retreated into the kitchen.

The sound of her housekeeper's sad, worried voice made Clarie's heart shrink. Perhaps she should have confided in her. Rose had been a pillar when Henri-Joseph died, sitting quietly by Clarie as she mourned; offering food, sympathy, devotion. Clarie kissed her son as she tried to quell the sadness in these memories. She shook her head as she rubbed noses again with her son. No, no matter how faithful Rose had been,

Clarie could not get her housekeeper involved in her differences with Bernard. Resolved in her decision, she set Luca on the ground and told him it was time to go.

After more than an hour of swinging and trying to introduce Jean-Luc to a few other little boys in the park, Clarie was ready for a rest. Most of the children were in the charge of nannies, whose close-fitting hats signaled their profession. They banded together, happy to be out from under the eyes of their mistresses. Mothers, gathered in twos and threes, seemed to know each other too. Had Clarie been less distracted, had it not been getting so hot, she might have tried to penetrate one of the closed circles. At noon, the sun beat down on the playground and on the new church atop Montmartre, making it as white and shiny as an alabaster moon. "Let's sit down and see if we can figure out when they will finish Sacré-Coeur," Clarie said to her son as a way of getting him to join her on a bench in the shade, some distance from the others.

When they settled down, Jean-Luc pointed his finger. "I wanna see. I wanna see." She nestled him on her lap as they both looked up toward the growing church and its scaffolding.

"Perhaps one of these days we will climb that big mountain and you will get to see it. For certain we will go when it is all finished." She tousled Jean-Luc's hair. Bernard would argue against introducing a child to a building he considered the very symbol of reaction. But then he would give in. After all, the finished basilica, in all its ornate grandiosity, promised to be the kind of place that would amaze a little boy. Clarie sighed. How nice it was to have that kind of disagreement. One that had Bernard grumbling and her coaxing, and both of them ending up in laughter. Clarie patted her son's sturdy thigh. How different from what was happening now.

Suddenly a strange hand brushed Jean-Luc's head. "What a beautiful child."

Startled, Clarie looked up and gasped. The scars that rippled up one side of the tall, thin intruder's face were so deep and severe that his eye had almost disappeared. Her shock seemed to please him, and the pleasing frightened her.

"I'm sure you love him very much. And want him to be safe."

"Go away." Two words were all she could muster against the intruder. Her heart began to pound as she recognized the raspy voice of the man at the back of the café. There, she had not seen the terrible burns on his face. She put a protective hand on her son's head and hugged him to her breast. She was desperately grateful that Jean-Luc had his back to the terrifying apparition.

"Beautiful day, isn't it? Just like the day of the Charity Bazaar fire. Horrible, don't you think, what happened to those pretty, high-born women and girls?"

"Yes." She inched to the edge of the bench.

"They screamed and ran but they could not escape the fire roaring toward them. And the smell. Oh, the smell of burning flesh." His hand trembled over his right cheek.

He should have stopped, just gone away. Instead, he added "And yet they were doing what women—ladies like you—should do. Work for charity. Not slumming."

Clarie jumped up from the bench, holding Jean-Luc tight against her, wishing she could cover his entire body with her arms. "Please leave me alone."

"I'm only trying to warn you," he said, and laughed.

She turned her back on him and rushed toward the playground. As soon as she reached a group of women, she swirled around to see if he was following. But he had disappeared.

"Are you all right?" a short woman in a plaid dress asked. "Here, sit down."

Clarie must have looked a fright. She was damp with perspiration and felt faint. She collapsed onto a bench, still gasping for air. "I'm sorry, a strange man was very rude to me." The women peered back to where Clarie had been sitting. "He's gone," another taller woman offered. "Would you like one of us to walk home with you?"

"No, no, thank you. I'll be fine." Clarie got up and set her wriggling child on his two feet. "Perhaps tomorrow we can sit and chat." She tried to sound bright and optimistic. "I should not have let him bother me so."

The women seemed unconvinced. But it wasn't them who needed convincing. Clarie had to find the courage to walk through and out of the park. She smiled again at the women before saying good-bye. Holding Jean-Luc's hot, sticky little hand, she urged him forward, talking to him, trying to sound happy, while being utterly aware of every branch that stirred, every shadow crossing her path. When they got to the end of the block that comprised the park, they had only to cross the street and soon they'd be home, safe. She picked up Jean-Luc and wove her way through the traffic. When she reached the other side, she almost broke into a run. She didn't care if people stared or had to step aside.

Entering her courtyard, she spotted the darkening shape of an unfamiliar shadow. When Séverine stepped out to meet her, Clarie fell against the wall of the building, panting.

"What are you doing here?" she demanded. "You shouldn't come here."

"I had to see you, my dear. The concierge told me that you had gone out. So I waited. I didn't mean to frighten you."

"You talked to the concierge?" Clarie grimaced. If Mme Peyroud knew that a notorious woman had come to visit her, who would not know by the end of the day?

"We can't talk now."

"We must."

Clarie caught Séverine's eyes with her own and led them toward her son.

"Oh." Séverine shrugged. "I can wait."

Clarie wasn't sure what to do. It seemed impolite not to invite Séverine to her apartment, yet that would bring Rose into it. Jean-Luc was struggling to get out of her arms. When she let him down, he started toddling toward the stairway, announcing his need to make pee-pee. That helped her to decide. "I'll take my son upstairs," she said to Séverine, "and then we can meet at the café."

Séverine shrugged and nodded, not at all interested in the requirements of maternity. Clarie grabbed her son and carried him up the stairs. Her mind was racing as she pounded on her door. When Rose answered, she explained that Jean-Luc had to go to the potty and she had to talk to Mme Peyroud. A good story—one always had reason to talk to the concierge—and, of course, dear Rose readily accepted the deception.

Descending the cool, dark stairway gave Clarie time to compose herself. At the bottom she took out her handkerchief and dabbed her forehead and cheeks. She wasn't sure what she was going to say to Séverine, the woman who had gotten her into so much trouble. One thing for certain, they should not meet again. That resolved, Clarie strode out of her courtyard, holding her head high, in case she passed someone who had witnessed her unseemly homecoming.

Séverine was at an outdoor table already enjoying a coffee. "Join me?" she asked.

"No, I really can't stay."

"Your husband found out, and he's angry," Séverine said, before she took a sip.

"The police too," Clarie said coldly.

"Oh! And they told him. My, my." Her eyebrows reached almost to her impertinent too-blond curls. She set her cup in its saucer.

"It was unfair that he had to be humiliated in that way," Clarie saying to Séverine what she should have said to Bernard.

"What did they tell him?"

"That he should control his wife. That I might be in danger."

"Anything else?"

Clarie was stunned. Didn't Séverine understand how difficult she had made life for her? No apologies, just questions?

"Sit. Listen. I came here to warn you about someone."

Clarie pulled out a chair. "Warn," the second time she had heard that word today. The fear that she had felt in the park came back in turbulent waves. "What do you mean?" she whispered, as she sat down.

Séverine leaned toward Clarie. "I've made inquiries along two lines. About the two street musicians and about the men I suspected of being provocateurs." She laid her hand over Clarie's. "One of them was not. And he may be a little mad. Moreover, according to my sources, he may live in your neighborhood."

"The man with the scars on his face." Clarie stared across the way to the Square d'Anvers.

"Yes. You've seen him?" Séverine gripped Clarie's hand more tightly, trying to retrieve her attention. "Oh, poor dear. That's why you were so frightened in the courtyard. He's approached you already?"

"Yes. Today. In the park."

"What did he say?"

Clarie thought for a moment, wanting to explain, not only what he said, but how he had said it. "He warned me. Suggested that a lady should not do the things I do. He touched my child's head. And when I told him to go away, I could see he was enjoying himself, enjoying frightening me." She wriggled her hand free.

"Oh, dear." Even Séverine seemed a little nonplussed.

A waiter came up to them. "A coffee for Madame," Séverine said quickly, "Or," she turned to Clarie, "would you like some brandy in it?"

"No, just milk." Brandy is not what she needed for fortification. Information, assurances, that's what she needed.

"*Une crème*," the waiter shouted toward the interior of the café.

Clarie closed her eyes, waiting for him to leave.

"You think he lives near here?" Clarie asked as soon as they were alone.

"Yes, in the special housing for the employees of the Gas Company on rue Rochechouart."

"Oh, no." Clarie's chest caved in as if someone had knocked the wind out of it. If this were true, he lived only a few blocks away. She could have crossed his path a hundred times. "How do you know?"

"Well," Séverine stirred more sugar into her coffee, "anarchists are not all one breed, all innocent idealists or union men. Some form tight cells and can be every bit as cunning as the police. I'm in touch with one such group. That's how I knew what café to go to. Apparently they were suspicious of this man's story. He appeared out of nowhere about two months ago and told them he hated the bosses because he had lost an eye in an explosion at the gas works. They didn't think he looked or talked like a stoker. Too weak. Talk too educated. So they followed him home one night. The fact that he lives in company housing gave enough plausibility to his story and enough assurance that he wasn't a police agent for them to let him be, especially since he seemed to hang on this Pyotr Balenov's every word."

"Two months ago." Clarie wrinkled her brow. "That's about the time of the Charity Bazaar fire. He talked about that again. It was so horrible, as if talking about it gave him pleasure." Clarie shivered. "Could he have been injured there?"

"I don't think so. The dead and badly injured were all women." Séverine took another sip from her cup. She seemed to have regained her calm. In analyzing, in demonstrating her awareness of events, she was in her element. A journalist to the core.

"But don't you think there's a possibility that something about that fire set him off? Made him seek out violent people," Clarie pressed. She was neither calm nor in her element.

"My dear, remember, we believe that these people are not violent. Besides, if he talks in an educated way, works at the Gas company and lives in their housing, he's probably a clerk." Séverine shrugged. "What was he wearing?"

Clarie had to think. For one panicked moment, all she could remember were the scars and the voice. "A bowler, yes, and a suit coat, and a vest."

"Just as I thought. A mere clerk who leads an unsatisfying life, adding up other people's bills." Séverine's mouth screwed up in distaste before she took another sip.

Clarie was taken aback by Séverine's condescending dismissal of men who earned their living as "mere clerks." She suspected that this disdain extended to all of the so-called petit-bourgeoisie, who exist between the very poor and militant workers Séverine championed, and men of her own class, professionals, or men of wealth or adventure.

"If he leads such a gray, uninteresting life, why do you think he had the nerve to threaten me?" Clarie challenged.

Séverine put her cup down. "He could be disappointed in what he has become. He may simply be a man, who, because of his failures in love, hates women. Who knows, maybe those burns are a result of some lover throwing acid in his face."

Clarie shuddered. Despite her unfair presumptions, Séverine's hypothesis made a certain amount of sense. Bernard had told her of incidents in the working-class districts of jealous or angry lovers, mostly women, who used acid as a cheap and effective means of revenge. And if the scarred man really hated women. . . . "Do you think that he would use acid?" Clarie asked, her voice trembling.

"My dear, I don't know what to think, except that we need to work it through from every angle. I wouldn't be worried about you, except. . . ."

"Except what?" Clarie might have raised her voice even more if the waiter had not arrived with the coffee. She had to stay calm. While he lingered, Clarie sipped on the foamy edges, hoping to gain some comfort in the familiar, warm aroma. But she couldn't. Her stomach was churning. Séverine paid the bill and sent him off.

"*What?*" Clarie insisted.

"Normally I would assume that someone who approached a beautiful, young defenseless mother in that way was merely a weaselly coward. But there is more. I don't mean to alarm you, my dear," Séverine paused, "but my informants tell me that this scarred man is every bit as interested in the musicians and their song as we are. He says he knows the boy."

"Maura."

"Yes, apparently your Maura. Do you know if there was any other time she masqueraded as a boy?"

Clarie shook her head. Her lips remained slightly parted as she tried to imagine what all of this could mean. *He knows the boy?*

"This is why I think he may be dangerous. Even insane. We know that Angela was stabbed. You say that the girls insisted that the Russian boy was also killed. By a bomb. Two different methods. Someone with a bit of education could pull this off. Now he seems to be on Maura's trail. But why? As you said, my dear, why kill Angela—or Pyotr—in the first place? If we knew that, we could make a case against him."

And you could become a heroine for all the public to see again. Clarie held her tongue and grimaced. What did she care about Séverine's adventures or ambitions? She might have just encountered a killer. Someone who was hunting for Maura. Someone who had touched her child.

"That's why we—" Séverine began.

"No." Clarie got up and pushed back her chair. "Not *we*. I need to go." She had her own life to worry about. And Maura's. And maybe even Jean-Luc's.

"Would you like me to walk you back—"

"No. Please. I have to say good-bye."

"All right, then." Séverine gave a little pout. "Be careful. If I were you, I would not return to that park, nor would I go out alone."

Clarie did not even acknowledge this last warning as she left. She had to get home. Only then could she think about what she should or shouldn't tell Bernard.

16

Climbing the stairs to her apartment, Clarie came to her senses. It was preposterous to think a killer was after *her.* She refused to believe she was in mortal peril. She lived in a good neighborhood. She was a thoroughly respectable woman. She never intended to go out alone at night again. She paused when she reached her landing. If Bernard insisted on warning her about the dangers of getting involved with the Laurenzanos, he was doing it out of love, to protect her, or, she reminded herself with a frown, just being a husband. As for Séverine, dramatizing was her stock in trade.

The trembling of Clarie's hand as she searched for the key in her cloth purse made her realize she was still a little afraid of that awful man. Yet, she thought, as she pulled out the key and held it suspended in her hand, he must be more crazy than dangerous. If Séverine was right, he was probably a clerk. Anarchists, even policeman, had been known to kill. Office workers were not killers. He might want to find Maura because they had both been friends of Pyotr. He might want to console her, praise her for wanting to find the real killer. Clarie thrust the key into the lock. Besides, there were ways to deal with this unpleasantness. She'd take precautions.

She turned the key and opened the door.

"Oh, Madame Clarie, it's you." Rose must have heard Clarie's clumsy hesitations in the hallway.

"Oh, yes, I had trouble finding my key."

"You should have rung."

"I didn't want to disturb you." Clarie hoped Rose would not ask about the pretend conversation with the concierge. Entering the parlor, she stopped to study her son absorbed in pulling his little wooden horse on its wheeled platform.

That's when her resolve began to crumble. She imagined the man's hand hovering over Jean-Luc's head.

"Did our Madame Peyroud have any complaints about me or Jean-Luc?" Rose asked as she followed Clarie into the parlor. Their grumpy concierge had become a companionable source of amusement between Clarie and her housekeeper, and Rose worked hard to stay on her good side.

"No, nothing like that. Has Jean-Luc had his lunch?" Clarie asked, changing the subject. She hated lying, evading. Without even waiting for an answer, she went to her bedroom, threw her purse on the bed, and began yanking off her gloves.

"I was just about to feed him. Then I was planning to take him shopping with me before his nap."

"No!" Clarie closed her eyes and took a breath. "Sorry, I think I have a headache." She didn't turn, because she was afraid Rose would see her fear. "Why don't you do the shopping, and I'll feed Jean-Luc." She wasn't making any sense.

"If you are feeling up to it." Clarie heard the doubt in Rose's voice.

"Oh, yes," Clarie said, recovered enough to face her housekeeper. "I've been thinking too much about school, the new courses for next year." Another lie. "Watching our Luca make a mush of his lunch will be the perfect cure."

"Very well. I'll go right now."

Clarie gave out a sigh of relief, as she watched her short, portly housekeeper take off her apron and waddle into the kitchen to hang it up.

A few minutes later, Clarie announced to her son that they were going to have lunch.

"Not hungry. Horsey hungry," he said, pointing to the wooden toy.

There was no reason for this slight resistance to throw Clarie off balance, but it did. "Come, Luca," she said reaching for him. He pushed her away. "Horsey hungry!"

For a moment, she didn't know what to do, then she almost laughed at herself. "Well, let's feed horsey," she said, getting down on the floor beside her son. "Ham or an apple?"

"Apple."

With the pretend apple delivered from her hand to Luca's and into the horse's mouth, Clarie was able to urge her child into the kitchen by promising eggy bread. "Your favorite," she said as she gave him a kiss. He circled his finger in the air and made an umm sound with closed lips to demonstrate his agreement.

She put him in his high chair, sliced some of the morning's baguette, cracked and beat an egg, dipped the bread in it, and lit the stove. She melted a pat of butter in a pan and fried the bread, all the time carrying on a one-sided conversation with her son. "Maman should cook more often, it's fun." "Maman loves eggy bread too, maybe I'll make some for myself." "Oh, Luca, this is going to be so good." She didn't like the tinny brightness in her voice, but she had to keep talking, to entertain Jean-Luc and to lift her own spirits. When she was done frying the bread, she slathered it with her son's favorite strawberry confiture, cut it into little pieces, and warned Jean-Luc that his lunch was still hot.

He played with the pieces of fried bread for a moment, before putting one in his mouth and making another umm sound. Once he was thoroughly engaged in smearing and eating, Clarie could stop talking and start thinking. It wasn't *what* she was going to tell Bernard or *when*, but rather *if*. So many ifs. If she and Jean-Luc weren't in danger, why upset him? That was the best possibility. She picked up another egg. And if she had put them in peril, it was her fault. She felt fear, but more, she felt shame. Shame that she had gotten herself into such a mess despite everything that Bernard had tried to tell her, shame that she may have put her son in danger, shame that Bernard had been humiliated by the police because of her. And, if she told Bernard, what could he do? Insist she stay at home? The egg collapsed in her hand as she made a fist. There had to be another way.

"Maman, messy!" Jean-Luc pounded on the table and pointed at her.

"Oh, look what Maman did! That's not the way you crack an egg," she said. Clarie stared at her slimy hand. "I don't think I'm hungry anyway!" she exclaimed, as if that were a fine thing, instead of the result of her turmoil. She ran her hand under the faucet and cleaned up the table before pulling up a chair to watch her son's chubby face being painted with sweet red jam.

If only Emilie were here. If only she had someone to talk to. Emilie would try to alleviate her fears, and then insist on forming a protective phalanx around her. The notion of Emilie, five-year-old Robert, and Emilie's quite rotund mother acting as a shield, brought the first genuine smile to Clarie's lips in hours. But the Franchets were in Normandy. And Papa, Clarie's father, who would understand why she tried to help the Laurenzanos, was in Arles, even farther away. "Oh, dear!" She had promised Bernard she'd be inviting his mother to come to Paris. "I'm going to write your grandmother today," she announced to Jean-Luc, covering up the dismay at almost forgetting. "When she comes, won't that be fun?"

He nodded as he stuffed the last piece of bread into his mouth. Of course, it wouldn't at all be fun. And Adèle Martin was certainly not a woman you could talk to about getting mixed up with "improper" people, like the lower-class Laurenzanos or the flamboyant Séverine.

At least, once her mother-in-law arrived, Clarie and Jean-Luc would be safer, the three of them going everywhere, absolutely everywhere, together.

Clarie dampened a towel to wipe off Jean-Luc's face. A pious woman would go to a priest to ask his advice about what she must tell her husband and when. But Clarie was not a pious woman and did not have a confessor. She needed to talk to someone who understood what it was like to be her, overwhelmed by obligations and emotions that pulled in different ways. Someone wiser and more experienced. Of course! Clarie picked her son up and kissed each damp cheek before setting him on the floor. It had all begun at school. Tomorrow, despite the risk that Mme Roubinovitch might think less of her, Clarie would go seek out her principal.

17

"WHAT A BEAUTIFUL MORNING," CLARIE declared after Bernard had left for work. "I think we should all go to the Square Montholon before it gets too hot."

"All of us?" Rose was bustling about, clearing the breakfast dishes.

"Yes, I need to stop at school to talk to Mme Roubinovitch." That was one reason for choosing the park that was farther away. Clarie sucked in a breath. The other was that they'd be distancing themselves from the Square d'Anvers, where she had met that terrible man. "I don't think you've been there with Jean-Luc since school ended, and we could all use a nice walk."

Flustered, Rose wiped her hands on her apron. "You are sure? I still have—"

"Oh, let's leave them," Clarie said as she picked up the remaining dishes and put them in the sink. "Madame Martin will be here soon, and you know, once she arrives, we will have to keep everything in perfect order. Now is our time to be spontaneous, to be on vacation." Clarie hoped the false cheer in her voice did not alert Rose to the troubles churning in her mind. "We haven't had a walk together for a long time," she added to stave off another protest.

"Well," a smile worked its way across Rose's worn face, "I haven't been there for weeks."

Within minutes, they had dressed Jean-Luc and carried him down the stairs. Because he insisted on walking as soon as they reached the courtyard, progress was agonizingly slow. Clarie was only able to persuade him to "take a ride in her arms" at the busiest intersections. "Let's settle you two at the park first, then I'll run up to the school," Clarie shouted over the noise of traffic to Rose, purposely choosing the route that did not go by the gilded gates of the Paris Gas Company's administration building. She did not want to take a chance of running into the tall, scarred clerk. If indeed he was a clerk.

Upon reaching the Square Montholon, Clarie suggested they take the path around the inside of the park to see if there were any prospective little friends to play with. The three of them promenaded slowly, she and Rose on either side of Jean-Luc, holding his hands. At midmorning, the Square was almost entirely populated by mothers, nannies and children. Clarie scoured every bench, tree and bush for anyone who was out of place. Satisfied that it was safe, she set Jean-Luc down in the sandbox to play with two boys, close to Rose and two nannies. After giving him and Rose a quick kiss on each cheek, she dashed to the stone steps leading to the block above the Square. At the top of the stairs, she paused to survey the park from above. She caught sight of her son's dark curls, as his hands dug into the sand, and of Rose, faithfully looking on. It was agonizing to leave him, but she had to be sensible. That terrible man had not gotten a very good look at her son. After Clarie repinned her hair, pressing back all the strands that had fallen from her bun, she strode up the block and around the corner to the Lycée. Mme Sauvaget, the school's plump, amiable bookkeeper, answered the bell.

"Is Madame Roubinovitch in?" Clarie was still a little out of breath. At that moment, everything seemed to depend upon the principal's presence.

"Yes, Madame Martin, in her office."

"Good, I need to speak to her for a moment."

"Of course," Mme Sauvaget said as she stepped aside.

Thanking her, Clarie wove her way through the familiar labyrinth of the centuries-old mansion. Without the shouts and whispers of the girls who were the school's lifeblood, the building was eerily quiet. Upon reaching the office on the second floor, Clarie paused to gather herself, then knocked and listened for an invitation to come in.

"Ah, Madame Martin, how good to see you." Mme Roubinovitch rose from her chair. "But what a surprise. You haven't gone away?"

"No," Clarie said, standing just inside the door. "We're spending most of the summer in Paris."

"Ah. As must I." The principal gestured to the piles of papers on the huge desk, which would have dwarfed a lesser woman. "I must prove to the Ministry of Education that we are functioning efficiently."

Clarie nodded, unsure of how to proceed.

"Please come, sit."

Clarie sidled past the long table used for student seminars and teacher meetings, and took the chair in front of Mme Roubinovitch's desk. She maneuvered to more clearly see her superior beyond the books and papers. The sun was shining directly into the room, but Mme Roubinovitch gave no concession to its wilting heat. The part in her hair was as straight as ever and the bun on top of her head as controlled; the collar on her starched white blouse rose stiffly half-way up her neck.

"I've come to you about one of our family at the school, a charwoman."

Mme Roubinovitch removed her gold-rimmed glasses and put them on the desk. "Yes?"

Surely she would have heard about Francesca's troubles, Clarie thought, her pulse beginning to race. Her superior was not making things easier.

"Francesca Laurenzano."

"Ah, yes. The murdered daughter."

"And Angela's presumed connection with a violent anarchist; and now Maura, the younger daughter, is missing."

"Terrible events, but, my dear, what do they have to do with you? Are you saying that we should not continue to employ Francesca?"

"Oh, no!" This cry came out before Clarie could stop herself, and quite in spite of her pledge to keep her emotions in check.

"I see."

"What do you see?" Clarie asked.

"Madame Sauvaget mentioned that Francesca had left you a message. I hoped, then, that you had not gotten involved." Mme Roubinovitch's wide, almost Slavic face could be kind or, more often, stern. Even before really beginning to say what she had come to say, Clarie felt the force of her principal's judgment.

Her mind split into warring factions. Should she cut her losses, by lying and saying she had only come merely to express her concern? Should she object, and point out the hypocrisy of teaching about virtue and charity if one did not plan to employ them? Or should she admit that she had come for advice?

Clarie straightened up and looked right into her superior's dark, penetrating eyes. "Yes, I have become involved, and this has caused some difficulties. I came to you for advice and counsel." There, she had said it. She had taken the step that would forever confirm her concern for Francesca and her daughter.

Mme Roubinovitch relaxed back into her chair and slowly shook her head. "Clarie Martin, what am I going to do with you? That heart of yours. So open. How did it happen?"

With a calm and order that surprised her, Clarie narrated the history of her relationship with the Laurenzanos, her surmises about the crimes that had touched their lives, and her meetings with Séverine. She admitted that she had proceeded against the advice of her husband and, now, a small part of her feared that she was in danger.

When she was finished, Mme Roubinovitch leaned forward. "You haven't told your husband about your encounter with this man?"

Clarie shook her head.

"But, my dear, why not?"

Clarie stared down at her lap and twisted her plain gold wedding ring around her finger. "I suppose," she whispered, "I feel ashamed." Her cheeks were burning.

A moment of silence followed. Mme Roubinovitch was not one to speak without consideration. Finally, she said "I cannot get involved in your marital problems."

"There are no problems," Clarie interjected. Not yet.

"I was going to say," Mme Roubinovitch continued, with the impatience of one unaccustomed to being interrupted, "that you need to ask why you allowed yourself to get involved in these 'adventures.'"

Stung by Mme Roubinovitch's tone, Clarie bit down lightly on her lower lip. For one humiliating moment, she felt almost as if she were twelve years old again, being chastened by her confessor for disobeying the nuns at her school. Clarie shook off that memory. She was no longer a girl. She was a grown woman. She did what she thought was right.

"I wanted to help Francesca when she said her daughters were missing. I had lost a child. I understood her anguish." Without really seeing them, Clarie gazed at the books lining the shelves behind the principal's desk. Slowly, haltingly, she continued. "Going to Francesca's home, writing to Séverine . . . I had to do something. I think after I lost my baby, I lost a part of myself. The part that was compassionate, yet unafraid." *The part of me that Bernard fell in love with, the woman I thought I would be.*

"And do you think, by these acts, you regained something? Your courage?"

Clarie shook her lowered head. "I'm not sure." No one with courage would be quailing like a coward.

Mme Roubinovitch got up, walked around her desk, and laid her hand on Clarie's shoulder. The hair on the back of Clarie's neck prickled under the scrutiny of the woman she admired with all her heart.

"I've always felt that you've underestimated yourself. Coming from your background, achieving so much. But perhaps that's why you felt compelled to help someone like Francesca."

Clarie sat up, alert. "My background?" Someone *like* Francesca?

Mme Roubinovitch removed her hand and strolled back to her desk, where she remained standing as she spoke. "Your father a blacksmith, an immigrant, no mother."

"I don't see. . . ." Were some people worthier than others? Should a professor care only about the bourgeois girls who inhabited her classrooms and ignore the fate of someone like a Maura Laurenzano, who had so few chances in life? Was Francesca expendable because she was an immigrant, or because she was a charwoman? It was no longer shame that was fueling Clarie's passions, it was anger. She squeezed her hands together in fists, willing herself to silence.

"I had no father," Mme Roubinovitch continued. "Such things make us stronger, after they almost defeat us. The fact that you and I have become professors is proof of that."

"But are you saying we shouldn't care about the lower classes?" Clarie's heart pounded in revolt. She could not accept this. Not after what she had seen in the Goutte-d'Or. She was, after all, her father's daughter.

"No," Mme Roubinovitch shook her head. "That is not what I am saying. However, I would advise you to choose your battles more carefully, because there are going to be so many. I expect a few will be pitched right here at our school in the fall. There are rumors of an all-women's newspaper that will try to recruit my teachers as writers and supporters. Some in the press are hinting at revisiting the Dreyfus verdict. If that happens, we will again be under pressure not to recruit and keep our Israelite students. And through all this," she said, sweeping her hand over the papers on her desk, "I must keep the Minister happy with us, while assuring him that I plan neither to 'rein in' my staff nor bow to prejudice."

"I can see you have a lot to deal with," Clarie murmured, thinking that Bernard, too, had chosen the battles that were most important to him.

"Problems enough, without one of my staff getting tarred by the black flag of anarchism."

Clarie stood up to leave. She shouldn't have come. What if she had jeopardized her position at the school?

But Mme Roubinovitch did not sit down, did not pick up her papers again, did not, by these actions, dismiss Clarie. Instead, she sighed. "Clarie Martin, I wish I didn't like you so much. You are a fine teacher. A good colleague. Never forget that."

"Thank you." Clarie realized she had stopped breathing. Her hands and face were covered with a thin veneer of perspiration.

"And to say that you have courage does not mean that you have no fear. All of our boldest actions may cause us to fear their consequences. In your case, there is even the possibility of a physical threat. Since you came for my counsel, I can only advise you to talk to your husband as soon as possible."

"Of course, you're right." Clarie began to pull her gloves over her dampened hands.

"I'm sure it won't be easy. But he is no more your master than I am. Didn't you tell me he gave up his judgeship to come to Paris with you?"

"Yes, but that is what he wanted."

"I'm sure it was. I believe you told me he took the risk of giving up a prestigious position in order to do what he thought was right: help the oppressed." Mme Roubinovitch paused. "Apparently," she said with a rueful smile, "that makes two of you."

Clarie stared at her superior. Can one disapprove of something you've done and still admire it? Point to what you thought was dividing you from the person you loved most in the world, and aver that it is exactly what should bring you together? In the world that Clarie came from, the rush of emotion, *the gratitude* she felt at that moment would have led her to do something foolish. At the very least, try to take her superior's hands and press them warmly. But this was not Mme Roubinovitch's way. Her way was to make sure that lessons had been learned, admonitions had been heard.

"We teach our students, we were taught at Sèvres, that our duty in life is to reach a greater and greater moral perfection. So much is changing in our world, with the talk of women's rights and workers' rights and the rights of Israelites, sometimes we are confused about what path to take to make the world better. I don't think you've been wise, but I don't think you have anything to be ashamed of. Courage is often foolish." Mme Roubinovitch sat down, put on her glasses and raised her head. "Please find a way to keep yourself safe. I so look forward to seeing you back here in the fall."

Clarie thanked her superior again before turning and quietly leaving the room.

She rushed down the stairs with every intention of quickly getting back to Jean-Luc. Her pace slowed as she traversed the corridor that led to her classroom. She could not resist going in. She lightly touched the wooden desks as she made her way to the front of the room. How she loved this place. The way the sun streamed in making her students' faces glow with an eagerness to learn. How the Alphonsines in their black and white uniforms evoked the memory of her own desires and frustrations when she was their age. Her world had been much more limited, by the teachings of the nuns, by the prejudices about what women were capable of. She had struggled so hard to gain knowledge, wisdom, even a new morality. And her job, her wonderful profession, was to impart what she had learned to her students.

She glanced at the empty desks. Would she ever come here again without thinking of Francesca's daughters, girls excluded by the circumstances of their birth? How many girls like them would she ever be able to help? Clarie stepped back against the blackboard. She hadn't been able to rescue Angela. But she could start with the one who remained, was alive, somewhere. If Mme Roubinovitch and Bernard had the right to see their battles through to the end, so did she. She could not give up her search for Maura.

By the time Clarie returned to Montholon Square, Jean-Luc was a very cranky little boy. To placate him, she bought a baguette from the nearest boulangerie and tore off an end for him to chew on. Then she and Rose took turns carrying him through the sun-drenched busy streets. More contented, he gnawed on the bread in between pointing and naming what he observed over their shoulders: the *potato* in the cart, the *hat* in the shop, the *boy* selling a newspaper. Rose beamed and Clarie patted Jean-Luc's back, both of them delighted at his pride in showing off new words. Telling Mme Roubinovitch the truth about the last few weeks had eased the tensions threatening to sap the joy from Clarie's life.

But the sight of her apartment building dampened Clarie's spirits. It reminded her that the scarred man could be lurking nearby, and it drew her closer to the moment she would have to tell Bernard everything. She insisted on carrying her son up all three flights, since she was younger and stronger than Rose. When she reached her door, she could hardly breathe. Her chest had tightened up again. Stepping inside, Clarie set Jean-Luc down and gave him a kiss. "Want to go play with horsey before lunch?" she asked.

He pulled on her skirt, urging her into the parlor as he repeated "horsey, horsey."

"Just a moment, Luca," she said, tousling his hair. "I'll be there in a minute. I promise."

His eyebrows came together and his lower lip stuck out in a pout as he considered this. Then he turned and toddled off toward the wooden horse. "Rose," Clarie said, before her housekeeper left the foyer, "when we put Jean-Luc down for his nap, I have something to tell you."

Rose's brown eyes searched Clarie's. Her face, older and more wrinkled than it should have been for her fifty years, was filled with concern. Good Rose, faithful Rose, she'd never ask, she'd wait. She had waited. Clarie did not intend to discuss her disagreements with Bernard. But she needed to explain her mysterious comings and goings, and to make sure that Jean-Luc was safe. It was a beginning. Clarie no longer wanted to live in a home diminished by secrets.

18

THE MORNING CLARIE SOUGHT OUT Mme Roubinovitch, Séverine was watching men in bowlers go into the administration building of the Paris Gas Company. She stood in front of a haberdashery, across the street from the gilded entrance, wearing a chestnut wig and black-rimmed glasses. She also had on a wide straw hat belonging to her servant, Augustine, and a charcoal-gray dress, plain, save for the line of tiny buttons parading up to her chin. Being frumpy rather than fetching was her disguise.

Suffocating under the high morning sun, Séverine consoled herself with the fact that she had suffered and survived much worse. Seven years ago, to report on the condition in the mines, she had climbed down a shaft fully garbed in miners' helmet and overalls. She'd spent three sweltering hours amid the smoldering ruins left by a fatal explosion. Her article, "The Descent into Hell," was her proudest achievement, the apex of a career dedicated to oppressed workers. Séverine sighed. Since then, she had aided a fugitive, marched on picket lines, and written countless columns seeking charity for those most in need. But nothing had compared to her heroism in the mines. Now, though, if she could catch a killer and prove the innocence of the Russian anarchist, she'd once again be the talk of all Paris.

She took out a lace handkerchief and fanned herself, hoping she had chosen her vantage point well. The gates of the Gas Administration building faced a confluence of four streets. Her sources had said that the man at the back of the café lived in company housing. When he approached the lovely Clarie Martin at the Square d'Anvers during a lunch hour, he had worn a bowler and a vest. Her instinct and logic told her he was a clerk, worked for the Paris Gas Company, and would be traveling to work along the rue Condorcet. Her instincts were seldom wrong.

She spotted him striding up the street, a head above most of the others, as if he were a man with important business to transact, instead of a clerk about to add a column of figures on someone's gas bill. After he turned into the gates and was safely inside, Séverine slipped her magnifying glasses into the purse dangling from her wrist, crossed the street and, lifting her thick skirts just a bit, set out for the rue Rochechouart. This led, halfway down the block, to the Cité Napoléon, Paris's only government-sponsored worker housing.

Before ringing the bell, she gathered herself, getting her story straight. Somehow she was going to have to find someone in the complex who knew the scarred man.

The concierge, a big woman with haughty suspicion written all over her coarse features, opened the door. The facts that she was wearing shoes rather than slippers, that her broadcloth dress was neat and pressed, and that she needed no apron to fulfill her duties indicated the relative importance of her position.

Séverine thrust out her hand and introduced herself as Augustine Petitbon, a reporter for *Le Temps*, the most staid newspaper in Paris.

"I haven't heard anyone was coming," the woman answered, keeping her hands firmly planted on her ample hips.

"You haven't?" Séverine said, feigning surprise. "We understand that you are doing such an excellent job, keeping things in order here. A good report in our paper will assure that the municipal council continues to fund you at the rate you deserve." Séverine loved playing roles. And this certainly was one. She was sure she wouldn't like the model housing. None of her anarchist friends would dream of living in it, because all of its well-known benefits—the baths, the laundry, the drying room, the child care, and the spacious grounds—came at a price: surveillance, discipline, even a ten P.M. curfew. The concierge, along with a city-appointed inspector and a doctor always on call, had to be chief among the disciplinarians.

Seeing that the woman was softening, Séverine added more sugar. "To tell the truth," she said, which was hardly the truth, "I accepted this assignment because I so wanted to see the grounds and the buildings for myself and to talk to some of the staff who have made this such a good place for our workers to live."

Without saying another word, the concierge stood aside and allowed Séverine to enter. "I don't have time to take you around," she said gruffly, "but I can get one of the charwomen and maybe the doctor is free."

Séverine went into the long entryway and walked up to peek at the courtyard, which was surprisingly green and lush with trees and shrubs. "How lovely," she remarked. "You must be so proud." Seeing the four separate buildings that comprised the complex made her heart sink. She'd have to get lucky. Or be very clever.

"Do you distinguish by employments, here?" she asked. "Do the lamplighters and stokers and clerks all live on separate floors?"

"No," the concierge grumbled. "It's according to what they pay and if they have children. Let me take you into this building. It's our best. We'll see if a char is around."

The big raw-boned woman trudged into a hallway that was as surprisingly pleasant as the courtyard. The building was made up of parallel rows of apartments reached by a series of bridges. This allowed the overarching skylight in the roof to illuminate every floor. Séverine took out a notebook and made a scribble she hoped her companion would take as a note. "Clean and impressive," she remarked. At least she would not slip on a potato peel on a darkened stairway.

The concierge's only response was to yell for a Louise. A head popped up by the railing on the second floor. "Yes?"

"Someone who wants to be shown around."

Séverine was already resigned to the fact that this concierge, unlike most belonging to her profession, was not a gossip. She had to hope the chars were more talkative.

"I know you're busy. I'll be fine," Séverine said, eager to please and get rid of her severe escort. "Thank you." Before the concierge could respond, Séverine was on her way up.

Louise, in her fifties, short-haired, almost balding, and portly, was talkative, but, at first, not very helpful. Masking her purpose, Séverine began by asking the charwoman if she knew any stories that would amuse her newspaper readers, how families got on here, what it was like to bathe and to do the wash in a model community, and how she felt about the ten P.M. curfew. Louise had opinions on everything, especially the families. "Little devils," she called their children, resentful of the dirt they dragged in and the noise they made.

"What about the bachelors?" Séverine asked, circling closer to the information she needed.

"Bachelors," Louise said with a knowing smile. "You want to know about bachelors, don't ask an old married woman like me. Go upstairs to Elise. She's probably doin' the toilets by now."

Something in Séverine's expression must have alerted Louise that she had made a slip, for as Séverine turned to go up the stairs, the charwoman caught her by the sleeve. "You ain't going to repeat what I said, are you?"

"Heavens, no," Séverine said innocently, as she wriggled away. "I just need to see more of the building." And she needed to get to this Elise before Louise could warn her friend that she had given her away.

When she reached the landing of the next floor, she saw a charwoman on her knees, scrubbing.

"Elise," she said softly.

"Yes?"

"May I speak to you?" Séverine said, approaching her.

With some effort the woman got to her feet, dropped the rag she had been using in the bucket and left the cloth she had been kneeling on beside it. She wiped a lanky strand of mousy brown hair from her eyes and pinned it into her scraggly bun. She had a pockmarked face and sad gray eyes. Although she was probably barely thirty, about the same age as the vibrant Clarie Martin, she looked worn down.

Séverine introduced herself as Augustine Petitbon and said that she had come to learn about the charwoman's routines and work at the Cité Napoléon.

"You can see it," she responded with a weary wave of her hand. "The stairs, the hallways, and the toilets at the end of each hall, four on each floor."

"Do you live here?" Séverine asked, taking out her notebook, calculating that this question could lead to revelations about the woman's life.

"Yeah. Over there." Elise gestured toward a door across one of the bridges.

"Alone?"

"Yeah."

"Could I see your apartment?" A private place for a private talk.

The woman shrugged. "I've got work—"

Séverine reached in her purse and took out a five-franc note. "Can I tell you a secret?" she said, raising her eyebrows.

"What?"

"I'd be willing to pay for some information."

Elise stared at the banknote, which easily represented a few days' work. She met Séverine's eyes and nodded. "Let me dump out the pail, and I'll take you to my place."

Elise bent over, picked up her knee rag and her bucket, and plodded to the communal toilet at the end of the hall, where she wrung out and folded her rags and poured out the dirty water. Watching these slow, deliberate movements took every iota of Séverine's patience. She fingered the money and prayed the woman knew the right bachelor.

Wiping her hands on her apron, Elise led Séverine across a bridge to her apartment. It was a single room with a one-burner stove, a window, and two gas lamps on the barren walls. There was a narrow bed and a wooden table with three rickety chairs, a pantry and armoire. Aware that Elise was observing her, Séverine felt compelled to remark that it was very nice.

"I've worked here five years. I'm saving to get a room with a fireplace. It's cold in the winter," she said, standing before Séverine, waiting to be handed the banknote. Once she got it, she went over to the table and wearily dropped into a chair. Séverine took this as a tacit invitation to join her.

"Well, then," Séverine said, as she sat down, "let's get started. What's it like to live among bachelors who work for the Gas Company?"

Elise glanced aggressively at Séverine. "You're not from the Moral Police, are you? Or sent by that building inspector?"

"Of course not!" If only this Elise knew the history of Séverine. She was as far from the Moral Police as you could get. But how to convince her? Séverine retrieved another wrinkled five-franc note from her purse. She assumed the inspectors did not give or take bribes. "Look," she said, taking a chance by changing her story, "I'm not really reporting on life at the Cité Napoléon. I want to write a series on the violence that men do to women, and women do to men. It's going to get some people angry, so I need you to keep what we say just between us."

Elise's eyes roved suspiciously between the money and Séverine's face.

Séverine bit down lightly on her lip before taking the plunge. "I'm particularly interested in finding out about the man I've seen going into the Gas Company, the one who had acid thrown in his face."

"Acid?"

"Burned, all up one side."

Elise shook her head, puzzled. "Are you talking about Michel?"

A name! Not wanting to frighten off the charwoman, Séverine braced herself to remain calm. "Michel who?"

The woman shrugged. "Michel Arnoux."

"And you know him how?" With two gloved fingers, Séverine edged the banknote toward Elise.

Elise placed her hand over it. "I like the clerks. They're cleaner than the stokers or the lamplighters. Smarter, too. More educated."

From the way that the charwoman refused to meet her eye, Séverine assumed there was more to her relationship with Michel Arnoux than a mere passing acquaintance. Séverine could not believe her luck. Or was it simply, once again, her unfailing instincts? "So the man with the burnt face and the closed eye," she said carefully, "is Michel Arnoux."

"Yes, but no woman did that to him. It was the anarchist who did it. The one who threw the bomb in the fancy café."

"When?" It was Séverine's turn to be puzzled. The only recent bombing was the explosion in Pyotr's cart.

"You know, the famous bomb, years ago."

"The Hotel Terminus?"

"Yeah, that one."

At last, a new clue. Despite the wig, the hat, the heavy dress, Séverine felt light, as if she could soar. Of course, she remembered the 1894 bombing. Everyone did. Thrown into a crowded café on a cold February night. The explosion that had terrorized Paris. Séverine dropped her hand to her skirt and clawed at it, reminding herself not to show her excitement. She was on the verge of uncovering a motive: revenge.

"Was he bitter about what happened?" she asked, almost holding her breath. "Did he talk about that night?"

"Well, not so much about the lamp that caught fire on their table. But about his fiancée, the one he lost. The one that was so perfect, so good. Except she couldn't have been that good. She couldn't bear to look at him any more, even after he saved her." The tone was bitter. Whatever her relationship with Arnoux, she would never live up to the phantom of his imagination. Elise kept flattening out the banknotes against the rough wood of the table. "A pretty little blond thing," she added. "At least according to him."

"Do you think he hated all anarchists for what one of them did to him?" Séverine pressed.

"Oh, yes. He said, all the time, his life would have been so different. He should have been a manager. He should have had a real apartment. He should have married . . . that woman." Her hand stopped. Her voice drifted into silence. Something must have happened. Some hope must have been dashed. Perhaps the hope that by marrying a bitter, mutilated man she would improve her life, enjoy a warm apartment in the winter.

Séverine decided that a show of sympathy was probably the best way to pry more information out of the charwoman. "Oh, my poor dear, was he ever violent with you?" She reached for the woman's hand.

"No," Elise said, pulling away. "He used to be nice to me."

"*Used to be?*"

Elise began chewing on one of her broken fingernails.

"What happened?" Séverine urged. What had brought Michel Arnoux to Pyotr's café?

Elise closed her eyes, as if deciding whether or not to answer.

"Did he hurt you? We can—"

"No! It's not like he hit me. I don't want you to think that."

"Well, then."

Elise nodded to herself before beginning slowly. "It's the way he talked. It was bad enough that he kept telling me about his fiancée or how he could have become a big shot. But after that fire happened in May, when all those ladies got burned, he couldn't stop talking about it. How their bodies were charred, how their jewels melted right into their flesh, what they smelled like." She shook her head with distaste. "He went to see them every day they were laid out after the fire. He tried to get me to go. It was as if, as if . . . he liked it." She wrinkled her nose as if she could smell the flesh burning and shot Séverine a glance of horrified perplexity.

"Does he still talk about the Charity Bazaar fire?" Séverine asked, perfectly aware that he did.

The charwoman shook her head. "We don't talk anymore. I couldn't stand it. It's too gruesome."

Séverine stood up. She had gotten what she needed. The room was stifling, and she was perspiring heavily under her wig. "Thank you, you've been very helpful. And it is very important that you tell no one what we've been talking about." She glanced at the banknotes under the guard of Elise's fingers. Her only guarantee.

Séverine bid the charwoman good-bye and dashed down the stairs as fast as her heavy skirts allowed. She needed to go home. Get out of the awful clothes. Think. Write notes. Then go to Clarie Martin with what she had learned. She had struck gold.

19

HOURS LATER, A BEEF STEW simmering on the stove, Rose and Clarie carried Jean-Luc downstairs to play with his horsey in the courtyard. They had devised a plan that would allow Clarie to talk to Bernard alone and, at the same time, keep Jean-Luc from any possible harm. Clarie asked Mme Peyroud if they could borrow her stool for Rose to sit on in the courtyard as she watched their Luca. This was an unusual request. But it was an unusual day. Fortunately the concierge didn't ask any questions before she retired to her lodge to prepare her own meal. After Clarie showed Jean-Luc how much fun the horsey would have riding over the cobblestones, she went upstairs to wait for her husband.

Within minutes, the doorbell rang. Puzzled, Clarie put her book down. Had Bernard forgotten his key? Or did he have Jean-Luc and the wooden horse in his arms? Clarie swung the door open to discover, much to her dismay, the audacious Séverine.

"I must come in."

"No, you can't. Bernard will soon be home and. . . ."

Ignoring Clarie, Séverine stepped inside the foyer and pushed past her into the parlor. She swirled around. "We may both be in danger," she said, with a certain imperiousness. "I know who the scarred man is, and I think I know what he has done."

Even though Clarie was afraid of what Séverine had come to say, she had to listen. Fear thudding in her chest, she walked to one of the chairs by the reading lamp and gestured to Séverine to take the other. "How did you find out?" she asked, holding on to the arms of the chair as she slowly settled into the seat.

"I'm an investigative reporter. I investigate," Séverine said briskly, as she yanked her gloves off, one finger at a time.

"And?"

"As I surmised, my dear, he is a clerk at the Paris Gas Company," Séverine said with an impatience that Clarie assumed had to do with her guest's less-than-gracious reception. "I waited on the corner of the rue Condorcet this morning until I saw him go in. Then I went to the Company housing on the rue Rochechouart and talked to a charwoman who knows him, shall we say, quite well."

Séverine paused, eyebrows arched, waiting for praise or encouragement.

"Please go on," Clarie urged. She had no time for Séverine's dramatics. She was hardly breathing. The fireplace, the floral rug, the familiar walls seemed to be vibrating with the possibility that the worst was true: the man who approached her worked at the Paris Gas Company, a few blocks from her school. He lived nearby.

"His name is Michel Arnoux. And his friend told me that his face was burned in an anarchist bombing, the famous one at the Café Terminus. You know about that, of course?"

Clarie shook her head, still stunned.

"February 1894."

"I was in Nancy, teaching," Clarie whispered. "I remember something—"

"Well, it was quite notorious. This slightly crazed Emile Henry threw a bomb in a new posh restaurant as everyone was sitting around having a good time, drinking, eating, listening to the music. The place was packed, about 350 people. The explosion was so powerful, it went through the roof."

"How awful," Clarie said. "How many died?"

"Fortunately, only one. Many injured. What was really terrible is that all the anarchists were blamed for the act of one fool."

Clarie stared at Séverine. "What was terrible is what happened to the person who died and people like this Michel Arnoux."

"Oh, yes," Séverine waved her hand dismissively, "that's why everyone was so up in arms. Because Henry wasn't aiming at the army, the police or the government. He targeted ordinary people. And what could be more ordinary than a clerk?"

Shocked by Séverine's callousness, Clarie repeated: "What happened to this man, this ordinary clerk, was terrible."

"And it gets worse," Séverine went on, undeterred by Clarie's disapproval. "Apparently he was there with his fiancée, got her away from the fire and, then, she rejected him because of his disfiguring wounds. I can see exactly the way it was. He must have been near the orchestra—that's where the bomb went off—a special table for a special night. Something he could ill afford. Maybe he wore a top hat for the first time. Perhaps that's when he asked her to marry him. Or, didn't get the chance to ask before the explosion. Her rejection, that's why he's so bitter. Bitter enough to hate women, bitter enough to kill," she concluded triumphantly.

Clarie could see Séverine exactly, too. Imagining the story in her head. But she wasn't interested in hypotheses: Clarie wanted to know everything Séverine had found out. She had to know. "So you believe he killed Pyotr and Angela?"

"Yes, I'm almost sure of it." Séverine began counting on her fingers. "He is educated. He works for the Gas Company. It wouldn't be hard for him to build a bomb. Undoubtedly he saw Angela and your Maura with the Russian. And here's where you were right," she said, leaning toward Clarie: "the Charity Bazaar fire. Something about that set him off. Apparently he was obsessed with going there and looking at the victims. He kept trying to describe them to his little friend."

"He saw the bodies," Clarie murmured. He had tried to describe them to her, too.

"And smelled them."

Clarie touched her cheek, remembering how his hand had hovered over his wounded face. "He couldn't help himself," she said suddenly.

"Yes, I suppose. He may be mad."

"Yes, mad," Clarie said, her mind racing over a path she had been avoiding, "but in a certain way. In Nancy, Bernard worked with the famous Dr. Bernheim, who used hypnosis and suggestion with his patients. He believed that suggestions, images in our minds, if introduced correctly by a psychotherapist, can be so strong, they can cure neuroses. Or, left unattended, they can lead a person to commit horrible crimes. Those poor women laid out for everyone to see must have brought it all back to him: the smell, the pain, the hurt, the anger. He had to strike out. Find a way to strike out." Clarie realized that she was talking as if in a trance. What she was saying was frightening. "If that's what happened. If seeing those women made him envious and revengeful, he is a dangerous man. Pitiful, but dangerous. What would stop him?"

Séverine slumped back with a sigh. "If only I could prove all of this. What a great story that would be."

"What!?" Clarie got up and crossed her arms, clutching her elbows. Despite the way the summer baked the parlor in the afternoon, she was cold, chilled and clammy. "A *story*? These are people's lives." Her life, Luca's life, Angela's life, Maura's life. Maybe the lives of other anarchists making speeches in that café.

"I know this is about real lives, my dear," Séverine retorted. "But certainly you, of all people, having been married to an investigating magistrate, know how important solving crimes is to building one's career."

"Bernard never felt that way." In fact, he had given up *that* career.

"Well, then your Bernard must be the exception you believe him to be."

Séverine's retort felt like a slap. "Yes," Clarie said curtly, "he is."

Sighing, Séverine got up and put her arm around Clarie's shoulders. "Look, my dear, we shouldn't be arguing. We should be talking about how to keep ourselves safe. What if the charwoman tells this Monsieur Arnoux that I talked to her? He may go wild! You need to figure out how to take care of you and your child. You can leave the solution of the crime to me."

"Or to the police," said Clarie.

Séverine shrugged. "Do you think they'd listen to me, after all my run-ins with them? I doubt it."

"Then Bernard will go to them." She moved away. She and Luca and Maura were not a *story*. If anyone could persuade the police to investigate this man, it was a former judge.

"If you insist," Séverine said, plopping back into a chair, "I'll wait to tell him what I know as long as he keeps me informed about what the police are doing. I want to be the one to break the news."

"You can't wait here," Clarie objected.

"Why not?" Séverine stuck her chin up and Clarie suddenly understood the kind of impudent charm the famous investigative journalist must display when she wanted something. She hadn't noted the elegance of Séverine's outfit when she forced her way into the apartment. A white cotton dress with a scattering pattern of periwinkles that perfectly matched her eyes, the tightly corseted waist, the fetching bow at the neck, and, adding a certain piquancy to the whole, a lavender toque small enough to accentuate the stunningly white-blond curls. None of this mattered to Clarie. It was the simple question "Why not?" that changed her mind. Of course Séverine had to tell Bernard everything. He knew how to ask the right questions, and he would have to listen.

"You're right. You should stay. But let's not pounce on him. Give me a chance to tell him that you are here."

"If you insist." Séverine sighed and stretched out her legs, wiggling her feet, as if she had been hard at work the whole day.

"Would you like a cup of tea?" Clarie didn't really want to make a pot of tea. She wanted to run downstairs to prepare Bernard.

"That would be lovely," Séverine answered as she laid her head back on the chair.

Clarie was pouring the boiling water into the pot when the key rattled in the lock. As she put the kettle back on the stove, she heard the exchange in the foyer.

"You must be Maître Martin." Clarie imagined Séverine thrusting her hand forward to be shaken.

"And who are you?" Bernard was too polite to refuse the gesture. But, considering his opinion of Séverine and her flamboyant life, he was not about to give her the satisfaction of recognition.

Clarie dashed around the corner into the foyer. "Bernard," she said, "this is Séverine. I've told you about meeting her." Their guest stood between them. In the relative darkness of the foyer, Clarie envisioned a cloud passing before Bernard's eyes and a storm brewing behind them. "She's come to give vital information about something that happened to me yesterday."

His expression changed from anger to concern. "You?"

"I was waiting for the right time to tell you. That's why Jean-Luc and Rose are in the courtyard." The words tumbled out. She needed to say them as quickly as possible. "Why don't you two sit, and I'll pull up a chair from my desk." Surely he had seen Rose and their son in the courtyard. If he didn't believe her, there was nothing she could do about it now, not with Séverine between them. Clarie picked up her wooden desk chair and carried it across the room to set in front of the two armchairs. If she kept her eyes on both of them, she'd make sure they stuck to what was important: finding a killer, keeping safe, saving Maura, not their dislike or distrust for each other.

Séverine retook her place in Bernard's usual chair. He was slower in coming. Clarie leaned forward to watch him take off his bowler, hang it up, and loosen his cravat. He was a thoughtful man, a tactful man. He'd do the right thing.

He strolled behind the two armchairs and settled into Clarie's usual place. "So tell me what happened," he said in a measured voice.

"I was in the Square d'Anvers with Luca yesterday, when a man came up to me and said awful things, about the women in the Charity Bazaar fire. He said they had suffered despite doing the things that ladies should do." She didn't say he had touched Luca's head or that he had implied she deserved punishment. What she told him was frightening enough.

"What did he look like?"

Bernard's voice was surprisingly gentle, considering what must be going through his mind, that she had once again kept something important from him.

"He had scars, burn marks, all up the side of his face, so bad that one of his eyes was closed."

Bernard froze for an instant. If she hadn't known him so well, she wouldn't have noticed. When he unclutched his hands from the side of the armchair, she saw that he had regained his composure. "Had you ever seen him before?" This time his voice carried less love and more authority.

She hated saying it. "I'm not sure. Perhaps at the café in the Goutte-d'Or. It was dark," she ended in a whisper.

Bernard's nod said "later," as if he already knew, as if once more she was to blame for having gone on that foolish venture. He shifted his focus to Séverine. Always eager for center stage, Séverine repeated what she had found out. She also mentioned Clarie's remarks about Dr. Bernheim.

"Bernard," Clarie asked, "do you really think the Charity Bazaar fire could have set him off? The timing seems right. That's apparently when he first got to know the Russian boy, perhaps started to observe and follow him, and Angela, and Maura." What a terrible idea. Being watched by someone waiting for the opportunity to kill. Was the same happening to her? The thought of it brought her to her feet. She began to pace.

Bernard watched her with worried eyes. "I think both of you may be right," he said.

She paused to listen, wanting to hear how he, the former judge, analyzed the situation.

"If, as Madame Séverine says," he began, "the suspect was bitter about being left by his fiancée, he might have something against pretty young women and would have been very envious of an anarchist, someone he hated, being surrounded and admired by them. And, as we know, the smell, the sight, the imagined screams of the women who died in the Charity Bazaar fire powerfully affected everyone who went to see their bodies after they were laid out in the Palace of Industry. For someone who had gone through a similar trauma. . . ." Bernard shook his head, thinking. "There's a good chance you are right."

"Then they were and are the targets—Pyotr, Angela, and now Maura." Clarie said this with a mixture of shame and hope. She did not want to believe that she was among those being stalked. She had only been *warned*.

"And, if he's not caught, other anarchists and the women who dare to admire them might also be in danger." Bernard looked up sharply. "He may think you admire them. You mustn't take any more chances."

Clarie sat down again. "Then you must go to the police and have them question this man."

"Why doesn't Madame Séverine go?"

"You must know why I can't go," Séverine said, striking a rather coquettish pose.

Bernard had managed not to sound sarcastic. That was his way, even though Clarie was fully aware of the grievances behind his question: he didn't like Séverine, he didn't like Clarie's relationship with her, and he had already been embarrassed by a run-in with the police. But Clarie was not about to let Séverine's pride in her reputation for disreputability nor Bernard's barely repressed irritation interfere with what needed to be done. "I'm sure they'll take what you say seriously," she insisted to her husband.

"Of course I'll go," he said. Their eyes locked. Clarie had the feeling that if they had been alone, he would have apologized for insinuating, even for an instant, that he did not intend to do everything in his power to keep her safe.

"And," Séverine said, interposing herself, "I hope you will keep me informed about any arrests or new developments. I want to be sure I'm the one who reports the story first."

The silence following her remarks was palpable. Bernard turned ever so slightly to block her from his view. Clarie didn't want to look at her either.

"It's my living," Séverine said. This time without a touch of archness or frivolity.

"Of course." Clarie got up, a peacemaker, moving closer to both of them. Séverine had never hidden the fact that Clarie's plea for help fed into her ambitions. And there still was work to do. "What about Maura?" she asked.

"*My* concern is for you and Jean-Luc," Bernard said dryly, distancing himself from any concern about the Laurenzanos.

"My friend, who has been following them, says she is performing around Montmartre at night and in the Parc Monceau in the daytime," a subdued Séverine responded. "I'd better go."

Clarie walked her to the door and watched while she put on her gloves. Séverine clasped Clarie's hands in hers. "Tomorrow night, I promise, I'll find an escort and go look for Maura on Montmartre." She kissed Clarie on each cheek. "Stay safe, my dear," she said.

"You too," Clarie answered.

"I hope this is not good-bye."

Clarie shook her head. "I don't think so." She embraced Séverine. "Be careful," she whispered.

Séverine squeezed Clarie's hands one more time before turning and leaving.

Taking a deep breath, Clarie went into the parlor to talk to Bernard. She soon found out that he, too, had a secret. He had not told her that Jobert warned him about the scarred man. He hadn't wanted to alarm her or to believe she was in danger. This admission made it easier for Clarie to tell him everything she had done in the past few days. He did not ask, and she did not promise, to give up the hunt for Maura. Perhaps he assumed she would. What he did not understand was that for her, giving up on Maura would be like surrendering a piece of herself.

20

"BRAVO!" MONSIEUR ANDRÉ CALLED, AS if he were some high-class gentleman instead of the head of a rascally ragpicking family. "Bravo!" echoed his wife. Others clapped and banged on pots and pans.

Maura held her hand to her waist and bowed, joining in the mockery of those who thought they were better than the motley crowd that surrounded her. She and Nico, the street musicians known as Piero and Nicoló, had taken to performing for the ragpickers each night as they waited for the ten o'clock hour when they were allowed into the streets of Paris to hunt and gather. In the last few days, the commencement of the ragpickers' work had become the end of Nico's and Maura's.

To her amazement, her plan had worked, and she and Nico had made more money than they needed to survive, especially as they gained the courage to perform in wealthier neighborhoods. It helped that she had grown up with many of the songs that Nico knew. It also helped that he was so willing to sing of Pyotr and Angela.

"Sing your song, we like it!" Jacques, one of the strays, yelled.

"Nicoló, strike up the chord." Maura stretched out her hand toward her companion.

Pieter, a boy from Tzarist Russia
Loved mankind with all his heart. . . .

More amazing to her than her success was the fact that she had learned to like some of the ragpickers, although she'd never dream of wanting to live among them, or rather among the stinking mounds that undulated out of their doorways. Her first friendly exchanges began with the women who had worried about Nico being alone and told her they were happy he had a companion. For them, sleeping five or six or seven in the one room they called home was not only hardship, it was companionship, protection, warmth in the winter. Maybe that's why the families so willingly took in the strays, the lice-ridden, emaciated runaways that eventually found themselves in "the zone," the ragpickers' quarters. To share while having so little. To be so honest in plying their trade, when everyone treated them with contempt. She almost began to believe the words she had written.

Why can't we all be free
To work with joy and dignity
To earn our bread and all we need
To live, to love, to play, to breathe?

Someone heard the ten o'clock bells, and the ragpickers began to move, waving good-bye to the women who had to stay with the smallest children, and to Maura and Nico, who started off toward the vineyard. Nico had told her he chose to live alone because he loved the well, the quiet, and, until she came, spending his waking hours at peace, wandering or playing music and thinking of his Jeanne. He said he knew that she would leave some day, and he would be fine. She doubted this. He was so old. But she was worried about her mother, who was also alone. Sometimes she had fantasies that they could all live together.

More than anything, she was too young to give up her ambitions. Playing in the Parc Monceau had reignited her dream. She'd never be like the women in silks who strolled through the park with their top-hatted gentlemen. But she wanted to make something of herself. Not to beg all her life. Yet she could not leave the zone until they found Angela's and Pyotr's killer. Then, and only then, would she be safe.

21

"YOU WON'T GO BACK TO the Square d'Anvers?"

"No," she promised.

"And you'll always go out with Rose."

"Yes."

Martin took an ebony curl that had fallen out of one of Clarie's pins and wound it behind her ear. "I want nothing to happen to you."

"Don't worry. On your way, Maître Martin." She picked up his bowler and plopped it at a jaunty angle on his head. Martin knew that she was trying to lighten the mood. But her chest was heaving ever so slightly, so he held her in his arms again, feeling her heart, trying to make her feel safe. "Don't worry," he assured her, "I'll track down Inspector Jobert if it takes all morning. He's clever and competent. He'll drag in the man before noon, I promise. Or at the latest by the time the bastard is back from lunch. And in the meantime—"

"We won't go out."

"Promise?"

"Promise." This earned her a light kiss on the lips. When he stood back, he caught a fiery glint in her eyes he hadn't seen for years. In it he glimpsed the girl he had fallen in love with, the impetuous Clarie Falchetti. Not the responsible, hard-working mother and teacher he had so come to cherish. Nor the subdued Clarie she became after she lost Henri-Joseph. When it was all over, he'd try to understand what had happened to her in the last month. And, in turn, he'd make her understand that he was capable of loving all the Claries. As long as she was honest with him and kept herself safe from harm.

Martin raced down the stairs and through the courtyard. He wound his way through the busy streets and struggled through the crowd in front of the Gare du Nord to get to the train station's post office, where he looked up the address of the precinct that served the Goutte-d'Or and sent a pneu to the Bourse, telling them he would not be in until the afternoon. Then he headed north on the street that ran between the giant train station and the equally elephantine Hôpital Lariboisière and continued on whatever route pushed him north toward the rue Doudeauville. This was unfamiliar territory to Martin. He breathed in the fetid odor of open sewers and felt the suspicion the inhabitants exhibited for well-dressed outsiders. He was chagrined, once again, at the notion of Clarie walking the same streets, alone or, at night, in the company of Séverine. It was a relief to reach Doudeauville, a lively commercial street. Address in mind, as he strode along, it only took him a few minutes to spot the iron gates in front of the police station. He rushed through the courtyard into the station. Rushed, only to wait. Impatiently. For more than an hour.

Martin could not resist rising from the bench every fifteen minutes to insist to the mustachioed receptionist that he had to see the inspector. What he got in return, from the indifferent uniformed man, was a shrug. Being a defense attorney did not help in this environment. Another bitter reminder of the power Martin had once had as a judge.

"Where is he?" Martin asked for the third time, more of a shout than a question.

"Out. As I told you. He said he would be in soon." The mouth hardly moved under the hair covering the burly man's upper lip.

Martin paced. In the best of all worlds, Jobert would have had "his man" follow Arnoux and know what he was up to, even have arrested the bastard. In the worst, Jobert was out on some other case, investigating a petty theft or assault, or just making someone else's life miserable with his feeble, sarcastic jokes. As Martin waited, his doubts grew. He should have gone to the precinct in the ninth arrondissement, closer to his home, or he should have gone straight to headquarters in the Palais de Justice and found an inspector he had worked with during his time there. Why was he trusting that Jobert was doing anything useful? Waiting was insane. Clarie could be in danger. Martin swiped his bowler from the bench and was about to leave when the secretary said "Maître Martin, I think I heard someone come in the back door." The man got up and lumbered down the hallway that opened beside the counter that hid his desk. His return was equally, agonizingly slow. "I told Jobert you were here. He'll be out in a minute."

Martin took off his hat and settled on the bench *again*. He placed his hands on his thighs, closed his eyes and waited, trying not to count off the seconds. Trying to keep his mind clear, ready for his meeting with the irritating inspector.

"Maître Martin." Jobert's jocular, all-too-knowing voice.

Martin got up. "Inspector Jobert, I have an urgent matter to discuss, in private."

Jobert scrutinized him for a moment. "Well, Maître, your timing is good. I happen to have someone in my office you will want to meet."

Michel Arnoux? Did Jobert have the bastard in custody? Martin moved forward. "Let's go, then."

Jobert nodded and ambled down a narrow gray hall to his office. Martin followed impatiently, hoping every step of the way that he was about to confront Clarie's tormentor. But when they arrived at the doorway to Jobert's tiny, tidy office, the man who stood to meet them was neither tall nor thin nor scarred. He was stocky, with a stubble beard and a nose that looked like it had been broken more than once. Although he wore a shabby worker's smock and cap, Martin realized at once that this rough-looking character was a police agent.

"Maître Martin, Agent Torcelli," Jobert introduced them as he maneuvered behind his desk. "Please, sit," he said, pointing to the two wooden chairs that took up most of the remaining space. "Torcelli, tell Maître Martin what you have found out." Jobert picked up the cigar that had been left smoldering in an ashtray.

Martin took his watch from his vest. Ten thirty. He calculated that there was time for him to learn what the police knew before they went to the Gas Administration building to arrest Arnoux. All his training and experience as a judge had predisposed him to listen first and give his version of events later.

"Well, sir," the agent said as he scraped his chair closer to Martin, "the night your wife, Madame Martin, came to the café was the first time I noticed this guy, the one with the scars on his face. It was only my third time there. It's true," he admitted as he ran his fingers around the rim of his cap, "I decided to follow your wife that night, especially since she and that woman, Séverine, said they were looking for the Laurenzano girl. But as soon as I figured out who she was—your wife, that is—I hurried back to the café, hoping to have a little tête-a-tête with the guy who had been talking about planting bombs."

"Go on," Martin muttered, jiggling his knee. At least the fool seemed contrite that he had stalked a respectable woman instead of an idiot publicly advocating violence.

Torcelli swallowed hard. "Unfortunately, when I got back, he wasn't there. The bartender snickered that he had had to go home to meet a curfew, that he was like a pussycat having to slink back to the Gas Company housing every night right on schedule. Turns out, quite a few of them laughed behind the guy's back. He'd come in, trying to be the big man, saying he was a stoker who had been in an explosion. From the way he talked, from the way he dressed, no one believed him, except the Russian, who trusted everyone. This Balenov took the man under his wing, so to speak, and tried to make a disciple of him. I almost decided then and there that the man with the scars wasn't worth investigating. That is, until I talked to my inspector."

Torcelli glanced at Jobert, who was leaning back in his chair, chewing on the last stub of his cigar and nodding approval.

"The inspector thought this guy could just be very wily, fooling everyone, and that I should press him to see if he was in a dangerous cell. Remember, at that point, we thought Angela Laurenzano was killed by an anarchist to keep her from talking."

At that point. "What do you believe now?" Martin was about to burst. This was taking too long.

Jobert held up his hand to calm Martin. He pointed to Torcelli to continue.

"Wednesday night he came back to the bar. He seemed grateful for anyone who would talk to him. So I stood him a few drinks and asked if he really believed that Balenov had been lying the whole time about being against violence. He assured me, he knew the Russian was violent."

"How?" Martin straightened up. "Did you ask how he knew?"

"Sure, I asked. He said because the Russian and his 'little friends' had killed Barbereau."

"Those 'little friends' would be Angela and Maura Laurenzano," Jobert interrupted, shooting Martin a meaningful look. "Do you think your wife knows anything about that?"

Martin ignored Jobert. He wanted Torcelli to get to the point. "Do you think he was part of their cell, of any cell?" he asked the undercover man.

Torcelli shook his head. "I don't think so. He didn't really talk like an anarchist. More like a crazy man, a loner. When I asked point-blank if he knew anyone who could build a bomb, he said that he was plenty smart enough to build one himself. He'd learned enough from reading one of 'their' pamphlets. I noted that: not 'our' pamphlets, 'their' pamphlets."

"That's when I got involved." Jobert leaned forward. "I wasn't about to let Torcelli lose his cover by going to the Gas Company making inquiries, so I went myself. With that face, it was easy to find out who he was."

"And who is he?" Martin knew. He wanted to hear it from them. He did not want to believe that Séverine had found out as much, if not more, than the police.

"Michel Arnoux, injured in the bombing at the Hotel Terminus three years ago. Presumably because of that, no friend of anarchists. A clerk in the accounting department, who, according to his boss, has gone a little bit off the rails lately. Missing days, coming in late other days—"

"So he can go stroll through the neighborhood and threaten my wife. I want the man arrested." Martin could no longer contain himself.

The inspector looked up, startled. "When did he approach her?"

"Two days ago. You should be out there right now, hauling him in."

"What did he say exactly?" Jobert no longer wore that irritating, insouciant look. This was serious, immediate. And Martin was sick at himself for not having made his demands as soon as he saw Jobert. "He talked about the Charity Bazaar fire, he warned her she wasn't behaving like a proper woman."

Jobert and Torcelli exchanged glances.

"You should make sure she keeps away from him, sir," the brutish-looking Torcelli said, with surprising gentleness. "He's funny about women. Last night when I got a few more drinks in him, he kept going on and on about how unfair life was, how the worst men attract all the pretty girls; and how good men, like him, are betrayed by bad women. He sounded as if he hated women. So I took a leap. I asked him if Angela Laurenzano deserved what she got. He turned all red, took a big swallow of whiskey, and clammed up. Said he had to get home. Very suspicious."

"So why haven't you dragged him in?" Martin got to his feet. Did this madman think his Clarie was a bad woman, a betrayer?

"Maître Martin," Jobert sighed, smashing the stub into the ashtray, "I tried this morning. He wasn't at work. Nor was he in his room at the Cité. I came back here to consult with Torcelli. And lo and behold, you were waiting for me. That's when I told Torcelli we were in luck."

"What do you mean?" That infuriating sarcasm. Martin would have shouted again if Jobert's expression had not turned deadly serious, even hostile, as he added, "Since you already seem to know something about Arnoux, and your wife is involved with Maura Laurenzano, we thought perhaps you could tell us where to find two murder suspects."

It was time to cooperate fully. To keep Clarie safe, and to get a madman off the streets.

The next fifteen minutes was filled with a rapid exchange of information. Martin found out that the Russian girls had been questioned for days without the police being able to prove their involvement in subversive activities. Nevertheless, they had been dispatched on a train back to their homeland. Martin spoke of Bernheim's work and explained how powerful mental images can lead to violence. Arnoux, he surmised, was reliving his own fiery trauma through the tragedy of the burnt women. The images, the sensations, the pain, the bitterness all compelling him to seek revenge for what had been done to him. Martin also told them that Maura Laurenzano was the "boy" street musician claiming Pyotr Balenov's innocence. "It may be," he concluded, "that Arnoux is searching for her while we are sitting here. All I know is that she has performed near the cabarets in Montmartre and at the Parc Monceau."

Jobert ordered Torcelli to round up a few uniformed men. "We'll go to the Gas Company, then to his apartment. And if he's still not there, we'll start looking in the parks." Jobert offered Martin a ride back to his neighborhood, but he demurred. He had no desire to be seen in, or to be in, a police wagon. He'd walk.

As the police were gathering themselves to leave, Martin sank into the chair. *Thank God Clarie is home.* He had to hope with all his heart that she would not get it in her head to try to find and warn Maura.

22

Clarie spent the morning in a state of restless anticipation, agonized by questions: What if Maura was being stalked right now? If they all waited for nightfall, when Séverine promised to go to Montmartre, would it be too late? Knowing the killer was out there, how could Clarie not warn Francesca's daughter? Clarie thrust her book aside. Why hadn't she urged Bernard to tell the police to look for Maura first, before anything could happen to her? Maura was the one in danger. This had to be true.

"Maman?" Jean-Luc toddled into the living room from the kitchen.

"Yes, darling."

"Play horsey?"

Clarie smiled and got down on her knees. All her anxiety might be totally unwarranted. Bernard had promised they'd track down Arnoux this morning.

Still, her unsteady hand toppled her son's latest wooden-block formation.

"Maman bad."

"No, Jean-Luc, we must not say that," she chastened her son before planting a kiss on his forehead. *Maman is only nervous.* Clarie frowned as she restacked the blocks. *You would have thought life had taught her patience by now.*

But it hadn't. When the noon church bells rang, there was still no message from Bernard. Clarie had no idea what this could mean, but she was finding the waiting and indecision unbearable. She had to act. "Maman has to talk to Rose," she whispered to Jean-Luc. "I think we are going to have an adventure today."

Jean-Luc gaped up with big eyes, one drop of saliva hanging from his lower lip. He did not know the word "adventure," but he seemed to understand that something new and exciting was going to happen. Clarie got to her feet and headed into the kitchen.

She told Rose they were about to take an excursion to the Parc Monceau. When Rose looked shocked, Clarie asked, "Have you ever been?"

Rose shook her head, not fully hiding her skepticism.

"It's so beautiful. An oasis. Acres and acres of green, flowers growing wild in the English style, ponds, fountains, statues. Even a carousel. Luca will be thrilled. And I haven't been since last summer."

"But Monsieur Martin said—"

"It's past noon. Everything must be fine. We'll be together. There'll be plenty of people around." She could have gone on, said she could not bear waiting, that this was her best chance to find Maura. She didn't have to say more, she rationalized, for there was every good reason to take Rose and Luca to the Parc Monceau on a hot, sunny day. She wasn't really lying. And she didn't want to upset her dear, faithful housekeeper.

Her housekeeper's hands hovered over the bow that tied her apron, as if she couldn't decide what to do. Finally, she pulled on the tie and managed a smile.

"Oh, good," Clarie said as she turned toward the parlor. "We'll be on our way soon." She bent down to tell Luca that they were going to ride a tram, which is *almost* a train. And they were going to see a merry-go-round with big painted horseys. She left him solemnly considering all this as she hurried to her bedroom to get ready.

Clarie's first hesitations came as she was pinning her straw boater to her hair. Staring into the mirror, she wondered if she had worn it two days ago when the man approached her. She couldn't see herself clearly on that day, but she saw him. Saw his hand over Jean-Luc's head. His deeply wounded face, the bubbling flesh around his missing eye, the reddened ripples of tortured skin on his cheek. Heard the words, those horrible words. And his laugh. She touched the side of her face. She wasn't burning, but it crinkled with pain. She rubbed her temples to relieve the tension and put on a cheerful face before going into the parlor to get Rose and Jean-Luc.

Once they were outside, she assured herself, the worst would be over soon. They'd have to go past the Square d'Anvers to get to the tram that ran along the outer boulevards. Even though she assumed that Michel Arnoux was already in custody, she could not bear to go through the park. Instead she went around it, picking up Jean-Luc and hurrying, despite the fact that their presence would be obscured from any lurker within by the trees and iron fences. She breathed a sigh of relief when she reached the Boulevard Rochechouart and got in line for the tram. It was good to be surrounded by people.

"Horsey!" Jean-Luc pointed with delight at the white beast trotting toward them.

"Yes, Luca, he is going to pull the tram along the tracks." She bounced her son in her arms and gave him a kiss. She felt the comforting presence of Rose behind her.

When the Etoile-LaVillette tram came to a halt, several men tipped their straw boaters and stepped aside to allow her, Jean-Luc and Rose into the carriage ahead of them. Clarie and Rose sat on the thinly cushioned leathery seats and faced the north side of the street. Jean-Luc, standing on Clarie's lap, looked over her shoulder. Although the Parc Monceau was only four stops away, each link in the chain of the outer boulevards opened onto a different world. The vast park was in the middle of a new, very wealthy and fashionable neighborhood. To get there, the tram passed a line of some of the city's most garish cabarets. Clarie winced as they pulled by the Place Pigalle, a name almost synonymous with prostitution. Poor girls, she thought, and hoped that Maura would never be among them.

She patted Jean-Luc's back, grateful that the most flamboyant edifice behind her was the Medrano Circus. She held on even tighter as they lurched to a stop across from the false windmill and crimson front of the Moulin Rouge and the gigantic, hungry devil's mouth framing the entrance to the Café of Hell. The ugliness of it made her shudder. "Only a few more stops," she whispered as much to herself as to her son. For his part, Jean-Luc didn't seem to mind that the car was hot and stuffy, redolent of perfumed women and sweating and smoking men. He was fully absorbed in the moving picture of the city.

Finally, the Parc Monceau was announced and Clarie reached up to pull the cord. Passengers stepped aside, making sure that Clarie and her entourage got out in good time. After she and Rose hopped off the iron grille staircase, they crossed to the entrance, went through a gate and passed a large stone rotunda, once used to collect taxes when the park formed a northern boundary of the city.

Clarie took a deep breath. The air seemed so clear here. The park, once belonging to a king, preserved much of its royal elegance and went on and on. The three of them could take any of the intersecting, serpentine paths and find something interesting and beautiful to look at and things for Jean-Luc to do. "We're here," she said to Rose. "Isn't this lovely?" she added, even as she tried to calculate which path was the most open, the safest. She couldn't move because she could not decide.

It was Jean-Luc who broke the spell. He spotted the merry-go-round and gasped "What's that?"

"That is a carousel. With big wooden horses. Maybe we'll ride on it later."

Jean-Luc kept pointing and moving forward, fascinated by the hurdy-gurdy music and the shiny, painted steeds going up and down and around all at the same time. He took hold of his mother's skirt and began dragging her toward the wondrous machine.

"I think we should walk for a while and see what else there is," Clarie urged Jean-Luc, not wanting him to do the best thing first and lose all interest in the rest. "We might see some real horses you could pet, and sandboxes and other little boys."

"Wanna ride horsey," he insisted and pulled harder, while reaching and spreading out his fingers as if aching to receive the magic. Clarie picked him up and started down one of the undulating paths. "You'll have fun, little Luca," Rose assured him, walking slightly behind them.

"Look, water and boats," Clarie said to distract Jean-Luc as they approached a basin where children were launching their toy sailboats.

"Want horsey," Jean-Luc insisted.

"And music, singing." Clarie stopped and listened. "I know that melody. It's an old Italian song."

Rose listened, while Jean-Luc wriggled in Clarie's arms. She put him down. The music filled her with joy and sadness at the same time, the joy and sadness of the past. "My father used to sing it to my mother," Clarie explained to Rose, "and then he'd translate it for me so I'd understand he was teasing her because she worried too much. It went something like this:

"I would have taken a wife, but have repented
'Tis well to change one's mind before too late
I'd rather be a bachelor alone and contented
Than be consumed with the cares of an anxious mate

"It went on and on in that vein. He always thought my mother had too many cares. Of course, after she died," Clarie said, staring down at the ground, "he never sang it again." Clarie understood now how her mother had felt. Life brought many worries, and fears.

Jean-Luc kept pulling on her skirt. Now he was interested in joining the boys and their sailboats.

The melody had thrown Clarie off balance, into the past, and when she returned to the present she realized the clear, young voice might be Maura's. She, too, may have heard that song when she was a child.

"Rose, would you mind taking Luca down by the water with the other little boys?" Clarie said, relinquishing his hand to Rose. "I want to see who the musicians are."

"If you're sure."

"Oh, yes, there are lots of people around. I'll be right back."

Rose nodded and took Luca's hand. Who could worry on such a glorious day?

Clarie followed the music around a bend and saw a gathering of spectators. She approached, stretched and craned her neck, and there, hair shorn, dressed in pants, a shirt, a vest and a cap, was Maura. Alive and strong. She had found her!

At the end of the song, while her companion, a bent-over white-haired man, played his concertina, Maura collected money in her cap. Some listeners left, and Clarie moved to the front. When Maura spotted Clarie, her eyes flickered with recognition, but Clarie could not tell if they conveyed hostility or fear.

Maura strode back to her companion and picked up a bundle of papers from a sack on the ground. "I'm going to sing a new song," she said, legs apart in a stance of bravado. "It's our own song, about freedom and justice, about a crime that has been committed in our city. You may buy a copy if you like it and help us spread the truth."

Clarie shook her head and pursed her lips. So this is how that brave, foolish girl had been testing fate, putting herself in danger. Clarie was tempted to run up and tear the sheets away from her. Maura shot her a defiant look. The girl didn't need protection; she needed a good talking to.

"Pieter, a boy from Russia," Maura began, "Loved mankind with all his heart." Maura's face softened as she sang about her prince. When the chorus came, the old man, suddenly revitalized, joined in with touching conviction. Maura had found a protector, perhaps even a teacher. Or, simply, someone who loved her for who she was. Clarie hoped she would not have a hard time persuading her to leave him.

"Do you like this song?" A rasping whisper. That voice. Clarie's heart jumped up to her throat. He was so close, she smelled his sour breath and sensed his nervousness. He blew on the back of her neck, separating the soft hairs that never got caught up in her bun. "I asked, do you like it?"

She opened her mouth, wanting to scream for help. Then she felt something sharp, jabbing her side by her breast. "Don't say anything. Don't make one sound, or I will stick it in you."

This could not be happening. Didn't everybody see?

But everyone was watching the musicians sing about a murderer.

"I like that song," he murmured. "I'll soon get her too."

She wanted to shout. Her mouth was agape, panting. Drying up. Useless.

She turned far enough to see that he had tipped his boater to obscure his scars. One of his arms was extended across his chest, leading to the hand that held the knife. He was using his other arm, aimed down, flat against her body to conceal his weapon. She felt him groping and heard him mutter "We're going to walk away, side by side, as if we were lovers." He took tight hold of her forearm. Now her arm, pulled down and locked in his hand, was helping to hide the blade pointing at her. She wondered if it was the same knife that had penetrated Angela's heart. She shuddered, afraid that her teeth would start chattering and make him angry. She shouldn't be wondering. She should be thinking.

"Smile. Or would you prefer I go find your baby?"

She shook her head. *No, not that.*

"Let's stroll," he said, as if he were one of the gentlemen in a top hat languorously enjoying the day.

The hand gripping her forearm directed them around and onto the path. She lowered her head, swallowed hard, and pressed her lips together. At first, all she saw was the gravel beneath her slowly moving feet. He was so close, his arm against the side of her body as stiff as a rudder leading a ship.

Think. Her terror rolled in waves from her chest to her stomach. "Where are we going?" she whispered.

"To a quiet place." His voice had grown calmer. "Smile," he insisted. "Don't stumble."

She lifted her head. She had to see where they were. They passed lovers holding hands; boys and girls in sailor suits, rolling hoops and carrying balls; women laughing together in big hats, which shaded their eyes and obstructed their vision. His hold got tighter as her body sprouted with sweat. The knife jabbed deeper, threatening to cut through her corset into her flesh. *Think.* The red and white flowers lining the path had turned into rivulets of blood. She was crying.

They changed directions, into a narrower path, a more deserted way, lined with shrubs.

"Why are you doing this?" Her voice trembled.

"To keep them from killing, from destroying people's lives."

"Who?" Maybe if she could keep him talking, someone would notice the knife.

"The anarchists. I came here to get her, the little singer, the girl dressed as a boy. But then I saw you. Trying to warn her. A good woman wouldn't be on their side against me." Whatever nerves he had felt in capturing her had disappeared. He spoke with deadly purpose.

"But Maura is innocent, just a girl." Surely he realized that.

"Stop lying," he said as he poked the blade through her corset. "You know they killed Barbereau. They like to destroy."

Clarie desperately looked around for someone, anyone to stop him. The gray path, the too-blue sky, the jade leaves on the shrubs were closing in on her. She tasted the metal of fear. She heard their feet crunching on the stones. And music. Someone singing "The Fiancés of the North."

Was that the last human voice she'd hear? Was that now or then? That night when Bernard sat across from her, so proud, so happy. Bernard. She'd never see him again. Or Jean-Luc. Her baby! The music was getting louder. Closing in. He heard it too. He was trying to push her into the bushes. Her baby. Jean-Luc. A motherless child. Motherless. No! No! "No!" She thrust her foot sideways and sent him reeling. His knife tore into her as he fell. "Help!" she cried. "Help!"

She saw half his face as he thrashed about. The eyeless half. And his hand wildly groping for the knife.

She felt burning, ripping from the back of her breast to her chest. She stepped back and held her hands against her wound. Bumped into someone.

"I told you he was following that teacher." Maura's voice. The music had stopped.

"All right. We got her. It's Madame Martin."

Clarie turned to see a rough-looking man with a stubbly beard and crooked nose holding on to her. Suddenly Maura appeared in front of her, and all of Clarie's bottled-up emotions burst out in a cry. "You!" Clarie broke away and grasped the girl by her shoulders. "You have to go back to your mother. Now! Do you hear?"

Stronger hands pulled her back and she saw the imprint of blood, two red cat's paws, on Maura's shirt. She examined her hands, streaking with red. She glanced to where Michel Arnoux had fallen. He had stopped struggling. A uniformed man held him down. Another stood above him. She smelled cigar smoke.

She heard a second man's voice behind her. "Now that you've stopped giving orders, we're going to sit you down."

Someone gently helped her to the ground. Another man crouched down and told her to let him have a look. His bowler was tipped to one side, revealing a full head of ginger-red hair, which matched his bushy eyebrows and mustache. Clenching a cigar in his mouth, he set to work, pulling her hands away and peeling back the shreds of her blouse and corset. He took out his handkerchief and told her to hold it tight against her side. "I guess it was a good thing that Adam gave Eve his ribs," he said. "That and your corset. It will sting for a while. But you'll be all right." He was matter-of-fact, which comforted Clarie, and jocular, which annoyed her.

"I'm Jobert, incidentally," he added.

"My son," she said through gritted teeth. She felt like a slice had been taken out of her.

"We'll find him and bring him. You sit for a while." The man stood up. "Get that bastard out of here and send for two cabs," he ordered. Two uniformed men began dragging the strangely silent Michel Arnoux away.

"You all right?" Maura bent over to peer at Clarie. There were other faces. A small crowd had gathered.

"How did everyone get here?" Clarie asked, pressing hard against the burning cut.

"Your friend," the voice boomed from above, "ran up, got a policeman and then led us around like a god-damned pied piper until we found you."

"And you?" Clarie tried to will the fuzziness out of her head as she looked up at Jobert.

"Me? When your husband came to talk to me this morning, he told me that Arnoux might be coming to the Parc. Didn't say anything about *you* bein' here. Fortunately, you had a friend keeping an eye on you. You're a very lucky woman."

Or a foolish, brave girl, Clarie thought, remembering Bernard's words of many years before. No, she stared at her shaking fingers, red with her own blood. She was confused. The foolish, brave girl is Maura.

"Torcelli will stay with you until we find your son and send you home in a cab. In the meantime," he reached and grabbed Maura, "we'll be taking this one with us. She needs to answer some questions about Barbereau."

Maura tried to yank herself away, but Jobert was too strong.

"No," Clarie protested. "Don't take her. Let me up. Don't—" She struggled to get up. Again, the rough-looking man helped her with gentle hands.

"She's a good girl." The old musician stepped forward and pleaded. "Don't take her to prison."

Maura kept trying to wrench her arm away and didn't stop until Clarie stood face to face with her. "We will help you," Clarie said. After she told Bernard that Maura had likely saved her life, he'd have to help.

Before responding to Clarie, Maura turned to the musician. "Nico, don't worry. They'll help. I'll see you soon." Clarie saw Maura's strength and determination, even a new kindness. She was a girl so worth saving.

When she looked at Clarie, her green eyes were neither hostile nor skeptical. "When you see my mother," she said before Jobert dragged her away, "tell her I'll be home soon."

Epilogue

Sunday, 6 February 1898

Clarie read to Jean-Luc until his eyelids drooped in peaceful surrender. Her boy had had a busy Sunday morning, visiting his idol, the six-year-old Robert Franchet, and walking home through the cold, gray drizzle that was Paris in February. Clarie waited to make sure he was asleep before pressing the blankets around his shoulders and neck. Rubbing her hands together for warmth, she went into the parlor where Bernard had just built a fire.

"Done," she announced in a whisper. She glanced at the papers waiting on her desk and decided she could take an hour from her work to enjoy the fire and her husband's company. He was already settled in his chair, reading *Le Temps*.

She picked up *La Fronde*, *her* newspaper, from their reading table. "So," she asked Bernard, "how do you think Edgar is doing with his alone-Sundays?"

"Not exactly alone. There is his mother-in-law, the nanny, the maid, as well as little Robert."

"And us," Clarie added, laughing. "You two had a lot to talk about today."

Bernard shook his head and frowned. "We're not at all sure how it is going to turn out. Zola's trial starts tomorrow. What if they find him guilty and try to put him in jail?"

"They won't."

"The army, the courts, and most of the Chamber of Deputies claim that what he wrote about their railroading Dreyfus was libelous. They don't want Dreyfus's guilt to be questioned."

"Are you really worried?"

"About Zola? No, not really." Bernard was a great admirer of France's most famous writer, whom he had met during his first big case. "He'll be all right. I don't think they'd dare imprison him, or, at least, not for very long. World opinion would be totally against them. But. . . ."

"I know," she reached over and laid her hand over his, "the riots and the scurrilous articles in the newspapers about Israelites." There had even been a fight in the Chamber of Deputies.

"And—"

"Most of the men at the Labor Exchange consider this a battle between two different factions of the bourgeoisie," she said, putting into words what troubled him the most. "They will come around eventually, when they realize what the Army did to an innocent man. And then you'll be able to be more open about your commitment to the cause."

He kissed her hand and screwed his mouth into a wry smile. "Well, at least your colleagues seem to be on the right side of things."

"You've been reading Séverine!" Clarie teased. Her columns in the new all-woman's newspaper campaigned against anti-Semitism almost every day and were avowedly pro-Dreyfus.

"I meant at the school," Bernard said, still unwilling to give the journalist her due. "Mme Roubinovitch protecting her Israelite students and teachers. And Emilie, of course."

Clarie lowered her head to hide a grin. She had overheard Edgar and Bernard talking about Emilie's new venture. Edgar Franchet was alone on Sunday because Emilie was at *La Fronde,* writing a column on education and taking part in the fencing exercises that the publisher, Marguerite Durand, had set up in one of the rooms in the newspaper's building. *In principle,* Bernard and Edgar believed, or thought they *should* believe, in her right to take Sunday off, consort with female journalists, and even learn swordplay. But, *in practice*, both of them seemed a little uncomfortable with her decision and its consequences: a weekly assignment for Edgar to stay with a six-year-old and a loquacious mother-in-law.

"You could work for the paper too, you know," Bernard said, reacting a bit defensively to her obvious amusement.

"No," she shook her head. "I only have Rose to help, and with Maura, it fills my days."

"Is Maura still doing well? I forgot to ask."

Clarie basked in the warmth and genuine concern in his voice. He was so busy at the Exchange and with the meetings dedicated to reopening the Dreyfus case that he seldom saw Maura when she came for lessons. But he knew that Rose and Clarie considered her almost part of the family. And Jean-Luc adored her.

"She still wants to work at the Bon Marché."

"As soon as she's ready. The salary, the security would be a great help to her mother."

"And?"

Just as she could fill in his sentiments about his colleagues at the Exchange, she knew what he could leave unsaid about her and Maura. "And she's still young. Strong. Willful. And all I can do is help," Clarie conceded.

If Bernard hadn't turned back to *Le Temps*, after nodding his agreement, she might have gotten up to kiss him. *He* had been the best help of all, rescuing Maura from the criminal courts. With a contented sigh, honoring the peacefulness of their Sunday afternoon, she turned to her favorite part of *La Fronde*, Séverine's column.

She hadn't read much of the newspaper before she heard a loud knock. *Maura?* The girl still hadn't gotten into the habit of ringing the bell. "I'll get it," Clarie said, and hurried to the door.

It was Maura, shivering in her heavy shawls, and crying.

"Maura, my goodness. What's wrong?"

She only managed to sniffle and gasp, before another sob erupted from her lips.

"Your mother? Is your mother all right?"

"Nico."

"Yes?"

"Nico's dead. He died yesterday. They just told me. They brought me his concertina."

Clarie took Maura in her arms and hugged her tight, feeling Maura's damp curls graze her cheeks and smelling the wet wool of her shawls. "Come, come," she soothed. "Let's get you warm."

Bernard was already standing when they walked into the parlor.

"Nico's dead," Clarie explained.

"I'm sorry," he said to Maura. "Let me take those wet things."

Maura stood passively as Bernard lifted the outer garments from her shoulders. Then Clarie gently led her toward the fire. "Here, warm your hands."

Maura extended her hands over the flames. Her lips trembled. "I should have been there. I should have made him come live with us."

Clarie kept her arm around Maura's waist. They both knew that Nico's moving in with Maura and her mother was impossible. Maura had dreamed of making enough money to move to two rooms. But there hadn't been time. Dear Nico was dead.

"Let's go into the kitchen and get you a hot cup of tea," Clarie said. Bernard stood aside, a grave expression on his face, as they passed by. Once in the kitchen, Maura took the usual place at the table, where she learned her numbers and went over spelling twice a week. Clarie struck a match and lit the stove, then reached for a tin of biscuits. She set them in front of Maura and spooned tea into a pot. They didn't say anything until the water had boiled, the tea had steeped, and Maura had her cold hands wrapped around a warm cup.

"Do you know how he died?" Clarie asked as she sat down.

"In his sleep. They said he was smiling. Maybe he was dreaming about Jeanne or Italy."

"Or you."

"I should have—" Maura bowed her head and pressed her lips together. It was so unlike Maura to cry in front of anyone. Clarie was glad that she felt she could do it now, here, in her place.

"Maura," Clarie leaned over to peer into the girl's eyes, "didn't you go at least once a week to see him?"

Maura nodded, staring down at her cup.

"Didn't he say you didn't have to come, but that it gave him great joy?"

Another slight nod.

"You gave him so much. You made his last days very happy. You know that."

"He didn't need me to be happy. He was happy because he was so kind and good."

"But you were a gift, an unexpected blessing for him."

Maura sniffled and took a sip of tea.

"And you didn't abandon him. You could have, you know."

"Oh, no, I couldn't, I—" Maura almost smiled. Between the arithmetic and the orthography, Clarie had often taken time to tell Maura that she was a smart, good, brave girl who would grow into a fine woman. The smile seemed to be proof that she was beginning to believe it.

Maura grabbed Clarie's hand. "But why do all the good people die?"

Clarie sank back in her chair. This was not a question she addressed between lessons. She could not help but picture all the deaths in her life: her mother, her baby, Bernard's father. All beloved. She squeezed Maura's hand and leaned forward again. The girl had suffered so many losses. Pyotr, Angela, now Nico. And who knows what had happened to her father, or the Russian girls?

"I don't think they die really, altogether. They stay inside us, are part of us. Just as when you grow up, the young Maura will be part of the older Maura. They'll all be there inside of you, helping you to be a wiser, fuller person. And besides," Clarie tugged on Maura's hand to try to get her to look up, "not *all* the good people die. Some are still with us."

Maura pulled her hand away and stared into her cup. "I know that," she whispered. "I know that now."

"This doesn't mean," Clarie said, still trying to meet Maura's eyes, "that we should not mourn, that we should not be sad. We must be, because we'll miss them. And sometimes it's very unfair that they leave us so early."

They both sat there in silence for a few moments, until they heard a commotion in the parlor. Bernard knocked on the doorframe and entered the kitchen with a very grumpy Jean-Luc in his arms.

"Look who's here," he said to his son.

The pouting toddler rubbed his eyes until he could see clearly. And then he smiled.

After all, it was Maura.

Historical Note

Readers may wonder which of the characters really lived and which events actually happened. Séverine (Caroline Rémy de Guebhard) was a famous journalist of the time, and Mmes. Roubinovitch and Sauvaget did serve the Lycée Lamartine. *La Fronde* (The Sling), mentioned in the Epilogue, was an all-women's newspaper edited and published by the enterprising former actress and salonnière, Marguerite Durand. The first edition appeared in December 1897. The Charity Bazaar Fire (May 1897) and the bombing in the Café Terminus (February 1894) were important and traumatic events in the history of Paris.

If you explore Clarie's Paris, you will find the gilded entrance to the Gas Company Administration building, the Moulin Rouge, the Lariboisière Hospital, and, of course, the Gare du Nord and Gare de l'Est railroad stations. The building once dedicated to a model workers' community still remains, marked by a plaque, on the rue Rochechouart. Lycée Lamartine also lives on in a very different guise. It is no longer a breeding ground for proper bourgeois girls in uniform, but a public co-ed institution, with teenagers "hanging out" as they would near any American high school. Farther away, the Bourse du Travail (Labor Exchange), near the Place de la République, is an impressive center for labor activities. The laundry and the tenement on the rue Goutte-d'Or are long gone.

The two Italian songs in the story are loose translations of traditional lyrics reprinted in *The Folk-Songs of Italy* (Arno Press reprint, 1977). "The Fiancés of the North" was one of the many popular songs written to protest the killing of nine demonstrators in the northern industrial town of Fourmies on May Day, 1891. The rapturous reading of Proudhon that Clarie heard in the working-class café is taken from one of the anarchist's articles quoted in James Joll's *The Anarchists* (New York, 1964).

To say that the rest is fiction does not relieve the author of striving for authenticity. This means piecing together innumerable sources: general and specific histories, biographies, travelers' accounts and guidebooks, photographs and paintings, dissertations, nineteenth-century novels, and the ever-handy Internet. Rather than present a tedious "select" bibliography, I'll give some examples of sources that fueled the narrative, sometimes in surprising ways.

John Savage's dissertation on the legal culture of the Paris Bar (New York University, 1999) provided me with a number of wonderful details about the arduous path to admission (including the house inspection) and the Labor Exchange's attitude toward lawyers. On a much smaller scale, Matilda Betham-Edwards' *Home Life in France* (London, 1905) confirmed that, indeed, a Parisian housewife could buy a ready-to-eat chicken.

Emile Zola is essential. It was only after I chose to have Maura live in the Goutte-d'Or that I remembered it as the locus of his 1877 working-class novel, *L'Assommoir.* Guy de Maupassant offers a sardonic look at Paris journalism in *Bel-Ami* (1885), loosely based upon the life of Séverine's most notorious lover, Georges de Labruyère. John Merriman's *The Dynamite Club* (Boston, 2009) details the words and deeds of Emile Henry, the Café Terminus bomber. For what Clarie called the "noise of Paris," there are innumerable books on Montmartre and Vanessa Schwartz's wonderful *Spectacular Realities: Early Mass Culture in fin-de-siècle Paris* (Berkeley, 1998), with photographs and analyses of popular ghoulish entertainments like the Paris morgue. Finally, the best source in English on the notorious lives and impressive achievements of Séverine and her friend and colleague, Marguerite Durand, is Mary Louise Roberts' *Disruptive Acts: The New Woman in Fin-de-Siècle France* (Chicago, 2002).

Acknowledgments

FIRST THANKS MUST GO TO the members of my wonderful writers' group who have saved me from countless embarrassments and infelicities as the book developed: Mabel Armstrong, Faris Cassell, Kari Davidson, Elizabeth Lyon, and Geraldine Moreno-Black. The next line of defense were willing readers of the first completed draft: Linda Frederick, Freddie Tryk, Pam Whyte, and especially George Wickes, who keeps me attuned, on pitch, to the cultural mores of late nineteenth-century French culture. My editor, Jessica Case, offered an incisive critique, as always, with a deft and gracious hand. Mollie Glick, my agent, continues to be the support system that any author would be grateful for.

One of the pleasures of writing this book was exchanging emails with far-flung colleagues in French history. I thank Claire Germain, Benjamin Martin, John Merriman, and Jo Burr Margadant for the work that has been important to the Martin series and for their prompt, friendly responses. Tom Kselman gets a special thanks for sending me to Zola's short story, "The Way People Die," on the different social strata of nineteenth-century Paris. As for non-historical help, thanks to Dr. Lee Davidson, who graciously and promptly shared his experience with knife wounds.

Finally, I thank my husband, Daniel Pope, for his technical help, enthusiastic support, and for just being there.